PRAI...
Do I Kn...

'Many authors can write compellingly about falling in love . . . but it takes a deft hand (or two, in this case) to write compellingly about staying in love. Luckily, we have Wibbroka, who have crafted a novel about marriage that is honest to the bone, refreshing and – like a long-term relationship – deliciously surprising'

Jodi Picoult, *New York Times* bestselling
author of *Wish You Were Here*

'*Do I Know You?* shows the pure magic of that pivotal moment when two people make the choice to fight for each other. This book is more than a story of a marriage in trouble. It's the story of a spark rekindled, and the new flames deliver all the warmth you could want in a novel. Full of humour and heart, *Do I Know You?* had me in my feelings!'

Denise Williams, author of
The Fastest Way to Fall

'*Do I Know You?* offers the fresh twist on a marriage in crisis that I didn't know I needed! Wibbroka does it again with a magnetically raw and intimate portrayal of where love begins, fades and begins again. Flirty, sweeping and hopeful, readers will clutch their chests and root for Eliza and Graham until the very last page'

Amy Lea, international bestselling
author of *Set on You*

'Reading Wibberley and Siegemund-Broka's prose is like sliding into the crisp sheets of a luxury hotel bed. *Do I Know You?* is such an inventive take on a "marriage in trouble" story, showing the fragility that can sometimes hide behind familiarity. By the end, I cared about the fate of Eliza and Graham's relationship like I knew them personally'

Alicia Thompson, bestselling
author of *Love in the Time of Serial Killers*

'Readers won't be able to turn the pages fast enough'

Publishers Weekly

Titles by Emily Wibberley and Austin Siegemund-Broka

The Roughest Draft
Do I Know You?
The Breakup Tour
Book Boyfriend

EMILY WIBBERLEY

Book Boyfriend

AUSTIN SIEGEMUND-BROKA

PAN BOOKS

First published 2025 by Berkley,
an imprint of Penguin Random House LLC, New York

First published in the UK 2025 by Pan Books
an imprint of Pan Macmillan
The Smithson, 6 Briset Street, London EC1M 5NR
EU representative: Macmillan Publishers Ireland Ltd, 1st Floor,
The Liffey Trust Centre, 117–126 Sheriff Street Upper,
Dublin 1, D01 YC43
Associated companies throughout the world
www.panmacmillan.com

ISBN 978-1-0350-2038-6

1 3 5 7 9 8 6 4 2

A CIP catalogue record for this book is available from the British Library.

Book design by Kristin del Rosario

Printed and bound by CPI Group (UK) Ltd, Croydon, CR0 4YY

Visit **www.panmacmillan.com** to read more about all our books
and to buy them. You will also find features, author interviews and
news of any author events, and you can sign up for e-newsletters
so that you're always first to hear about our new releases.

Book
Boyfriend

1

The elevator opens. I walk out into the lobby, ready to get dumped.

Honestly, I've known the dumping was coming for a while. I have no emotional connection with Jordan, no deep passion, very few shared interests. I probably should've dumped him myself already. Instead, I've let one chance exchange of phone numbers in a coffee line draw out into six months of increasingly unenthusiastic dating for one reason.

Hope.

No magic in the fantasy novels I've cherished practically my entire life, intertwining them with my personality and now my livelihood, is as powerful as *hope*. Human, ordinary, and devastatingly enchanting. Especially, in my case, when it comes to my relationships.

At least I call it hope. Others might have other names for it. *Idealism. Sentimentality. Naïveté.* I'm well aware I'm a dreamer. The problem is reality never manages to match my dreams.

Was I *hoping* Jordan Jenkins would change into a completely different person overnight, embodying romance itself with his devotion and graceful kindness? Was I hoping we would fall madly in love and start planning an incredibly romantic elopement in Ireland?

Yes.

Even when our relationship is over in approximately five minutes, will I keep dreaming of the Ireland thing?

Probably, yes.

For now, though, no green hills or whitecapped waters wait for me. The lobby of the West 56th Street office building housing Parthenon Publishing Group, where I work, smells of linoleum with hints of stale coffee. The summer sunlight coming in the plexiglass windows heats the wide room uncomfortably. The corporate décor of marble floors and couches no one uses complete the picture.

I wait while people in suits pass me, swiping into the elevators on their return from coffee runs or late mornings working from home. Parthenon takes up five floors of the high tower, with other offices occupying the rest, giving me an audience of plenty of people I've never met during the joyous occasion of my dumping.

Would I have preferred we do this literally anywhere else? Once more, yes. Unfortunately, however, my office is right next to Jordan's place, where he works from home. We planned to get lunch this afternoon, like we often do.

But Jordan's hesitance to either pick a restaurant or meet at his apartment has indicated there shall be no lunch.

Which is disappointing, as I packed nothing to eat today. Not that I would prefer eating ramen in the place nearby, waiting to be dumped after the bill. Or worse, sitting down only to be dumped before the food even comes out.

Oh well. Even without the powerful magic of hope defending me from the conversation I know is coming, I'll manage. I remind myself of how Queen Kethryn doesn't possess any magic of her own. Only perseverance. Sure, the heroine of the Elytheum Courts book series never got dumped in front of her office elevators, but our circumstances are close enough.

While I'm mentally encouraging myself, Jordan enters in the glass doors, and—

Wow. It's even worse than I imagined, which is saying something.

Jordan is carrying a medium-sized cardboard box. I recognize my coziest hoodie, one of my scarves, even my Halloween costume peeking up from the top. He has, I realize, consolidated my possessions from his apartment. *How considerate.*

Now I'm going to have to haul my Just-Dumped box up to my office for the rest of the day, in front of every single one of my colleagues. Including—ugh, I know Scott's going to make some comment. Probably write it down in the notebook he's never without. *J. Worth dumped today. Very entertaining.*

When Jordan comes closer, I force a smile. I'm not expecting the pang I feel despite the dark comedy of the occasion. Giving up hope never *doesn't* hurt, I guess. Even irrational hopes.

"Wow. All my possessions that I keep at your apartment. Is that my toothbrush in there? My pajamas, too," I marvel sarcastically. "How did you know this is exactly what I needed to get through my workday?"

Yes, I could make this easier for Jordan. I won't, though.

"Where do you want to go for lunch?" I continue cheerfully. "Ramen?"

Jordan winces, like he legitimately worries I might not have grasped what's happening here.

"No to ramen, then," I continue. "Pizza?"

"I'm sorry, Jennifer," Jordan says. "I think we should break up."

I gasp theatrically. "No. You don't say! I'm shocked!"

Jordan drops my gaze, understanding now. With every literal passing second, I forget what I saw in him. Is he cute? I guess. Light brown hair, perpetual stubble. He's in his ordinary zip-up, T-shirt, jeans WFH ensemble. He's five ten. He never pretends he's six feet. He just says *I'm five ten*. Then he changes the subject.

He has the grace to meet my comedy routine gently. "I figured it was better this way," he says, nodding to indicate the box.

I notice the books I left on his shelves, having learned I needed reading material for when *Call of Duty* or *FIFA* consumed him. Yes, even on the nights I stayed over. I hope it's very heavy.

"Now you don't have to come by later for it all. This is less awkward," he explains.

"So much less awkward," I agree.

I do not offer to receive the parcel from him. Instead, I decide, if I'm going to get dumped at work on a Friday—just hours from the good part of Friday, no less, when everyone soft-decides it's the weekend and emails stop coming—I'm going to have the full fucking horrible experience. "Want to tell me why?" I invite him.

"Um." Jordan shuffles, either under the weight of his considerate packing efforts or the unexpected masochism of my question. "I guess. I just think that, like, you don't really like me."

I pause. *Okay, fair.*

"I think you're hot and we have fun together. It's cool how much you're into in the bedroom," Jordan elaborates generously. I flush the color of the end papers in the special edition of *The Shattered Court*—pink. Very pink. I pray to every fantastical god that we're not in earshot of any of my coworkers. "But, like, I think you like the idea of a boyfriend more than you really like *me* as your boyfriend," Jordan says.

I narrow my eyes, surprised. The observation is . . . unusually insightful coming from him.

"I'm not like the guys you read about." He hefts the box, indicating the books inside. "Honestly, Jennifer, I don't think anyone is. They're not real."

Instantly, my enjoyment in my own dumping disappears. He didn't need to invoke my favorite books. I know the guys he means. Lord Valance, in particular, and his fictional counterparts—the ominous, reserved, intimidating, ultimately incredibly noble, devoted men of my romantic fantasy favorites.

"How would you even know what they're like? You never read the books," I point out indignantly.

I won't pretend Jordan's disinterest in my fantasy favorites, especially the Elytheum Courts series, didn't hurt. When I invited him to read one—*Just one!* I entreated playfully—he explained he "didn't read fiction," which meant he didn't read anything.

I didn't need him to love them. I didn't need him to share my every interest. He knew they were important to me, though. I would've played *Call of Duty* if he'd offered to let me, let alone asked me.

"I don't need to read them," Jordan protests.

I cross my arms, pissed. "So you're saying it's impossible for you to be emotionally available, charming, flirtatious, kind, sexy, devoted, and loving?" I clarify. *Just to get it on the record.*

Hands pinned under the cardboard, he nevertheless manages to shrug. "I mean. Yeah."

Infuriated now, I wrest the box from him, ignoring his visible relief. Yes, I know the men in the fantasy novels I like to read are a *little* exaggerated. But the core of who they are shouldn't be impossible to find in the real world. Should it? Not every hope needs to feel like magic, evanescent and unrealistic.

Does it?

It's not like I need a literal strapping fae warrior. The man of my dreams doesn't need wings. Obviously.

"Thanks for my stuff," I say. "I hope you find a girl willing to settle for everything you're willing to offer her. Barely texting me back, showing up late to half our dates, never taking an interest in my interests. What a total package!"

Jordan glares. I guess he's finally had enough of my self-deprecating enthusiasm for this conversation. "Yeah, well, if you want the kind of fantasy love story you read about, I hope you're ready to wait forever," he retorts. "I'm going to go *live* my life."

Without hesitation, he leaves, evidently planning to start right now.

Regrettably, I have no comeback or perfect rejoinder. It was a respectable dramatic flourish, I have to concede.

Nonetheless, I won't dignify it by watching his retreat. I'm *done* with Jordan. Not interested. Over him. He's a foolish hope, a failed enchantment. A fantasy not worth having.

Holding the heavy reminder of our ended relationship, I start for the elevator—only to run into the last person I want to see right now.

2

Of course, I drop the box—full of hefty hardcovers—right onto his foot.

"Ouch," Scott Daniels says.

Not *yelps* or *exclaims*. No, Scott simply *observes* the experience of my possessions falling onto his foot with the droll dispassion he's reserved for every one of our interactions over the past year.

"Sorry," I say, matching his enthusiasm.

He eyes me warily, like he doesn't really believe I'm sorry. Which, yeah, I'm not. He's Scott. He deserves it.

Ever since I knew publishing was a job, I've wanted to work in it. I networked and interviewed hard for the internship I managed to secure after college, which several years later led me to work in commercial fiction marketing for Parthenon. Now, I love every single part of my job—except for one arrogant, rude coworker.

Scott Daniels started in my department a year ago. While we work on different titles in different genres, we and the other marketers work closely on coordinated plans, allocation of department resources, and other joint efforts. I remember my excitement when he was introduced during the weekly interdepartmental meeting.

A handsome man my age who loved literature? Was this the American Dream? Of course, I expected we would get along.

Until we didn't.

The man regarding me with disinterested displeasure in our office lobby should be my type. Cute in a nerdy way. Muscular in an unshowy way, his nice shoulders visible in the stretch of his work shirts. Intelligent in an eager way, quick to endorse or expand on every one of our colleagues' ideas *except* mine. A perfect Excel spreadsheet of a man.

Instead, after our first interaction, my professional relationship with Scott Daniels descended from strained to outright unpleasant. Every meeting, every discussion, neither one of us can help frowning, or pointedly contradicting the other, or deliberately putting our titles in competition for promotional opportunities. I am forced to deal with him every weekday, including work-from-home days, when he shadows my Outlook inbox like the worst demons let loose on Kethryn's court.

"Nice box of personal possessions," my demon remarks. "Either you're planning to move into your cubicle more seriously or you just were dumped."

I purse my lips. I hate how quickly he catches on. How effortlessly he pairs wry humor with hidden delight for my misfortune. Yes, I'm definitely going in the notebook. *J. Worth dumped. Dropped heavy shit on my foot. Still a win.*

Notebook worthy or not, I'm relieved that his question means he didn't overhear my breakup. "That's a personal question," I return with Scott's dismissiveness. It's what we do. *Return.* Displeasure. Dismissal. *Dislike.* "We have no obligation to answer each other's personal questions because we are only colleagues. And look," I observe, "we're in the lobby. Technically outside of work. I'm surprised you even want to talk to me."

I give him a meaningful glare.

He doesn't look embarrassed, because he's not. "I do consider the lobby to be part of our professional sphere," he replies.

"Elevators, sure, but we're outside the card swipers," I point out. "I think you're in the clear."

Scott genuinely considers my observation. I watch pros and cons, rebuttals and concessions neatly arrange themselves in his eyes the way they do in meetings or on dreaded team calls we have to join in Parthenon conference rooms. Pretending we've never met is the only way I endure them.

Finally, he nods once, conceding my point. *Hooray, me.*

Except, I can't help myself. I remember his phrasing. "Why do you assume I was the dumpee?" I ask.

I'm really one for masochistic questions this fine Friday. Scott, of course, looks ready to indulge me. He pauses, regarding his *favorite* colleague, chin raised in the unconscious way he does, sunlight glinting off his glasses' gray frames. "Because I know you," he finally says.

Leaving me fuming. What was I expecting from Scott?

I notice, despite the early hour, Scott has his leather shoulder bag. If he's going home early, the day has its silver linings. I put on a smile. "Have a great weekend, Scott," I say.

"Actually, I'll be out all week," he informs me with reluctance, like the orderly imperative of work staffing is feuding with his hesitation to provide me information or welcome news.

Which it is. I don't force my smile now. "A whole week," I say. "What a treat for us both. Me because I'll be free of you, and you because you'll be . . . where?"

"A friend's wedding," he replies hastily.

"You have friends?"

Scott glares.

"Personal question, Jennifer," he reminds me.

I don't laugh. I would never give him the pleasure of knowing I find his reprise clever. Instead I purse my lips, defeating the urge, while Scott stoops down to pick up the box. I hurriedly pull it from his hands before he can examine the details of my Halloween costume, which was, shall we say, *provocative*.

I'm not fast enough. Scott's eyes widen. Then they move to mine.

Wait, I order myself, controlling my reaction. Why should *I* be embarrassed in front of Scott? I would have to care about his opinion to be embarrassed.

"You want to ask, don't you?" I say.

Scott says nothing, visibly warring with himself.

"Your colleague who you strongly dislike has a box of her possessions, and what's that? It's strappy and leathery? How interesting," I continue. "What could it be? I wonder if she looks hot as hell in it. Alas, if only such a line of inquiry weren't—what's the word, again?" I exhale. "Oh yes. *Personal*."

Scott's frown deepens when I hit the final word with victorious venom. I grin.

"I'm not that curious," he grumbles.

"You're well within your rights to lie to me, of course," I remind him sweetly. "Since we aren't friends."

Scott looks like he's deliberately not agreeing with my assessment. "Have a great weekend, Jennifer," he replies instead.

I smile. Knowing Scott won't join me in any conference rooms or malinger in my inbox for the next nine days, I really will enjoy the weekend. Ending things with Jordan feels like a distant memory. Who cares! Not me. I've just defeated Scott Daniels at pointless verbal sparring.

Hoisting my personal effects, costume included, I return to the elevators. I ride the high of my perfect comeback up to the Parthenon offices, which were recently remodeled in comforting modern shades of glass and wood. I continue down my hallway, feeling more optimistic now. If a couple coworkers notice what I'm carrying? Whatever. It's Friday.

The fragile magic doesn't last long.

It's worn off when I reach my desk. Instead, sentimentality and discouragement have set in.

I put the cardboard box down, noticing, under my costume and my hoodie, the Oklahoma keychain I got for Jordan early in our relationship on a whim in the airport on my way home from visiting my family. Whenever he noticed it and thought of me, I explained, he would remember how I spent the week thinking of him. I felt like if we got married one day, the keychain, the humble "first gift of our relationship," would make good wedding-website material.

What a fool I was.

If hope is magic, I don't know if I'm happy under its spell. I'm in the unfortunate habit of projecting more onto my relationships than they deserve.

Except, if I were to stop . . . well, I'm starting to fear I would have to give up dating altogether.

Hurting and frustrated, I shove the box's painful reminders out of sight under my desk. Impossibly, I find myself wishing it were *Monday*, or even the dreaded Wednesday morning, when the momentum of work is its most stressful. I could stand to lose myself in deadlines or complicated correspondence right now.

Instead, I have only Friday's lazy continuum. It's 11:15 a.m., leaving me plenty of empty hours. I jog my computer on, then spend fifteen minutes halfheartedly reorganizing my desktop files.

When my phone's vibration hums on my desk, I seize the source of welcome distraction.

It's a photo from my friend Amelia, my former work wife, once my favorite Parthenon marketing coworker. Amelia Gupta, like me, loves Elytheum. It forged our friendship fast, in memes DM'ed during meetings and weekend readathons with cheesecake. She's the Hazelheart to my Spindleshear, which is how we introduce ourselves at Elytheum events. It's hilarious if you're a fan.

In the dazzling morning, with the woods in the distance— North Carolina, I know—Amelia stands in a clearing, looking exhilarated. I notice handmade flags sewn in dark purple, wooden tables laden with scented candles and stage-prop swords. Yes, what surrounds Amelia is unmistakable.

The Elytheum Experience.

I've wanted to go since the Experience was announced. I pretty much worship everything Heather Winters has ever written. For the past decade, while Elytheum Courts has grown into one of publishing's most popular, enduring successes, I've hung on to every word of the unfolding epic of warring fae and mortals in the dark, magical, Regency-meets-medieval realm of Elytheum— especially the forbidden love story of mortal Queen Kethryn and her fae paramour, Lord Valance.

I'm not alone. Far, far from it. While Elytheum flourished, I found other fans online, at events and festivals, and eventually in my job, where I'm fortunate if unsurprised to have coworkers who share my fantasy favorites. I wake up every morning with videos of fan theories and funny reenactments of events from the series, and I procrastinate with Instagram scrolls of fan art and character memes.

Which is why the Elytheum Experience is literally a dream made real. About a year ago, a few fans decided they wanted to organize an Elytheum "immersive experience," complete with costumes, character actors, and scene-inspired events, held on Hollisboro's campus for how perfectly the Gothic architecture reflects Elytheum's darkly dramatic setting. For intellectual property reasons, the founders reached out for Heather Winters's endorsement.

Not only did Winters endorse—she offered to fully fund the Experience, even working in close collaboration with the founders in developing original lore for the expansive immersion.

Original. Lore. The very words make me feel like I've just downed espresso with nine sugars.

Which, for the record, I would never do. Cinnamon dolce lattes only, please.

It was the ultimate move of gratitude and honor for her fans. The Elytheum Experience was official. Nine months ago, Amelia got the worst and happiest news. She interviewed for a developmental role with Winters's IP—a coordinator position hired by Heather to manage and liaise with outside inquiries while the Elytheum brand expanded—and she got the job. We knew it was the right move for her professionally, but we cried her entire last day at Parthenon.

In her new role, Amelia was involved intimately with every step of the Experience's planning. While she couldn't divulge details, when the first Experience was scheduled, she *could* offer her dear friend a free invitation, which she did months ago.

Of course, I suggested to Jordan we go together. Of course, he produced the convenient excuse of his mother's sixtieth birthday. He invited me to her celebratory brunch at his parents' house in the suburbs. I knew it was important to him, and I was proud of the indication for our relationship, Jordan welcoming me into his family.

Guess I'm no longer invited to that! I have to remember to return the candle I got her—

Realization jolts into me. In my clumsy epiphany, my phone

falls from my hand, noisily dropping onto my desk. I don't care. New hope seizes my heart.

New magic.

I'm not with Jordan anymore. I don't have to go to Linda Jenkins's birthday brunch. There's no reason I need to spend the weekend at home crying over her son, either.

Instead, I snatch back up my phone. With fast fingers, I fire off my reply to Amelia.

Any chance you still have a ticket for me?

3

In Elytheum, no one ever has a hard time finding parking.

I've rounded the quiet streets of Hollisboro four times during my hunt, desperation growing with each circumnavigation—feeling probably much like Val when he knew Kethryn was captured within Nightfell's walls with the hourglass running out on her life. Except, of course, for the smell of the "Cherry Evening" air freshener pervading the interior of my sister's Prius.

When I *finally* find parking outside one of the neighborhood's overwhelmingly common frozen yogurt places, I'm frustrated. I *hate* being late. If you're late, you're late. If you're early . . . you've just given yourself extra time to read the book you have inevitably brought with you.

I have no welcome reading opportunity now. I'm late. *Well*, I remind myself, *isn't acting out of character the entire point?*

My new plan is very out of character, honestly. Instead of comforting myself about the end of yet another relationship with ice cream and my favorite Elytheum Courts chapters, I called my sister, Sarah, took the NJ Transit to her condo, picked up her fruit-scented Prius, and drove eight hours into the wooded heart of North Carolina.

I don't need another Jordan, I decided with new resolve. I don't need another relationship. I don't need to pretend dinner and Netflix and decent sex once a week is the height of romance for month after month.

Why do I keep dashing myself against the rocks of online dating when I have the love in my favorite series, where it's never disappointing? Did a date *ever* measure up to a night of reading about the passion and connection of Lord Valance and Queen Kethryn in Elytheum? Where men are noble warriors and devoted lovers?

Okay, not exactly men—what with the wings and horns. Still— when they say "I love you" it means something.

I didn't even return home from the office on my way to Sarah's. Very conveniently, I had the box of everything I needed from Jordan, toiletries and clothes and all. Plus, I didn't want to lose my nerve, which I worried would happen in my cozy apartment with favorite rereads on my shelves and peanut-butter-pretzel ice cream in the freezer.

I grab my cloak from the Prius's passenger seat, resenting the reminder of my ex when my fingers catch the Elytheum emblem I embossed into the fabric. When I made the garment for Halloween, Jordan said I looked hot, referring to what I wore underneath, the leather video-game-character costume I felt reasonably approximated Kethryn's Royal Vanguard armor.

The compliment helped me ignore the obvious fact that Jordan had no idea the cloak was from my favorite series. Honestly, I'd liked how I looked—how my dark brown hair fell over the stripes of leather crossing my skin. For the night, I wasn't average-height, average-everything Jennifer. I was a heroine.

I pull on the cloak over the blouse and jeans I wore to work. I could use some less strappy Elytheum options for the week, honestly. Fortunately, Amelia says the Experience will include opportunities to buy or craft other Elytheum-appropriate costuming.

Hollisboro is wonderfully warm in the summer night, cooling off enough for me to fling the cloak over my shoulders without overheating. I hustle down the quaint streets with Google Maps' guidance in the direction of the College of Hollisboro's campus, ignoring how my driving-wracked stomach yearns for coffee—the Experience started an hour ago, and I won't miss one second more.

Passing grad students and college-touring families, I feel a little ridiculous. *A grown woman, walking around in her costume.*

I hate the ingrained reaction, knowing I wouldn't feel the same if it were a sports jersey. It's just hard to fight when I hear often how embarrassing my reading preferences are, from guys I date, and even from colleagues—including, of course, Scott Daniels. He's never outright mean, just dismissive and occasionally judgmental whenever Elytheum or romantasy comes up in office conversation. I'll read whatever I damn well please, Scott!

Whatever. None of my exes are here. No grumbling coworkers. No judgmental literati. No one is here who will make me feel uncool for loving Elytheum. I don't have to hide my cloak *or* myself.

The College of Hollisboro's high gates finally appear amid the college town. They're just like the caricature rendered them on the Elytheum Experience website. I must admit, they're the perfect entry point. Imposing, wrought iron, stretching high into the air, they say, *fantasy awaits.*

I step onto campus emboldened—and am impressed. The Experience's location is perfectly chosen, with sculpted archways of gray stone under intricate Gothic spires. Ironically, the grounds look fit for the courtly intrigues, clandestine cunning, and dark magic rituals of Elytheum, not for Economics 101.

Reaching the dining hall, I pause, remembering how I felt in my office. How foolish, idealistic, and delusional. How *hope* has led me right into the stupid, painful, frustrating end of another relationship.

I fight the feeling. *No.* I'm not hurting. I'm in Elytheum.

Pushing open the door, I walk into another world.

None of the vivid dreams I've had prepare me for what I find inside. The Elytheum Experience is . . . enchanting. Intricate production design has converted the college's dining hall into the Great Hall, the imposing room where fae declarations of war are delivered and queens mourned. Only candlelight illuminates the hall, into which romantic violin music plays quietly from musicians near the fireplace. Everyone is dressed much more elaborately than me.

At the front of the room, a stunning woman in armor sits on an actual throne.

Chills spread down my arms. *Kethryn*. Which means . . .

Heart pounding with excitement, I gaze eagerly around the room until I find him.

With prosthetic horns peering out from his sweep of ebony hair, he's unmistakable. The man in ornamented dark garb watching Kethryn from the corner of the room was the central preoccupation of a good number of my aforementioned dreams—or, his character was.

Lord Valance is exactly how I imagined him.

I find I'm grinning my first grin of the day. Elytheum really is magic, one way or another.

"Okay, I'm amazed you got here in time."

Only Amelia's voice pulls me from my unabashed scrutiny of Val. I haven't seen her in months, and just hearing her has me immediately emotional. I spin, crushing the clipboard she's holding with the hug I sweep her into.

"You did *not* exaggerate," I say when we part, referring to the room.

Amelia shrugs, smug. She's shorter than I am, and even the heels she's wearing as part of her impeccable courtly look don't bring her to my eyeline. Her hair is braided into an elaborate black crown, her thick mascara accentuating her dark eyes. "I really didn't," she says. "Here, I snuck your key from check-in so you can go up after this."

While the key card she offers me is plastic and obviously non-magical, reasonably required for use of the dorms for the summer week, it's painted to resemble a playing card, one whose design I recognize from fan art. *Of course.* Demoniaca is the recreational card game of Elytheum, a cross of poker and Pokémon over which deals are struck or secrets exchanged. *Spindleshear*, mine reads, with the demon's portrait. I hold it up.

Amelia smiles. "Cool, right?"

"God, I've missed you," I say.

"You too, girl." Her expression shifts into hesitant sympathy. "Are you—is everything . . . ?"

While I know she means well, I don't welcome the distraction of the hurt welling up in me. "We're not supposed to talk about the outside world here, right?" I reply. It was on the email confirmation's list of rules, emphasized to prevent "bleed" from the real world.

Amelia's mouth flattens with my evasion. "Convenient for you," she remarks. "Well, we're going off campus for coffee and you're telling me what happened," she orders me.

It's how Amelia is, always on the fine line separating domineering from encouraging and defending me like no one else in my life ever does. "It's really not worth talking about," I say weakly.

"Yes," Amelia replies. "It is." Excusing my further resistance, her eyes catch on a girl waving her over nervously. "Heather's assistant needs me," Amelia says with forced patience, her gaze returning to mine. "We'll catch up later," she promises me meaningfully.

I nod, my stomach knotting. Honestly, I don't want to discuss my pathetic love life—not when Elytheum is here to experience.

While I walk over to sit at one of the long tables, another epiphany descends over me in the rose-scented room. For the next week, I'm *not* Jennifer Worth. I don't have to be the woman who spent the past year dating a man who gave me only what a relationship *needed*—consistency, fidelity—while never giving me what I *wanted*. I don't have to be the Jennifer who wasted her time or had her time wasted.

No, I'm . . . *whoever I want to be.* Warrior. Princess. Fae. Demon. I don't know yet. I just know the options are exhilarating.

Sampling the cheesy stuffed mushroom one of the many footmen has delivered me, I listen, scouring the snatches of conversation surrounding me for inspiration. The man and woman next to me make illicit plans, their offers to "exchange sensitive espionage information" sounding like pretense to exchange something else.

I stay silent, still figuring out what I want my story to be.

Darting unhidden glances at Val in the corner, the women across from me swap fictional war stories from the Western Court Campaign. It's wonderful realizing I'm following every reference, every detail. Who knew a fantasy world could feel like home? I'm about to chime into their conversation when I hear a familiar laugh.

No. No way.

I look over my shoulder while the room seems to enter slow motion, as if under the Forgotten King's hourglass magic. The man who laughed is chatting animatedly with an older woman in elf ears, his grin upturned roguishly. In full leather armor, he looks like he's in the Queen's Guard.

Or, that's how I know he looks to everyone else here.

To me, he just looks like Scott Daniels.

4

I almost wonder if he has a twin. We've never shared *personal* information, obviously, so I would never know if Scott has an identical sibling who lives in North Carolina. Who loves Elytheum enough to dress in an elaborate costume.

Yes, it makes perfect sense. Perfect sense they would be opposites, even. Wasn't Lord Valance's late brother considered everything Val wasn't when they were young, leading Val to emulate his sibling's nobility when the elder was slain? Lord Resten was upstanding, where young Valance was cunning. Not-Scott evidently values the greatest fantasy series ever written, where his benighted brother doesn't.

I venture closer. I look hard, my heart sinking.

No. No sibling switcheroo.

It really is Scott. *My* Scott.

How? His absence from work checks out. His excuse doesn't. He said he was going to a friend's wedding. And, I remember, when I strode eagerly into my supervisor's office eight hours ago, pitching my weeklong adventure as research in case we ever want to organize something like this for one of our titles, she didn't say she'd already sent Scott.

He's here, and he's kept it a secret from everyone. Not just from me. *Why?*

Concentrating on the question instead of the displeasure of seeing him, I walk closer, curiosity compelling me.

More proof it's really Scott waits for me. I notice he looks—out of place.

I mean, of course he's out of place. He looks like he *knows it*, though.

His costume is right, I'll grant him, sinisterly formal with the vaguely period flair of Elytheum. Yet the man inside looks like he's . . . posing. He's standing with stiffness his leather pants do not entirely explain. He holds his jaw tight, his eyes on the middle distance in wistful, wary concentration.

When Scott joined Parthenon, I thought we could be friends.

Until Scott made it very clear he wanted nothing to do with me. I've been rejected romantically probably hundreds of times. But rejected for *friendship?* That was a new low, even for me.

The weeks went on, and I couldn't help standoffishness in the office. Scott returned the same, which was entirely unnecessary and unfair given *he* was the one who rejected *me*.

Ultimately, I found myself grateful we never got closer. I quickly realized how incompatible we are.

Namely, I realized how disdainful Scott is of the stories I love. I've unashamedly used my work at Parthenon to promote and legitimize my favorite genres. Why shouldn't romance and fantasy get the prestige marketing and universal renown general and literary fiction does? There's nothing wrong with loving them, and many, many readers do.

Then along came Scott. From his first grimace when I invoked Elytheum, or *The Crimson Rose*, or *Iron Clad*—I don't even remember—to repetitions of how he "didn't get the hype," he's waged petty war on my passions, my fandom, for the past year.

I could have gotten over Scott rejecting my overture of friendship. I really could have, even when his conversational manners left much room for improvement. I could have patched up my pride and determined to make aloof colleagues with my new coworker.

What I cannot forgive, however, is Scott rolling his eyes whenever I would summarize my newest reading obsession to Amelia in the pre-meeting minutes in the conference room. Or murmuring how *people shouldn't just read one genre* when I presume to push two romantasy titles in one month.

When I prevailed in my yearlong campaign to push Elytheum to the top of our colleague Raymond's TBR, only for Raymond to come in on Monday *raving* about Val and Kethryn's first night together, what did Scott say? *Repetitive.*

How dare he!

Now the pain in my professional ass props one foot up on the dining hall bench. Leaning forward awkwardly—like he's recovering from leg day at the gym—he's engaged in, well, flirtatious conversation with the woman next to him. She's pretty. Her Western Court costume is perfection.

I can't even enjoy the pained exertion in Scott's posture, or admire the details of his counterpart's cloak. His very presence, not to mention his chatting with attractive other guests, feels vindictive. Uninterested in fantasy and then intruding on mine? Pick one, please.

Frustration rises in me, urgent and uncontrollable. On the drive down, I'd really hoped this week could provide the healing respite I needed from the end of another relationship. I just wanted to forget the embarrassment, the hurt, with my favorite escape from reality's disappointments. Now I'm supposed to let Scott ruin my real-life daydream?

No. I need to hold my ground. The way Kethryn would.

Steeling myself with the strength of the warrior queen, I march right up to him.

"I knew you didn't have friends who would invite you to a wedding," I say with no waver in my voice.

I'm gratified when Scott startles. Less when he immediately recovers—plastering on a smooth, oil-slick smile I've literally never seen from the precise and polished, notebook-obsessed marketing coordinator I know.

"So sorry," he says to the Western Court woman. "Would you excuse me?"

The woman evidently intuits our conversation is *not* part of the Experience. She nods, slipping politely from our presence.

Scott's gaze shifts back to me. He isn't wearing his glasses, I notice. "What," he says with controlled frustration, "are you doing here?"

I gape. "This is my favorite book series, Scott. What are *you* doing here?"

He shakes his head, stubborn. "No," he insists. "When I arranged my time off, I was told you would be covering my titles."

I take a deep breath, fighting to control my racing heart. I *should* be admiring the enormous, intricate map of Elytheum on the wall, or speaking to the character actors right now. It's just utterly, damnably Scott to make a sticking point of *who's covering whose titles*. Could you drop it for one minute, Sir Organization?

"My trip was very last minute," I explain in exasperation. "Let me guess," I go on. "You're here for work research, but you were too embarrassed to admit it to everyone after insisting you would never get the Elytheum appeal. Finally realized you should pay attention?"

While Scott returns my glare, he has nothing to say in his defense. Finally, he looks away, which is perversely satisfying—almost enough for me to miss the unreadable flash of something crossing his features.

I also notice we're unfortunately starting to draw stares. Even Val himself is watching us with interest I consider, frankly, not character consistent.

It robs me of fight, the perfect reminder of how Scott's presence here cannot help messing everything up. "Forget it," I say, hiding my impatience. "I'm here now. I'll do the market research. You just—go home. Enjoy your week off."

Not understanding the imperative, Scott eyes me like I'm some particularly neat handwriting in his fucking notebook.

"You want me to leave," he clarifies.

"Obviously." Now I know Scott hears the frustration in my voice. The Lord of Night over there probably hears it. "I came here to escape my ordinary life. To live out a fantasy. *You* do not fit in."

When Scott's eyebrows rise, I realize I've said the wrong thing. "I don't fit into your fantasies?" he replies, sounding more amused than insulted.

"You're the antithesis of my fantasies," I inform him.

My irritation only increases when—instead of looking wounded, or perhaps combusting into nothingness like he's been struck by a foul curse—Scott looks . . . interested? "How, exactly?" he asks me earnestly.

I narrow my gaze. I'm here for the Elytheum Experience, not the Scott Daniels Experience. No, every second I spend stuck in some ridiculous feud with him is stealing from the week I wanted for myself. I redirect. "Look," I implore. "If you leave, it's a win-

win. I'll share my ideas with you. You can even take credit for them. Just . . . go home, and let me enjoy my fantasy week."

He regards me for a long moment, and I'm surprised to find he really looks conflicted. Despite the easy out I'm offering him, something keeps him in place.

Finally, he replies. "I . . . can't."

"You *can't*?" I repeat. "Why?"

"It's personal," he grinds out.

My eyes widen. Unfortunate as his arrival is, I'm curious now. The man I know is one-dimensional, an avatar of meetings and emails. Yet in this moment, Scott Daniels is wrestling with himself. It's admittedly intriguing. "Are you here to enjoy the Experience? Are you secretly a fan?" I goad.

"No," he replies without resentment.

"You do understand what this week is going to entail, right?" I charge on. "Whatever your personal reason, surely you can ignore it and go home."

Finally, he sighs, defeated. "I wish I could," he confesses. "But if my presence here ruins your week, Jennifer, then please, by all means, leave."

I wish I could?

I don't have the chance to decipher Scott's inexplicable determination. Long horns, impressively designed to look sculpted of ivory just like in the series, held to the mouths of impeccably costumed court footmen, call the room's eyes with deep, vibrating notes. With them, Kethryn steps onto the stage. Val follows her, evidently remembering himself despite my distracting work feud.

"Everyone be seated," he orders. No *please*. Val doesn't say *please*. Except, ugh, one incredible scene in Crimsonfell when—"Your queen wishes to address you," Val interrupts my fan-spiraling.

I hesitate. Does part of me want to drag Scott into the courtyard and figure out why he's really here so I can find a way to convince him to leave? Hm, I don't know—do demons cherish shards of fae souls?

Yes. Yes, very much.

The greater part of me, however, refuses to forgo even a second of the once-in-a-lifetime Elytheum Experience.

Ignoring his cryptic remark, I turn from Scott and take my seat, ready to listen to my favorite character in real life.

5

The stuffed mushroom nearly sends me over the edge.

The mushroom I was enjoying, specifically, from the servers dressed in Elytheum livery. The cook captured something unusual. Spicy, smoky, decadent with warm cheese. I could imagine Kethryn's courtly cooks concocting the appetizer—immersion even in dinner.

And now it's gone.

Cleared innocently while I fought with the one man I shouldn't have to deal with here!

Stomach rumbling, I decide I *won't* let Scott ruin the Experience. I just need to pretend he's not here.

Fortunately, I have the ideal distraction right in front of me. Kethryn sits regally straight on her throne, regarding us. Val's proclamation has spread reverent silence over the costumed crowd.

I'm used to reaching for escape in my favorite stories. I've found refuge in books, especially fantasy, for as long as I can remember. Growing up in Oklahoma City, I was, well—weird. I could never join casual activities or make connections easily. Definitely not compared to my sister, Sarah, who was athletic, supplying her a ready-made team of friends for every season.

I knew my peers found me shy sometimes, overenthusiastic at others. I just couldn't figure out how to control the extremes. When I finally did, entering high school, I wound up scared to distinguish myself in any way. If I was a knight in the kingdom of Oklahoma, they would have called me "Jennifer the Ordinary."

Finding friendship requires putting yourself out there. Putting yourself out there requires . . . vulnerability. I'm not good at vulnerability. I would really rather not show strangers exactly who I am, only for them to reject me. No way.

Instead, I wait for people to approach me. Has it made me the most popular twenty-six-year-old woman in New York City? My minuscule Instagram following would indicate not. Whatever. I have Amelia. I have college friends I FaceTime with approximately once every fiscal quarter. I *had* a semi-serious boyfriend to take me to dinner and give me orgasms.

And . . . here I am, dwelling on my mediocre ex.

No. I'm here for the companions who've never left me, the loves who've never hurt me. In the pages, I don't just find fictional friends. I find places where I can feel everything I won't let myself in real life, knowing the emotions could disappoint or mislead me. I can feel heartbroken or proud or excited, and it doesn't have to be more than a feeling. It doesn't have to scare me to see the well of emotion inside.

As I grew up, my favorite stories led me to my closest friends, to my career. They held my hand when my emotions got too big, or when I didn't know how I felt—or when I just needed something to look forward to after college, when life started to stretch in front of me in one long winding road with no more signposts or traffic lights.

They taught me what falling in love should feel like, what sex could be with the right partner.

Long before my unfortunate dating history, they taught me heartbreak. How characters I considered reflections of myself could journey on past unimaginable hardship. How they could lose love or family or destiny without losing themselves.

The stories I love led me here. They prepared me for this very moment.

I need only hold on to them now.

Kethryn rises, impeccably in character. She's everything, not in the vernacular sense—Winters wrote her as the embodiment of uncompromising, intending to prove how the Queen's elegant grace could cohere with her hard-core combat skill and her hard head for statecraft.

The actress is capturing her manner perfectly. Her lips part in fond indulgence of a smile.

"Welcome," she says, "to my court."

I lean forward. *Finally*, my hope of immersing myself, distracting myself, is *working*. It feels unimaginably good.

"Your presence here honors me and my crown. While I know you are here to enjoy the finest entertainments our court can provide—and you shall—I hope you find the greatest treasures among those seated beside you," Kethryn continues. "Elytheum's magic lives in every greeting between strangers, every smile among friends, every embrace of lovers."

Oh. Oh no. Jennifer the Ordinary might cry.

Did Winters herself script Kethryn's introduction? It's not a speech from the series, yet the message and the melody are pure Elytheum.

What *else* is pure Elytheum is the longing look Kethryn gives Val next to her. Her perfectly tortured paramour. I have the feeling of finding myself *exactly* where I'm meant to be. Just mere moments of dialogue in, the Elytheum Experience is proving to be everything I'd hoped.

For some reason, I glance at Scott. I guess the Queen's speech has moved me, despite my sounder judgment, to some fantasizing of my own. It's what inspiring writing does, right? In the fantastical version of this week, Scott comes to me saying he was a fool for rejecting me, apologizing for his unconscionable manner, and professing how wrong he was for *ever* implying the Elytheum books were uninteresting.

I would meet his eyes, finding the volatile combination of hatred and longing I know from Val fan art. We would have the perfect enemies-to-lovers romance where he ultimately changes every unlikable quality about himself and I *deign* to give him a chance . . .

Instead, Scott is, irritatingly, *not* looking at me.

Fantasy fail.

He's watching Kethryn. I don't know why I ever expected otherwise. Scott could never embody the heart-stopping, heart-rending perfection of my favorite scenes and characters. He's way too boring, introverted, and judgmental.

Why would I ever daydream otherwise? What was it Jordan said? *If you want the kind of fantasy love story you read about, I hope you're ready to wait forever.*

Kethryn continues, conjuring fantasy where Scott Daniels can't. "May your stay here prove nothing short of magical. On your final night in our illustrious court, we invite you to join us in the richest of courtly festivities," Kethryn entreats us. "A masked ball, in this very room."

I straighten, heart fluttering. From the *ooh*s and whispered chatter rising from my cohort, I know everyone is having the same reaction. Or, everyone except one improbably costumed marketing coordinator. Friends grab one another's arms, whisper in each other's ears, or squeal in anticipation. The Elytheum Experience's vague description on the website invited eagerness but was low on details—everything Kethryn shares of our schedule this week is the first we're learning of the particulars of the inaugural Experience.

"However," Kethryn continues.

A hush descends comically quickly over the room.

"One word of warning," she says. "We have enemies here at court who have hatched a devious plot against us."

Now I *really* can't help glancing at Scott. Once more, no return glance. He's fixated on Kethryn's performance. Pretending the world of Elytheum is oh so fascinating instead of the subject he's dismissed in every departmental meeting.

Enemies indeed.

"While you may rely on the protection of the captain of my guard, Lord Valance, standing to my right, I urge you to keep your eyes open," Kethryn entreats us.

With the first utterance of his name from Kethryn herself, or, okay, the Kethryn actress—whatever—everyone in the room indeed keeps their eyes open. Pointed in one direction, in fact. We needed no encouragement.

Val welcomes our regard. His dark gaze capturing everyone and no one, he straight-up *smolders*. I know no other word for the intense look he gives us. He's really good, honestly. Perfectly cast, with his ink-wash hair, his inhumanly symmetrical, combat-ready musculature. It's very hard to imagine this guy waiting tables or doing deodorant commercials instead of defending the court from demonic incursions, and I choose not to.

"In fact . . ."

Kethryn interrupts our collective fantasizing.

The playful note in her voice catches my interest. Like she's excited for what she's going to say next. I wonder if *she's* a fan. What if this is her dream made real just like it's ours, except differently?

"Our foes have hidden clues to their plan throughout my court. Perhaps you will find some. Find three, and you'll save us," Kethryn elaborates, her voice humming with precarious promise. "Of course," she goes on, "I would wish to reward such a hero and to relay such valuable information to my captain of the guard."

Clues.

Excitement hurries my heartbeat. Kethryn is promising us . . . a game. A hunt.

The room holds its breath, each of us realizing in the same moment what I have. No scavenger hunt is complete without a prize.

Hints on the next spinoff series? My eager mind starts outpacing my heart. *Deleted scenes for the winner's eyes only?*

"The first to find three clues," Kethryn says slowly—playing with us, pausing while we lean in—"will attend a private dinner with Lord Valance."

Oh, this is much, much more important than deleted scenes.

No one here needs this like I need this. Respectfully. Me, Jennifer Worth, who ended her six-month relationship this morning. I need the rebound to end all rebounds.

A dinner date with Lord Valance.

Val responds perfectly, pretending Kethryn's invocation really has surprised him. Of course, on his nobly unmoving, ever-wary features, incredulity registers only the faintest of reactions. One dark eyebrow quirks.

"Surely I'm no *reward* for these fine people," he replies. The crowd giggles. Pretending he finds Kethryn's orations irritating while honoring her every request is *very* Val. Even his voice, resonant in the first full sentence I've heard the performer speak, is perfect. Velvet the color of night. I wonder how many courses one would be permitted to order during the prize dinner.

"Don't play humble, Val," Kethryn chides.

"Are you saying my company pleases you, my queen?"

"On occasion," Kethryn replies drolly. "On others, it vexes me."

Okay, Winters *must* have scripted this.

Val crosses his massive arms. He regards Kethryn. The look he gives her is . . . impossibly dreamy. Inhumanly dreamy. Unfairly dreamy. I can practically see the sparks flinting off his charged gaze.

"Well, we can't have that," Val murmurs. "I aspire to vex you always and forever."

My heart melts. Like, into chocolate fondue. It is everything I've imagined in every reread of every favorite scene. *This* is what love should look like.

"*Ho-ly shit*," the woman next to me says.

The comment unlocks the table's collective chatter, like everyone's simultaneously realized we're watching the same shared dream play out.

And wishing the same wish.

"I wonder what kind of clues," my other neighbor says. "God, if only I was good at puzzles."

"Maybe they'll be, like, challenges? Sort of *Survivor*-style?" her friend offers. They're dressed in full demon garb. It's kind of intimidating, honestly, while they speculate on the clue challenges. Fierce competitors.

The first woman who spoke leans her elbows on the table. "If I have to balance on a beam for an hour to go on a date with my literal book boyfriend, I will. I don't care if I look ridiculous."

The chatter continues, its import settling upon me. Lord

Valance isn't just *my* book boyfriend. He's the paramour of the pages for . . . everyone here. If I'm going to win the dinner date of my daydreams, the cure for Jordan Jenkins and lobby breakups, I'll need to outplay the ultimate competition—Elytheum fans as avid as me, who've shown up for the very first immersion in our favorite fantasy.

They don't have heartbreak going for them, I comfort myself.

"In order to succeed in this task, one must possess secrecy. Loyalty. Temerity and aptitude," Kethryn counsels us, managing to cease exchanging lustful looks with her captain of the guard.

Despite myself, I wince. *Temerity and aptitude?* Kind of a mouthful, where I usually prize my favorite series' poetry. Guess Winters didn't necessarily script *every* line of dialogue.

"Work together, help one another, and embrace adventure," Kethryn continues.

Movement in front of me distracts me from her speech and from the continued murmur of strategizing and enthusiasm from the guests around me. Scott is no longer watching Kethryn— which I find frustratingly, satisfyingly predictable until I notice what he's doing instead.

Hunched over his lap, he's *writing*. In his ubiquitous black notebook, his companion for every marketing meeting. The notebook's presence here viscerally upsets me. In a profession devoted to sharing the writing we love, Scott manages to drab-ify every discussion with analytics pointedly presented from its pages, which invariably contradict whatever I'm proposing or excited about. Funny how that happens!

He has one of his favorite pens, the brand he praises for the easy, precise roll of the ink. I wish I didn't know him well enough to remember this detail. And he's . . . taking notes on Kethryn's speech?

I narrow my gaze. He's completely focused on the actors. *Why?* What game is he playing? He said he wasn't here for work . . . But what other reason could he possibly have for wanting to get dinner with fake Lord Valance? None. I expected competition from Elytheum fangirls. I did not expect it from him.

Immediately, I realize I can't just ignore him this week. Not amid the scavenger hunt. No, if he's going to play hard and I have to watch *Scott Daniels* win dinner with *my* book boyfriend, my Elytheum Experience will become a literal nightmare.

No. If I can't convince him to go home, I'm going to have to beat him.

In the same moment I make my resolution, Scott looks up. His eyes meet mine. I hope he reads the declaration of war in the glare I give him.

Scott smiles and fucking winks.

6

My room is five stories up. There's no elevator.

Well, at least the punishing climb is Elytheum appropriate. They don't have elevators in Kethryn's court, either.

I huff up the interminable steps with my small suitcase, which I collected from my car after leaving dinner. Notwithstanding the presence of one particular guest, our evening meal was delightful— especially dessert. In one of Elytheum's cutest scenes, Val escorts Kethryn into the shadowy city where he grew up. They have "night cakes" from the neighborhood's street stand. Every cake is different, and the constellation of sugared "stars" on the dark mousse of the delicacy "predict the fortune" of the eater.

What did I find when the servers deposited dessert in front of us? Rich chocolate mousse, decorated with smatterings of silvery sugar. Exactly how I envisioned the scene.

Me and everyone else, obviously. Gasps went up from my dinner companions. Congratulations to the chef, who I'm starting to feel certain has read Elytheum. I mean, wow.

The long communal tables permitted small talk with other participants, and over night cakes, I met some of my cohabitants of Kethryn's court. Erica with her daughter Nora, who shared their fandom when Nora went to college. Literary agent Nia, looking to remember what she loves in fiction. William, in his sixties, whose coworkers in insurance got him enthusiastically into the series. "I haven't slept in a dorm in forty years!" he proclaimed.

Their company, not to mention the chocolate mousse, distracted me well enough from the presence of one Lord Daniels, even if, watching him carouse with demonesses, I imagined potential fortunes his night cake could have given him. *You will fall down the college's grandest stone steps and split the seams of your new costume pants. You will discover an allergy to chocolate mousse causing horrific diarrhea.*

Mounting the stairs to my suite, I no longer have the relief of distraction. With every heavy stomp, I let the pain in my legs push out the frustration of Scott.

The stairway is shadowy in the Elytheum-*inappropriate* electric lighting. Finally, I reach the uppermost landing, where I find the hallway of the college dorm I'll call my fantastical home for the next week.

Only when I click open my door with the Demoniaca-painted key card do I realize Amelia gave me my room as a kindness, not for unwanted cardio. It's a corner suite in a literal Gothic tower, with windows overlooking the whole college. While night has left the campus in darkness, the pathways are lit up, illumination crossing the quiet expanse. I see people walking with friends carrying ice cream from town, grad students returning home from the day's research, couples holding hands.

It's idyllic. Magical, even.

I pull my shoes off in the doorway, finally relaxing. I leave my cloak on. For the first moment since I spied Scott downstairs, he feels wondrously far from here.

I explore my suite, which is nothing like my own college

experience—I commuted to Oklahoma City University from my parents' house nearby. Everything here feels new in an exciting way. Within the white walls, standard dorm pieces furnish the rooms sparsely. Past the frankly small and odd-shaped common room, I find two bedrooms. Whoever my roommate is, if I have one, they haven't arrived.

What leaves me marveling, however, are the Elytheum details. The organizers have enlivened the College of Hollisboro suite with flourishes I cannot wait to examine. Like, I do not know where I will start. The elaborately framed Elytheum landscape print over our couch, fan art in the guise of the work of a courtly painter? The sigils over the doors, instantly recognizable emblems of Kethryn's reign? The candelabra on the coffee table, surrounded with designer chocolates? On second thought, I do know where I'll start.

Amelia and the organizers have done everything to make the dorm feel like I'm living in the very finest of Elytheum. It's not just idyllic. It's epic. Ironic, perhaps, to find myself enchanted by a college dorm room when I have my own apartment, with views of New York City and furniture I chose myself—or maybe just the magic of the Experience.

I pick one of the bedrooms, where I hoist my suitcase onto the ebony coverlet, which manages to make my collegiate sleeping situation look opulent. I unpack my minimal luggage into the equally small wardrobe.

Finished, I don't even hesitate. I know exactly what I'm doing on my first night in my fantasy.

I'm going to fucking *read*.

I'm ready to start Elytheum Courts over with the perfect scenery surrounding me. *The Shattered Court* opens the series majestically with Kethryn, the youngest daughter of the royal family, surviving an invasion of the palace—the *only* survivor. Under the protection of an obsidian-eyed fae, she is crowned the new queen, fearing for her safety while investigating the plot against her family.

Perfection!

I've owned numerous copies in the past decade. The one I packed with me is my favorite, a special edition, the Wright & Camby's exclusive with full-color fan art on the inside of the covers and spicy extra scenes. In the quiet of my room, I lift the heavy volume gently from my suitcase and head into the weirdly shaped common room, where I curl up in my cloak on the couch.

I light the violet candle on the coffee table. I pop one of the designer chocolates.

I open the book. *Page one.*

With the fabulous day I've had in the real world, it should be freeing, immersing myself in Elytheum. In passages I could recite anywhere, anytime. *Kethryn wore black on the day of her coronation . . .*

No, it *is* freeing! Instead of stuck on the highway in my sister's Prius, caught in the horrible repeating memory of getting dumped in my office's elevator lobby like some demented time-loop movie, I'm here. Instead of reading on Jordan's couch while he plays video games—feeling quietly, exasperatingly stuck—I'm *here*. Cozy, wrapped in the candle's sweet leather scent, free from judgment.

I keep reading.

Kethryn wore black on the day of her coronation. The wrong choice . . .

Instead of Jordan nodding off while I keep the nightstand light on, wishing I wasn't engrossed in the manuscript Scott spent the day's meeting championing, I'm here.

Instead of watching Scott present using only his ever-present notebook, the only person in our meetings without a laptop, I'm . . .

The wrong choice . . .

God damnit. Yes, I'm here, but my mind won't pull me into the pages. I'm stuck on Scott.

Just like my compulsion to start my favorite series over again right after finishing it, endings always make me think about beginnings. My first real interaction with Scott, the real start of our delightful relationship, occurred in the nondescript hallway of one of our colleagues' apartments. How fitting—a decidedly uninteresting location.

I was heading to the birthday party of Charlene in Sales, who I do not particularly like. Her friends were hosting, not even Charlene herself. The only reason I'd even gotten invited was office chatter about the event. It would be awkward for Charlene not to invite everyone, including Jennifer Worth in Marketing.

I knew I had to make an appearance in order to not look like the office jerk who didn't come. However, I *really* didn't want to. I would not consider myself a comfortable partier under even ideal conditions, and an event in a random apartment, hosted by people I'd never met and would never meet again, were not ideal conditions.

Nevertheless, I went.

I hung out *near* people, pretending I was hanging out *with* them. I wished Charlene's friend had pets with whom I could distract myself. When finally I felt I could make my escape, having served my partying sentence, I left.

Absconding from Charlene's friend's apartment, I found him in the hallway.

Scott Daniels, I learned earlier in the week. The new hire. Like mine, his invitation to Charlene's party was no doubt out of office obligation.

And like me, he did not appear in the partying mood. He was approaching the door while I was leaving.

"Any signs of slowing down?" he asked me, nodding at the door in indication of the party, which was very much *not* slowing down.

"You . . . like to make an entrance only after a party has slowed down?" I couldn't help clarifying.

He had the good grace to smile, although not without restraint. Like the danger of making small talk with Jennifer Worth might pull him into the pit of partying. "I was on the fence about coming at all," he replied. "I'm hoping to make a friendly appearance when things are mostly wrapping up."

"We'll, you're in luck . . ." I said with the careful bedside manner needed to break terrible news, "if you think tequila shots mean a party is slowing down."

He rubbed a hand down his face. "Maybe your departure will start a party exodus?" he ventured.

Having spent the past exactly one hour and fifteen minutes standing awkwardly by a boarded-up fireplace, nursing a Sprite and hoarding a mediocre spread of cheese cubes, I laughed a little bitterly. "I'm guessing my exit will only spur the party on harder."

He eyed me then. Curiosity won out in him. "Why's that?"

I felt Scott taking in my corduroy dress and black tights. I knew what he saw—the quiet girl in every class. Or the nerd with irritating niche enthusiasm.

Why not own it? I remember asking myself spitefully. "I'm a perennial party pooper," I confessed. "A California-king-sized wet blanket."

He laughed—and it was joyous and free of judgment. Like we

were in on the same joke. And I guess I dared look closer. He wasn't wearing anything much different from the office—unshowy dress shirt, casual gray blazer—yet he carried the crispness off with an understated confidence. It isn't strictly possible for someone to look mild mannered—yet, he did. With his narrow nose, his inquisitive eyes, glasses that suited him.

"Well, what are you doing out here? You have to go back in there," he encouraged me. "Absolutely decimate the vibe. Oversharing, weird family anecdotes. Change the radio to the Sirius Met Opera station. Pick some fights."

It was my turn to laugh. "Only people who listen to the Sirius Met Opera radio station even know what it is," I pointed out, welcoming without shame the membership in this group my statement implied.

"In case it wasn't abundantly clear," he replied, "I, too, am unfun."

It pushed me over from curious into amused. "I don't think so," I said.

In fact, I was feeling the inklings of something like hope. Amelia was my only real work friend, and I wouldn't mind making another in the promising new guy.

"But I mean," I went on, "we could test it? We could go in there, team up, and find out just how quickly two uncool people can shut down a party."

My new compatriot eyed the door, weighing my proposal. I liked the hint of mischief in his eyes. In his whole nerdy, professional vibe, it stood out intriguingly. The first drop of watercolor paint into clear water.

Emboldened, I continued. "Or we could leave and get a drink. There's a bar across the street. Get to know each other."

He hesitated. I waited, proud of myself. I'm not usually one for putting myself out there, which was probably *why* Amelia was my only work friend. I felt unexpectedly good. Like Scott Daniels could be the start of something. I'd managed to conjure hope, my favorite magic, in the hallways of—

"No thanks," he replied curtly.

Startled, I blinked. The crestfallen hurt was delayed, not hitting me until moments later, when I was prepared to hide the reaction under casual deference.

"Oh," I replied. *What kind of person says* no *to friendly drinks with a colleague?* "I'm . . . just being friendly," I clarified, momentarily horrified by the thought he interpreted my invite romantically.

Scott retreated several steps, putting his hands in his pockets with square-shouldered defensiveness. He looked like he positively wished for the reprieve of Charlene's party, from which "Turn Down for What" was emanating powerfully. "I know," he said. "I'm just not interested."

Oof. Okay, while it wasn't like I knew Scott Daniels or was entitled to the pleasure—debatable now—of his company, I was a little shocked by the dismissal. Resentfulness flickered into my voice when I replied.

"You know what, you were right," I said. "You *are* unfun."

Scott eyed me, but he said nothing. Of course not—he'd gotten what he wanted. The end of this conversation with shy, nerdy, irritating Jennifer Worth.

We went our separate ways, him presumably into Charlene's party, and me home, quietly hurting from his rejection. I was embarrassed. It was, I decided, sort of like asking someone out and getting rejected . . . except worse. Attraction wasn't part of it. Nor were logistics, or commitment issues, or previous relationships. Just me!

Offering only the most casual of kindnesses, I *still* was someone

Scott Daniels didn't want to know. I'd just gotten *friend* rejected, and I was not a fan.

I close *The Shattered Court*, finally surrendering to distraction. Scott, unsurprisingly, quickly changed into the worst part of my workdays. Days stretched into a year of dodged eye contact, visible frowns whenever we're the first people in a conference room, and the occasional argument each of us absolutely knows isn't really about the virtues of one font placement or other.

The worst part is, I can't quite forget our conversation in Charlene's unremarkable hallway. It was . . . fun. We *could* have been friends, instead of the wretched game we play now.

Whatever. Ignoring flaws, or even romanticizing them, has only left me alone and embarrassed, again and again. Hope *is* magic—and magic is dangerous.

When I hear footsteps in the hallway, I remember I'm *not* alone here. In fact, people who love what I love surround me. *My* people.

I jump up from the couch, eager for company, or even just distraction. Perhaps it's my roommate, looking for our suite. Or it's another hallmate—someone I could invite over, getting to know my fellow fans, fulfilling one more college experience I never had. Hanging out until midnight, chatting about our favorite fandom. I would gladly share my artisanal chocolates in exchange for good *Elytheum*-centric conversation.

Okay, maybe not *gladly*. I would share, however.

Or I could go outside. I could meet someone new in an unfamiliar hallway. I could backspace over my memory of my first conversation with Scott, like Heather Winters does if characters' dialogue isn't working or interactions feel forced. I could rewrite the start of my failed relationship with . . . I don't know who.

Emboldened, recklessly hopeful, I open the door, and—

No one is in my hallway. Whoever passed my suite has gone into their own for the night.

Of course. I close my door, feeling foolish. I haven't just spent the day running from reality. I've spent the day chasing fantasy. Right now I feel like it's because fantasy never comes to me.

Returning to my suite, I remind myself how enchanting I found its perfectly rendered details. While the ember of my enthusiasm is weak, it's not extinguished. However, I know I won't find happy refuge in the pages of Elytheum. I need some sleep.

I head into my bedroom, telling myself it's okay if I don't feel like I'm living a fantasy just yet. I have the whole week here.

Tomorrow, I promise, your life will change.

7

I wake up under my obsidian coverlet, my heart light for one wonderful moment.

Then I remember breaking up with Jordan and running into Scott here. It's one of the worst feelings in the world—*remembering* what's going wrong in your life. There is almost an inexplicable obligation in it, like you haven't paid your debt of distress just yet. It's like when someone emails you "following up" on something you really don't want to do, except the email comes from your short-term memory into the inbox of your soul, and it has one of those horrid "high priority" exclamation marks on it.

Just following up!

No, damnit. My heart hits "delete."

I push sadness from my sunlit morning, refusing to mourn the end of yet another waste-of-time relationship. Discouraging though my romantic history is, the breakup brought me *here*, where I have the chance to win the date of my dreams with the man of my fantasies.

Only if I can win the scavenger hunt, though. I'm determined to find one of the clues by the end of the day.

My room is no less magical in the morning light. I'm convinced sunlight in small towns just hits different. It filters in the windows of the suite, lending everything gentle crispness. The warmth has even started to soften the wax of my Elytheum-themed candle, hinting the room with the perfect sweet, smoky-leathery scent.

Carrying my toiletries, I head into the hallway, which I'm unsurprised to find empty. It is presently six in the morning. I woke up early because I didn't want to miss a minute of clue-searching time, and because I've always been an early-to-bed, early-to-rise girl. I'm eager and a little nervous for breakfast, which starts in one hour.

The nervousness is mostly due to the scavenger hunt. I wouldn't consider myself very competitive. Okay, no, I'm very *not* competitive. Like, losing-card-games-on-purpose-so-I-can-enjoy-watching-my-friends-play-without-stress levels of not competitive, or hands-getting-sweaty-when-Jordan-challenged-me-to-Mario-Kart levels of not competitive.

Nevertheless, I *really* want the dream date. Which means going head-to-head with my fellow Experience participants. They're probably more confident, more resourceful, less . . . ordinary. Maybe even—*gasp*—more knowledgeable Elytheum Courts fans. In the ultimate Elytheum-off, I'm competing with many of the only people in the world I would really consider my competition.

So, yeah, some nervousness.

And my eagerness?

Winters is indulgent with descriptions of food in the Elytheum Courts series. In interviews and newsletters, she's explained how food connects us and stands out in our memories of our favorite places, whether home or away, and she wants her writing to reflect the same richness.

While I'm certain every fan's heart holds a different dream re-past, I suspect four little words have started to circle in everyone's heads. *Western Woods puff pancakes.* The signature comfort food of the main setting of the second installment in the series.

I reach the communal bathroom, ready to welcome another advantage of my early wake-up. I'm excited to meet new fans and friends, but I very much don't feel the need to make introductions while naked, heading for the shower. I hold my robe tight while I enter, expecting morning solitude.

Instead—

Of course the restroom isn't empty. Of course the only person in here isn't even a future friend. Certainly not a fan.

Of course, the only other person up at six a.m. in a college dorm is Scott.

I contemplate retreating. When Kethryn, captured in the Realms Past, competed in deathly gladiatorial games with un-speakable monsters, she survived one challenge entirely using stealth instead of hurling herself into the fray. I could go the queenly route of slipping out and heading downstairs to use one of the showers on another floor.

Then Scott's eyes—without his glasses post-shower—swivel to me in the mirror.

Now I refuse to give him the satisfaction of my fleeing any-where. Even from a slightly dark and mildewy communal college bathroom! Stealth is queenly. Cowardice is not.

I stride in, holding my chin high. Scott's gaze follows me the length of my short walk to the mirror next to his. He is unfortu-nately wearing only his towel. He is unfortunately wet.

Whatever! Who cares!

He's not here, I counsel myself sternly. Not to me. He is like a spider in a corner of the cavernous, shadowy Great Hall—best to pretend it's not there.

I unzip my toiletries bag. It happens I have very strong muscles of ignoring—enjoying reading in public while living in New York City develops them. I exercise my herculean powers pretending I'm the only person in the room. Just Jennifer!

Unfortunately, however, the novelty of post-shower Scott Daniels offers me no mercy. Regrettably, he smells good. Even from here, crisp soap combines with sweat into something assaultive on my soul's defenses. Disastrously, he has a nice chest, no doubt earned from working out.

Who cares! Stay strong, Jennifer.

I won't let such details distract me. I'm certain Val smells good after a shower as well. The idea makes me smile, which Scott catches.

"Happy to see me?" he asks.

I deign to spare him a look. "Hardly," I reply. "I was thinking about Val."

He grimaces. "Right," he murmurs. "He's your . . . book boyfriend, isn't he?"

The pointed use of the terminology condemns me to pink cheeks, not that the dewy sheen the shower has given his abs wasn't doing that already. He's definitely overheard my gushing conversations with coworkers, then. Whatever—Scott Daniels doesn't deserve my embarrassment. "Yes," I reply resolutely. "He is."

Undaunted, Scott presses on. "Made any progress on the clues, then?"

"Do you plan to always be in the bathroom at this time?" I reply evasively, determined to retake the upper hand. "It'd be best if I know what times to avoid it and, by extension, you."

He pauses, shaving razor in hand, and turns, eyeing me incredulously. Water beads down his chest—*nope*. I divert my gaze.

In fact, *gaze* is excessive. Winters would never write *gaze* when she meant *glance*. My *glance*.

"Sharing my showering habits feels *personal*, Jennifer," he reminds me. I refuse to even entertain the idea of humor or playfulness entering his voice. We're defenders clashing in combat. Enemies from sworn opposing courts. Nothing more. "Probably safer if you just ask for a room change. Amelia will do anything for you," he recommends.

I scowl. I loathe the idea of giving up my corner suite with its stunning views. Elytheum decorations or not, I am still living in a college dorm for a week. I don't know if any quantity of candles could make me enjoy lesser lodgings.

"I suppose I can subject myself to this sight if I must," I say, gesturing to his chest.

Scott's lips pull into a dangerous smirk. *Is he kidding with that? Since when does overly meticulous Scott smirk?* "How *will* you survive?" he replies, heartlessly droll.

Fighting self-consciousness, I face my reflection in the mirror. *It's the damn shower's fault.*

I'm not letting embarrassment silence me, however. If I'm going to win the scavenger hunt, if I'm going to compete with equally determined fans, I'm going to need to keep my composure and face challenges head-on. "You're not usually this full of yourself," I comment.

I didn't intend the implied compliment hiding in my retort, although I'm forced to recognize it's not inaccurate. Judgmental though Scott Daniels may be—and definitely willing to pick inane fights over font placement—the man I've gotten to know in our

offices is frustratingly graceful with creative criticism and an irritatingly good listener to our supervisors' suggestions.

His bravado seems to momentarily flicker, the pressed-and-
polished guy I know from work returning, until—

"Well, I'm not usually shirtless in front of you," he points out.

I clench my jaw, refusing to concede I walked right into the
comment. "Misfortune upon misfortune," I manage. Recognizing
I've done myself no favors in the conversation, I grab my toothbrush and start hurriedly to brush.

Scott says nothing. Deciding he's wreaked enough damage on
my morning, I would guess. He packs up his toiletries and heads
for the door, where, like he's warring with himself, he pauses.

"We're not friends," he starts.

You made sure of that, I don't point out to him. "Understatement," I hurry to agree around my toothbrush. *Understatement.*

Scott continues, undeterred, like fae cadets undertaking the
war magistry's fearsome gauntlet. "Still. It was rough watching
you get dumped," he says. "Are you holding up okay?"

My cheeks flame. Wow—he's managed to unlock even more new
ways of upsetting a morning I was supposed to be enjoying. I *wish*
we could return to sniping over me eyeing his chest. Except, no I
don't. I spit into the sink, pretending I'm expectorating the future
memory of this conversation. "I did the dumping," I inform Scott.

In the mirror, I notice his eyebrows join. "I'm curious what exactly Jordan was alluding to when he said it's cool how much you're
into in the bedroom, but naturally that would be such a *personal*
question."

I fumble my toothpaste so violently it clatters to the tile floor.

His eyes sparkle with laughter. "Clearly, I heard *everything*," he
says victoriously.

Fine, so me dumping Jordan was as fantastical as fae courts or dark magic incantations. "Okay," I amend, desperately fighting to keep my cool, "it may have been silent and only in my heart, but believe me, internally I had dumped him long ago."

I expect the doubtfulness I've come to consider one of Scott's main qualities when interacting with me. Instead, I'm surprised when only patience greets me on his keen features. "Why didn't you go through with it?" he inquires.

Having not exactly woken up planning on analyzing my relationship issues with my least favorite coworker, I frown. "Because I'm a coward. I don't know," I reply.

"I doubt that's true," Scott says.

The certainty, the conviction in his voice makes me find his eyes. I'm not ready for the measured intensity in them. I pin his stare, desperate to wrestle it into compliance. "Okay," I say—half-defiant, half-curious, and wholly disliking the combination. "Since we're so very close, tell me why you think I didn't?"

Scott's expression closes up. "You're right," he replies, regaining a little of the combativeness I anticipated. "I've overstepped. Too much temerity, I suppose."

I recall with irritation his focus on Kethryn's welcome speech. Of course he remembers the scavenger hunt announcement perfectly. I say nothing, and he leaves the room, his words hanging in the echo of the door clicking closed.

Too much temerity. Honestly, the comment was a gift. Scott has just reminded me he's my competitor. *Yes, Scott, you demonstrated very impressive temerity. However, you get no points for aptitude.* Anyway, who even needs *temerity* in a scavenger hunt—

Wait.

I noticed immediately, during dinner, the uncharacteristic oddity of Kethryn's phrasing. It doesn't entirely make sense in context, and it doesn't read like Winters's eloquent, understated dialogue.

Of course it doesn't. After all, *it's not just dialogue.*

Like I've just figured out a plot twist, I'm instantly convinced my deduction is right.

Kethryn has already given us the first clue. At dinner. And she's given it in a form Elytheum fans would know. In Winters's world, the fae love riddles, word games, verbal evasions. Like . . . anagrams.

Inspired, I hop into the shower Scott just vacated and turn on the water. In the fog steamed onto the door, I write the letters. *Secrecy, loyalty, temerity, aptitude.*

SLTA.

I hear Val's voice in my head, the same way Kethryn did when he slid some rather explicit scrolls under her door early in their courtship. Fortunately for every one of us readers, she remembered earlier instructions he'd given her on fae anagrams to decode them. I recall the same instructions now.

The first letter is not your friend, he counseled. *It guides you falsely. Start in the heart of the word.*

I stare. I sort out combinations.

With clarity's heady rush, I write what I've found in the condensation with my finger.

LAST

Quickly I erase what I've inscribed, irrationally worried Scott or one of my companions will come in and notice my deduction.

LAST. Last what? I'll figure it out. Regardless, I have something I didn't when I inconveniently found Scott Daniels in my bathroom.

Or *conveniently,* I guess. I could kiss Scott for sparking my discovery of the clue—except, definitely not.

I wash my hair, welcoming the warm water pounding over my

shoulders. Finally, I feel *good*. I held my own with the greatest enemy of my personal court. I found my first clue.

In fact, Scott doesn't realize his mockery led me to the clue, which only makes it even more satisfying. I knew I would enjoy solving fae riddles—I just didn't know I would enjoy it quite so much.

8

Western Woods puff pancakes.

The dream is real. The chef has surpassed even my wildest imaginings, and where fluffy cakes are concerned, my imaginings can get pretty wild. Flat like pancakes on their wondrously golden tops, they rise up whole inches from my plate.

I carry the delicacy the same way I cradled my copy of *The Ashen Court* at the midnight launch event, continuing from the servery into the dining hall with great care. I'm not costumed this morning, given I've got nothing to work with. This denizen of Elytheum just happens to wear a Proud Volunteer of the Oklahoma Public Library shirt.

Entering the high-ceilinged room, I notice details I didn't last night. On the wall across from the entrance hangs Val's sword, I know instantly from the ornamented hilt. Okay, I also know from the small crowd assembled under the mounted weapon. A similar group has gathered in front of what I realize is a painting depicting the series' climactic fight with the Darkness.

I promise myself I'll join them later. For now, I'm forced to obey the sweet scent wafting up from my food.

I head for the tables, where I discover my plate of pancakes is, surprisingly, *not* the most exciting element of the morning. With the fantastical fare comes something even more enticing— schedules at every place setting.

I put my plate down and snatch up the cardstock, finding the paper perfectly stained, folded, and softened to resemble courtly scroll-stock. *Is this hand-lettered?* First pancakes, now parchment. Another compliment I owe Amelia.

While the great hall fills with Experience guests chatting in the sunlight from the high windows, I lose myself in the descriptions of the immersive programming. Potion making—or cocktail mixing, the summary explains—horseback riding, even lessons in the Demoniaca card game.

While I peruse, I reach for the syrup carafe. *Fogberry*, reads the label. It's a nice flourish. When I try some on my pancakes, I find the chef has combined cherry and blueberry into the emulation of the fictional purple fruit said to bramble everywhere in Kethryn's court gardens.

I keep reading, savoring my pancakes. Archery, paint-and-sip, jewelry making. Some of the classes, I notice, require you attend with a "paramour," the Experience's way of making sure guests mingle with one another.

Of course, I have no paramour. I have one immensely irritating colleague, who is an ass. And I have one friend, who is ineligible to participate in the activities directly.

Fortified by my pancakes, I conclude there is only one solution. If I'm going to participate in the full extent of the Elytheum Experience, I'm going to have to start making friends.

Not *just* for the events, either. I remind myself it's good to socialize. Get out there. It'll distract me from Scott and help me feel more like myself.

I look up from my dish, attempting to make eye contact with

the other guests wandering in from the servery. Without staring weirdly, I work at mustering a winningly eager sit-next-to-me vibe.

No one does. My confidence ebbs. I hate the familiar feeling. Why is making friends as an adult so hard?

Okay, it's not like it was easier when I was younger. Still. I've gotten jobs, gotten promotions, gotten my driver's license, moved cities. Why is *this* hard? Even with fellow fans surrounding me, I feel frustratingly alone.

I feel the pull of returning upstairs to read. The first event requires no "paramour" and doesn't start until nine thirty. I hardly even started the first chapter of my full reread last night.

Kethryn wore black the day of her coronation . . .

I straighten up. No—no, I will not retreat. My favorite stories are stories of courage. Of confidence summoned amid adversity. Their heroines never let fear shake their determination. Maybe immersing myself in fantasy doesn't just mean lighting candles and eating fancy pancakes.

Maybe it means finding my own heroism.

I can't fight mythical monsters or wage courtly war. I can, however, find enough courage to make friends. If I want the kind of life Jordan thinks only exists in books, I have to start acting like a main character.

Mustering my nerve, I stand, fixing my eyes at random on two women probably in their twenties. They're costumed to the nines, one in impeccably crafted, not-fucking-around leather armor, the other red-gowned like she's going to whatever Elytheum's equivalent of New York Fashion Week is. In my civilian garb, I immediately vow to get more costumes later from the student center, where the map indicated I could find them. For now, however, I stride right to where the women are seated near the doors.

"Hey," I say. "Mind if I join?"

"Please," the armored one replies. Her voice is soft, and she speaks with quick precision. "I'm Laurel, and this is Brit."

"Jennifer," I introduce myself. I notice Brit reaching for the syrup. "Oh, you have to try the fogberry," I say.

"It's honestly delicious," Laurel concurs. "I'm going to make some at home when I want to pretend I'm up early for combat exercises instead of, like, work."

I laugh, knowing exactly what early-morning combat scene she's referring to. An hour of hand-to-hand exercises with Val in the court gardens ended with some hand-to-somewhere-else exercises right on the grass, getting the stains of the purple fruit everywhere.

"I'm literally going to dream of puff pancakes tonight," I offer.

"*Yes*," Laurel responds.

I feel relieved, regretting my misgivings earlier. I guess befriending fellow fans isn't so hard. It makes me suddenly sad—in six days, I'll return home to regular, non-fan friend making.

I push the idea from my mind. "I've read *The Exile Court* like fifteen times," I inform them, referring to the installment where our memorable morning meal is introduced. "It's probably my favorite."

"Me. Too," Brit replies emphatically.

"What are you planning on doing today?" I venture. "I kind of want to check out . . . everything."

"We were going to do the needlework class. I want to make a Western Court crest for my masquerade gown," Brit says. She raises her sculpted eyebrows in invitation. "Want to joint us?"

I grin. "I'd love to."

————

Two hours later, I have pricked my finger more times than I can count. But I am not abandoning my Northern Court crest.

Every Elytheum reader knows the regional courts surrounding Kethryn's Court of Elytheum—Northern, Eastern, and Western, since the Darkness destroyed the Southern—represent the personality characteristics of their famous rulers. The North, responsible for watching over Elytheum from their snowy vantage, stands for stoic self-reliance, embodied in the sword emblem I'm stitching.

Self-reliance. Yeah, it's the court of single people.

Right now my sword looks more like a slug. Nonetheless, I determinedly continue stitching the pattern with the auburn string I chose.

We're outside, the class held in one of the small quads. In the daylight, the grass gleams emerald, the stone of the campus shining white. I can imagine I'm a courtly noblewoman, enmeshed in Elytheum intrigues. Okay, a noblewoman who wears an Oklahoma library T-shirt—close enough. Perhaps I'm in possession of a dangerous secret, one I need to communicate covertly to queen Kethryn. Perhaps I'm plotting an assassination no one will suspect of a mere lady-in-waiting. Perhaps—

Ow. Fuck. Forget perhaps. I've *definitely* pricked my finger again.

I'm enjoying hanging out with Laurel and Brit. It's refreshingly easy to connect with people who share my same passions. People who, notably, won't make pointed comments about *book boyfriends*.

I'm the new member of their group, and other than loving Elytheum, I'm only just getting to know them. Of course we start with the important stuff—favorite scenes, favorite characters, favorite spinoff theories.

When I notice Amelia visiting our class, I realize how immersed I was. The real world—my regular life, my breakup, Scott—had fled my memory.

Amelia heads straight for me. "Okay, I have eight minutes until

I have to officiate the archery contest." She surveys the clearing, looking jittery with nervous excitement. Nervousness is uncommon on the no-nonsense Amelia—it shows me how invested she is, personally and professionally, in the Experience. "Incredible, right?" she asks me. "Did you see Val?"

I hear the reassurance she wants under the disguise of enthusiasm. "Amelia, Val is perfect," I say. "Everything is perfect."

She smiles, satisfied. The very mention of the fae bodyguard puts a blush in her cheeks. I recognize the reaction from my dinner companions and, okay, from myself. Everyone—except Scott—has a crush on the perfectly cast actor. Everyone will be working hard to win the date.

"Good." She permits my reassurance. "Do you love your suite?"

"It's amazing," I gush earnestly. "You've brought Elytheum to life. Only one thing . . ." I can't help adding. "You could have warned me Scott was here, and on my floor."

Amelia waves off my complaint. "Oh, he's not so bad," she replies, still flushed with pride from my praise of the Experience. "I figured you knew! He didn't mention it at work?"

"He did not. And *not so bad?*" I exaggerate my incredulity. "How can you say that? He's the worst. He . . ." I falter, remembering the Experience's rules about immersion and the outside world, which I especially don't want to violate with Amelia herself. "He is possessed of very evil magic. He would sell out his friends to the Inquisitorium for nothing. He makes Nightfell Ravens look like . . . fluffy ducklings."

Amelia laughs, evidently not appreciating the dark import of the Scott situation. She overlapped with him for a few months when we were all Parthenon colleagues, and of course I filled her in on the Charlene's Hallway Incident. Amelia was as affronted as l by Scott's unfriendliness as well as his attitudes in the office. But clearly her months away have made her forget how much he sucks.

"It's cool he's getting into Elytheum, though, isn't it?" she says encouragingly.

"I don't believe his motives are innocent," I reply.

"Who's Scott?" Brit interjects, no doubt intrigued by my ominous sincerity

"He's my—" I improvise, the Elytheum pretense coming easily. "He's my sworn enemy."

Reasonably, my meaning does not reach Laurel and Brit. Laurel leans in, looking intrigued. "Sounds sexy."

Horrified, I shake my head vehemently. "No. *Not* in a sexy way," I protest. "We are . . ."

Hm. What's the fantastical equivalent of coworkers? *Warriors from the same guild* sort of overstates matters when the only war we wage is during marketing meetings.

"We serve the same lord in our home court," I settle for weakly. "Laurel, Brit, this is Amelia," I introduce her, realizing I haven't. The perfect subject change from Scott. "She works for Heather Winters. She's the mastermind behind the Experience."

"Oh my god," Laurel says.

"No way," Brit says.

While they enthuse over every aspect of the Experience and their rooms, I watch Amelia's cheeks go pink with pride. It's wonderful, and I recognize the upside of the difficulty of finding friends who really understand you. When you do find them, they mean everything to you.

"Thank you," Amelia replies earnestly. "I just want the fans to love it. I mean"—she gazes out over the quad, fond and reverent—"it has been my entire life for the past year."

"Who needs a life when you have this?" I reply.

Amelia's eyes move from the quad to me. I recognize the concern in them. Whenever I mentioned offhand that I couldn't remember when I'd last spoken to my parents or was oversleeping longer and longer on the weekend, or whatever, Amelia's Ameliometer would go off, and she would offer me some gentle-yet-firm advice, on which she would inevitably follow up.

I focus on my shitty needlework, hoping Amelia gets distracted in the midst of the Experience.

She doesn't. "I'm proud of my work here, really," she says levelly. "But I'm excited to have more time to myself, too. I can't remember the last date I went on."

"You're not missing much," I grumble.

"Seconded," Laurel concurs. Something sharp hides in her voice, and I notice sympathy flicker on Brit's features. I start quietly filling in context—Laurel is another romance reader like me who's not in love with real-world romance.

"Well, I hope we meet Scott," Brit ventures. "Is he a rugged fae warrior?"

I snort. "No. Definitely not."

Like Brit has uttered a magic summons in the words *rugged fae warrior*, one walks right into the quad—or, the closest thing to one in our decidedly non-Elytheum world. Lord Valance is newly costumed for the day, the collar of his night-colored shirt hanging open. He saunters into our midst, swaggering and smirking up a storm. The man's smirk-per-minute ratio is unreal, honestly. He must spend some serious minutes practicing.

He approaches the needlework circle, where he crouches down next to us. Amelia, specifically. He perches on his heels close to where she's sitting. From his position, he peers at Brit's needlework.

"Western Court, I see," he observes. "You're going to be trouble, then."

Brit blushes fiercely. Laurel and I light up. The reference is impressive—Val in the series has enmity with the Western Court, the final court to join Kethryn's climactic alliance due to Kethryn having spurned the lord of the court romantically in favor of Val.

Val eyes my work next. Squints, more like. My sword is not looking so hot.

"Northern Court, I . . . suspect?" he pronounces. "Perhaps fewer . . . squiggles would aid you."

I grin, remembering one of Winters's key Val lines, now emblazoned onto hundreds of pieces of sharp-eyed fan art. *He makes mockery sound like sweetest praise.* The performer is fantastic, and he's clearly studied the source material.

The fun I'm having makes inspiration come easy. "I'm afraid I have other talents, Lord Valance," I reply.

He meets my eyes with an intrigued eyebrow raised. "Do you, now? Like what?" He leans in closer, drawing glances of interest and glares of jealousy from nearby guests. He smells just like the candle in my room.

I play it nonchalant. "Perhaps you'll find out when we dine after I've caught the court's spy," I say.

He licks his lips. "Perhaps I will."

He holds my gaze until I'm the one—me!—who ends our eye contact, returning to the shambles of my Northern Court emblem.

"My lady," Val continues on, addressing Amelia now. "I believe we are to judge some archery from the newest recruits among the court's defenders. Shall I walk you?"

Amelia, who has watched our interaction with nothing short of rapture, pauses. Her regard shifts from me to Val, like his offer has startled her. "No, go on ahead of me, Lord Valance," she replies. "I'll . . . join you in five minutes."

It's unmistakable. With her reply, Val's smirk falters. He looks . . . disappointed.

Then, with the poise the fae lord is known for, he shrugs away the momentary reaction, the same way he would easily fend off shots of dark magic from enemy warriors. He stands to his full height, passing one final assessing gaze over the group, and strides off.

"Oh my god," Laurel exhales, enjoying the view of his departure. "He's so good."

Then their eyes find me.

"*Other talents?*" Brit cheers. "Girl, who *are* you?"

I grin, hiding how their praise delights me. I honestly surprised myself chatting with Val. IRL, I'm not exactly known for my silver-tongued flirting.

I guess Elytheum just suits me.

One of the women next to us speaks up, likewise having for the moment abandoned her needlework in favor of watching the retreating Val. "I heard someone found a clue at breakfast," she says enviously. "Has anyone else discovered anything?"

My head whips up. My pride in my fantasy flirting vanishes.

Someone *else* has found the first clue? Or . . . *a* first clue? Either they unraveled the *LAST* clue already . . . or, likelier, the Experience organizers have left numerous clues in various locations on campus. Even if I find one, I won't have the only lead. And if I don't figure out what LAST is alluding to, I'll fall behind people who've already found their first clues.

Stress starts to steal into me, which definitely isn't what I envisioned for my week in Elytheum. I'm supposed to have fun, I remind myself. Still . . . I really don't want to lose out on the prize date.

Not when the two sentences I just exchanged with Val made me entirely, finally, forget about Scott.

Everyone else has started eagerly speculating, which makes me feel guilty for not wanting to join in and share the anagram I noticed. A couple of my needlework classmates have begun peering around, like they suspect clues hide among the needles—which, I don't know, maybe they do.

I catch Amelia watching it all. "I'm guessing you can't participate?" I ask.

"Considering I hid ninety percent of the clues, it would be a little unfair," Amelia concedes.

The wink in her voice doesn't quite hide the wistfulness. Her Elytheum costume is perfect, her dress embroidered to resemble Kethryn's on the *Shattered Court* UK cover art. She's like each of us—the ultimate superfan—and she's immersed herself in creating the Experience's marvelous world, yet she can't fully partake of it. The week, the realization of her efforts, must be bittersweet.

"Anyway," she continues, just a little like she's reminding herself, "it's not like the person who hired the performers could win the date."

Her eyes have drifted back to Val, who was receding from our group. It occurs to me I've never seen the look she's wearing. Not when Sam Heughan was on-screen during our marathon of the first *Outlander* season, not even when I commissioned her some very detailed Elytheum fan art in celebration of her new job. Her gaze holds something more yearning than the rest of ours.

The Experience, I realize, maybe isn't the only thing she's wishful and wistful for.

Whenever I'm lovelorn or frustrated or down, Amelia works to lift my spirits. Even when it's in the midst of her professional victory lap. I owe her the same.

"Hey, I mean, at least you get to hang out with him while judging archery, right?" I point out encouragingly.

Amelia smiles. "Yeah, no, I'm great," she replies with conviction. I guess she's as good at picking herself up as she is at consoling me. Still, her eyes don't leave the departing Val.

I follow her gaze while I line up my next stitches. Val's purposeful stride looks diligently practiced. Amelia probably designed his costume, which matches hers for detail. His cape features the complete crest of the Elytheum Courts, the new iconography forged at the very end of the series, which is interesting, as it positions the chronology of the Experience itself—

I stab my needle right into my finger.

The pain doesn't even hit me immediately. Because I've figured it out. The first clue. Or, the next part of it.

Val's costume features the *complete crest of the Elytheum Courts*. Commemorating the union of Northern, Eastern, and finally Western in order to defeat the resurgent Darkness, the new Elytheum crest incorporated the emblems of every court, including the thorned rose Brit is presently stitching.

Western Court. You're going to be trouble.

When the Western Court finally joined Kethryn's alliance, Lord Valance could not help giving them a sneering nickname, which caught on among Kethryn's courtiers.

Western Court? he chided in the heated negotiation scene. *More like Last Court.*

When my finger stings, I pop it into my mouth to keep from bleeding on my needlework. *West, Last. Last, West.* While I contemplate, I control my expression, not wanting my eager compatriots to know I'm on to something.

Amelia notices only my new injury. "You okay?" she asks.

"Mm-hmm," I reply hastily. "I . . . think I just need a Band-Aid. I'll catch up with you all later," I assure my group.

I abscond from the needlework class, retreating into the nearest corridor. Heart pounding with hope, I pull out the campus map I grabbed on my way out of my room. Either my deduction is right or I'm zero steps closer to my first clue.

West, Last. Last, West.

When I unfold the map, I find it instantly, far from the main quad.

West College.

9

The cicadas quiet when I approach. West College sits on the out-skirts of campus, close to the river. The dorm is small, with ivy crawling up the stone walls. While students have camped out to read on the lawn of the closest quad in the morning light, West College itself looks uninhabited, and only the rustle of leaves ac-companies my footsteps.

I ditched the end of needlework. The hunt for my clue will probably deprive me of the start of the History Masters' Seminar, which the description says involves an open mic opportunity for Experience attendees to read favorite passages aloud, with coffee served in the college library near the Great Hall.

Oh well. I've regained some of my confidence in my scavenger-hunt lead. Even if the walk demanded seventeen full minutes from our end of campus out to West College, it's only half-past ten a.m. I can't imagine many of my fellow fans have cracked other clues quite yet.

I check the heavy doors first, just in case. Like I expected, the handles rattle unproductively when I pull on them. Swiping the card reader, I receive a red light and an unfriendly chirp. *Locked.*

I'm undaunted. My clue is here—I know it.

Inspecting the premises of West College, I explore the courtyard in front of the hall. It's quiet, vacant in the daylight. Fortunately for me, it's unadorned, leaving few places where the clue could hide. There's another door, and . . . a statue in the center of the courtyard. My most promising starting place.

I walk up to the monument. It's an 1800s-y looking man, seated and reading. His plaque informs me he is the founder of West College. Cool. Does he have my Elytheum clue?

His stone pedestal seats him five feet above the ground. Knowing what I have to do, I feel a little ridiculous. It's a college, not a playground for imaginative grown-ups.

Nevertheless . . .

Hastily, I climb up onto the statue. It's what a heroine would do, I am certain.

If I were designing a scavenger hunt centered on a series of novels, I'd start with the statue's book. I peer inside, prepared for Elytheum inscriptions in the pages . . .

Instead, I find a small scroll taped inside!

Exhilarated, I seize the parchment. I jump very gracefully to the ground, hoping no one sees me. While other Experience-goers would need to be pretty intrepid to reach the anagram's coded location as quickly as I did, I don't want to explain myself to campus security. *You see, Officers, Queen Kethryn must uncover the spy in her royal court. She needs our help!*

I want to examine the clue, but I hear approaching footsteps. I decide to unroll the scroll in my roommate-less suite. For now, I need to get out of here. What's more, I would like to catch the History Masters' Seminar if I can. I speed my steps into the archway connecting the courtyard with the path outside—

Scott enters the arch at the same time.

I freeze. He freezes.

Scott's eyes dip to the scroll in my hand. His shoulders slump.

"Well, let's get it over with," he grumbles. "You found the clue first. I know you want to rub it in."

Shock has robbed me of the instinct to gloat. "How did *you* figure the clue out?" I ask. I mean, honestly. Realizing the speech represented an anagram—okay, I guess our conversation inspired him the same way it inspired me, and he made the same deductions. Connecting the LAST anagram to West College, however, would require actual knowledge of Elytheum . . .

No, no, no. Scott is methodical. I know from his pitches in promo meetings, from the neatness of the lists I've glimpsed in his notebook. He's organized. Focused. Diligent. I know he got up early. Instead of enjoying the Experience's programming, he's probably spent the morning hours searching *everywhere* on campus. We just happened to hit West College—

"The *Last Court*," he says easily.

His words silence my speculation.

"You've read the books," I venture.

"Skimmed them," he replies.

I'm not impressed. No way, even if Scott's clue deduction leaves me seriously wondering what his definition of *skimmed* is. "Did you enjoy them?" I prompt him, unable to help myself.

"I found certain subjects intriguing," he intones.

I frown. It's not the derision I expected, not the counterpart to the impatient grumbles I would overhear when I championed special editions and new interior designs for my romance favorites on Parthenon's list. Still, it's intentionally cryptic. More evasiveness from the man spending the week pretending he's Elytheum's newest fan.

Whatever. I have no interest in gloating, or prying into his story, or prolonging this interaction in any way. I move to pass him in the archway.

He steps into my path.

I pause. *Really?* With fragile patience, I reroute to the side.

Scott matches me, standing in my way with arms crossed. It is incredibly immature.

"Can I see the clue?" he asks.

I am aghast. "No."

"What a shame," he intones.

What a shame? Scott doesn't move. "Are you serious right now?" I demand, my voice pitching up.

He doesn't reply. He only steps closer, his eyes locked on mine.

Unfortunately, it weakens my knees. I've never seen pressed-and-polished, methodical Scott Daniels this assertive. Or . . . intense.

It is, frankly, a turn-on. Obviously, given who my favorite book boyfriend is.

"Cut it out," I demand.

His eyes never leave mine. His expression never wavers. "Cut what out?"

"You know what," I reply impatiently. "The whole persona. It's not you. Honestly, it's very unconvincing."

I aimed to cut him down with the remark. Frustratingly, Scott's composure doesn't falter. I'm—okay, underneath my exasperation, I'm impressed.

Not just impressed. I feel like a spoonful of sugar is melting in my mouth. *Happy, Scott?*

He isn't. He frowns. Not like I've hurt him. Like I've . . . disappointed him.

"I'm not leaving without the clue, Jennifer," he informs me.

His voice is low, rough, and hushed. It's miserably sexy. Disastrously sexy. I never once heard him speak this way at work. I mean, I would've endorsed more of his promo plans—enthusiastically, even—if he'd asked *this* way.

Right now it makes me resist him even harder.

"Say my name normally," I snap. "In a normal pitch."

"This is my normal pitch," Scott murmurs.

"You literally sound like Batman right now."

Scott looks like he wants to laugh. Instead, he only shrugs, dashing my small victory. "Oh, so you're saying I sound sexy," he replies.

I roll my eyes, hating how he's read my mind. *Scott Daniels, expert diviner of Elytheum.* I shake off the impossible, infuriating notion.

While I'm busy resenting his intuition, however, Scott uses the opportunity of my distraction. He reaches swiftly for the scroll.

Not swiftly enough. I clutch the parchment to my chest, swiping it from his reach. His surprise move has set my heart racing, and I chase the impulse. If he can move fast, so can I—I certainly don't need to wait around fending off more rough-voiced attempts at persuasion while he stands in my way.

I make a run for it.

For once, I'm glad I'm not in an elaborate costume. In my worn-in sneakers, I fly out the archway and down the path into the wide green outside West College. I hear Scott following me, having dropped his dark and domineering persona in favor of good old-fashioned schoolyard pursuit.

I race right onto the lawn, ignoring students' stares. For fleeting moments, my stride powerful under me, I feel like I'm going to make it. I have surprise on my side.

Scott, however, has long legs.

In mere seconds, I hear his footsteps close the distance my impulsive run gave me. Then his hands, reaching out, finding my waist. The context-confused collision of my *coworker*—my very cute coworker, my judgmental coworker, who vexes my every weekday—hits me hotly.

And then he's grabbing for me. I shriek, hating the fact I'm . . . having fun.

Scott collides with me clumsily. While we fall, I manage to hold on to the clue scroll. Scott rolls us somehow, and I end up collapsing onto his chest when he hits the grass.

"*Ooof.*" I hear him exhale, and I find the utterance hilarious. I don't even know why. I just do. I abandon my fury, just for the moment, and laugh.

"Real smooth," I chasten him.

Scott's hands haven't left my waist. He's pretending he's only reaching for the clue. Or maybe I'm pretending he's *not* only reaching for the clue. I don't know. I don't care which. "I sense you're being sarcastic," he replies while we wrestle, "but I'm not sure why."

"We literally just fell down in front of random college students," I remind him. Indeed, our spectators have not stopped watching us once while I struggle to stretch my clue out of Scott's reach.

"Yeah, *you* aren't being smooth, that's for sure," Scott returns. "I can only work with what's given me."

"Please." I gasp, pivoting to extend the clue out of reach. "I've known you for a year. You're *not* smooth." I do not, of course, credit him with the—*fine*—smoothness he's exhibited in our past couple interactions. No need to introduce that to the discussion.

"Maybe you haven't brought out the best in me," he retorts.

I roll my eyes. Then I roll fast to the side, wrestling to free myself. It doesn't work. Scott grips me tightly, his hands locked on my hips.

I hate how my resolve weakens with my muscles. Hate how good it feels, being entangled with him, even in this absurd, utterly unexpected context. *Hand-to-hand combat exercises, outside the courtly gardens . . .*

I guess I should have known play-fighting would not feel far off from other kinds of exertion.

"Grow up," I reply, not knowing which of us I'm admonishing.

Scott is unrelenting. "Let me see the clue," he demands.

He's dropped his dark, rough, Sexy Scott Voice. It's just Scott. Unfortunately, it's . . . still compelling.

I have the fastest-fleeting, hopeful, guilty vision of us collaborating. *An enemy alliance.* His methodical focus and head for problem-solving. My passionate drive and knowledge of Elytheum. We could join forces into the ultimate scavenger-hunt duo. Not unlike when a certain young queen, determined and fearless, allied with a certain fae lord, noble and cunning—

The idea vanishes when I remember what we're competing *for.*

"No way," I declare.

Scott meets my eyes. He reaches once more for the clue. Positioned the way we are, his effort is hopeless. I hold the scroll high overhead.

To the watching students, we probably look like scrabbling schoolchildren, and I want to reassure myself it feels like nothing more. Just competitors, dueling for the clue, refusing to give up.

Instead, part of me wonders whether I would *wrestle* like this— scavenger hunt or not—with someone whose body I didn't want this close to mine.

Who I didn't want pinning me . . . reaching up over my head . . . rolling with me on the ground . . . his scent everywhere, the sheen of sweat starting to slicken our skin . . .

Right then, Scott releases my hips.

It's a calculated risk. I could easily get up and run from him now. *Is he counting on my distraction to keep me here? No, no,* I comfort myself. I'm not even really that distracted. It was nothing. Half of a silly daydream. Nothing worth registering.

Unfortunately for me, the combination of his gambit and the warm weakness invading my limbs works. Scott is fast. With his freed hand, he reaches up, his longer arms finally surmounting my reach. Grasping onto my wrist, he wages war on my closed fist with prying fingers. I clench my hand, panting with the exertion, knowing my fight is losing—my precious clue now crumpled like a note passed in class, only seconds from the enemy's clutches—

Then I notice Scott's notebook.

In our scuffle, it's fallen from his pocket open onto the grass. The pages flutter invitingly in the light summer wind.

While Scott works on extracting the clue, I whip to the side, reaching for the Moleskine. Scott notices a second too late. Instantly, he abandons the scroll, rushing to defend his notebook.

He isn't fast enough. I seize the leather cover.

In Scott's flailing surprise, I've gotten free. I quickly scoot out of his reach, holding one of my prizes in each hand. Rising from my grass-stained knees to stand victoriously on the college lawn, I open the first page.

"Let's see," I crow. "So *this* is where you cracked Kethryn's clue last night. What other clues have you started figuring out . . . ?"

"No, Jen, don't—" Scott says urgently.

Jen. Not *Jennifer.* Scott's desperation has wrung from him the first time I've ever heard him use the nickname. Or—I don't know. It's probably not desperation. Perhaps he wants to confuse me. Wants to leverage the friendly moniker into hesitation or mercy.

Not today. While Scott struggles to his feet, I flip notebook pages.

At first, I can't quite make sense of what I find inside. It holds no anagrams. No *LAST*. No mentions of West College. No other puzzles, either. No locations, no questions. Nothing Kethryn said.

Instead it's full of observations . . . about Val.

Must smirk at every opportunity. No smiling except key moments. Leaning also important. Voice should be pitched low. Learn eyebrow thing.

It's—well, it's accurate. Scott has noticed everything the actor has perfectly imitated from Winters's descriptions of the character.

Which addresses none of my confusion regarding why the listed observations fill Scott's notebook. "What is this?" I inquire, honestly curious.

"None of your business," Scott snaps. He's flustered. The frantic fun of our war for the clue is forgotten.

He snatches for the notebook. Expecting the sudden movement, I dance out of his reach. I continue reading while Scott watches, helpless, knowing I won't give up my new acquisition easily.

"You're writing down notes on Val?" *Only one ha per laugh*, Scott's jotted, which, although precise, is not wrong. *Chin up, gaze down.* Character observations, rendered with impressive precision.

Is he . . . writing a book? Crafting his own romantasy character?

The hunch fades when I remember the changes to Scott's own demeanor. His Batman voice. His unfortunately effective smolder.

He *is* crafting a romantasy character. Just not for the page. "*This* is what your whole personality change is about," I say, realizing. "You're *imitating* him. Why?"

My pulse, which had evened out after my escape from Scott's clutches, picks up again, like my heart knows to distrust Scott's intentions even if my head hasn't figured them out yet.

"Give me my notebook," he orders me.

"Answer my question and I will," I say.

Scott crosses his arms. It's ironic—the exasperated glower he gives reminds me more of Val than any of Scott's recent posturing.

Until his shoulders slump. He sighs, defeated.

"I'm only admitting this to you," he concedes, "because I saw you get dumped. You do not have the upper hand on me." When I glare, he wisely goes on. "I, too, have found myself recently unsuccessful in romance. I . . . never seem to be able to get a woman to want to stay," he admits.

I've never heard the disarming honesty in Scott Daniels's voice. His downcast, defensive gaze skirts mine. I would find it pitiable, even relatable, if the confession wasn't coming from Scott.

I grin. "So you're saying you were recently dumped, too," I clarify.

"It was much less embarrassing than your dumping."

"Suuure." I stretch out the word. "So much less embarrassing that you're *here*," I point out, "trying to, what? Turn yourself into everyone's romantic fantasy?"

Scott squares his shoulders. He doesn't look like Val right now. He looks like the guy who frowns when someone says the e-reader experience is indistinguishable from hardcover. "How would you say I'm doing?" he challenges me. "You seem to enjoy my techniques."

"I do not!" I protest, scoffing, instantly determined to reveal nothing of how I felt wrestling with him.

The wounding comment works. Scott's frown deepens. "Whatever, Jennifer," he says. "Don't act all superior. I'm not the one trying to go on a date with someone imaginary," he points out.

Jennifer. He's right not to use the nickname now. We're very, very not friends. In fact, if I could elongate his name to demonstrate our unfriendliness, I would. Scottathon. Or Scottifer.

"You're trying to win this clue, too, buddy," I retort. "Probably so you can learn from him." I hold up the notebook. My prize. My hostage.

Scott glares, confirming my guess. "The difference is," he declares, his voice low, in no imitation of Val, "at the end of this week, I'll go home and use what I've learned to improve my real life. You'll go home hung up on something that doesn't exist."

On the lawn, the mid-morning sunlight suddenly shines too dazzlingly, the heat sweltering too insistently. Our spectating students undoubtedly notice the wrestling pair have progressed to fighting.

"What's *that* supposed to mean?" I demand. I intend the question to come out pointed, not pained. Instead, real hurt softens my voice. Scott shouldn't know me. He shouldn't know how to pervade the corners of my heart, how to hit my insecurities like he has Kethryn's aptitude for archery. He shouldn't know how foolish I feel when I romanticize undeserving parts of my life, right up until they leave me feeling hurt and naïve.

"Nothing," Scott replies.

I shake my head, compelled to vehemence. "Oh, don't start that 'it's too personal' crap now. We're clearly past it."

Scott watches me. The defensive posture in his expression never changes, and I half welcome its ominous promise. I want to retreat from whatever charged, personal place we're venturing into. I want to remember petty feuds over font placement and uncomfortable silences in the Parthenon elevator. I want to fight.

Of course, Scott Daniels doesn't give me what I want.

He hesitates, then speaks measuredly. "Fine. I heard what your ex said to you," he explains, "and I'm not sure being here is the best thing for you. I mean, you're trying to win a date with a *fantasy* so you can avoid the real world."

Hot, embarrassed anger heats my face. When will I learn? When will I stop asking Scott Daniels questions that only lead to him hurting me?

Now, I decide. In reply, I shove his notebook to his chest. Despite how eagerly he clasps the leather cover in his hands, I do not see relief in his gray eyes.

When I walk off the green, he lets me leave with the scroll.

10

This campus doesn't freaking end.

I want to unroll my clue in the privacy of non-college surroundings, where prying Experience participant eyes won't see me. I mean, the whole premise of the hunt is finding a court spy, right? I need to honor the narrative Heather Winters—and Amelia—have elegantly designed.

Also, I don't want anyone else to read my clue.

Unfortunately, however, the vast College of Hollisboro campus is inescapable. I just want to reach the end of the innumerable quads, where the salvation of sidewalk will lead me to a coffee shop or something.

I guess I've gotten turned around, because I keep passing imposing lecture halls I'm pretty sure I recognize from wandering by them two minutes ago. I don't have the greatest sense of direction, to be honest.

Frustrated, I settle for the nearest building with no visible Experience affiliation. It's modern, with high walls of huge glass windows and stainless-steel superstructure. It wouldn't work for the Experience, not unless Winters started writing some sci-fi crossover, which, *oh my god, how cool would—*

No. I need to focus on my clue.

I pass a handful of students descending the hall's wide, low steps. Heading in the open glass doors, I'm wondrously relieved when the cool curtain of the air-conditioning descends over me.

The engraved metal sign in the entry says I've found the science library. In the gray carpeted main room, under daylight slanting in the high windows, students work quietly. Postdocs, I'm guessing.

Scott has a master's of English literature, from Cornell. He mentioned it during no fewer than two department meetings. He probably studied in libraries like this one.

He hasn't worn his glasses once while here, I realize. It's a shame.

Except—I don't care how he looks, I remind myself. I don't care about him at all. *Ugh.* I need a little alarm on my phone, every five minutes. *Focus on clues. Not on Scott.*

I settle into one of the chairs near the windows overlooking the river. In the hushed library, I do one final surveillance sweep for Elytheum cloaks or costumes.

I find no one. I'm in the clear.

Pretending I'm genuinely hunting the Elytheum Courts' spy— why not, right?—I unfurl my scroll. My heart races when I read the hand-scribed missive, which is undoubtedly my next clue.

The Lord of Night cherishes me. Mounted with Glory. Watching over all.

Mounted . . . watching over . . .

The answer strikes me instantly. The Lord of Night. Val's sword! The intricate, handcrafted weapon I noticed earlier this morning, mounted in the dining hall! Of *course.* Amelia and the organizers wouldn't prepare the impressive replica without giving it some secret relevance. Winters has the same flair for repurposing memorable worldbuilding details into important plot points.

In the next moment, my high spirits descend.

I wasn't the only person who noticed Val's impressive sword in the dining hall. I recall the literal crowd *ooh*ing and *aah*ing over the piece earlier. For the past few hours, I've maneuvered and, yes, wrestled to preserve the secrecy of my clue . . . and now I'm going to have to seek out the most crowded place in the Experience.

Although I desperately want to, I can't investigate the sword right now without everyone in the entire Elytheum Experience knowing of the possibility of a clue. And if someone finds it first, I'll have to hunt the rest of the Experience for new leads. Worse, my greatest obstacle is Scott, who knows I have a clue and will be watching to follow me to the next one.

I curl my feet under me, gazing out the window, contemplating furiously. I'll need to examine the sword when no one else is around. Which means . . .

The middle of the night.

Fantastic.

While the idea of staying up late after getting up at six a.m. dismays me, I muster determination. I'm not going to let exhaustion stop me. How many sleepless nights do heroines go through? If I want adventure, I'm going to have to leave my comfort zone.

And coffee. I'm going to need coffee.

My plan forged, I walk out of the library, mourning the exit from the air-conditioning. With the river to reference, I now know roughly the right direction to walk in order to return to the Experience. Without a clue to hunt until nightfall, I could rejoin the programming. The History Masters' Seminar is unfortunately over, but once I find lunch, I'm ready to lose myself in jewelry making or embroidery.

Heading down the library steps, however, I catch sight of my own scuffed sneakers, speckled with wet grass from my morning chase with Scott.

I remember how I felt hanging out with my costumed new friends while I sat there in my Oklahoma Public Library shirt, wearing the reminder of the box of my possessions I brought here. Of how I didn't even plan on coming to the Experience until yesterday morning. Of how I'm only here fleeing a breakup. Sometimes literally, in a pair of grass-stained Adidas.

No longer! Feeling inspired from my resolution, I decide if I'm going to act like a heroine, I'm going to need to *dress* like one.

Lord Valance isn't the only fan art subject readers go wild for. Endless incredible renderings of Kethryn and her spinoff-ready ladies-in-waiting light-up fans' For You Pages with elaborate, glittering costumes. They're iconic. Sexy. Fierce.

With new eagerness, I check the Experience map. Yes, it's unhelpfully light on detail concerning how to get from campus to, say, CVS. But it's perfect for my purposes. Drawn in the fantastical style of the maps in the Elytheum books, it depicts the parts of campus the Experience is using for locations. The dorms, the dining hall, the main library, the archery range, and more.

I quickly find the destination I'm looking for—the costume boutique. It's set up inside the student center. The center is drawn like an ornate, multistory structure with dresses in the windows, exactly like a venturesome fae visitor would find in Kethryn's flourishing courtly city.

If Scott can suddenly act like an Elytheum leading man, I can change myself into an enchanting leading lady.

I hasten my steps, enjoying this plan. It's not enough to experience the fantasy—I'm going to become it.

11

"Are you sure?" I ask.

"Yes!" Laurel and Brit exclaim in unison.

Having exchanged our dorm room numbers during needle-work, I arrived at their door with a handful of dresses and robes, needing fashion consultation. They welcomed me in, and I found myself distracted from my fantasy-makeover project—their room is incredible. They've decorated their double suite with extensive Elytheum merch they packed with them. Apparently they live only an hour away, and they loaded their cars up with posters and figurines, candles, mugs, and maps. It's heaven.

Or, wait, no. It's Afterrealm, Elytheum's conception of the spiritual life after death, the dulcet realm from which fallen heroes gaze over their kin.

Anyway, it's amazing.

Laurel and Brit helped me choose from among the dresses I'd purchased—all fan-made, of course—and promptly started braiding my hair and applying purple shimmering glitter to my cheeks like I'm a demoness. Laurel commanded the effort while Brit, I noticed, retreated into the hallway for multiple phone calls with someone named Stephanie, returning harried yet with undimmed excitement for her and Laurel's handiwork.

Honestly, I needed their aid. After collecting a sandwich in the student store closest to the library, I hit the costume boutique, where I picked out my Elytheum attire for the week, then proceeded to spend the next hour indecisive in front of the mirror in my room.

Finally, I admitted defeat. I would have to impose on my new friends, who I knew were exactly the right people to ask. Earlier, I had learned Laurel and Brit run impressive social media accounts dedicated to re-creating looks from Elytheum and other series. I was moved when they offered me their expertise without blinking.

I evaluate myself in their lit-up vanity. Honestly, I'm not overwhelmingly confident right now. Hence my hesitation.

Nevertheless . . .

Laurel and Brit's work is incredible. I look like I could take on hordes of vicious demons, magic curses, ex-boyfriends, annoying coworkers, inboxes of over a hundred emails. The world.

Main character energy.

I'm wearing the outfit they helped me choose. The long-sleeve purple dress hits me mid-thigh. Pairing the dress with leather boots, I look badass—not how I ever imagined describing myself, not when my hobbies consist of rereading books and crocheting, and my tolerance for caffeine past five p.m. is nonexistent. From her own collection, Brit even lent me a snug leather vest that pushes my breasts together.

I look drop-your-plate-of-puff-pancakes-in-the-dining-hall good. I look like fan art come to life.

"I can't thank you enough," I say. "Honestly."

"Please." Laurel waves my gratitude off. "This is our favorite thing to do. I only wish Jordan could see you."

I smile. Her voice holds more wistfulness than Jordan—the man who once forgot to pick up dinner for my visiting parents because he was debating someone on Reddit—deserves, but I'm grateful for Laurel's kindness.

While they did my makeup, I shared with my new friends the real-world details of my "ex-paramour." They were sympathetic in exactly the right ways, indignant in exactly the right others. *Revenge is makeover magic*, Laurel pronounced, and I wondered if she spoke from experience.

Likewise, I learned about them. They're middle school teachers who started a smutty book club during lunch breaks, which is where they first read Elytheum. It brought them together, and now they're part of a whole broader bookish community.

The more time we spent together, as more makeup transformed me into the daring woman I see in the mirror, I felt more and more like we'd known one another forever instead of for eight hours. Hearing how Elytheum founded their friendship comforted me. It reminded me how despite everything in my love life, I have Amelia, and now I have them. Who knows how many other fanfriends I'll find this week? While I may have come to the Experience running away from the loss of my relationship, I'll leave here having gained something precious.

"Forget *Jordan*," Brit announces. "I can't wait for your coworker who you *hate* to see you. Your *sworn enemy*," she repeats with dramatic enthusiasm.

Under my demoness glitter, I'm certain my cheeks have gone pink. "Scott? Believe me, he doesn't care," I protest, remembering his judgment this afternoon.

"Enemies to lovers is always compelling," Laurel admits thoughtfully.

"Debatable," I offer weakly, as if my bookshelves aren't overflowing with the trope.

"You said he's here to become the ultimate book boyfriend to impress girls? Why don't you give him some personal feedback while using him as your rebound? Win-win-win," she proposes with a flourish. On each *win*, she swishes her makeup brush like a magic wand. "For Scott. For you. For fans of enemies-to-lovers everywhere."

"It's *really* not like that," I say coolly. "We got into an . . . unpleasant altercation today. Believe me, it's best if we don't speak for a while."

"Who said anything about speaking?" Brit asks, raising an eyebrow.

I'm definitely pink under my purple makeup streaks now. *A rebound fling? With a hidden enemies-to-lovers agenda?* The idea is obviously out of character for the Jennifer who drove down here, the Jennifer ready to romanticize every relationship into her OTP. I don't really do *rebounds*.

However . . .

I can't deny the frustrating spark I felt while we fought for the clue. And *out of character* is part of the point of this week.

"*Maybe*," I say. When Laurel and Brit promptly high-five, I preempt their perilously high hopes. "But he's probably not even attracted to me. He's made it pretty clear he wants nothing to do with me," I say.

"Don't even worry," Brit drawls her reassurance. "We," she says, "are going to do a little court recon tonight."

I meet her eyes in the mirror, wary, and—okay—excited. "What did you have in mind?"

12

With my new look complete, we cross the quad in the early-evening half-light. It's ridiculously pretty, fairy-tale vibes. I'll never forget how the orange fades from pink into purple over the roof-tops.

Tonight, I don't enter the dining hall alone. With me, Laurel and Brit wear fae gowns with glittering handmade headpieces. We share our favorite dialogue lines, finding out everyone loves one dark-horse favorite, the Oracle's speech to Kethryn in *The Shattered Court*. We pile our plates high with roast chicken in some sort of spiced glaze. We struggle to remember whether the culinary choices reference any scene for the series, then settle for our dinner's deliciousness regardless of its Elytheum relevance.

I don't look for Scott. My new friends, however, do. Finally, he enters when we're sitting down at one of the long tables.

I clench my jaw. He never passes up the opportunity for more fantasy-hero flaunting, does he? He's changed clothes since our scuffle on the West College lawn. He's dressed in all black, his shirt loose and billowing. It has the damnable effect of emphasizing the chest I could not help eyeing early this morning.

My friends notice. "Oh my goddess," Brit says without subtlety. "Is that him?"

I face my new friends, lightly embarrassed to be caught in my watchfulness. "Yes. Has he looked over yet?" I ask, losing the war with my curiosity.

"Not yet," Laurel confirms. "Jennifer," she adds indicatively, "maybe you could get us some napkins?"

She nods, and I follow the pointed gesture over my shoulder—finding Scott at the condiments station near the extra napkins.

I grin. Laurel is right. The excuse is perfect. I stand up from my seat and cross the room to the condiments, enjoying the marching rhythm of my new heels on the stone floor.

When I reach the napkins, I don't acknowledge him. I don't even look up, knowing my friends will catalog his every reaction, which they will describe to me in detail, exceeding even Winters's rendering of Kethryn's first venture into the marvelous icy city introduced in *The Ashen Court*. Yes, maybe I lean over the counter a little more than needed—I want to *enjoy* the descriptions, don't I?

Napkins in hand, I return to my seat, feeling like I'm walking off a battlefield victorious.

My friends affirm my expectations.

"He *literally* did a double take," Laurel informs me. "He definitely checked you out and looked pleased."

"Your mission was officially a success, *Lady Jennifer*," Brit concurs. "You've cast your rebound spell for sure."

"If you hook up before the end of the week, you're going to give us your clues so we can go on the date with Val, right?" Laurel presses me.

I laugh, although I admire her ambition for the scavenger hunt.

Relatable. Still . . . Scott didn't even want to be my friend, and that was *before* we hated each other for a year.

"Are we positive this is a good idea? I mean, he's Scott," I reply. "Surely there's someone *better* here for me to rebound with. Like, anyone."

As I say it, my friends' faces close up. Laurel shakes her head subtly.

It's in vain—the vow has left my lips. Needless to say, I know exactly who I will find when I look over my shoulder.

Scott stands over me. His expression is unreadable like the tearstained pages of a favorite book. I don't know whether he heard what I said—and if he did, what do I care? He rejected *me*. So what if I reject him now?

I think the enemies-to-still-enemies trope is severely underappreciated.

I look up expectantly, hoping the purple glitter on my face contours my cheeks imposingly. Of course, I refuse to speak first.

Scott clears his throat.

"You look nice," he says.

His voice is stiff. His compliment is, I reluctantly concede, surprising.

"Wow. You really are taking notes," I reply, only just managing sarcasm past the uncomfortable pounding of my heart. "A compliment from Scott Daniels. You didn't even burst into flames."

"Did I not?" His voice is . . . seductive?

Brit stomps on my foot under the table.

Fine. Message received. "You . . . um, look fine," I muster.

Actually, he looks good. Really good. The ebony shirt works for him. His pants are high-waisted, making him look much cooler than I'm used to. The "rebound spell" has indeed started to work, I fear—on me.

Scott nods in understated acknowledgment, his expression never once changing, and promptly walks off, saying nothing more.

What?

Brit voices my question. "Did he . . . walk across the room *just* to compliment you?"

It's not like Scott to be cryptic. I chew the inside of my cheek, hating that I know exactly what I'm feeling.

It's one of the favorite words of the fantasy canon. *Intrigued.* Everyone and everything *intrigues* romantically entangled characters. *Intriguing. I'm intrigued. I confess, my queen, you intrigue me.* Scott's done nothing all day except goad and fight with me. Now he's done something worse. He's intrigued me.

I shake my head. *No. No, he hasn't.* He's confused me, which is different. Calculus class confused me. Fixing my malfunctioning printer confused me—I mean, really, it was like a Swiss watch in there. Scott Daniels isn't my intrigue. He's just my fucked-up printer.

"No. No way. I mean, why would he even do that?" I demand. "There's nothing in it for him."

Laurel fixes me with a look. "Because it's just so true that he *had* to say it," she declares.

I laugh harshly. "I suspect you might be projecting some romance here," I say, like I wasn't just contemplating the same potential purpose for Scott's visit. "Believe me. We're no Kethryn and Val." I glance behind me, confidently checking for confirmation of my reading of events.

And I get it. Scott sits down next to a woman having dinner alone. I watch her clock his costume, his appearance, and light up. He says something introductory, which makes her smile. It doesn't surprise me. While he's not an extrovert, he's not a total shy nerd, either. I couldn't help noticing in the office how easily he could chat or persuade others with smart, plainspoken charm.

I whip to face my friends, kind of stunned how the sight stings. While I don't want to feel *intrigued*, I don't want to feel interchangeable, either.

"See?" I insist, fighting the waver in my voice. "He's not even interested."

"I'm sure that's not true," Laurel reassures me. "Remember him coming over here just to compliment you, like, five seconds ago? I still think you should get your rebound."

"Maybe," I concede without conviction. The truth is, I'm hesitant to put myself out there again with Scott, even if just for a no-strings rebound now that he intrigues me. Being rejected for friendship was unpleasant. Being rejected for something more would probably require me to quit my job, leave publishing altogether, and possibly move to New Jersey. "Whatever. It's fine. I'm not here for him. I'm here for *this*." I gesture to the servers, who have entered the dining hall in impeccable Elytheum costumes with the first course of dinner.

I wonder if my friends hear the forced nonchalance in my voice—until, I realize, maybe it's okay if they do. I only ever planned on coming to the Experience to immerse myself in the dream of handsome fae, powerful queens, and courtly indulgence. Now I'm left asking myself—which fantasy am I chasing? The one where I'm a fearsome demoness from my favorite realm?

Or the one where I'm Jennifer, and I'm fine? Where I've forgiven and forgotten and found confidence?

Even when I was with Jordan, I yearned for the chance to come here and pretend I was part of my favorite fantasy. What's the difference in conjuring up the life, the self, the hope I want in the real world? It's what even Scott is doing, isn't it? He's going to carry the fantasy home with him, conjuring it whenever he wants.

Could I do the same? Maybe the problem in my relationships isn't only that the men I pick don't live up to my dreams. Maybe *I'm* not living up to them, either.

Perhaps it's part of what stories like Elytheum offer. When I'm here, or when I'm reading, or when I'm perusing fan art, what if I'm learning how to find strength in fantasy? In imagining myself in the world of characters whose magic I'll never possess, maybe I'm practicing how to imagine *myself* as the person *I* want to be.

13

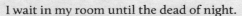

I wait in my room until the dead of night.

With the numbers on my iPhone clock into the three-digits, I get very sleepy. Nobody who's ever waited years for the next installment in their favorite epic fantasy series surrenders to sleepiness, however. Just like I knocked out the entire second half of *The Risen Court* in one night, I endure with the help of a can of espresso from the student store while rereading my favorite chapters. Whenever I need to use the bathroom, I diligently descend the stairs to avoid another run-in with Scott.

I didn't speak to him for the rest of the evening. I ended up having fun at dinner—I focused on Laurel and Brit, and we wound up eating with a couple who flew out from California, Michael and Alec.

It helped to be around other people. I haven't just felt hurt the past couple of days. I've felt unmoored. It's hard not to—like I've just wasted six months of my life and have to start all over again. Like I'm returning home to harsh reality after half a year of . . .

Well, fantasy can hurt as well as help, I suppose. It's perilously hard to know when *fantasy* is just another word for false hope.

Laughing with my group, I reminded myself that romance isn't everything. It's not the endgame of life, even if it's something I desperately yearn for. I focused on what I do have—community, fandom, friendship—which I'll have when I leave here, no matter whether I win the date with Val.

Still . . . I really want to win that date.

In my room, I rehearse the clue, wanting the exact wording on hand in case I need to remember its intricacies. *The Lord of Night cherishes me. Mounted with Glory. Watching over all.* I wait until I no longer hear any sounds echoing in my dorm's hallways. In the summer night, I don't need to pull my Elytheum cloak over my shoulders.

Jittery with excitement and caffeine, I exit my suite and steal quietly down the four full flights of stairs into the dining hall. It's entirely empty, the chairs pushed into the tables. The high ceiling looms overhead.

In the nighttime quiet, it feels like another Elytheum. One of secrets and shadow. One Amelia and the organizers wanted us to uncover on our own, I suspect. The candelabras are unlit. The landscapes in the paintings wait, unmoving. Alone in the dark, I lose myself in the hall's elegant, ominous grandeur.

With only moonlight coming in the Gothic stained-glass windows to guide me, I navigate to the front of the room, where Val's sword is mounted on the wall.

I click on my phone's flashlight. Yes, the harsh white emitted by Jennifer Worth's iPhone does upset the room's perfect moodiness. I'll return to enjoying the courtly vibes once I've figured out the clue.

The sword is magnificently detailed. Real, Hollywood-quality craftsmanship. Intricately woven leather covers the hilt grip. The scabbard is engraved with rose vines. The metal pommel glints in my phone's light.

It's gorgeous . . . and it yields nothing. I look the weapon up and down, inspecting for inlaid words, symbols, other directions or unusual features. I wrack my memory for Elytheum details or innovative approaches, like I've seen Jordan do with video-game puzzles. Alas, no ingenious solutions come to me. I was never much help in *Legend of Zelda*, either.

No, staring at the sword won't be enough.

I don't love the idea of messing with Amelia's impeccable decorations. However . . .

If the sword is a clue, the Elytheum organizers knew we were going to investigate it. Right?

Resolute, I return my Elytheum-inconsistent phone to my pocket. Gently I lift the sword from the hooks holding it on the wall. *Mounted with Glory*. It comes easily—I know instantly it's much too light to be a real weapon. I rotate the sword slowly in my hands. Nothing on the other side . . .

I unsheathe the sword from the scabbard. Dismayingly, no secret scroll slips out. Nothing is written on the sword itself.

My heart starts pounding with nervous discouragement. The clue is unambiguous. The Lord of Night is Val, his honorific. Mounted with glory, watching over . . . No matter how I ponder, strategize, and reorganize the words in my head, reflecting on the prop in my hands, I find no indication of another clue.

It's . . . a dead end. I was wrong.

"I let very few people handle my sword, you know."

The droll voice echoing from within the room startles me. *Val*'s voice.

I jump, managing not to drop the aforementioned weapon. Whirling, I find him—Val—here in the hall with me.

He's leaning against one of the tables, the moonlight perfectly painting him in blue.

How did he do that? Why is he even here?

Without my sword clue, I only have the West College clue. It's very likely another more intrepid, intuitive Experience participant will outpace me and win the date. Which means here, right now, might be my only one-on-one time with Lord Valance of the Elytheum Courts.

I have to make it count. I have to know if Jordan was right—if what we had was all I can expect in life and romance, or if there's something more out there.

I compose myself. *Heroine time.*

"I guess I'm one of the few, then," I reply airily. "Lucky me."

Val smirks. He actually smirks!

I can't help noticing how ridiculously good he looks. No fae magic or demon incantation could match how captivated I am. Val is made of muscle, his impeccable costume emphasizing every contour. His hair falls rakishly loose, framing features like cut obsidian. His intense eyes watch me expectantly.

While I'm dying on the inside, he pushes up from the table. He walks over to me, his unhurried footsteps falling heavily in the darkness. Crossing his arms, he nods at the sword in my hands. "You must think little of me if you imagine there could be a clue on my own sword," he chastens me.

I shrug, perfectly nonchalant. "I'm merely of the opinion," I say, "that everything should be . . . thoroughly inspected." I rake my eyes over Val, hardly recognizing myself.

He grins. "You're good at this," he remarks.

Stepping closer, he comes right up in front of me. It's overwhelming, and validating. Deep down, I feel like I'm proving something to Jordan. And maybe to Scott, too. I *am* entitled to my romantic dreams, damnit.

"You are not, however," Val continues, "finding a clue tonight."

He plucks the sword gently from my hands. Honestly, he could've lifted my phone or wallet and I would have handed them over to the dark power of his eyes. "I recommend sleep," he comments.

I forget to be disappointed by his verdict on my scavenger hunting efforts. How could I, with my very favorite bookish dreams unfolding right in front of me?

His eyes don't leave mine while he sheathes the saber. Did he see me shiver? How could he not? Does he know the warm weather could not possibly have induced the reaction? *How could he not?*

Gaze remaining on mine, he reaches behind me. The mass of him comes even closer to me, perilously close, while he gently hooks the sword where it rested on the wall with one hand. I exhale, then inhale. Just normal respiration. Like people do. Definitely not intentionally smelling the black-leather violet musk of him.

When he's returned the sword, he eyes me one moment longer, and then turns and walks away.

I of course disintegrate into espresso-flavored mush. What my interaction with Val has reaffirmed is exactly why I'm here. Fantasy *never* disappoints. It was *exactly everything* I ever imagined it would feel like. It was amazing. I can't even speak as Val strides away, heading for the shadows.

I know it's not real—I know it's not Lord Valance of Elytheum, fae warrior and smoldering, swaggering consort to the Queen. I know the man portraying Val probably has nothing in common with his persona, either. He's an actor. He's playing precisely the part designed for readers like me, and he won't cross lines of professionalism.

Nevertheless—the feelings I have are real. Why not? What's wrong with a real crush on a fictional personage? How is it different from a crush on a celebrity or a stranger?

It isn't. And it feels wonderful. I'm not embarrassed to flirt or daydream. I'm not afraid of what he's going to say, how he's going to reject me, or find me quiet or uninteresting or annoying or obsessive or everything I worry about in ordinary life. I feel accepted, and acceptance gives me the courage to be my truest self—who, I'm finding, is bold and sharp-witted.

I like her. I like *me*.

Inspired, I call out to Val, who's nearly reached the doorway to the dining hall. "I know you can't respond," I start. Val pauses in the archway, facing the shadowy corridor. "I just wanted to say . . . whoever you really are, you're doing an incredible job," I say, speaking from the heart. "I really appreciate it."

He sends me a quick smile when he looks up. Not a smirk—a smile.

The next moment, the familiar curtain of my favorite character falls over him. Val watches me from the darkened hallway.

"You have a kind heart as well as a courageous one," he comments. "Like another woman I know. Which is why I'm going to offer you a word of advice."

My excitement flags. Insecurity rushes over me. It's never far from even my fantasy version of myself, I guess. Advice? *Remember, none of this is real.* I know. I know, Scott.

Instead, Val eyes me with his usual gravitas. "If you're intent on hunting for secrets, I've learned the Queen may have something planned in commemoration of my birthday," he confesses, with character-consistent reluctance. "I would recommend you participate in her efforts," he concludes indicatively, peering out from the shadows and holding my gaze.

I need a moment to understand what he's really saying. *If you're intent on hunting for secrets* . . . Clues.

Val's not criticizing me. He's . . . helping me!

I straighten up, flush with delight. "I thank you for your valuable information," I say.

Val nods once in perfectly cool acknowledgment. He starts to leave.

"Oh, and"—I grin—"happy birthday, my lord."

Val rolls his eyes in the impatient, pleased way he's described as doing with Kethryn, and then disappears into the shadows.

It is perfection.

14

Over the coming day, I do not rest on the helpful hint from my favorite fae. While I'm eager to pursue whatever event Kethryn announces, there's no guarantee I'll find the clue Val insinuated was involved. Even if I do, I need one more.

Hence my efforts on the second full day of the Experience. My scroll counts as one clue, and if I could solve it, I'd find one more. But instead of puzzling over the riddle and wasting time, I decide to look for other clues spread out in the Experience.

I participate in every class and event I can. Fortunately for me, my new strategy is very enjoyable. I go to the Demoniaca card game class, where I duel with Laurel, and where we each get to keep one richly designed card as a souvenir. It's incredibly fun despite confusing me worse than my uncooperative printer.

Brit doesn't join us, and Laurel fills me in. Brit had her first child eight months ago, and the Experience is her first extended absence from her daughter, who is in the care of Brit's mom, Stephanie. In Laurel's estimation, Stephanie is very well-intentioned, but hardly less needy than the infant.

I'm impressed. Proud, even, of Brit gifting herself self-care and the opportunity to reconnect with her passions. I have no doubt leaving home for the week wasn't easy—although I would guess puff pancakes and magic makeovers compare favorably to spit-up and sleepless nights.

She rejoins us for lunch, which I follow up with jam making. I do momentarily lose track of the scavenger hunt in favor of making as many jams as possible to take home with me, intending to have fogberry on every foreseeable piece of toast.

The high point is the Elytheum folklore seminar, during which Amelia giddily explained features new worldbuilding legends Winters herself scribed. It's literally exclusive content in seminar form.

The event is held in a real Hollisboro seminar room, one of the old ones dating from the college's 1800s founding, with high windows letting the sunlight warm the rows of seats. Listening fascinated in the lecture, I seriously consider reviving my grad school dreams . . . for about fifteen minutes, until I reality-check myself. Most classes aren't about my favorite subject in the entire world anyway.

While I find no clues, I do have my nicest day of the Experience yet. Not coincidentally, it is free of Scott. The only events I avoid are the ones I notice him attending—and horseback riding, of which I steer clear despite lots of attendee interest. Horses frighten me, and I'm content to let someone else find *that* clue.

I enjoy dinner with my new friends. I hang out until late in Laurel and Brit's room, where I help them edit their "Elytheum Experience Day One" video for social media, and we join Brit for a moment on her FaceTime home. I return to the roommate-less peace of my own suite, where I relax under the covers in surprisingly uncomplicated joy.

I find myself wondering if enchanted queens or noble fae, when they're not out defending the realm, ever wish for nights working on videos with their friends, or whatever the equivalent is. I would guess they do.

Only the next morning do I start to feel stressed. I've made no progress since my West College escapade, while Laurel and Brit have found one clue each. My lead is disappearing.

My friends notice my dispiritedness. "Cheer up, Jen," Brit encourages me over our puff pancakes in the dining hall. She, I've found, is the chattier and older of the pair. Laurel, quieter and easier going, is only twenty-four. "You'll figure your clue out. I'm happy to look at it, if you want?"

She watches me with eager, innocent eyes.

I pour more fogberry syrup on my pancakes. "And what's to stop you from figuring it out and claiming the next clue for yourself?" I inquire, matching her forced nonchalance.

She grins slyly. "I mean, it's a date with Val so . . ."

I can't help laughing with them. "All's fair in love and fandom," I finish. Of course, no one can be trusted with *this* prize on the line. Shouldn't every story of courtly intrigue have subterfuge and suspicion? It's very in-plot, really.

I just have to keep remembering how my favorite heroines would do it. Diligence. Determination. Endurance. No alliances? No problem. I'll just go to *every* event today.

Okay, not horse ones. How can consecutive days feature the horses?

While I'm strategizing, Kethryn stands from her throne.

My mind instantly quiets. *I've learned the Queen may have something planned . . .*

Yes. I only have to follow exactly whatever Kethryn says.

"We have a slight change in the day's entertainments," the Queen announces.

Promising.

"Someone very close to me is celebrating his birthday today and being very difficult about it. As usual," she says. *Perfect.* Val does a very commendable job of appearing touched under his usual scowl. "I have offered him the finest delicacies and drinks," Kethryn continues, "and cloaks, and weapons—"

"And I have already assured you I have everything I want," Val interrupts her. They lock eyes. The look they exchange is heated.

"You deserve more," Kethryn returns, her voice low.

Ugh. The sexual tension is delicious. Only a couple like Vethryn can find the fire in discussing birthday plans. For *my* birthday, Jordan promised me somewhere nice for dinner, then took us to *his* favorite pasta spot. There were no drawn-out, fraught looks. Not one. I would have contented myself with some nice cheesecake, even.

"My contentment cannot be surpassed," Val insists.

"If you're not going to cooperate," Kethryn responds, softly stern, "I shall settle for granting you what you've never dared to wish."

A combination gasp-*aww* rises from the crowd. I am part of it. It's just, Kethryn's invoked one of the couple's very final conversations in *The Risen Court*, the end of the series.

You're everything I've ever wished, Kethryn sighs, her confession in the quiet of morning after their climactic victory.

I have my work set out for me, then, Val replies. *All I am left is granting every wish you've never dared.*

Watching the fantastical couple, my heart swells in my chest. Where would I be without fictional love? If I didn't have reminders like Elytheum to find comfort in, I would probably never want to date again. Which I do, I know I do. Even amid the embarrassment of my recent, unfortunately public, breakup, I want to find my own noble, swoony love interest.

Just like the characters in front of me. It's fantasy that helps us face the uncertainties and pains of reality. Anyone who says fiction is just something to hide in doesn't understand how much hope and strength it can inspire. It isn't just practice in imagination. It's a reminder of what I deserve to imagine.

"And besides," Kethryn adds with vigor, "*I* wish to celebrate the day of your birth, and I am the Queen, so we shall!"

Everyone glimpses Val grin as Kethryn faces us again.

"We will have a competition," she declares. "A race over difficult obstacles, sure to greatly amuse attendees and test the strength and perseverance of the competitors."

Val purses his lips, looking charmingly intrigued. "I admit, this would please me," he replies.

Well, it would not please *me*.

I have gone stiff in my seat. What Kethryn has announced is unambiguously the celebratory clue opportunity Val hinted at the other night. It's just . . . *really* not the proposal I wanted to hear. I'm confident no amount of fantasy-inspired reinvention can change the fact athleticism is not my strong suit. In fact, "athleticism" in my case often consists only of hurrying in the halls at work when I'm late for meetings. I've never wanted to work out with friends, knowing I would feel self-conscious.

Val poses the obvious question. "Will there be a prize?"

Kethryn pretends to consider. "Interesting . . . I suppose it would heighten the stakes . . ." Her eyes land on her paramour. She smiles.

The room hangs in suspense. Well, except for me. I know where the conversation is going. It's as unpleasant a feeling as when I inadvertently open to the wrong page and catch a spoiler.

Kethryn plays coy. She shrugs one nonchalant shoulder. "It's your day, Val," she remarks. "If it's a prize you propose, a prize we shall offer. Whoever wins our obstacle race shall receive the court's favor."

My gaze snags on the fae lord himself. Silently, I will him to dramatically change his inclinations, declaring no, he needs no obstacle course. In the quiet of his heart, he wishes nothing except to pass the day reading with his closest companions. Especially Jennifer.

Instead, his lips upturn in the shadowy semblance of a smile. They *quirk*, his author might describe. Okay, not might. She definitely would.

Val winks directly at me.

He's unquestionably reminding me of our conversation. *It's good*, I tell myself. I'm now the only person here who knows a clue waits at the competition's finish line—although others will probably guess.

"Eat. Relish the company of your friends," Kethryn encourages us. Her eyes glimmer with the perfect combination of her character's conspiratorial charm and intimidating cunning. "For when the sun rises directly overhead, you shall call them your competitors."

Noon. I have until noon to prepare myself for my first fae-inspired obstacle course.

Prepare myself *emotionally*, I mean. Not physically. Physically, I'm a goner.

I think of the ways my favorite writers deal with characters like me, who nearly didn't graduate high school for lack of PE credits. Could I please get one of those time-collapsing training paragraphs? A *Time passed, days drew into weeks, Jennifer's powers grew* kind of thing.

"If you wish to join the fray," Kethryn instructs the room, "please write your name on the scroll in the entryway by the end of breakfast." She returns to sit next to Val, whose hand she clasps with shy sweetness.

"We're doing this, right?" Brit prompts.

"Um," I say.

Laurel, I'm reassured to find, mirrors my nervousness. "I'm not sure I'll be very good at obstacles involving upper body strength," she admits.

"You can do it," her friend encourages her. "It's like when mothers do impossible things like lift cars to save their babies. We can do a ropes course to win a night with Val!"

I have to smile. While her logic is iffy, her earnest support is endearing.

When Laurel looks heartened, I decide I feel the same. Fandom *has* pushed me to limits I didn't know I could reach. In English classes, I fought to compress hundreds of pages of Dickens and Dostoyevsky into finals week. Now I crush volumes of Winters like it's easy. Release events and cliffhanger chapters have powered me past exhaustion into early-morning hours. I've even discovered I know how to flirt.

Minutes passed. Jennifer's powers grew.

"I'm in," I say confidently, shooting Laurel a smile.

"Yeah," she replies. "Fuck it, right?"

"In love and fandom," Brit repeats.

We stand from our plates of unfinished pancakes. Like conquering heroines, we march for the sign-up scroll.

15

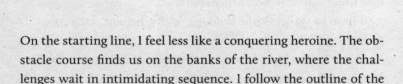

On the starting line, I feel less like a conquering heroine. The obstacle course finds us on the banks of the river, where the challenges wait in intimidating sequence. I follow the outline of the imposing events—the course involves crawling under ropes, climbing over high fences, balancing on logs in the mud, and more.

Honestly, it looks like something from *Survivor*. I love *Survivor*— watching it, I mean, preferably with hot cocoa, in pre-errands free time on weekend mornings, with my computer on the couch.

Not, you know, competing in it.

Not even for Val.

With my nervousness joining forces with the sun—shining directly overhead, like Kethryn described—I'm sweating, and the race hasn't even started. I haven't competed in anything athletic since middle school soccer, so I'm not sure why I let Brit convince me this was a good idea.

Half of the other sign-ups look equally unnerved, which is encouraging. The other half look intimidatingly excited. No one is in costume. In an omen of how seriously everyone is taking the event, they've exchanged leather armor and demoness gowns for activewear. Honestly, it looks like the Elytheum guard has a sponsorship with Lululemon out here.

I did not pack activewear. Instead, I went to the nearest running store off campus twenty minutes ago.

I picked the first thing I tried on, fighting insecurity and self-doubt as I took in my unfamiliar reflection in the far too well-lit changing room. While I desperately yearned to leave all spandex behind, I refused to lose my nerve for the obstacle course. I figured if I purchased running clothes—if I really committed—I would *have* to follow through. Otherwise the black nylon, incriminatingly unworn, would remind me of my cowardice.

Now here I stand, in my very first pair of activewear shorts, which are already rolling up my thighs and climbing into my butt. I'd better win so this is worth it. With everyone busy assembling on the starting line, I attempt to discreetly resolve the wedgie situation.

Quite naturally, this is when Scott comes up next to me.

"Surprised to see you here," he remarks.

I straighten. Forget the wedgie in my shorts. Scott is the wedgie in my soul.

I prioritize accordingly. "Why?" I demand, hands on my hips.

His eyes never leave me. The look he gives me is curiously fraught. Like he's angry with himself for how he feels. Like . . . Well, if circumstances weren't otherwise, I would say he looks like he missed me yesterday.

His sharp-edged voice says nothing of the sort. "Because this is an obstacle course. Outside," he replies. "Doesn't exactly feel like a Jennifer Worth activity."

Okay, no, he didn't miss me.

"You don't know anything about my activities or what I'm

capable of," I protest, meeting him spite for spite. Sarcastic sword fighters on the ramparts of our unfortunate working relationship. "I could easily compete in Ironman races in my free time—you know, the time I spend outside the office as part of my *personal* life?"

"How many miles does one bike in an Ironman?" Scott returns.

I've spent the past days living the fiction of Jennifer the main character, lady of Elytheum. What's the difference in conjuring a Jennifer who competes in Ironman races? "Twenty," I reply firmly, despite having no clue.

Scott laughs. I scowl.

"Would you like to know the real answer? I actually did do an Ironman, you know," Scott informs me.

Fuck.

He's going to be good at this obstacle course, isn't he? "Are you trying to impress me?" I demand, sidestepping his question.

Pulling one arm in front of his chest to stretch his shoulder, Scott eyes me with purposeful dispassion. "Impress you? Why would I care to do that?" he retorts. "Hey, found anyone better to hook up with yet? I'm just *honored* you entertained me at all, considering I never volunteered."

I flush fiercely. Great to know he heard everything. I mean, of course he did. He was standing right there. I guess I just hoped some Elytheum magic would shroud my words or something.

Unfortunately not. No, I've found myself in a nightmare. Kethryn-captured-in-Nightfell-level disastrous. Scott Daniels heckling me over my friends' unconcealed plans for me to rebound with him. I have the urge to go walk into the river and fall face-forward into the mud to hide from the world forever.

I make the closest reasonable escape. "Please just forget you ever heard that," I say, heading for the starting line, leaving Scott and his supercilious remarks and his shoulder-stretching.

"What if I did volunteer, though?"

I round on him slowly, ready to glare. He's . . . He's messing with me. Just playing some cruel Scott Daniels game.

Instead, I find him watching me, eyebrow raised. Just *one* eyebrow. Just like Val.

Which he physically could not do when we arrived here. I remember the notebook I seized from him. *Learn eyebrow thing.* Scott has succeeded in putting one of his most important observations about Val into practice. He actually fucking learned how to raise his eyebrow.

"How did you learn to do that?" I ask quickly. I'm genuinely astounded enough to abandon our petty debate.

Of course, he revels in my reaction. "Oh, is it supposed to be hard?" he replies, indulging in sarcasm like I might indulge in fogberry jam.

He raises it once more. Then once more in fast succession.

No way. I will not stand here while Scott quirks his damn eyebrow like he earns credit card points every time he does.

I reach forward automatically to his forehead and push his eyebrow down. Childish, perhaps, but I do not care. "Cut that out," I order him.

Scott grabs my hand, deflecting my prodding. He raises his eyebrow again. "It appears *you* are the one who doesn't know what *I'm* capable of," he replies, clearly enjoying every drawled word.

While he holds my wrist, I wrestle in vain for his defiant eyebrow. The struggle only pushes us closer together, chest-to-chest in the midday humidity. His face comes close to mine, his scent inescapable in the afternoon air.

"This is only one on a *long* list of things I've mastered since coming here," he informs me.

I feel surprising heat spread through me. I go weak in his grip, waylaying me momentarily.

"Oh yeah? What else?" I challenge him, renewing my efforts. Am I mocking his accomplishments? Or daring him to give me an unforgettable answer? I don't even know.

"Another pity," Scott replies. "You won't experience them. Since I'm at the bottom of your rebound list."

Of course. Now I understand. He's mocking me, returning the favor for the comments he overheard. Pretending he wants to hook up with me, hoping I'll embarrass myself the way I embarrassed him. In real life your enemy doesn't want to hook up with you. They want to embarrass you. I may be prone to romanticizing, but I won't forget that. Suddenly I feel like I've just plunged off the logs over there into the cold water of the river.

I withdraw my hand, no longer having even grudging fun now. Scott can eyebrow me freely if he wants. I frown and face the starting line, keeping him in my peripheral vision. His stare never leaving me, he rolls his neck like a fighter entering the ring.

I roll my eyes like my life depends on it.

One of Kethryn's footmen standing to the side calls out, sparing me from further bickering with Scott. "Competitors ready!" With ceremony he obviously enjoys, the footman lifts to his lips one of the large horns the courtiers held in the Great Hall on our first night.

Some of the other participants crouch like Olympic runners. I don't chance it. I don't need to look like Spider-Man, not when I'm genuinely unsure what consequences such a stance would visit on my new shorts. Everyone looks intense, focused—especially Scott, whose competitive glare I do not dignify with one of my own in return—until, out into the afternoon, the foghorn rings loud and low.

I run.

No, I *fly*. I pick up momentum fast on the grassy hill where the course opens, leading us to the river under the cover of the campus's impressive oaks. Even when my feet start to skid on the slope—even when I notice a few of my competitors wipe out on the wet grass—I stay upright. I don't let myself panic. Forget the date with Val. Right now, I'm motivated by beating Scott.

Inspired or not, exertion hits me hard. I expected I would get—I don't know, farther without knifelike pain in my windpipe and dull stinging in my legs. It's embarrassing, which only makes me more uncomfortable, which only makes running hurt worse. I'm an unathletic self-fulfilling prophecy.

Nearing the ropes challenge, which waits alongside the river, I correct myself. When I got here, I marveled at how I could be anyone. Not someone—*anyone.* Princess. Demoness. Lady. Warrior.

I'm *not* Lady Jennifer right now. I'll return to Lady Jennifer when I'm recuperating from my sporty outburst with my friends. In fact, I deeply look forward to it. Right now, though, with each furious footstep, each push of power in my miserable legs, I re-imagine myself.

This isn't a race. I'm not in North Carolina. I'm rushing into combat to slay the demons stalking the realm. And if my annoying co-worker catches a stray sword slash—well, it happens.

In a stroke of unexpected genius, I manage to distract myself with my fantasizing. I reach the ropes, surprised to find my legs moving less strenuously. While I'm far from the lead, I'm not last, either. I can't see Scott, which is probably good.

In front of the ropes, I hit the ground. Wooden poles frame the obstacle, the ropes connecting them a foot off the ground at odd angles. A few of my fellow racers decide to go right into the ropes, loping and ducking to pass the heavy woven cords.

Not me. I wiggle on my stomach under them the entire way. I know I'm getting grass stains everywhere, but I don't care. Would a courtly lady of Elytheum? Certainly. Would a vengeful warrior, charging into the fray to hack up horrid demons? Hell no.

And don't I have the most horrid demon of all to face down?

When the end is in sight, I pull my arms in tight and roll the rest of the way. Staggering to my feet, I find my strategy has worked. Not many other runners are in front of me now. If I push—if I stay inspired—I could win.

The fence, the next challenge, waits only yards in front of me. Unfortunately, the obstacle is imposing. The wooden wall rises nearly to the height of the younger oaks hemming the river. We're meant to use the spaces in the wooden slats to climb up, then heave ourselves over the fence.

Whatever. I'll manage it. I sprint.

Only, when I'm seconds from the fence—Scott passes me.

Devastating. Disastrous. The dismay I felt when the Darkness claimed Val's oldest comrade in *The Risen Court*'s most emotionally wrenching scene. *How could this happen?* When Scott dares to shoot me a victorious glance over his shoulder, I'm just glad he does it without his eyebrow stunt.

I hit the fence moments later, straining every muscle in me to push faster, ignoring the severe cramp in my side. This fearsome warrior is yearning to hunt down some vitaminwater right now. I'm next to my competitors, each of us grunting and gasping as we surmount the tall wooden slats.

With finger strength forged from flipping pages, I manage to pull myself up over the fence. Scott, I'm distraught to discover, has surmounted the obstacle entirely. He's dropping nimbly to the ground, landing solidly on his feet.

Knowing my chances are disappearing, I make the calculated decision to fall off the fence onto the other side. Who needs gracefulness when you have gravity? I release my grip, plunging the fifteen feet to the ground. The drop knocks the wind out of me.

Scott does a double take at the sound of my impact on the grass. He stops, then . . . *abandons his lead*. He rushes to my side while dull pain pervades my upper body.

"Ow," I say.

"Jen, are you okay?" he asks.

"Ugh," I say.

I would have preferred losing. I would have preferred his victorious laughter while he lopes on his long runner's legs to the finish line. I would've preferred he cock his left eyebrow fifty million times. I would have preferred anything instead of what he's doing now.

"Jen," he murmurs again, urgently. When I start to sit up, only to drop down again from the ache of impact stinging in my side, Scott crouches swiftly. He's right next to me. Kneeling over me, really.

He reaches out. Concern, or something—it couldn't be concern, not for his arch competitor, his rival—sharpens the gray in his eyes, like lightning hiding in the clouds.

He hesitates a moment, and then, firm and sure, he wraps his hand under my shoulder. Like he's going to help me up, or pull me into an embrace. Just like on the starting line, his scent is everywhere. Slicked now with sweat, like . . .

No, Jennifer.

It's absurd for him to pretend this way. People pass us left and right. Our lead vanishes. I struggle onto all fours while Scott, supporting my shoulder, his frame bent close to mine, watches me intently. Like he's nervous. Like he actually cares! It's more fantastical than the notion of real live fae in enchanted Elytheum regalia coming to heal my wounds with magic.

Which is why, the moment Scott withdraws his hand, I spring to my feet and sprint past him, laughing.

It feels fucking wonderful. Imagining myself fighting fearsome demons can't even match this pure exhilaration.

Scott is startled for a moment—I can tell from the footsteps I *don't* hear pursuing me—until he remembers himself and reengages, sprinting to catch up.

Still, I'm in the lead when we reach the next obstacle. Logs are laid lengthwise over a patch of thick mud. We have to dash the length of one without falling off.

I step onto my chosen log. Quickly, I learn what I lack in running power, I also lack in coordination. On my first attempt, I wobble. I'm forced to drop off the log and plant my feet in the mud. Impatiently, I renew my efforts.

I get frustrated when Scott passes me, walking the length of his log with precise paces. My irritation only makes me clumsier. When I fall for the second time, I pause. I close my eyes, collecting myself. Daring to walk the log more slowly, I manage to reach the other side.

The instant I land on flat ground, I'm sprinting again. The course leads sharply uphill. I give the incline everything I have, outright ignoring my unrelenting cramp. With the slope slowing everyone down, I seize the opportunity to make up ground, passing wearier competitors.

Nearing the height of the hill, however, I realize the worst has happened.

Scott is *literally* in the lead.

It's incredibly frustrating. Personally and philosophically. I contemplate shouting out *He's not even a real fan!* and everyone would drop everything and pile onto Scott like zombies.

I don't, obviously. I want to win using the nobility and perseverance Val prizes in warriors. Sweating profusely in the humid heat, I scramble up the hill, using my hands for extra stability. I know I look like hell. I'm proud of it, honestly. Hill dirt coats my hands. My hair has come chaotically loose from my ponytail. Glittered cheeks are for making Scott notice me in the Great Hall. Grass stains are for a different kind of victory.

Unless Scott wins, of course. I straighten up, preparing for disappointment or salvation. The hill opens onto the final challenge.

Relief rushes over me.

For the end of the obstacle course, we only need to toss three beanbags into a black bucket.

I beam. *This* I can do. I did not spend my childhood dashing over logs or recreationally surmounting high fences. I *did* spend summers under the Oklahoma sun playing cornhole.

I confidently grab my first beanbag. In the same moment, Scott overhands his and it lands way wide of his objective. *Promising. Very promising.* The man is out here looking like he's playing darts. Meanwhile, I step, swing, and—neatly score my first.

My progress visibly frustrates him. He glares. I even hear him *growl* watching me outscore him. Either he's overcommitting to the Lord Valance storminess or he *really* doesn't want to lose.

Scott is no quitter, however. He's also irritatingly disciplined and determined. His scavenger hunting proves it. I'm not surprised when he refocuses quickly, reassesses his throw, and lands his first *and* second shots impressively.

The crowd cheers us on from the finish line. I will *not* lose out now, not when this is something just regular Jennifer excels at. I exhale—I wind up—

Scott does the same—

Of course, we land our beanbags in our buckets at the very same instant.

No one else has finished the challenge. I lock eyes with Scott. We hold each other's gazes for a split second—and then we both take off, flying for the finish line.

Disappointment draws on me immediately. With yards until the finish line narrowing into feet, I watch victory slip out of my grasp. Scott is faster than me. He just is. *Stupid annoying Ironman experience.*

I see the finish line nearing, see how Scott will get there first.

And I decide impulsively, the Jennifer who defends Elytheum doesn't accept defeat. Screw nobility and perseverance. I can't pass Scott. But I can keep him from winning.

Drawing on my very last reserves of strength, I throw myself forward, leaping and grasping onto Scott's shirt.

The snarl of fabric flings him off his stride. He flails, crashing to the side, and poetically, we go down together. "What the—" I hear him grunt-gasp. He catches sight of me, and his eyes widen. "Why—?"

He doesn't get to finish the question. Unfortunately, we . . . *keep* going down. I'd not considered how close we were to the edge of the hill we just surmounted.

I clutch Scott, and we roll all the way down the slope and onto the muddy shore, right into the river.

16

My head lands on Scott's chest. The rest of me lands in the mud.

"*Ufh*," I hear him exhale.

"*Ew*," I declare.

I push myself up, feeling the wet squelch of mud everywhere. I'm *covered* in river muck. Forget pride in my filthiness. I regret everything.

We're right where the grassy incline meets the murky current of the river. It's calendar-page worthy, with swaying green foliage overhead, rocks dotting the river's edge, and the cloudless sky overhead. Comically lovely, except for the pair of mud-covered intruders.

When I wrestle to my knees, I find Scott similarly coated in mud. It's small, grim consolation. At least I have this sight as a cherished memory forever.

Scott sits up, grimacing at the grime on his hands. His eyes meet mine, and—

He laughs. *How dare he*.

"You look worse," I inform him.

Scott stands. "Do I?" He doesn't sound furious, which I can't quite make sense of. He holds his arms wide, showing off how, yes, he's completely mud-covered.

Yet the grime is not what I notice most. It's how unfairly endearing his smile is.

Unfairly. I cling to resentment like I clung to the obstacle course fence. "I would have won if you weren't here," I say.

Scott nods, like, *Yes, reasonable point, Jennifer.*

"Alternatively," he remarks, "*I* would have won if a certain irritating colleague of mine hadn't thrown herself at me."

I flatten my gaze, hearing his double meaning and in no mood to entertain it. He's here for one reason. Here at the Experience, here at the obstacle course, here in this muddy river. "Did you know the winner would get a clue, or were you just determined to outdo me?" I demand.

His expression doesn't change. If the clue reveal was new information, he conceals his reaction well. Or I don't know—perhaps he had the same knowledge. He could have had his own nocturnal flirtations with Kethryn in the dining hall. "Your competing was reason enough for me to sign up," he replies, evading the question.

"Don't we do enough competing at work?" I return. It's funny— we've never outright discussed the quiet war we wage in every presentation and departmental meeting. Until now, covered in river mud. "Itemizing your objections to my pitches for every weekly meeting wasn't doing it for you? Had to add obstacle courses into the fun?"

"I did think it would be amusing to beat you," he admits. "As it always is. But no. You were avoiding me, and I wanted to quickly follow up on the rebound comment."

It's equal measures annoying and darkly comic, how he's co-opting email phrasing for our present, very unprofessional discussion. *Just following up.* Just like he does in our inbox exchanges when he pings me on an unfortunately overlooked deadline, with everyone cc'd.

"Sorry, I'm out of office today," I imitate. "Could we circle back or connect live? How about end-of-day never?"

He watches me like the Scott I know, but fraught with emotions I don't recognize on him. Familiar, yet unknown, like the new installment in an old series. One I'm not sure I'm going to enjoy. *Scott Daniels, the next chapter.*

"Cute," he replies, droll. As I study him, he holds out his hand to help me up.

I hesitate. Ultimately, not wishing to incur further embarrassment by slipping onto my ass on my way up, I reach up and put my hand in Scott's.

He starts to pull. The mud makes our fingers slick against each other's, and Scott needs to grip me hard to get purchase. The contact is firm and gentle, warm and rough—and *damnit*, I want him to hold on.

"Gross," Scott comments.

Meaning the mud. "Disgusting, yes," I reply hastily.

I drop his hand as soon as I'm on my feet, feeling like I'm losing something instead of releasing it. Hating my unreliable heart, I storm off—only to hear Scott's footsteps following me up the wooded hillside.

"So returning to our discussion," he prompts.

"We weren't having a discussion, Scott," I say. "I don't even want a rebound, honestly. I'm not a rebound girl."

Seconds pass in which only our footsteps crunching dried leaves fill the silence, until Scott speaks up. "Sure, that makes sense," he says.

Wow, I nearly comment, *your first ever instance of agreeing with me. What character development!* Then I decide I do not wish to prolong the conversation, if possible.

Scott's stride once more easily outpaces mine. He comes up next to me, then slows to fall into step.

"For my research this week," he ventures, "I'm curious *why* exactly you were so opposed to me. As a hypothetical hookup, of course," he clarifies.

I'm quietly relieved. He's not playing with me. He only wants to know for his little *book boyfriend* project.

"You're going to write what I say in that journal of yours?" I inquire.

Scott nods once. His stride is loping and comfortable next to my muddy stomping under the North Carolina forest cover.

"*Everything* I say?"

"Yes, Jennifer," he replies with put-on patience.

I feel the muddy squelch of my steps less now. The sun seems to shine warmer on my drenched clothes despite the heavy canopy of leaves overhead. "Well, *hypothetically,*" I commence, "I think it has something to do with your face."

Scott stops.

Innocently, I pause with him, turning to him in inquiry.

"My face," he repeats.

I keep my expression neutral, mustering my most reasonable countenance. Like he's just proposed sharing our presentation templates with each other instead of hoarding our own files in pursuit of PowerPoint domination. Reasonableness, not rivalry. "Yes, your face. It's just off-putting," I reply. "Thank you for being so professional about constructive feedback. It's a skill I'm pleased to see you progressing on."

He scowls while he wipes sweat and mud from his forehead with one precise hand. It's almost like he's—drawing my eye intentionally. "I don't think my face has anything to do with it," he informs me. "In fact, I think you *like* my face."

"Wouldn't be the first time we disagreed," I reply.

Scott shakes his head, undeterred. "No. I've watched you watch *me*. Our morning outside the showers. Wrestling on the green. The way your eyes . . . linger," he describes slowly. "Yes, I think you like my face just fine."

Hot irritation flames in me. *Presumptuous much?* I wish I could reply with withering sarcasm.

Except then Scott would press me on whether he was wrong. I'm not confident I could convincingly lie—not when I do, in fact, find his face less than loathsome. "It's your personality," I return stubbornly. "Hypothetically, it sucks."

"I'm working on that," Scott replies. "Would you say I've improved or worsened since arriving here?"

I stop, thrown. Nothing in his earnest response sounds sarcastic or performed. I wasn't expecting him to . . . take my insult seriously.

Still, it's impossible to imagine he's not pursuing some agenda, some subterfuge. Remembering the Jennifer I envisioned dashing into combat with demons, I decide I need to reassert myself. "Well, your personality couldn't possibly worsen," I say. "Nothing's worse than rudely rejecting someone who was just trying to be friendly."

Instantly, the memory of our first conversation stings me. The embarrassment hurts even now. In hindsight, invoking Scott's dismissal of me perhaps was not the wisest avenue for insulting my nemesis.

He studies me. "When?" he asks hesitantly. "You mean—"

"You know exactly when I mean," I snap. "Charlene's party. When I invited you out for drinks, hoping to make a new friend in the office, and you acted like I was . . . nobody."

Scott falters. I don't dare wonder whether I catch the faintest hint of regret on his familiar features. The forest stillness descends over us. When Scott opens his mouth, I resent how I know I'm going to hang on to his every word.

"I would just point out . . ." he says, "considering you did want to get drinks together, my personality can't be *that* bad."

I utter a cry of frustration. *Of course* he doesn't care. Of course my shame is his punch line. "Clearly," I say, "it was a mistake I am continuing to suffer for."

Furious, I spin on my heel and march off. I refuse to wait for whatever painfully precise retort I'll receive from Scott.

Of course, he follows. We continue along the river, heading away from the obstacle course finish line, where the winner, a six-foot-two woman I saw overcome the fence challenge in five seconds flat, is receiving a rose from Kethryn.

Scott lets a few moments pass. Until—

"You want to know why I said no, don't you?"

My cheeks flame. I stomp forward, decimating leaves underfoot with deliberate vengeance now. "Not at all," I reply.

Of course, I've only wondered for the past year why he said no.

What's more, I've given him the opportunity for the perfect comeback. He could say my face. My personality. It . . . would hurt, I realize, which makes me regret my own insults flung his way.

Instead, Scott responds with his infuriating calm. "I heard you and Amelia talking in the lounge on my first day," he says.

I don't reply, having very much not expected his answer. *What could I possibly have said?* I wrack my mind. Were we shit-talking someone he was friends with? No, we very rarely complain about people. Only when they've done something egregious—like, say, rejecting me with only a judgmental dismissal. "What conversation?" I finally surrender to asking.

"You were talking about a guy who had just broken up with you. It was . . . a shitty way to dump you," Scott elaborates. Even wandering in the forest, winded from the obstacle course, I hear unique hesitation strain Scott's voice.

I struggle to remember. Fact is, sharing my romantic misfortunes with Amelia in the Parthenon lounge on extended visits to the coffeemaker was not unusual. "I'm afraid you'll have to be more specific," I say.

"You had, um, gone down on him," Scott clarifies, "and when you asked if he'd return the favor, he said that actually he was thinking you two should break up."

"Oh. Right," I say, sighing. "Malcolm." Of course. I'd completely blocked him from my memory, for understandable reasons.

"Him. Yeah," Scott says hastily. Glad the only uncomfortable part of this conversation is over for you, Scott! "I remember you were recounting this, and then . . . at the end, you said you wanted to give it one more shot because you thought he might really be the one."

"Obviously, he was not," I say. I don't understand, though. What does Malcolm have to do with Scott? "*That story* made you hate me?" I ask, uncomprehending.

Scott shakes his head. "I never hated you," he says. "I understood you. And I was right."

We're nearing where the slope up from the river rejoins campus, the end of our muddy journey. "Enlighten me," I say, hiding my curiosity under sarcasm. "You *understood me*?" I repeat.

"I mean, yeah," Scott insists. "You were the kind of girl who wouldn't let anything be casual. You fall fast and sweep yourself up in the idea of a love story that doesn't even exist. Malcolm was clearly shit and you were still ready to commit to him."

Stomping up the hill, I consider his assessment. Scott . . . isn't wrong, I guess. Nevertheless—"What did that have to do with us?"

He shrugs. "We had no common ground. You're a romantic. And I'm not."

"Books. Publishing. New York City. Yes, no common ground at all," I reply.

I don't even know why I'm debating him. I don't want to be his friend anymore. I guess debate is just my habit when it comes to Scott Daniels. One could even say it's our *common ground.*

He exhales in impatient discomfort. "Is it such a crime to just want to show up to work and do my job and go home? I didn't need any more than that. I didn't need to listen to you romanticize everything that actually just sucks. And you didn't need a friend who either lied to you about what he thought of your choices and philosophy or constantly scoffed at everything you were swept up in hope over." He shakes his head, frustrated. "It was better for both of us to remain . . . nothing."

I'd never known why he rejected me the way he did. Nonetheless, it doesn't matter. I'm not going to let Scott off easy for the embarrassment I felt leaving Charlene's—and if I'm honest, for weeks afterward. "Well, we didn't remain nothing, Scott," I say coldly. "We don't like each other."

"I *know* that," he replies. "Look, you asked me why I thought you didn't dump Jordan when you knew you should. It's not because you're a coward. It's this," he concludes. "You're desperate to treat every day like you're living in some romantic fantasy, and if we'd become friends when you asked, I would have told you this then. Happy? Was I wrong to say no to you?"

I say nothing, stunned.

No, indignant. So I sometimes get swept away! So what?

I find my voice while we continue up the hillside. "Being a romantic isn't a flaw, you know," I say, vehement.

"Has it made you happy?" he retorts.

"I—" I swallow. "I'm happy. Not right now. Rarely in your presence," I snipe. "But yes, I'm happy."

"I think you're so obsessed with a fairy tale that you overlook reality." Scott's voice matches mine for intensity now. "You're stuck in a dream, Jennifer. You need to accept that reality sometimes sucks or you'll never know how to have a *real* relationship," he declares. "And I was right, because Jordan said much the same thing."

"Being on the same side as Jordan is not something I would brag about," I inform Scott. "His favorite book is his *Call of Duty* strategy guide."

"Oh, Jennifer," Scott replies. "See?"

I fall silent, understanding his point.

Okay, yes—maybe I am a romantic. Maybe I let the magic of hope enchant me instead of wallowing in discouragement or embracing the dullness of the ordinary world. *It doesn't mean I can't have something real,* I insist in my head, promising myself with fraying confidence. *It just means I'm optimistic.* Optimism is good, isn't it? Positivity?

I have to fight the whispers of doubt infiltrating my reassurances. Haven't I felt uncertainties just like the ones Scott is describing? The dangerous magic of hope, casting a spell I no longer know if I want enchanting me? Jennifer Worth, fending off demons like none found in Elytheum now.

In the end, it's Scott who strengthens me. Not in any encouragement he offers. Definitely not. My defense against Scott's words is remembering it's *Scott* who said them. I neither need nor want any life advice from a guy with a notebook of things he thinks he can do to distract women from his shitty personality. He was right. I never should have wanted to be his friend.

"Don't worry," I say quietly, my voice sword-edged. "I know very well how much reality can suck, Scott. I have you to thank for that. Good luck getting any woman to fall for your whole book boy-friend scam. You're no Val," I say, "and you never will be."

I don't let myself imagine his face falling. I don't permit myself to wonder whether I've wounded him. He's certainly wounded me. I start walking faster now, marching toward campus. I feel my in-tention is clear—I'm obviously walking *away* from him now, not walking with him.

Scott doesn't pick up on my standoffishness.

He follows me on his long legs, like he's keeping pace on a course of obstacles much more complicated and harder to see. "You really don't think I could find someone who thinks I'm as amazing as a dude with goat horns?" he inquires.

"They're not *goat horns*," I reply. Honestly, how dare he insult Val's polished ebony horns, pride of the Elytheum Courts?

Scott says nothing.

"Well, so what if they are!" I amend. Flustered, I stomp up the path, welcoming the sight of the familiar campus commons nearby. When I pick up my pace, Scott matches me. Fortunately, it means we reach our dorm quickly. We're still dripping mud and river water on the walkways.

In front of our building's entryway, Scott reaches his arm out ahead of me. He pulls the door open for me, his movement abrupt, like he was polite on instinct and then remembered he was angry.

I nod angrily in thanks.

Our shoes quelch unpleasantly on the stairs with every stomp up the four goddamn flights. "My point is," I say, feeling confident I've composed myself, "a real Val, *goat horns* and all, would encourage romanticism. He would believe in a true love."

Once more, the *hmm* Scott makes sounds pointedly growl-ish. "A real Val doesn't exist," he grinds out.

"Actually, I plan to go on a date with the real Val this week, thank you very much," I announce, holding my head high as we round the stairwells. "That'll be all the rebound I need."

"You're going on a date with an *actor*," Scott rejoins. "And you're not even going on the date with him, because you're not going to win the scavenger hunt. You clearly haven't even figured out your scroll clue yet."

I fume. We're finally reaching our floor. I would dash the rest of the way up if the obstacle course hadn't left my legs utterly decimated.

"You know what I think?" Scott goes on as we approach my door. "Forget Malcolm, or Jordan, or whoever else. Staying with shitty guys isn't the worst problem with romanticizing everything."

Surprise keeps me from offering Scott the retorts I otherwise would, like, *I don't want to know what you think* and *You have no right to say "whoever else" like that.*

Unfortunately, he knows I'm curiosity's captive. He continues on. "It's writing off the *right* person," he says, his voice low. "If you can't accept that your dream guy is a fantasy, then when you do find someone great, you're not even going to realize it if they don't fit into the story you're telling yourself. You'll eventually push them away after you've stopped romanticizing them because they don't live up to the fictional character you've built up in your head."

I've reached my limit for Scott's dismissals and judgments, his exhausting condemnations. I have nothing more to say to him—I want only to get into the shower and wash the mud and this whole conversation off me. He's just claimed the last ounce of fight I have.

At my door, feeling like I've only barely survived the battlefield, I reach for my key card—

And find the pocket of my shorts empty.

No, no, no. I hide how the misfortune makes my heart pound. The key must've fallen out in the obstacle course fiasco. Of course it fucking did. We pretty much *Princess Bride*-ed it down the entire hill into the river.

Hoping I'll fool Scott with my nonchalance, I grab the door handle anyway. I figure he'll assume I'm going inside and finally freaking leave.

He doesn't. I push down on the handle.

The door does not move. Neither does Scott.

Fuck. I'm going to have to march all the way down to the river, get on my hands and knees, and rummage around *in the mud* for my key card. *Perfect. Remind me again how reality is supposed to live up to fantasy?*

"Having trouble?" he inquires, like he hasn't just reduced my entire romantic outlook to rubble.

I refuse to dignify his impertinent politeness with a response. Instead, I settle for pushing hard against the door, slamming the lock lightly. I don't know, maybe I can push past it, or dislodge something, or—I don't know! I *just* need to change out of my clothes. If I could just—

I'm wrestling with the handle when the door opens.

No, *someone* opens the door.

The man standing on the other side is . . . well, he's hot. He's very tall, his dark hair perfect, his jawline impressive. He looks like—Val.

He's not dressed like Val, however. He's dressed normally. Although, I mean, the word *normal* does not apply for the newcomer. Nothing he's wearing is fantastically ornamented. His jeans and heather-gray T-shirt don't scream "Elytheum." They're impeccably fitted, though. He looks ready to coach high school sports or sing on a Nashville stage, not spar with recruits in the Elytheum royal guard.

He's gorgeous. And he's . . . real.

At least I think he's real. I suppose it's possible I hit my head when I fell off the fence.

"Hi," he greets me with pleasant amusement. "Why are you trying to break into my room?"

"I'm—" I say, then stop. *My room?*

Which means . . .

"I'm your roommate," I say in realization.

While my heart races now for entirely non-frustration-related reasons, his confusion clears. He smiles a smile capable of stopping the Northern Court's infamous archers' arrows midair. "Of course!" he exclaims warmly. "Jennifer, right?"

"Yep," I say.

He opens the door wider. Grinning, I cannot help glancing at Scott.

His dismissive demeanor has disappeared. He's scowling as my oblivious roommate retreats into our suite.

"Maybe," I say, "I don't have to solve the rest of the clues. I think fantasies are real after all."

Scott says nothing. He only gapes with storm-clouded eyes while I follow my ripped-from-the-pages-of-a-favorite-book roommate into our suite.

17

His name, I learn, is Erik.

He introduces himself while I close the door. I can see into his bedroom from the small common room. Yes, I am snooping a little bit, but he's been in this room with all my things who knows how long without me. His suitcase is open and empty on his bed, his wardrobe full of hanging shirts, jeans, and what looks like costumes.

The contrast between the two of us at this particular moment is tragically humorous.

He glances at me, appearing to notice my disheveled look for the first time. Admittedly, dripping mud and river runoff in uncomfortable athletic shorts, which are not satisfied with riding up my ass and have started pushing into new territory on my thighs, is not how I envisioned meeting my hot roommate. However, I'm not complaining.

"I'm feeling a little overdressed," Erik comments.

I flush. "I'm sorry. I promise I'm not usually this dirty."

"Too bad," he replies.

My mouth drops open. Again—not complaining. The shameless flirting from my catalog-model-worthy new roommate just stuns me.

With the change in my expression, Erik looks guilty. Or, half-guilty. "Sorry," he says. "Sometimes the Val slips out of me. It's hard not to stay in character here." He gestures around our adorned suite. "I actually auditioned to play him in the Experience. Didn't get the role," he admits. "Please tell me the guy who did is terrible."

I hesitate.

Erik reads my expression, his shoulders slumping.

"I'm sure you would have been amazing, though," I reassure him. "You really . . . look the part," I add sincerely.

Erik grins, and I catch more than actorly vanity in his reaction. I decide I like the inexplicable hunk sharing my suite. His enthusiasm is inclusive and infectious. "I hadn't read the books before my agent sent me to the audition, but I got really into them," he shares.

I light up. "They're so good, right? What's your favorite part?"

"The part of Val!" Erik exclaims like it's obvious. "It's, like, an absolute career-maker. I could be the next Sam Heughan."

I push aside my annoyance at his superficial response. People can enjoy stories for all sorts of reasons, I remind myself. What's important is he's excited. We have the coming days for discussion of the Nightfell rescue, and the masquerade, and plenty of other key Val moments.

"I can see you as the next Sam Heughan," I reply. Again, *very* honest on my part.

Erik looks genuinely touched. "Thank you for saying that," he says.

This is the point in the conversation with my inordinately hot roommate when I would usually skitter off into solitude and the comfort of reading, unable to imagine someone like him finding me interesting enough to earn more conversation. Right now, however, I'm covered in mud, standing in the middle of a dorm room. My first impression is what it is.

"So is that why you're here? To study the character?" I ask Erik with nonchalant interest. *Pretend he's just Val in the dining hall*, I remind myself, *instead of . . . your roommate who looks exactly like Val in the dining hall.*

Erik smiles. No, grins. No—smirks? "Nah, I've got Val on lock," he assures me. *No argument from me.* "When I auditioned originally, I was told Heather Winters would be here. I didn't get to perform in front of her, unfortunately. Who knows who would have gotten the part if I had."

He chuckles immodestly. I'm into it. Kethryn would be, too.

"Thing is, the Val at the Experience isn't the only Val," Erik explains.

He pauses indicatively. I wait.

"If you're here," he says slowly, "I'm guessing you've heard the TV rumors."

I gasp a little. Not very coolly, I will admit. Whatever. Yes, of fucking course I've *heard the TV rumors*. They've occupied every Elytheum forum, every fan art account, every fandom group chat for the past year since it was announced producers were developing Elytheum Courts for the screen. The sort of mega-adaptation fans know will change our longtime fave into a worldwide franchise.

The aforementioned rumors have followed every stage of development. First the addition of an in-demand showrunner after her *Star Wars* miniseries exceeded commercial expectations and earned Emmy consideration. Then discussion of whether it would go streaming or somewhere like HBO or Showtime, which is still unresolved.

And nothing—*nothing*—has exceeded the casting chatter. Who among us hasn't fancast every it-girl and internet boyfriend as Vethryn for the past decade?

When the producers confirmed they would consider relative unknowns as well as famous names, speculation went into overdrive. Everyone has opinions on who would make the perfect Kethryn and Val.

Including, apparently, the man in front of me.

He reads the look on my face. "I'm here," he confirms, "in humble submission of myself for consideration. I figured I could show Ms. Winters my stuff up close. Impress her, hopefully."

Humble is not the word I would use. Everything else is music to my ears.

"I planned on coming at the start but I booked a last-minute commercial," Erik adds. He sounds genuinely nervous. "I hope I haven't missed too much."

I want to reassure him, except I'm finding it increasingly difficult to remain a human capable of speech. Erik is physically just like I imagined Val. And if he is any good at acting, and he *does* impress Heather and get the role . . . he could be the closest thing there is to Val in real life.

The universe, I conclude, is giving me exactly the sign I need right now. Written in enchanted lettering, decorated in the white roses of the Elytheum Courts. My favorite sort of sign.

Don't write off your dreams, it reads. *Fantasy can be real.*

"No," I manage to say. "No, you haven't missed much." *Only me and a guy I work with wrestling on the lawn, rolling down the hill outside, and other embarrassing episodes I would not want the next real-life Val to witness.* "Heather hasn't really been around much yet anyway. Everyone has been trying to win this scavenger hunt," I elaborate. "Find three clues and you win dinner with Val."

At the mention of his rival, Erik makes a face. "No thanks," he pronounces.

I have to smile. It's just, it's very Val. Every time visiting envoys play suitor to Kethryn in the halls of the court, the Lord of Night is described looking exactly this way.

Erik paces over to the window. "Although . . ." he starts.

He gazes out, the light dappling his features. Does he really have dark brown eyes exactly like Val? Or is he committing to contacts for the role?

Either way, it's amazing. You could paint a book cover from the commanding way he overlooks the campus from our vantage.

"If I win the scavenger hunt, it *would* get Ms. Winters's attention," he muses.

He puts his hand to his chin, deep in thought.

I take a breath, for an idea has formed in my head. A *daring* idea, like the raid on Nightfell.

Fantasies are *real*, I remind myself. You just have to reach for them.

"We could work together," I propose.

Erik looks up. He eyes me.

"I'll take the dinner and you have a shot at impressing Heather," I explain calmly, hiding how uncalm I feel. In fact, Erik has presented in himself the answer to the question lurking in my head since morning. How can I recover my lead, my command of the scavenger hunt? With every passing hour, I've been forced to realize my fan knowledge combined with my intuition—with fairly minimal help from my athletic coordination—have not proven enough. I need something new. My next move.

Like a partner.

Erik looks—oh, what's the word?—intrigued.

When he replies, I hear the seriousness of his consideration.

"And why should I work with you?" he queries. "I don't know anything about you."

"I figured out the first clue on the second day," I reply.

Erik nods.

"Impressive," he admits. "You must be, like, a superfan or something."

"Proudly," I say.

I mean it. And when Erik grins, I know it was the right answer. He studies me, looking enticed if not quite convinced. I do wonder if my present state has something to do with his hesitation. I don't exactly look like I have my highly competent shit in order. I look like . . . well, like someone who just rolled down a hill into a river.

I straighten anyway. Heroines look badass covered in mud.

"An alliance?" Erik asks.

"Yes," I confirm.

Finally, he sticks out his hand to shake.

Yes. When he opened our door, I was exhilarated just to have a hot roommate. Now I may have lucked into so much more. *Don't give up. Reach for it.*

Confidently, I put my dirt-encrusted palm in his.

18

Needing very much to shower, I head into the stairwell, prepared to seek out my usual sanctuary on one of the lower floors. Then I stop.

Why should I steer clear of Scott? Why should I go downstairs while he enjoys the convenience of showering on our floor?

Not today, I decide. Not when I'm obviously winning our endless competition right now. He only has the memory of losing out on the obstacle course, while I have the dreamiest scavenger-hunting partner I could want.

Scott has come close to ruining my time here, hasn't he? Well, now I don't mind ruining his shower.

I spin on my heel and march to the bathroom on *my own* floor. Inside, sure enough, I recognize Scott's towel hanging on the hook outside the first shower stall, the one I remember wrapped around his waist when we had our inconvenient first run-in here.

We're the only people in the steam-filled room. Without my barging right into his shower, however, Scott won't know I'm in here, especially when I've avoided this bathroom for days.

While I want to gloat, I don't want to just speak up. No, I want

Scott to *want* to know why I'm in ebullient spirits. Then I'll nonchalantly volunteer the information. Obviously.

So I do the mature thing. When I get into the hot water of my own shower, I start to sing.

Years of choir in school have made me melodious enough to hum the tune of "Since U Been Gone." While I'm not exactly ready for Carnegie Hall, I don't care. I'm enjoying myself. There's no embarrassing me today. I met a hot guy while covered in mud and fighting with my rival. I'm past embarrassment. I'm embarrassment-proof!

However, I earn no response from Scott. He ignores me for several minutes. Undeterred, I continue. Only when the water coming off me is running mud-free down the drain does Scott speak up.

"Not sure why you're in such a good mood," he comments gruffly. "You lost."

I smile to myself, then speak over the hiss of the showers. "You did see my roommate, right?"

Honestly, Scott couldn't possibly have set me up more perfectly. He grumbles something I can't hear over the water.

"What was it you said about reality not living up to fantasy? I think it's objectively clear Erik *is* the fantasy," I point out. "*And* he's my roommate. I don't need to project anything to make that into a fantasy. Thank you *so* much for turning down my offer of friendship. Imagine if I let you wear me down until I was as miserable as you and unable to appreciate this moment."

He humphs once more. I'm ready to encore my Kelly Clarkson performance when he interjects. "Two things," he starts.

I find myself once more envisioning our emails. *Two things*. It's very Scott. The eleven-point Calibri, Arial's playful cousin and

Outlook's former-default, would precede numbered items *1.* and *2. For ease of organization*, Scott would say. *To look tight-assed and ultraorganized*, I would amend.

"First, I'm not miserable," he says.

"Well, you're miserable to be around—"

"And second, you think if we'd become friends, I would have snuffed out your romantic idealism? I thought your hope was made of stronger stuff."

Hm. Didn't intend that implication. "You missed the point of my statement," I insist, withdrawing from the stream of the shower and sticking my head out. "Imagine I'm putting it in bold and underlining it in an email to Harrison. *Erik is the fantasy*," I reply.

I don't dare wonder whether I hear him chuckle. Executive Manager Emeritus John D. Harrison, whose job specifics nobody really understands, is—ironically, in publishing—not known for his reading comprehension. Important points in emails require every possible emphasis.

"Please." Scott matches me, sticking his head out enough to meet my eyes, his hair slicked back. "Tell me how your romance with Erik is going to go. Will you talk long past midnight in your common room, making the hours feel like minutes with everything you have in common? Will you do every activity and spend every meal together, not wanting to be apart even for a moment? Will you *make love* on your twin bed when the sexual tension in your room becomes irresistible?"

I glare. It's important he see no change in my expression, none whatsoever, at him saying *make love*.

"I think all of that is very possible. As long as he's not as miserable as you," I finally declare.

He holds my gaze. "*I* could never be your fantasy. Of course," he states. I can't help hearing the edge in his voice. Unexpected and sharp.

"Exactly," I exhale.

Scott's eyes flash.

"You have soap on your ear," he says.

Furious, I withdraw my head. I wash the soap off, and when I'm confident I've resolved the unfortunate ear situation, inspiration comes. In weekly meetings, some of my most successful rebuttals of Scott's skepticism for my proposals have come from asking him the very same shrewd questions he puts to me. "What's *your* fantasy relationship like, Scott?" I inquire.

"I don't do that," he replies immediately.

No. No way will I give him the easy out. I stick my head out of the shower once more. "You don't fantasize?" I ask, my question heavy with incredulity.

Never one to withdraw from conflict—as I expected—Scott follows my lead, sticking his head out again. "Of course I do, when it comes to physical fantasies," he says, in the driest intonation anyone has ever used for the words *physical fantasies.* "Who doesn't?"

I cannot stop the stray thought that invades my head. *Just what are Scott's fantasies in the bedroom?*

"But otherwise, I don't daydream," he says, issuing the final word with unmissable disdain. "I live in the moment. In what's real."

His eyes couldn't possibly skim down my exposed skin when he says *what's real.* He couldn't possibly linger in the echo of his words while his gaze hangs on to me. No, when Scott withdraws his head abruptly into his shower, I'm one hundred percent certain he means only judgment.

I do the same. Has the shower water gotten hotter in the past few seconds? It couldn't possibly have.

Desperate, I grasp onto the fight we're in the midst of. I *have* to win this argument, I decide with sudden vengeance. I have to prove that fantasies are worth holding on to.

I have the perfect evidence waiting for me in my dorm, I remember. "Erik is an actor," I say pointedly over the water. Pausing, I prepare to play my ace—or whatever the champion card is in Demoniaca. I found the workshop very hard to follow. "*And* he's a huge Elytheum fan," I announce.

Scott laughs. I hear nothing warm in the sound.

"Well, as long as he's a huge Elytheum fan," Scott repeats sarcastically. "Might as well save the wedding venue now. In fact, this campus would work. You could do a whole Elytheum-themed wedding."

"Maybe we will!" I retort.

Our voices have increased in volume, echoing in the harsh acoustics of the room much louder than the water. "You clearly have *so* much in common," Scott comments, heavy with patronization.

"We have Elytheum," I protest.

"*And?*" Scott asks.

"Does there need to be an *and*?" I shoot back in frustration. If you don't share each other's passions, your connection is like calling an impressive pile of wood a fire. It's missing one important piece—the fire.

Whereas a fire is . . . a fire. No matter how small, fraught, or hidden.

Of course, Scott douses mine. He laughs ruefully.

"Did you even have a real conversation with this guy? I know it's not the stuff fantasies are made of, but real relationships are built on getting to know someone beneath what's on the surface," he says.

"I know what real relationships are," I snap. *Enough*, I want to say. Scott proclaiming himself the authority on *real life* and *real relationships* is comical when he's literally here because he can't keep a girlfriend.

Nevertheless, while I would prefer rolling into another river over admitting it to Scott, his words have struck a nerve. Erik . . . didn't ask me any questions about myself, did he? My introduction to my eye-catching roommate suddenly seems insubstantial and one-sided. What if it was only fireworks, not fire?

What's more, what about my fantasies of Val himself? Not Experience Val—*Val* Val. When I'm daydreaming, the Lord of Night isn't asking how my day was, or wanting to know about my family or my childhood, or encouraging me in my work, or . . . everything else the person I love should do.

Scott shuts off his water. Pulled from my contemplation, I shut off mine.

We step out simultaneously, wrapped in our towels. Scott's eyes meet mine, the emotion in them clouded like the steam-fogged mirror. "I don't think you do know," he declares.

I swallow. I have nothing to say, not when I'm focusing every filament of myself on keeping my eyes from dipping to his naked chest. Glistening, no doubt, with shower water . . . The towel he's holding carelessly up with one hand . . .

I should have used the downstairs showers.

He steps closer. In the narrow space, only about a foot separates us. The humidity is intense. Or, I'm pretty sure it's the humidity. Yes, definitely—the damnable heat is only from the shower water.

Not Scott's face, inches from mine. In a hazy, weakened corner of my mind, I wonder if *this* is one of his fantasies. In a public restroom.

Or maybe it's only one of mine.

His gaze wanders to the towel I'm clutching around myself. Refusing to resist like I did, evidently. From the look in his eyes, I know I'm not the only one with humidity-haunted memories. "I think if you knew what a real relationship was," he grinds out, "you would realize what I've known all along."

"What?" I whisper. "That I'm incapable of love or happiness or whatever?"

I intend the question to come out hissed. Instead, I only sound husky with need. I guess I need to practice my whisper like Scott did with his eyebrow. I'll need my own notebook, no doubt. *Details for Demonesses.*

Scott's eyes flash. There's no fantasy-hero flourish when he speaks.

"The real thing *can* be so much better than anything you can imagine," he says. "Better than any fantasy."

His quiet conviction startles me. He isn't chastising or making fun. The strangled note in his voice echoes formlessly, like a cry in the fog.

My mouth goes dry. "Then why are you here?" I get out.

Scott's expression falters, the look of a man wrestling with his own contradictions. I would have had sympathy for him, once.

He reaches up.

Whether out of instinct or desire, I know what he's doing. I feel his intention. The promise of the movement. His hand nears my face, like he's going to caress my cheek or my forehead or—

Instead, he stops, his hand in midair. I ignore the shocking pull of want.

I force myself to remember what got me here. "Maybe you need to stop settling, Scott," I say. "It's okay to want more from life. From love. Dare to fantasize. Don't close yourself off to it."

It's the end of the final chapter. The end of this argument. The end of all our arguments, maybe. I start to leave.

Scott grabs my elbow. I only just manage to keep my towel from falling. Startled—with his grip yearning on my skin—I look up.

"I shouldn't have rejected you," Scott replies. "I'm realizing our friendship could have been . . . *interesting.*"

My mouth drops open. The steam-filled restroom suddenly feels far away. Like we really have entered some other realm. Not fantasy, exactly. Just not reality, either.

I say nothing, daring to search the storm in his eyes. *Fuck the final chapter,* his expression says. I have a rogue imagination, and in the literal heat of the moment, I'm pretty sure he's going to pull me to him and kiss me—only our towels separating us, and perhaps not even—until he lets me go.

"I hope Erik is everything you dream of," he goes on. "Goodnight, Jennifer."

He walks out, leaving me reeling. I exhale, shuddering out my surprise. No matter the harshness of his words, I felt the undercurrent in them. He wasn't just furious or judgmental. He spoke like someone who . . . wanted. He isn't the final chapter. He's ripped it out.

I stand in the steam, no longer certain of the ending, clutching the place on my elbow where his fingers had held me.

19

Fortunately, I have other riddles to preoccupy me. Real, literal riddles, not emotional riddles like smoldering, yearning Scott. The infuriating riddle on my West College scroll, for instance.

While Erik is hot, I'm not stupid. He knows I have one clue. He *doesn't* know the clue contains an as-yet unsolvable puzzle leading to *another* clue. He does not know this because I have not shown it to him.

I'm planning to, really. I just need to know if I can trust him first.

It's like the third or fourth rule of fantasy, if not the first. If an enigmatic hot guy enters your heroine's life, he's either an unforeseen ally . . . or exactly the deceiver the audience expects from such *convenient* hotness.

I decide I'll evaluate him over the coming day. If he collaborates with me on leads or strategy, I'll consider myself allied. If I catch even the faintest whiff of double-dealing, however . . . well, let's just say my favorite fantasy novels have other lessons on how to deal with saboteurs.

Okay, I don't really know what I mean by that. I'm not going to fling him off the parapet Val-style.

If I show Erik my clue, he *might* be trustworthy, but even then, I don't really think he'll be able to crack the clue I, a longtime fan, haven't. Maybe that makes me conceited. Either way, there's no real point to showing him the clue right now.

No, the main advantage to having an ally isn't in code breaking. It's that I can now partake in the "paramour" activities on the Experience schedule. Morning finds us rafting down the campus river, which, as I suspected, is lovelier when you're not wading in it. The cicadas join with the rustling leaves in accompaniment of our clear-skied journey down to a picnic, where Laurel finds her *second* clue in the ice chest. I'm excited for her—or I pretend very hard to be.

Erik, for his part, doesn't double-deal. In fact, he doesn't deal, period. He passes the morning preoccupied with sitting up very straight and gazing out over our surroundings in flinty, Val-inspired intensity. When I mention Laurel has found a clue, watching for shrewd interest in his eyes, I only receive a smoldery nod.

Despite the discouragement of Laurel's progress and my ally's, frankly, uselessness, I enjoy the one welcome development of the paramour activity. Scott isn't here.

It delights me knowing he couldn't find a partner. The paramour requirement isn't serious—it doesn't necessitate any actual romantic involvement. Laurel and Brit have accompanied each other, and of course I have Erik. Nevertheless, the fact of Scott's absence indicates he could find neither ally nor friend. How surprising!

Or perhaps Scott could find a partner and he's avoiding me after what he admitted.

Fine. Honestly, I don't know how I feel about it, either.

Anyway, he's absent. He noticed me with Erik during meals over the past day, which seemed to annoyed him. It was enormously satisfying—perhaps more satisfying than the meals themselves.

While walking down from our suite with my daydream guy was enjoyable, hanging out with Erik was . . . less so. He remained focused on catching the eye of Heather or, when she's absent, every fan in his vicinity. Every conversation we've had has centered on how perfect he is for Val, and how he just has to be noticed.

I found myself wondering deep down whether Erik's companionship really is lackluster—or whether Scott's words have wormed into me, eating away at the fantasy I wanted to find in my roommate. Scott knows nothing of my disappointment, however. Which is what matters. As far as he's concerned, my fantasy is everything I ever wanted, and definitely has not involved walking into our common room multiple times during one of Erik's "mirror hours," in which he practices facial expressions.

It certainly has never, ever involved me replaying over and over the moment where Scott reached up outside the showers to caress my face.

Never.

Not when I'm unwinding from the rafting day with a reread of the masquerade, my favorite romantic part from *The Ashen Court*.

Not under my obsidian covers in the darkened hush of my room.

Not even when I zone out during Erik's self-centered monologuing over a plate of pancakes the next morning. As we walk out of the dining hall after, I patiently permit him to regale me once more with his Experience audition story, and how his haircut ruined his chances. In fairness, it was interesting the first time. Less so now. Doesn't exactly have the rereadability of a Heather Winters book.

When we get outside, I am enormously relieved to spot Amelia heading for the gates, leaving campus. "Hey, Erik"—I interrupt him, perhaps rudely—"I think we'll have better odds of finding the next clue if we divide and conquer. We can cover twice as much ground."

Erik falters, surprised I'm cutting short his story. He recovers gracefully, nodding with what I know he envisions to be Val's Queen's Guard command.

"Good thinking, Worth," he pronounces. With new excitement, he drops his put-on demeanor. "Can I take the tattoo booth? It would be so badass if Heather saw me with Val's back tattoo," he enthuses.

"Great idea."

He pumps his fist, invigorated. "Do you think if I don't shower for a couple days, the temporary tattoo will last through the week?"

"You know," I say, "there's only one way to find out."

Erik grins dazzlingly. He marches off with purpose, leaving me to head in Amelia's direction. Yes, I suppose I should hunt for clues, like I implied to Erik I would do. But . . . since the scavenger hunt started, I haven't had a moment to hang out with my best friend. If living with an unshowered actor for the rest of the week means I can sneak away for coffee with Amelia while he searches for clues, it's a fair price to pay.

I catch up with her right outside the gates. "Hey," I greet her, slowing my jog. "You going for coffee?"

Amelia smiles in surprise. She pulls out her AirPods. "Yeah," she says. She eyes me in pleased curiosity. "Are you actually going to join me instead of searching for clues?"

I shrug her off. "You can't fault me for playing the game you literally designed."

Grinning in concession, Amelia loops her arm through mine.

We cross the street, heading into the college town. I can enjoy the cobblestone sidewalks and towering birch trees more now that I'm not hunting for parking, late for my fantasy weekend, or in need of athletic shorts. The cute shops have uniform facades of stone with white, old-timey trim. We pass jewelry stores, sandwich places, shops with College of Hollisboro gear in the window, ready for football season when summer ends.

"How many clues have you found?" Amelia pries. "You must be close if you're willing to step away from the hunt."

I eye her, playfully wary. "I'm not about to tell *you*," I say. "And as for stepping away, I have my roommate on it. We're in an alliance," I inform her proudly.

Amelia laughs. "An alliance. I love it." She raises her eyebrows. "An alliance with benefits, perhaps . . . ?"

"I won't lie. I did think about it," I admit.

We round a corner I clocked on my drive in. Our destination waits ahead.

Coffee. This place is the only feature I could imagine *improving* the wonders of Elytheum. How many coffee-shop AU fics have I read? Countless. The only detail I ever have issues with is Val's drink. While I understand fic writers' impulse to give him something night black and uncompromising, like cold brew, I'm not convinced. Val knows how to indulge, and he secretly yearns for the sweetness life hasn't left him.

I . . . feel like he might be a pumpkin-spice-latte man.

I hold the door for Amelia. The Hollisboro cafe is large, with plenty of seating for college students to camp out during finals. In the middle of summer, the shop is nearly empty. It's almost jarring being around people who are dressed only in regular clothes, with nary a fae lord or demoness to be found.

Amid the pleasant indie pop playing from the speakers, the

rattle and hiss of the counter, and the wondrous smell of coffee everywhere, we walk up to the register. The offhand familiarity of it jumbles up my emotions, the happy echo of the hundreds of coffee runs we made to the cafe on West 54th, closest to the Parthenon offices.

I've lost my dearest coworker and now my relationship in the past nine months. I haven't lost our friendship, though. I have Amelia. And we'll always have coffee.

I order my customary cinnamon dolce latte, Amelia her cold-brew concoction with oat milk and caramel. It's very good, from the sips I curiously asked to sample. It's just not my drink of choice. We post up in front of the wide windows, where we can people-watch the unhurried pedestrians.

"So," Amelia prompts me impatiently, "you thought about a roommate rebound, but not feeling it?"

I sigh over my drink. "He's hot, and I like that he's interested in Elytheum, but he's an actor and a little self-involved and . . ." I hesitate. "Well, I feel like if we were to hook up, he would treat it as character work."

Amelia eyes me like I've just announced my new favorite is *The Ember Court*—with due respect, widely regarded as the weakest installment. "Yeah, but . . . for a hookup, does it matter? Shallow is sometimes better. You can fill in the depths with whatever you want."

I smile hollowly, wishing I could do exactly what Amelia's suggested. Wishing *Scott* hadn't gotten into my head about whether I know what's real. Somehow, though, I expect hooking up with my hot actor roommate who happens to closely resemble my favorite fictional character wouldn't help me with such second-guessing.

"We'll see," I demur. Not wanting to spoil our coffee run with my romantic woes, I usher the conversation on to more welcome subjects. "I'm focused on the Experience anyway. Does working for Heather ruin Elytheum at all for you?"

Amelia sips her cold brew, considering. "It changed it, for sure," she starts, like she's still figuring out the answer herself. "I do sort of miss the days where Elytheum wasn't my job. When it was just an escape from my everyday. Not . . . my every day." She laughs. "Mostly it's just so much more work than I expected."

Just then, Val walks in.

Except it isn't Val, exactly. My mind works falteringly to comprehend what I'm perceiving. The actor who plays Val has just walked in, wearing . . . glasses, shorts, and a UNIVERSITY OF PENNSYLVANIA BASKETBALL shirt.

He notices us—or, notices Amelia. His eyes light up when he finds her. He waves boyishly—way more boyishly than the Lord of Night would. Amelia waves back, and after he quickly puts in his order, he comes over to us.

I watch him with fascination. He approaches us almost hesitantly. "Am I allowed to say hi or am I breaking the rules?" he asks Amelia.

"Fred, we're not going to control your time when you're not on the clock," Amelia says with humorous patience, like they've perhaps gone over this previously. "You're free to live."

The actor—Fred, I guess—grins, appearing indeed very free to live. The next moment, his eyes fall on me and his expression clouds with inquisitive concern. "Does it bother you, Jennifer?" he asks. "I don't want to break immersion for you."

I blink, genuinely touched he knows my name. I guess I figured our . . . interactions this past week, while fantastical and fantastic for me, were nothing out of the ordinary for him. Forgettable, even.

Admittedly, it is a bit weird to meet him outside his Val performance. I knew it was just a performance, of course, but having the proof in front of me is different. Particularly because Fred is nothing like Val. He's kind of a bro, honestly. A sweet one. I wrack my fan memory for Elytheum Courts referents for an earnest, youthful Val, and find nothing.

"It's kind of you to ask, but no," I reassure him. "You're no more distracting than the work emails I've been answering on my phone at night."

He nods in relief. Then his gaze darts to Amelia, like powerful fae magic compels him. "Amelia, I watched that episode of *The Vampire Diaries* you mentioned. I'm learning so much about smoldering. But also, it's just really good," he marvels. "I have to know what's inside the tomb!"

I can't help grinning. With every word Fred says, it's easier and easier to separate him from his character. He's definitely not the method actor Erik is.

Amelia responds accordingly. "Right? It's such a good show!" When she eyes him seriously, I know she's going to ask the big question. "Are you Team Damon or Team Stefan?"

Fred hesitates, considering with the depth the inquiry demands. "I mean, I get the Damon appeal," he finally says. "But how can you not love Stefan? He's her original love interest, and he's just a good guy, you know?"

Fred doesn't realize how meaningful it is when Amelia only nods in measured respect for his choice. I happen to know she had a poster of Damon *framed* in her first apartment.

I watch them chat, noticing how animated Amelia is—which *of course* she is, because *The Vampire Diaries* is amazing. But she's visibly at ease talking to Fred, like they're old friends. It makes sense, given they've collaborated on the Experience for months.

Nevertheless, I'm glad she gets to work closely with such a kind-hearted, friendly guy. His eyes light up when Amelia laughs, and he smiles when she smiles. He's focused on her, watching her like . . .

And it hits me.

He's watching her like Val watches Kethryn.

When Fred's order is called, I don't miss the fleeting disappointment on his chiseled features at the interruption of their conversation. "Well, I'll see you back on campus, then," he offers Amelia. It sounds like a promise and not a prediction. He glances at me. "Or rather, *Val* will, with goat horns shined," he amends with amusement.

"I look forward to it," I say. "But Fred is cool, too."

"Thanks," Fred replies, sounding genuine.

Amelia waves goodbye, then faces me when Fred has exited the shop. "What were we saying before Fred came in?"

There's no hint of color in her cheeks. No traces of a secret grin. No final stolen looks out the window at the himbo crossing the street with his coffee. Her whole focus is just back on me.

"No way," I say, incredulous. "We're not just going to pretend that didn't just happen."

Amelia blinks. "What? Fred? I'm sorry, did it ruin the Experience to see him like that? You could have been honest when he asked you. Fred is really understanding."

"Forget understanding! Although that's very nice of him. Amelia, the dude is into you." The sentence practically explodes out of me. Wasn't she just telling me how she can't remember the last time she went on a date? And now the perfect thespian jock with glasses has a massive crush on her!

Amelia laughs like I've made an incredible joke. I frown. Until—

Yes, there it is. She's blushing.

I lean back in my chair, Cheshire-cat pleased.

"No. No way," she protests, while her cheeks flame brighter. "I'm basically his employer. He's just being friendly. I promise he's not into me."

"Excuse me. Do you not *see* the way he looks at you?" I fan myself dramatically.

She rolls her eyes. "You mean like a human speaking to another human?" Her voice is way too dry.

"Like he's smitten. My god, Amelia," I say. I'm desperate to have her match even a fraction of my enthusiasm here. This isn't even my love life. In fact, my love life is in shambles, and *still* this fills me with soul-nourishing joy.

Now her expression flattens. She is unamused by my enthusiasm. "Please be serious," she says sternly. "He's an actor playing a part. That's it."

Sitting forward, I restlessly rotate the coffee sleeve around my cup. "Look, if you're not into him, that's different, and I'll respect it. But if you really just don't see what's happening, then I have to open your eyes to it. There is no reason why an actor playing a part can't develop real feelings for his very hot employer."

Amelia scoffs. Her gaze darts to the window. When it returns to me, there's something dark in her eyes, something like buried hopes.

"That's not realistic." Her voice is brittle in a way I've never heard it. "We work in romance novels. We don't live in them. I promise you it's not like that." She lets out her breath, then checks the time on her phone. "I should probably head back in, speaking of. Heather and I have to talk masquerade plans."

I fall silent. I know a conversational closed door when my best friend slams it in my face.

I just don't understand why. Clearly, Amelia is refusing to entertain this idea, and I'm not going to press her on it. Not now anyway.

Putting on a smile, I down the rest of my drink. "Masquerade plans," I echo. "I can't wait."

She shoots me a grateful look for dropping the conversation, then gets up to recycle her cup. While we walk back to campus, we return to safer subjects. Brit and Laurel's latest fashion creation. Heather's mysterious attendance at dinners, where the author is present yet never says much. Whether the grad students here have figured out why half the campus population is in gowns and glitter.

When she turns into the administration office she's made her headquarters, I can't help wondering if Amelia is so focused on building this fantasy for everyone else, she's forgotten to hold on to any for herself. Maybe when fantasy becomes your normal, you stop being able to see what's extraordinary.

It makes me sad for my friend. Amelia deserves to live the kind of stories she loves. She deserves to feel like the desired heroine she is.

20

It's probably an alliance warning sign that I'm not eager to regroup with Erik. While we need to coordinate for the rest of the day, I have a dark foreboding that much of my afternoon and evening will consist of taking photos of his new temporary tattoo.

As I walk to the large Gothic archway where volunteers stain custom Elytheum designs onto guests' various body parts, I console myself with the thought that I would look pretty badass with a thorned violet from the Northern Court on the back of my neck. I could wear my hair up to display it during the—

I ascend the steps to the archway and find Erik talking to *Scott*. Goddess damnit.

I shouldn't have let Erik out of my sight. Of course Scott was just waiting for his first opportunity to approach my roommate on his own. I didn't even warn my own alliance that we have an enemy. I prepare for worst-case scenarios—Scott warning Erik off me due to a crush I don't even really have anymore—or worse, sharing embarrassing details like when I intended to send a fairly . . . revealing piece of fan art to Amelia, only to absentmindedly cc the entire departmental listserv. My hot roommate, who I reserve the right to maybe or maybe not want to hook up with, cannot know of Listserv-Gate.

Except when I get closer, what is happening is worse than unintentionally mass-emailed fae dick art.

Scott says something to Erik, which makes him laugh. They look comfortable. *Friendly.* Like they've been hanging out for hours.

In what feels like horrible slow motion, Erik pulls off his shirt, then Scott proceeds to snap pictures with his phone while holding up a number of large, wolf-based Elytheum Guard designs to Erik's chest and back. They are hideous—not his chest and back, which are chiseled and definitely waxed. No, the tattoos are ridiculous. And yet Scott is giving him the thumbs-up. Like he *wants* Erik to look bad.

Sabotage.

When Scott notices me, he grins victoriously. He is so going to pay for this.

I won't retreat or surrender, though. I'm the lead of this story. *He's* just the villain. No, not even the villain. At best, he's an annoying antagonist. Chin held high, I walk up to them.

"Hey, Jen," Erik says. "What do you think? I know Val doesn't have this tattoo, but don't you think it fits him completely? And looks fucking hot, too."

It does not. But I don't need Scott to know that. Erik has handed me on a silver platter the opportunity to check him out. I can still make Scott *think* he's lost this battle.

"I need a better look," I say, my tone thoughtful. Smiling sweetly, I hold my hand out to Scott for the wolf tattoo. "May I?"

"I can just show you the picture," Scott says grimly.

I turn to him, blinking feigned innocence. "I'd like to see it in person. Up close."

Scott scowls. He's wearing sunglasses, and the tips of his hair brush the dark lenses. I wish I could see his eyes just to watch him glare. The gray in his irises really pops in a good glare. I content myself with the consolation prize of the tendon in his jaw straining delightfully. Honestly, it's sort of hot. Hotter than a wolf tattoo anyway.

"Why not both?" Erik asks obliviously. "It's important to compare how something looks in real life to how it photographs anyway."

I nod like I very much respect that opinion. When I clasp the top of the tattoo sheet, there's a moment where Scott doesn't let go and we're locked in a secret game of tug-of-war. He raises that damn eyebrow. I raise mine right back. Okay, maybe I sort of half raise both of them, but I think the effect is the same.

He releases the wolf with what looks dangerously like a half smile of amusement. My lips can't help twitching, too. Still, I walk the tattoo sheet over to Erik. He turns around so I can hold it up to his back. "Hmm," I muse, pressing the flimsy paper onto the hard ridges of Erik's very broad, very muscular shoulders.

Behind me, I hear Scott shuffling his feet. He clears his throat impatiently, no longer amused. While I don't know what Scott has said to Erik in my absence, I know I'm owed revenge for *something*. I take it in the form of brushing my fingertips lightly against Erik's back as I adjust the tattoo. When I feel Scott has suffered enough, I step back and hand the tattoo to Erik.

"Well?" Erik asks, his voice grave like he's awaiting a serious diagnosis.

I open my mouth, then realize that I just spent nearly ninety seconds touching a hot man and I didn't actually observe anything. I was more focused on Scott's micromovements than the sight in front of me.

"Only you can pull this off," I say somewhat honestly to Erik, my thoughts still stuck on Scott.

Erik exhales in enthusiastic relief. It's ironic how even as an actor, he puts every emotion out there with no artifice. "Excellent," he says. "I'm going to get it." He raises his hand for me to high-five. "Thanks, alliance partner."

Oh, perfect.

Scott's jaw tenses further. I no longer enjoy the sight. I realize now I should have specified ours was a *secret* alliance. Secret from everyone, and especially secret from Scott Daniels.

I guess I figured it was implicit. Not the Scott part, I suppose. The rest of it, though. Hasn't *Erik* ever watched *Survivor*?

"You're in an alliance?" Scott asks.

"Yeah," Erik replies, oblivious and undaunted. "To win the dinner with Val. Although Jen can take that part—I'm just in it for the glory. Are you competing?"

Scott faces me, a very worrying glee in his eyes.

"Yes, I'm competing," he confirms. There is nothing casual in his casualness. "I almost beat Jennifer to her first clue, in fact."

He's speaking like he's commenting on the weather. Only I know he's predicting storms.

Erik just looks sympathetic, I'm reassured to find. Not won over by Scott's pretty obvious vaunting of his own half qualifications. *Good*. "Ah, close one, man." He claps Scott on the shoulder. "Next time."

Scott doesn't look put off from whatever strategy he's enacting. No, he looks confident. He dips his head down so his eyes lock with mine over his sunglasses.

"So Jennifer showed you what was on the scroll, I assume?" he prompts. "Have you figured out the next clue?"

The air in the archway feels cold in the summer day. The shadows lengthen. *Damn him.* I want to stomp on Scott's foot, but Erik would see, and the damage is already done.

Of course Scott knew I wouldn't trust a stranger with the details of the clue I found. The scavenger hunt isn't the only game he's playing.

Erik rounds on me, his eyes wounded.

"You withheld your clue from me?" he asks. "Why? I thought we were going to the end together."

Okay, his plaintiveness is a little much. We're hardly Val and Lord Everbane, Val's closest military companion until Everbane's heart-wrenching death in *The Risen Court*. I only met the guy a couple days ago.

Still, I feel guilty. Whether Erik is overreacting or not, I have no doubt his emotion is genuine. I hurt his feelings. And . . . I don't want to lose my new partner.

"I was going to show you tonight," I venture.

Erik shakes his head. "I know a performance when I see one," he accuses me woefully.

Scott laughs.

"Oh yes," he joins in, no doubt finding our interaction more enjoyable than any character actors' this week. "Jennifer's no fun to work with. Trust me."

"Hey!" I protest.

Scott ignores me. No, he's—eyeing Erik, I realize. "*I* wouldn't keep clues from you, though," he promises my partner. "Want to join *my* alliance?"

"You don't want to join Scott's alliance," I interject, unable to restrain myself. "Trust me." Honestly, I hope Erik does not interrogate my reasoning. What would I say? *Scott, he's . . . very observant. He's very focused. He's patient and dedicated when he puts his mind to something. In conclusion, you definitely would not want to partner with him on the scavenger hunt.*

Erik doesn't press me, fortunately. He wavers, looking at both of us in the way I sometimes look at my TBR pile on my nightstand.

"Hey," Scott says, his approach changing. I recognize the measured manner of his voice. The appeal to reason. The appeal not to read *just one more chapter* when it's half past midnight. "I would understand if you want to stick with Jen despite her betrayal. I really would," he informs Erik. "She's exceptionally creative. Driven. Ingenious. I can't count the number of times she's outdone me at work."

Quiet hesitation catches his final sentence, making me look up in surprise. He sounds . . . sincere?

Is Scott . . . *complimenting* me? It astonishes me more than any fake fae or stage-designed Elytheum court.

Unfortunately, I'm not the only one surprised. The stain of suspicion casts over Erik's Val-worthy gaze. "You and Jennifer know each other?" he asks Scott.

I close my eyes. *Well, crap.*

Erik rounds on me. "You never said your work friend was here," he states, like I needed reminding.

"We're *not* friends—" I start.

"Definitely close acquaintances, though," Scott speaks over me, cheerfully unhelpful. "We work together in publishing. I've known her for a year. Wow, time sure does fly."

Erik has no appetite for cheerfulness. "I don't think we were in a real alliance, Jennifer," he goes on, heavy with judgment. "You didn't share clues, adversaries—anything with me."

I can't even muster a weak reply. *It's not you. It's me,* I want to say. I doubt it would help. I know it's over.

Yet again, Scott has foiled me. Yet again, Scott has driven his observant, focused, patient, dedicated foot right into something *I* care about. I'm the only Elytheum fan here—or, okay, I guess I need to give Erik credit. I'm the only *longtime* Elytheum fan here.

I roll my eyes when Erik extends his hand to Scott.

"Yes, I accept your offer of an alliance," he states formally, in what is obviously more Val practice.

"Wonderful," Scott replies, shaking on their misbegotten new pact. "Go get your tattoo and then we can strategize." He half smiles in quiet delight. I expect the expression is somewhere in his notebooks.

Wait.

I won't give up my alliance easily. No, I'll make Scott's subterfuge hard-won. I'm out for revenge. With no rivers nearby right now, I will make do with what I have. "Congrats, you two," I say, my voice like poisoned fogberry syrup. "Well, Scott, why don't you share your *notebook* with your new partner?"

I have to give him credit. Meeting my eyes, Scott doesn't wince when I mention what is probably the most cringeworthy effort to up one's game in the history of humankind.

"Of course, Jen," he says. He smiles for show as he pulls his notebook from his pocket and hands the journal to Erik. "Happy to."

He holds my gaze. Behind his sunglasses, I know ingenuity is working furiously in his eyes. Scott isn't just observant. He's inventive and determined, everything he said I was, and he's going to need his resourcefulness now. I've upped my improv game at the Experience. Scott's going to have to do the same if he wants to explain his Introduction to Val-ology notes.

Except Erik is reading the notebook and . . . nodding, like Scott's serial-killer-style jottings make perfect sense.

"I can help with this," my roommate says.

In unison, Scott and I whip to face Erik.

"Wait, what?" Scott asks.

"You can?" I say at the same time.

Erik nods, remaining improbably casual. "Yeah, of course," he assures us both. He flips a few pages, evaluating the material, until something compelling captures his notice. "Here, we can tackle 'the lean' right now."

While Scott and I wait in confusion, Erik walks off to hand the tattoo print to one of the attendants, promising he'll get it applied in a couple minutes.

"Okay," he says, returning. "The lean is, like, crucial for Val. It keeps Kethryn pinned between him and the wall so that he becomes her whole world. Which is how he likes it, because of course Kethryn already is his whole world."

I feel my eyebrows rise. Plural, not just the one. Erik is . . . completely right in his reading of Val.

"You have to make sure you go in with the right mindset, understand?" Professor of Romance Erik elaborates. "It's not just about the physicality. It's deeper than that. If you get the mental part right, the rest will fall into place."

He hands Scott the notebook.

"Watch," he says.

Erik paces over to the Gothic archway, where he evaluates its height like he's measuring it for a shelf.

His concentration is endearing, I have to say. It's easy to forget he's the guy who's done nothing except regale me with stories about himself for the past day. In earnest pursuit of his craft, he reminds me of . . . Well, *not* Val, I guess. More like the best version of himself.

Satisfied with his archway assessment, Erik rejoins us.

"Jen," he says, "may I?"

I startle like I've gotten called on in class. *May he what?* I nod, wary but curious.

Erik gently pulls me with him into the arch. Under the stone curve, he positions me with my back against the rough wall.

It is now that I realize the day is very much about to turn around for the better.

Erik lines himself up in front of me, in position for *the lean*. He is over six feet tall. He is the living likeness of my favorite fantasy love interest. He is shirtless. Dazed, I consider the coffee-shop AU fics I was just remembering. I'm pretty sure I've just stumbled into one.

Until Erik waves Scott over.

"You have to get close," Erik counsels him. "Observe my micro-choices."

Is there no fantasy Scott Daniels won't leave alone? No dream he won't devastate? Honestly, while Scott might be taking notes on Val, every villain intent on world domination or realm devouring or whatever could take notes on *him*.

For what it's worth, when Scott shuffles over, he does not look pleased, either. "Shouldn't you have a shirt on?" he grouses to his new alliance-mate.

I glare at him. "That's not necessary," I reassure Erik with absolute selflessness and zero regard for my own—um, circumstances.

Erik eyes us in confusion, evidently not understanding our dynamic. *Yeah, me too, buddy*, I want to say. I mean, really. Scott seems jealous, the way he grimaces when Erik positions his own Hemsworthian frame over mine. *Why?* Could Scott Daniels really be . . . jealous of Erik flirting with me?

Possessiveness, urgent and unmistakable, pushes past his usual reserve. He scoops up Erik's shirt from the ground and, with a warning glare, tosses the garment to Erik, who, ceding to his new *alliance partner*, shrugs and pulls on the shirt. *Alas.*

All is fortunately forgotten when Erik faces me again. He gives me his full focus. The way I look at fan art is the way he's looking at me.

"Hi," he says.

"Hi," my dry mouth permits me to reply.

Scott frowns behind him, pulling my focus.

Erik moves closer, hemming me in. I'm pleased we're not in the period of his unshowered state. He smells incredible, like clean sheets and aftershave. I've ordered plenty of custom-made Elytheum-scented candles from Etsy—"Lord Valance," "Lord of Night," "Fae Guard." I need to bottle this scent and send it to the fragrance artists. "Val's Lean."

Erik rests his arm against the wall near my head and—*wow*, he seems way taller now. I feel my back pressed into the stone, forcing me to look up to meet his eyes.

He holds our eye contact. The effect is . . . powerful. My knees weaken. My power of speech has abandoned me like the Western Court abandoned its allies in the Western Court Campaign.

I feel fantasy drunk. Euphoric on vesperynthe over rosewater cocktails. Indulgent, like I've eaten my fill of sugary night cakes. Dizzy from the high air in the Northern mountains.

And I love it.

Erik keeps up the performance. He sweeps his free hand through his hair like he's struggling to collect himself, overwhelmed by our proximity. *He's good.* It's working. I feel like my favorite descriptions of Kethryn, emotion and hunger written on my heart in secondhand ink.

The spell is shattered when Erik steps away suddenly. Looking to me and Scott, he preens like a Labrador who has performed a trick. I straighten up, feeling shaky. It's a nice shaky, a welcome shaky. Espresso with nine sugars.

"Alright," Erik prompts Scott encouragingly. "Your turn."

I can't help myself. I look to Scott, curiosity and expectation warring in me. His expression is dark, the shadows in his eyes gathering into thunderheads. It's what I expected. I could write Scott's reaction like Heather Winters writes courtly intrigues or veiled flirting—perfectly.

"Oh, no, I got it," he demurs. "Thanks for the demonstration. It was very . . . helpful," he grinds out. "I've made a lot of observations."

Although he holds up his journal, indicating he only means observations on Val-worthy conduct—Val-orous? Val-icious?—the inflection of his final word and the way his glance flits to me indicate something else.

Observations on how instantly swept up I was when a hot guy who resembles my favorite fantasy character flirted with me? Yeah, news fucking flash, Einstein. I refuse to feel guilty for indulging in the exact fantasy I'm here to indulge in, even if it comes from my roommate instead of the performers.

Erik, however, is resolute. He shakes his head patiently. Walking over to Scott, he places his hands on my rival's shoulders and physically steers him in front of me.

"You gotta practice it, man," Erik insists. "It's the only way to improve."

Scott fidgets.

And despite everything, sympathy hits me suddenly. In Scott's self-consciousness, I'm reminded how out of his comfort zone he is. Elytheum is *my* fantasy, my escape, my refuge. Not his. And it requires courage to admit something isn't working in your life. Not the courage of fae guardsmen fighting demons or Kethryn avoiding assassination attempts, either. Real courage.

Right now, I realize, Scott's courage is faltering. Deep down, I . . . want to help. His noble effort is impressive, or whatever. Charming, even.

Of course, it's not only selfless admiration inspiring me. If Scott decides he can be a romance-novel-worthy hero, he'll realize he was wrong—and more importantly, I was right. Fantasy is worth *everything*.

He just needs a push.

"Don't tell me you're scared," I goad him.

I'm not expecting the flash of determination on Scott's features. He removes his sunglasses, fixing his gaze on me. "Hardly," he intones. Without breaking eye contact, he shoves his notebook into Erik's chest.

"You got this," Erik encourages him.

Scott doesn't need it. He strides up to me—no, *stalks*. Paces.

What the hell? I'm writing romance description in my head for Scott now. He *is* proving me right, and I've never felt more confused.

In surprise, I back up, only to remember the wall behind me. It's just, I've realized this is a terrible idea. Even if it helps his self-growth or whatever, I do *not* need Scott to try to turn me on.

He places his hand on the stones next to my head. I turn slightly to look at it—the hand I've watched inscribe countless lists into his notebook in his impeccable penmanship, the hand he's gestured with in maddeningly compelling presentations. Scott's hand, I could probably draw the veins from memory if pressed to. I feel my breath catch in my chest. He leans closer.

"Is this okay?" he asks quietly.

I nod.

His gaze has captured mine, holding me hostage. I feel the space between our bodies, every shrinking molecule of it, while everything else disappears. The cicadas sawing in the grass, the sweet summer humidity of the day, the respite from the sun in the arch's shade. Even the rough stone hemming me in.

Everything vanishes into the enchantment of—Scott.

He looks into my eyes. Really looks, like I *am* his whole world.

He's become far too good an actor, I decide. He looks like he wants nothing more than to . . . lean down and take my mouth with his.

Or do I just want him to?

In the confines of the archway, it would be so easy to hide from my own wiser judgment. I could permit myself to forget every argument and petty clash we've ever had. I could plummet into his, yes, *smoldering* eyes, not knowing what I would find in their depths.

Instead, I remind myself *he rejected me.*

He claims he regrets it, yes. But he's been talking like Batman and dressing like Val, too. Is he just pretending? Doing everything he can this week in service of his goal of becoming the perfect romantic hero, the book boyfriend?

Of course he is, I realize. Of *course* he hasn't uncovered some year-old regret for the way our first conversation ended. He's just reciting the right lines. None of it is real. He's performing, just like this lean.

If I were to let myself want him, he'd just reject me again at the end of the week.

It hurts. Which makes me want to hurt him. I want to laugh, to dismiss his efforts, to derisively say he'll have to work harder to impress other girls.

Unfortunately, I'm not an actor like Erik, or even Scott. I know I couldn't pull off disdain. Not feeling the way I am now.

I put my hand on Scott's chest, experiencing the heat of him for just one moment, the connection humming like the cicadas' roar.

Then I push him lightly backward.

I address Erik when I speak. "No notes," I say honestly. "He's mastered it. You two really will make a formidable team."

Decisively, offering no invitation for either of them to follow, I walk away without another word. I head farther into campus, needing something—anything—to replace the overwhelming heartache of fantasy and reality colliding.

21

Night finds me reading in my dorm, unsurprisingly.

Erik is in the common room working out. Or I hope he's working out—otherwise the amount of grunting coming under my door is worrying. I would go out and watch except I have given my roommate the cold shoulder since he returned to our suite after sitting with *Scott* for dinner.

Curled on my comforter, I feel like I did in my childhood room in Oklahoma when I first fell in love with reading and fantasy. When even a dismal day could end with something wonderful, as long as I could escape into another world for an hour or two or five.

It's comforting. I may not have the constant of a boyfriend in my life, but I'll always have my relationship with books. I've relocated the common room candle onto my nightstand, and the wax warms the space with its reading-appropriate, smoky, sweet scent. It's what passes for perfect right now.

When a knock sounds on our door, I don't get up or close the cover. "If that's your *alliance member,*" I call coldly into the common room, "can you please get it? I've had quite enough of Scott."

It's a lie. If anything, haven't read one paragraph without

remembering Scott's lean—how his proximity and the wounding memories of him worked on me today.

And if I can't find distraction in *The Shattered Court*, I can't find it anywhere. It's utterly unnerving.

The fact is, Scott has weakened me. Even now, this moment, part of me considers asking if he meant what he said—our friendship could have been interesting. I'm forcing myself to stay strong.

Although . . . maybe he's right. I *do* need to stop romanticizing people. People like my work rival, who already rejected me once and proceeded to pain my workdays with his vexing focus and occasional, irritatingly good ideas. Am I just helplessly drawn to his new Val talents? *Valents.* What is wrong with me that I'm even considering hooking up with him?

I hear Erik get up from whatever he was doing on the floor. His heavy footfalls thud through the wall. Then the door opens.

"It is not Scotty," Erik announces.

I grimace. "Oh my god, do *not* call him 'Scotty.'" I close the book cover with less reluctance now and head into the common room. Erik, in gym clothes, holds open the door while Laurel and Brit stand in the doorway.

"Erik. Hello," Brit says with frosty formality. Despite her hoarseness, probably earned coaching Stephanie through another sleepless night, her hair and makeup are characteristically perfect. She really would make a good lady of Elytheum. Laurel skulks, eyeing my roommate with suspicion. If she had an Assassins' Convent dagger, I expect she would spin the point on her fingertip or something else intimidating.

Dagger or no dagger, the message isn't lost on Erik, who wilts.

He rounds on me plaintively. "Jen, don't bad-mouth me to people. I'm nice, I promise!"

He flashes our guests a grin. It doesn't work. Because he's right.

He has identified literally exactly what I was doing over dinner. While we shared the evening's stew, I informed my *real* Elytheum friends of Scott's usurpation and Erik's betrayal. Okay, was the high-stakes discussion of changing alliances under the grand ceiling of the Great Hall a little fun? Yes. Was the fun overshadowed, given the unfortunate context of my Val dinner being in jeopardy? It most certainly was.

I cross my arms, resolute against his friendliness. "Scott and I," I remind Erik firmly, "are on opposite sides."

My friends nod emphatically. Erik, newcomer to the Experience, does not understand the importance of his decisions. In allying with Scott, Erik has allied against each of us. Laurel and Brit have come by their rejection of my roommate honestly.

Unfortunately, Erik is not discouraged. He mopes theatrically. "Opposite sides of what, though?" he presses.

"Everything!" I declare, hoping to match my friends for ominousness.

Now Erik's expression shifts, and I'm the one left with foreboding. He fixes me with a sly stare.

"I don't think that's true," he says. "I saw the look you and Scotty shared."

I feel my face redden. Once a betrayer, always a betrayer, I guess! No redemption arc for Erik.

Brit's sternness falters. She stares at me, openly intrigued.

Laurel perks right up. "What look?" she asks.

What the hell! I want to protest. I feel like I'm in *True Blood* from how everyone is Team Erik now.

My roommate, for his part, has noticed his opportunity to be accepted. "Scott was practicing some moves on Jennifer," he says slowly, with delighted hush-hush, "and there were some definite sparks."

When Brit gasps, I recognize my defeat. "I knew it!" she exclaims.

Erik shrugs, visibly proud to have delivered the good news. He opens the door wider. "Do you two want to come in?" he offers, like they're here for him.

"Oh, were you planning on hanging out with us?" I ask him sarcastically.

The rhetorical question glances off Erik like archers' arrows deflected off powerful shield magic. It's no less discouraging. "I mean, it is my suite, too," he points out coolly.

I frown. Okay, he's right. I've got nothing.

Nevertheless, Erik sighs in what sounds like genuine remorse. "Please don't be mad at me, Jen," he implores with anguish in his eyes. "I forgive you for not showing me your clue. I hate it when people are mad at me. It throws off my game completely. I'm going to be so focused on winning your friendship that I'll blow my chance to impress Heather."

Laurel's eyes widen. Brit starts to smile.

I let out my breath. Yes, Erik did renege on our pact, but I did withhold information from him. He wears his heart so visibly on his sleeve—it makes him impossible to stay mad at.

"Fine," I say on a long exhale. "I'm not mad at you. Just don't ever invite Scott into our suite," I warn him.

Erik crosses his heart, looking moved and relieved. "I swear it on my honor, I shall not," he pronounces. Then his solemnity changes to a smirk. "You'll be the one to invite him in first," he promises.

I roll my eyes, retreating farther into the common room to escape the ridiculousness of *that* prediction . . . even if I'm guilty of considering it just minutes ago. Laurel and Brit follow me in while Erik closes the door. "What's up?" I ask my friends.

Evidently recalling why she's here, Brit bounces on her heels in excitement. "You're about to receive an invitation," she explains urgently. "We got ours ten minutes ago. Except, Laurel didn't. She wasn't in our room. She missed it, so we need to be here for yours."

Erik eyes them with amused interest as he stretches on the floor. He doesn't look *too* sweaty from his workout. Maybe I can use my forgiveness to ply him into showering at the expense of his wolf tattoo . . .

"What are you even talking about?" I ask Brit.

She opens her mouth to explain when footsteps sound on the stairs. She squeals instead. "It's happening!"

She hurries back to the door. When she flings it wide, I'm treated to the sight of the door across the hall opening.

Scott sticks his head out. Admittedly, I do not fault him with the noise my friends are making. "What's going on?" he asks warily.

Erik interjects, positioning himself in the doorway. "Scott, I'm sorry," he announces seriously. "I have sworn an oath not to admit you to our suite."

Scott's eyes shift to me, then return to Erik in dispassionate incomprehension. "That's fine. I'm okay right here," he replies.

I glare. Feeling my wrathful look, Scott finds my eyes. *He* glares. Our glare-off reminds me of plenty of scenes I've read in my enemies-to-lovers favorites, where heated glances hide passion behind facades of resentment. I have to say, it's the only experience I've found more fun to read than to live.

Into our midst steps the Queen herself. Kethryn, in her elegant, gem-encrusted gown from dinner, enters the hallway from the stairwell.

Everyone looks her way immediately, including others on our floor, who have emerged from their rooms due to our commotion. Kethryn looks unsurprised to have wordlessly captured our focus. Even fantasy queens have the effect of real royalty.

"Good. You're all here," Kethryn pronounces imperturbably, showing no surprise at our impromptu hallway congregation. "We've come to deliver your formal invitation to a special supper tomorrow night, which shall include dance lessons."

Val has entered next to her, like he was following her. "My queen," he chides fondly in his velvet voice. "You insult our guests in your assumption—"

His drawl dies when his eyes fix behind me.

Expression contorting, riven with surprise, he stares straight forward. While I know Fred is skilled, it's hard to imagine his stunned displeasure is performed.

Even harder when he speaks.

"*Erik?*" he gasps. "What the *hell* are you doing here?"

22

All eyes swivel to Erik, who, for his part, does not look startled. Instead, something gloating comes over his expression. Like he's pleased to watch Val—Fred—falter.

Of course he is, I remember. He considers Fred his competition. It was cute when Erik wanted my reassurance of his leading-man viability, exciting when he confessed his ambitions for the Elytheum TV series.

Now . . . I don't much like the look on my roommate's face.

Fred, fortunately, recovers nimbly. He clears his throat and glances at Kethryn, his fae-lord demeanor restored. "Apologies, I thought I knew this man from a war long ago," he demurs. "I was mistaken."

With agile professionalism, Kethryn doesn't react, only guides them easily into the scripted scene they've come here to play out. "Well, if he's any acquaintance of yours, he certainly is going to need dance lessons," she replies.

All traces of Fred have vanished. Val steps backward, jokingly affronted. "I'd say I learned fast." His voice is low. It's hard to find any critique of his performance—except for the careful way he avoids looking at Erik. When Val's eyes sweep the room, they skip seamlessly over the six-two man leaning on our doorframe with his arms crossed.

Kethryn pretends to consider, her eyes sparkling. "One can always improve," she says teasingly.

Val laughs, then holds his arm out to her. "You heard my queen. I will be in attendance with whomever comes to take lessons. I hope to see you all there." He ushers them both toward the stairwell with a tad more eagerness than fits his character. Only when they've descended the first steps does he turn just enough to dart one final questioning look at Erik.

The rest of our hall-mates retreat to their rooms, leaving the rest of us to round on Erik.

Suddenly, I don't feel so bad about withholding information from my former alliance member. It's pretty clear Erik has his own secrets.

In fact, for the first time since I met him, Erik looks like he doesn't want to be the center of attention. He's shoved his hands in his pockets and stood up from the doorway, hunching his shoulders.

"Well, I need to shower. Goodnight, everyone," he says stiffly before entering our suite.

On the one hand, *thank god* he's going to shower. On the other . . .

I hold the door open after him. "No way. You can't just pretend that didn't happen."

Brit and Laurel follow me in. With unexpected decisiveness, Scott—I guess curious and cautious of his new ally—joins them, walking unimpeded into Erik and my common room. So much for Erik's oath!

I would insist Erik uphold it except I don't want to give him any opportunities to change the subject. I'm stuck with Scott now. What else is new?

"How do you know Fred?" I demand when we're all assembled in the common room.

Scott whirls to face me. "How do *you* know Val's real name?"

Regrets flash in front of my eyes—letting Scott into my room, not leaving the moment I saw him at the Experience, trying to be his friend, et cetera. "It may shock you to know, Daniels," I reply archly, "but some people actually like talking to me. I am likeable."

Scott snorts, then drops down onto our couch. He crosses his ankle over his knee, getting far too comfortable. The posture is startlingly familiar to me, a flashback to the occasions I would find him working on the couch in the Parthenon lounge when I went to use the Keurig. Wanting to clear his head or change his perspective, I guess. I would skitter out with my refilled coffee, feeling like I'd seen something I wasn't supposed to—Scott, ordinary and unguarded.

I pull my eyes from him, focusing on the more pressing matter in this common room. Folding my arms, I level Erik with a questioning stare.

He lets out his breath in defeat.

"Fred is my brother," he admits morosely.

Brit and Laurel gasp. I'm stunned speechless. Of course objectively Erik and Fred resemble each other. They're both perfect walking Lord Valances. I just wrote off the similarity as nothing more than names on the same casting call sheet. To know Erik wants to take this part from his own brother! I mean, it really is drama befitting an epic fantasy novel.

"Did your brother not know you were coming?" Brit asks innocently.

"Oh, are you surprising him?" Laurel follows up. Neither of them knows Erik's rivalry with Fred. I was more focused on relaying what happened with Scott than getting into Erik's backstory. Honestly, I didn't think it would be relevant or interesting. I should have known backstory should never be ignored.

Erik winces. "Sort of."

I glance to Scott, who's been surprisingly silent in this reveal. He's watching Erik, his expression thoughtful. I wonder what pieces he's slotting into place. Does he want to break up his alliance now that he knows Erik has an ulterior motive here? But then, so does Scott. Maybe this will just bring them closer together.

I'm so screwed.

"He got the part over you. You both auditioned," I say to Erik. There's an implicit accusation to my observation, but I'd rather Erik voice it than me.

Erik collapses on the couch beside Scott, crossing his arms like a petulant child. "We have the same agent," he explains, his words coming quicker now that he's made his confession. "We used to go out for things together. Like when casting calls were for brothers. Our agent said we looked so perfect for Val . . . Fred got it over me. But have I shown you the haircut I auditioned with? It—"

"*Yes*," every other voice cries in unison.

Erik looks startled, but in classic Erik form he doesn't get self-conscious. He merely sinks back in the couch. "Glad my story is memorable," he says cheerily.

Laurel offers him a sympathetic smile. "You both really do look like Val."

"Yeah," Brit continues. "If the TV show happens, maybe you can *both* be in it. One of you can play Val and the other can play Resten. You know, his brother."

Erik, who has probably studied Val's character more than any-one in this room, does not need the clarification. He waves the suggestion off.

"As long as I'm Val," he replies, his voice blatantly bitter. In fair-ness, Resten doesn't have a whole lot of page—or rather, screen—time, since he's killed before the events of the story.

Scott laughs, but the sound is humorless. He's uncrossed his legs, and he leans forward onto his elbows. "You're perfect for Val," he says. His expression has darkened to match his tone. "In the shadow of the brother who is effortlessly everything you want to be."

I expect the comment to offend Erik. Instead, my roommate perks up. "You're right!" he exclaims. "I can absolutely use this in my character work!"

When auditions give Erik lemons, he makes vesperynthe over lemon water cocktails, I guess. Laurel laughs.

"It's perfect," she agrees. "Let's not go too far, though. There's no need to have your brother killed so you can then align with en-emy courts in order to avenge his murder."

Erik nods, undoubtedly glad the impact of his revelation is wearing off and, of course, eager to discuss Val's characterization and the effect of Valance's brother thereon. The conversation con-tinues, Brit and Laurel delighted to find a fellow Elytheum fan in the gorgeous guy who shares their friend's room.

I don't join in. I'm stuck on Scott.

Scott, who delivered what I have to say was a surprisingly good Elytheum diss.

I remember he said he only skimmed the series. Either he hap-pened to skim some very key pages, or . . . he read with more focus than he admitted. He's mentioned enough specific details over the past few days for me to suspect the latter. I remember his deduction of the West College clue when I realized his deciphering of the "Last Court" required knowledge he wouldn't have just from overhearing office chatter.

Feeling my eyes on him, Scott looks over. I avert my gaze, feeling ridiculous, like my crush caught me watching him in the middle of fourth-period French. *Moi? Mais non.*

Honestly, my curiosity is growing. The series is thousands of pages long. One wouldn't keep reading unless one . . . liked them. Even if one said they didn't in numerous Parthenon marketing department meetings. How far has he gotten? The full details of Val's relationship with Lord Resten aren't revealed until the third book, which opens with a prologue when Val was a child and his brother—

I gasp.

Everyone looks at me.

A fraction of a second later, I swat my arm. "Mosquito," I pretend.

It's poorly done. Erik frowns, his dramatist's intuition picking up on my weak performance.

Brit, I'm relieved to find, is none the wiser. "I have some cream if you need," she offers.

"Thanks!" I reply hastily. "I'm going to grab some ice from the kitchen real quick."

With everyone's eyes on me, I hurry out into the quiet of the hallway. I head into the seclusion of the stairwell, where my heart starts pounding without my setting foot on even one step of the four flights of stairs.

I'm not going to the dining hall. Instead, I pull out my clue scroll. Yes, I keep it on me always. There's no knowing who might go through my things. I've memorized what it says, of course. Nevertheless, I need to ensure the wording matches *exactly* the ingenious idea I've just had.

The Lord of Night cherishes me. Mounted with Glory.
Watching over all.

The prologue of *The Ember Court* is a flashback of Val and Resten—who, as the older sibling, holds the honorific "Lord of Night" until his murder. In the opening, a young Val finds his brother mounted on an ebony horse . . . whose name, I remember now, is *Glory*.

It's why *Glory* is the only improperly capitalized word in the clue, I realize. It's not an error. It's a *name*. Just like in *National Treasure*. I should have known—Amelia is a huge fan of the franchise.

And "Mounted with Glory" and "Watching over all" don't describe a sword. They describe a *person*. They confirm that the "Lord of Night" referenced in the clue *is not* the series' famous Lord of Night, Valance—rather, it's the man who held the title before Val. The Lord of Night we meet mounted on Glory, and who, after his death *watches over* Elytheum from Afterrealm.

The Lord of Night cherishes me.

The object of the clue is whatever Lord Resten cherishes.

In the prologue, Winters elaborates movingly on how the noble, deep-feeling Resten cared for nothing the way he cared for his . . .

Oh no.

His horse.

The answer is in *the stables.* Of fucking course it has to be horses.

23

I hope horses sleep in.

The possibility consoles me on my walk out to the stables at six in the morning, clutching my dining hall coffee for fortitude.

Honestly, I hardly need the caffeine. I'm plenty awake from the combination of nervousness and admiration of how stunning the campus is early in the morning. In the crisper temperature, the cicadas have gone quiet. Slick with dew, the lawns fill my lungs with their clean, sharp scent. Of course, no postdocs or curious families cross my path in the young day.

With the Gothic towers lit by the rising sun, I feel like Keira Knightley at the end of *Pride & Prejudice*, walking across the grassy slopes leading to Mr. Darcy.

Unfortunately, in my case, no good-fortune-possessing single landowner awaits. Only the temporary stables on the edge of campus. When the pasture enters my view, however, I don't see horses.

Instead, I see a man.

I recognize him from just the shape of his back in the soft morning glare. Quiet and unhurried, I descend the gentle incline down to where he gazes over the stables, waiting.

"Do you press your ear against your door and listen for me to leave my room to shower or something?" I ask.

The question comes out with more warmth than irritation, undoubtedly the result of my finding a familiar silhouette instead of a four-hoofed monster.

Scott turns his head, smiling faintly and unsurprised. "Good morning, Jennifer," he replies.

I come up next to him, where I lean on the pasture railing. Steam rises from the small opening in my plastic coffee lid. I sip, looking out across the grass, where fog is still coating the ground. Scott stands with me in what feels like contented silence—I'd find his easy manner suspicious if I weren't finding it comforting instead—until finally, I have to ask the obvious question. "Where are all the horses?"

"The stablemaster isn't here yet," Scott replies. "I imagine he brings them out from wherever they sleep."

I wonder how long *he's* been waiting out here, watching the fog in silence. What has he spent the morning contemplating?

He doesn't leave me alone with my speculation. His gaze shifts to me. "You prepared?" he asks.

Rivalry doesn't reach his voice. His competitiveness is playful.

Whether I'm enjoying the distraction of our conversation or mornings just make me soft, I don't know. Whatever it is, I do something I haven't yet in response to Scott's interference with my week. I play along. Narrowing my eyes, I turn and lean back on the fence, arms wide on the railing. "What led you to the stables?" I redirect. "I assume you're here for the clue."

Scott shrugs.

"Maybe I'm just here for the pleasure of your company," he says.

I roll my eyes, hoping I'm not blushing. Goddess willing, the chill of the morning fog will cool my cheeks enough to hide whatever pinkness Scott's words have put there. When I meet his gaze impatiently, indicating his flimsy pickup line is no substitute for real intel, Scott smiles in concession.

"Fine. Yes," he says. "I'm here for my next clue. When you beat me to the one from Kethryn's speech—West College—I realized the first letters of temerity, aptitude, secrecy, and loyalty don't just spell out *last*," he explains. "They also spell *salt*. It led me to the kitchens, where I found the chef."

Silently, I'm struck by the cleverness of the clue. I know I shouldn't be. Of course Amelia working with Heather Winters would yield impressive riddles.

"Let me guess," I preempt him. "She gave you a scroll."

Scott nods.

"*The Lord of Night cherishes me,*" he repeats. "*Mounted with Glory. Watching over all.*"

It's very easy to picture Scott pacing in his room, repeating the words long past memorization. Analyzing every angle like the Friday we were forced to reconfigure countless plans when we got unexpected budget reallocation news. Hours spent in the conference room, grudgingly cooperating, editing file-shared spreadsheets. Scott removing his glasses to rub his eyes from laptop strain, then replacing them. His hair springing up where he rested his head in his hand while he concentrated.

Not that I noticed.

Remembering the Scott of my workdays, my impulse is to one-up him, prove I figured out the clue first or have some other hidden advantage.

Instead I decide to just . . . give myself a rest. Give *us* a rest. Maybe, like our exhausting Friday in the conference room, I could just . . . spend time with him.

I'm either overtired or undercaffeinated, because it feels won-derfully, unexpectedly easy. "Did you check the sword?" I ask.

"I did," Scott confirms.

"Middle of the night?"

"During the Val picnic, actually. Everyone was gone."

I nod in impressed acknowledgment. "Nice."

In the midst of a fantasy experience, I'm surprised how much I enjoy the unadorned pleasure, the comfort in casual conversation. Especially with someone I unironically called my sworn enemy earlier this week.

"Like you, I couldn't crack the clue for days," he admits.

All pleasantry of casual conversation aside, this confession nourishes me. Puff pancakes for the soul. "Until your observation about Erik and Val," I finish, realizing.

Scott smiles. "I should have known saying it out loud would bring you here, too," he remarks.

The note of pride in his voice warms me in a way I'm not pre-pared for. The cooling fog doesn't stand a chance. I'm *definitely* pink cheeked from the flattery now. I cock my head, curiosity van-quishing the last of my competitiveness. "What do you really think of the books?" I inquire. "Now that you've read them."

I expect more playfulness from him. Instead, his smile slips. Something serious and unguarded enters his eyes, like there's something he wants to say but he's hesitating or warring with himself or afraid of my reaction. It only makes me more desperate to know his answer. He's opening his mouth to reply—

The clopping sound I've spent the morning dreading inter-rupts him. Facing away from the pasture, I hadn't noticed the stablemaster coming closer until now.

I turn to the sound, finding the squinting stablemaster looking like he didn't expect spectators at six in the morning. He holds the reins of two *very* large horses, leading them with him. The horses' eyes rove over us with gentle dispassion, inky marbles in the animals' enormous heads.

Sweat springs to my hands. I press them to my leggings. I hope Scott doesn't notice—I know he does.

"You're here early," the gravel-voiced stablemaster comments. "Must be for the clue."

Yes. The clue. I straighten, grasping onto the distraction. Or the motivation. Or some of each, I guess. "So you have it," I confirm urgently.

The stablemaster nods. "Hold on," he says. He notches the horses' reins to one of the fenceposts, then scrounges in his pocket. While Scott and I watch intently, he produces a crumpled piece of paper. "*The path is long to where knowledge continues,*" he reads. His narration leaves a little to be desired, although I know I'm spoiled from Val and Kethryn's sonorous performances. "*Yet only four feet separate you from your destination.*"

Four feet. "Feet," I say, unable to help my excitement, even under the revelation's circumstances. "Four feet. Hooves. It's not distance. *Four feet separate you from your destination.* We need to ride the horses somewhere."

Scott chews his lip contemplatively. "We need to ride them to *where knowledge continues,*" he ventures, not to be outdone. "What if it's not referring to the clue itself? There's a graduate college outside the main Hollisboro campus. I noticed it while looking for West College on the campus map. *Where knowledge continues.*"

I nod, heart racing no longer with just horse-related panic. If we were, say, errant knights in the countryside, or courtly inquisitors hunting deadly invaders, or a fae lord and an imperiled queen—instead of Jennifer Worth and Scott Daniels, from marketing—I would say we make powerful allies.

The unceremonious stablemaster crumples up his assignment and returns it to his coat pocket. "The grad college, yeah," he confirms. "It's just across the field. The horses will walk the path on their own. They love it," he says with his first real enthusiasm of the morning. "Lots of clover in the grass."

His ministration accomplished, he unhitches the horses' reins.

I know what comes next. While I'm very happy for our clover-hungry, four-footed friends, I find I can't move. Part of me was harboring hope we would only have to see the horses. Perhaps pet the horses.

No. We have to *ride* the horses. It's very unnecessary, I console myself in vain. Many courtly ladies of Elytheum don't ride horses.

Heroines do, though, a whisper from within reminds me.

Scott eyes me. While I may feel like we could make a great team, the truth is we're not a team. We came down here under the compulsion of rivalry. He's not going to help me. Certainly not. No, he's gauging me. Wondering why I seem like I'm chickening out.

Oh, I dearly want to. I feel the powerful pull of chickening.

If I do, though, I know I'll essentially hand the clue over to Scott. He's figured out the riddle. He's got no problem with riding horses, I assume. Nothing stands in his way.

I can't do it. I *won't* do it.

The stablemaster jingles the reins impatiently. "So you both want to mount up, then?"

Scott's eyes haven't left me.

"Yes," I say, feeling brave.

24

Her name is Jelly Bean. She is nineteen years old. The stablemaster shared this information with me while I mounted the massive brown mare. I think he expected I would find her seniority and the cuteness of her name comforting, or maybe he just enjoys divulging the details of the animal. Either way, I am not about to let my guard down.

At least Jelly Bean strides slowly down the path, which carries us over the grassy hill to the Gothic outpost of the graduate campus. Nevertheless, every one of her steps jostles my whole body, reminding me of the dire consequences if she takes off running.

Reading the liability waiver before getting on the horse felt like grim foreshadowing of the consequences of horseback riding. In the Western Court, "omens" hold potent import—crows flying at sunrise, full moons on the eve of combat. I felt similarly superstitious signing away my right to sue if Jelly Bean acts like the wild animal she clearly is at heart. When I climbed the short set of wooden steps to mount her after bidding farewell to my coffee, I'm pretty certain I blacked out.

Mounted with Glory. Yeah, right. *Mounted with Pants-Shitting Nervousness* is what my clue descriptor should read.

Still, I remind myself, what am I supposed to do? Surrender over the clue?

Not going to happen.

As we continue over the rise, I wish I could enjoy the scenery. It looks right out of medieval legends, epic fairy tales, or classic romances—all the stories I grew up reading, which inspired my lifelong love of books. Shaggy foliage hems our path on one side. On the other, green hills roll far into the distance. In the summer, Hollisboro kind of resembles Hobbiton.

Clouds overhead keep us from overheating under the rising morning sun. Jelly Bean and Scott's mare have stopped a couple times to pluck clover from the ground—the only moments when my fear cedes to finding their grazing, okay, pretty damn cute.

Otherwise, while we clop along, I find myself wondering who could ever enjoy horseback riding. I mean, the obstacle course will have felt like a massage compared to how *this* will hit my inner thighs. And how does everyone else cope with the fear? I feel like I'm riding a military cannon while holding a lit match. What excitement could one possibly find in the ominous swaying of a thirteen-hundred-pound animal with a mind of her own?

Yes, thirteen hundred pounds. Larger horses grow to fifteen or even seventeen hundred. I googled it. Not one of my wiser or prouder moments. I don't know what reassurance I expected to find under the covers at 12:37 a.m., googling "weight of horse."

Scott rides confidently ahead of me. However, he keeps stealing glances over his shoulder.

Consequently, I have to hold in my fear tears, wanting to appear completely at ease atop Jelly Bean.

"You okay back there?" Scott finally ventures. Mocking my obvious discomfort, of course. The way he would if our supervisor caught me spacing out in a meeting or something. *Care to join us, Jennifer?*

Well, I refuse to be mocked. "Wonderful," I reply, stiffening my voice. It comes out piano-string sharp, unfortunately. "I . . . love horseback riding," I manage. "What a fun, and safe, hobby. Maybe I'll move to Montana and take up a life of ranching."

Hopefully Scott knows I'm mocking his mocking. Nevertheless, he presses me. "You're not . . . scared of horses, are you?"

My denial is forming on my lips when, unfortunately, Jelly Bean stops abruptly, no doubt about to throw me to my death. Startled, I shriek. Then I clap my hands over my mouth when I realize my horse is only eating some clover.

Scott, I will grudgingly credit him, does not laugh. Instead, he looks . . . sympathetic. Worried, even.

Ugh. Way worse. I must look pathetic if Scott Daniels is pitying me, which only reminds me more of the peril of every kind in which I find myself right now. "Don't give me that look," I admonish him hotly. "I'm fine. I can do this."

He considers me, atop Jelly Bean, and then wry playfulness replaces the sympathy in his expression. Almost like he . . . knows our petty rivalry is the distraction I need right now. Or something.

"You could get down, you know," he calls out. Now he obviously knows what he's doing. Tempting me with reassurance! "Why don't you let me go ahead and get the clue? I'll let you look at it," he promises.

"No you won't," I reply as witheringly as I can currently manage.

He laughs. "We could work something out."

I narrow my eyes. He can't see my glare from yards ahead, but it's worth it.

My weaker judgment entreats me to hear him out, though. Even if Scott Daniels's patronizing concern is embarrassing, I do really want to get off Jelly Bean. "What could we work out?" I ask, making sure I sound like I'm only sussing him out dispassionately for information.

"I'll let you look at the clue," Scott offers, "if you admit you're glad I came to the Experience."

I scoff to cover my shock. Is this fighting or flirting?

Why is it so hard to tell them apart?

"Glad? Why would I be glad?" I retort desperately. "If not for you I would have gotten the obstacle course clue. I would have Erik as my alliance partner." *I would be alone right now*, I can't help adding in my head, *terrified*. "You're a distraction this week," I promise him, and myself. "Nothing more."

A distraction. Welcome or unwelcome remains, uncomfortably, to be seen.

Scott doesn't pass up the opportunity I've presented him. "When exactly do I distract you, Jennifer Worth?" he asks, and *damn* is he getting unnervingly good at the Val drawl. "When you're lying in bed at night, remembering the times I've come close to touching you?"

My eyes fly wide.

Admitting to that—well, I'd rather Heather Winters arrive at dinner announcing she was retconning the ending of *The Risen Court* and Val ends up with the devious Lady Dymestra. I'd rather Erik leap out of the forest in front of Jelly Bean, wearing a frightening mask, and leave the rest of my horse ride in fate's hands.

Not . . . because it isn't true. I'd just rather not *admit* it.

"I have my books," I say coolly. "I'm fine in bed."

"Is that so?" Scott's reply is droll. "Fictional Lord Valance has some good lines," Scott concedes, "but he can't touch you."

I literally feel my lungs clench in surprise. *He can't touch you.*

No, he can't.

"Well, you have one of those things in common," I return.

Scott falls silent and faces forward.

I smile at his back, pleased with my comeback. Relieved, even. No chance at all this is flirting. Why would we be flirting anyway?

While I ponder the question, something wet lands on my arm. I look up, finding the sky has darkened.

In dealing with Scott, I didn't notice how heavier gray clouds were closing over the morning sun. They look . . .

Like storm clouds.

Sweat coats my hands on Jelly Bean's reins. I really, really hope we can reach the graduate college before the summer thunderstorm hits.

Honestly, however, I don't know if we will. In my near decade of living on the East Coast, I've learned summer storms come on fast and unpredictably.

Nervousness weakens my resolve. "If I tell you when you distract me," I call up to Scott, "you'll give me your clue and I can get off this horse?"

Scott hesitates. When he faces me once more, he looks characteristically victorious. As if his alliance is not just him and Erik, but also includes the fucking weather. "I'll let you *look* at my clue," he negotiates.

While I consider—*really* consider—he slows his horse to walk next to mine. I feel the humidity thickening, reminding me I don't have long to consider the consequences of inclement weather.

I take a breath. Scott waits. "You don't distract me at night," I say.

He frowns. "Well, fine—"

"It's when we're not fighting," I say softly.

The interruption quiets Scott.

"When the real you slips out," I go on. "The sort-of-nerdy you, who's trying so hard to act cool and like he doesn't care. But beneath it all, you care so incredibly much." I make myself look over at him instead of hiding from my own honesty. "I want to talk to that Scott. Sometimes it makes me forget everything else."

He glances down. I'm in his peripheral vision, and I glimpse something pained in his eyes. For the past year, he's concealed everything in combativeness or carelessness. Every flicker of friendliness or compassion or camaraderie he may have felt, rendered over to rivalry instead. I guess I've done the same around him.

"You can talk to me," he says.

I laugh nervously. "And say what, Scott? *Thanks for stealing my alliance, dickhead?*"

He straightens, as if in relief at my change in the somberness of the conversation. "It's not exactly what I had in mind, but I can work with it," he replies earnestly.

I'm instantly grateful for his humor. While the clouds haven't shifted, his response has let a little light into my mood. In fact—I realize he's distracted me, and we're not far from the grad college now. I'd . . . almost forgotten I was on a horse.

Almost.

"Well, what if I texted, *How are your goat horns looking? Oh wait, you don't have any,*" I offer.

Scott fights his smile. "Can't imagine a better way to end my day, actually."

"What about, *For someone good at finding clues, you sure are clueless with women?*"

He's fully grinning now. "Careful," he says. "With insults like those, you'll have me falling for you in no time."

His heart-stopping words sound sarcastic and sincere at once.

The memorable description of Val flashes in my mind. *He makes mockery sound like sweetest praise.* Fighting or flirting. Sarcasm or sincerity. Scott Daniels, ever the man in the middle.

I'm thinking of my reply when the clouds split open.

Rain douses us, coming down in heavy sheets. I restrain the urge to shriek from the sudden downpour, relieved to find Jelly Bean is not reacting to the water itself. Our horses plod on, water pasting their manes to their necks.

Everything is fine *until* the first roll of thunder echoes in the distance. The animals start to spook, shaking their heads and stepping with nervous liveliness, and *holy shit, my heart has leapt in my chest.* I ride sitting ramrod straight, rigid in fear—

"Shh."

Scott has noticed the horses' fear and mine. He hushes our mounts, and incredibly, it works. Either from the authoritativeness in his utterances or the evenness of the sound, his shushing settles them, and they fall into steadier footsteps once more.

It works on the horses anyway.

I'm still hyperventilating. Anxiety is one of those feelings where once the not-okay switch is flipped, it comes with devastating, pulse-pounding, never-ending force. It's hard to unflip it even when your surprisingly kind coworker has removed imminent danger.

"There's going to be more thunder," I say, rambling now. "And oh my god, did you read the waiver we signed? Would it be worse to fall off the horses or have the horses kick us in the heads? Heads? Head? Is it *heads* or *head*? Heads, right?" Even grammar doesn't distract me for long. "Maybe I should stay on, but what if—"

Scott leaps athletically down from his mount. With his horse's reins in hand, he reaches, gentle yet sure, for Jelly Bean's, removing them from my sweaty grip. He stands—fucking fearlessly—in the middle of the path, slowing the horses.

The animals follow his lead. He's calming them, I realize, keeping them from running off.

It's just enough to ease my panic. We're no longer moving. I feel my pulse start to slow. I can speak without fear pinching my every hasty word.

"Thank you," I say.

Scott nods. In the downpour, we're drenched. His hair sticks to his forehead. Even in my extremely nervous state, I cannot help thinking that if Pemberley were to emerge around the path's next forested corner, Scott Daniels would not look out of place.

"I—I wasn't always afraid of horses, you know," I say. Rambling comes easily to me when I'm hoping to divert myself from this dangerous, Scott-related line of thinking. "Growing up in Oklahoma, some of my friends had them. I thought they were cute. I didn't ride one until I was twenty. My boyfriend at the time and I went on a trip to Mexico together. It was my first vacation on my own with a guy. I was so excited, of course. I wanted it to be perfect."

My efforts have started to work. I'm managing to distract myself—from our equine situation and from Scott. I remember the weekend-long excursion Victor planned for our six-monthiversary. I'd read four vacation-centered rom-coms in a row in emotional preparation. I was determined to have my own.

"He was sweet. He booked us horseback riding on the beach. I was thrilled, but then when I got up there, I started to have a panic attack. Obviously, I didn't tell him," I recount. "I didn't want to ruin it for him."

Scott watches me closely in the downpour, intuiting something is compelling my spontaneous storytelling. "It wouldn't have ruined anything, Jen," he finally says. "At least, it wouldn't with the right guy."

I swallow. His kindness just making him more attractive in the rainstorm, which was *not* the point of my rambling. "I'm proud of myself, though. I haven't even cried while on Jelly Bean. Progress," I announce while Scott steers us under the forest canopy to escape the rain. He holds the horses' long reins, one in each hand.

The posture accentuates his shoulders unfairly. I suspect if he knew how he looks right now, he would consider a career change. Jelly Bean, on whom I remain seated, walks obligingly with him while water glues my ass to the saddle.

"Just wait," I say. "Next time I am forced to ride a horse with a cute guy, I'll be unstoppable."

Scott sends me a smile over his shoulder.

"Cute, you say?" he repeats. Under the leaves, he watches me like he very much wants me to elaborate, raising one eyebrow in inquiry.

And for once, it isn't Val eyeing me. Scott isn't imitating a fictional sex symbol or playing a game or whatever. His newly mastered expression isn't performed smolder. It's just . . . him.

Our eyes remain locked, water beading in our eyelashes while thunder pounds in the skies and in our veins.

"Gracious me," cries the stablemaster, breaking the moment. The man we spoke to before has run up behind us, his boots caked in mud kicked up in the rain. "Sorry about that! These two"—he rubs Jelly Bean's flank, coming up next to me—"are usually pretty unflappable even in weather, but I can take them from here."

He retakes the reins, and the horses huff like they're glad to return to his more experienced hands. Well, that makes four of us.

Or, possibly five. I won't speak for Scott, although I expect he was enjoying the company of his horse.

"The clue is in the quad. I won't tell anyone that you didn't technically ride there." The stablemaster nods up at the nearby grad college. On the hill under the dark clouds, the ominous edifice looks like it would suit Dracula, not Darcy.

Nevertheless, clue information is clue information. The quad is close, close enough to run on foot without getting hopelessly drenched or exhausted.

I say a private thanks to the weather for sparing me the rest of the ride. Maybe it's not in Scott's alliance after all. Maybe I have atmospheric pressure and solar patterns on Team Jennifer. Except—then I remember I have to dismount without the step stool I used to get on. Jelly Bean has one more opportunity to fling me off in the meantime, causing certain injury. Or at least certain embarrassment.

You can do it, I urge myself. With all the courage I have, I stand in the stirrups, reverse engineering my process of getting on. I swing my right leg over the saddle to join my left. *Okay, halfway there. Now how to get from the horse to the ground . . .*

Why do they have to be so tall?

I know I have only one option. I lower myself down with my right leg, ready for impact. I'm definitely going to come up short of the ground, probably leaving me dangling in ungainly helplessness until I drop into the mud—

Instead, I meet a hard body behind me.

The firm interception halts my fall, steadying me. Scott's hands find my waist. With him . . . *holding* me, I continue my descent more evenly, reaching the ground without issue.

I turn in his arms, hesitantly, not wanting to face how much I want him exactly where he is.

"I had it," I say.

He's close, only inches from me in the hushed murmur of the storm. We're dripping wet. Rainwater has plastered Scott's shirt to the planes of his chest and soaked his hair and his face. His mouth. He doesn't move, doesn't step away, doesn't release my hips—he could, but he doesn't.

"You would have fallen in the mud. We did that once already this week," he replies. "Let's move on to something else, shall we?"

Obviously, it's fucking hot. It's right out of a fantasy. "Like what?" I ask breathlessly.

The stablemaster has started leading the horses back to the pasture. Jelly Bean's huge flank no longer hems me in. Which means I could also step out of Scott's reach, easily.

I don't. I don't want to.

His fingers tighten on my hips. Then his eyes dart to the quad. I know exactly what the mischief in his gaze promises. "Don't think because you helped me, I'm going to just give you the clue," I warn him.

"Now, that would hardly be fun," he replies. His eyes return to me, and I guess Elytheum's magic has followed us out here. Only under fantastical skies could I imagine fireworks dazzling even in the rain.

"Agreed," I say.

He grins, and I can't help doing the same—until, in the same moment, we take off, dashing out from the forest cover.

Into the rain, we run. Free of horse-related panic, the giddy fun of the ridiculously inconvenient weather seizes me. My shriek changes into laugher as the rain pelts my face and I keep my frantic footing in the muddy ground, managing to hold Scott's pace. Finally, I find salvation under the first archway leading into the graduate college.

It's smaller than the main campus, architecturally similar but with only a couple connected quads. *Whew.* Despite the mad-dash fun I'm having, I don't want to spend hours out here scrounging around in the rain.

I start in the archway itself, progressing into the first main quad. Frantic and with water warping my vision, I search the statues, the Gothic corridors, the lawn—every nook and waterlogged cranny—while Scott does the same.

Of course, we hit different spots, each of us wanting to stake our success on our own strategy. While Scott hurriedly inspects the corners and perches of the statue of another seated college founder, not unlike the one we found in West College, I lift up the cinder-block doorstop outside a now-closed door. *Nada.*

Fortunately, he's no more successful. Spinning in the rain, searching for my next opportunity, I notice a tree near him, limbs low enough for the clue to perch there, trunk thick enough for its whorls to hide what I need.

It's promising, but Scott is presently closer to it. If I run for it, *he'll* want to look there. This week has proven multiple times that he can outpace me if he wants.

Stealth, not strength, I remind myself. Fighting my shaking hands, I do the unimaginable. I stall. I diligently inspect the stained glass, practically certain no clue hides in the corners of the windows. In my peripheral vision, I watch Scott finish rummaging around the benches near the statue. He stands up, surveys the rest of our surroundings, then moves on to the second archway, undoubtedly figuring he'll get a head start on the next quad.

It's my moment. The second he's gone, I rush to the tree.

I roam my hands over the large, knotted trunk, searching for hollows. I find none. *No, no, no.* If I'm wrong, Scott's very real head start on the next quad might cost me the clue. *How is he so good at this?*

I reach up, inspecting every angle, ignoring the rain—

There. A scroll is tied with twine to the cradle of a bough!

Euphoric, with fingers clumsy from the cold, I fumble to untie the string. I gently extract the scroll, which only the leaves of its resting place have protected from the downpour. While I know the organizers have planned for *nearly* everything, I doubt even Amelia foresaw the possibility of her friend dropping the graduate college clue into the mud and eviscerating the scroll's handwriting.

With my prize clutched carefully in my hands, I retreat.

Of course, my steps carry me exactly into the line of the archway leading into the connecting quad.

Quite naturally, Scott looks up when I'm in view, glimpsing the scroll in my hands.

Right then the rain starts sheeting down harder and faster. Okay, the weather is conspiring against both of us, clearly. Scott races for me, and I race for the corridor along the side of the quad, heading for cover in which to wait out the rest of the deluge. I have no idea when we'll be able to return to the main Experience campus. Luckily, summer storms often dissipate as fast as they come on.

When I get inside, the rain is waterfalling down the apertures. My breath is fast with adrenaline. Knowing I have only moments to collect myself, I slick my wet hair back from my face with my free hand. With the other, I put the clue scroll into my back pocket.

Pounding footsteps suddenly stop in the archway.

I whirl, finding Scott watching me from the rain.

"Looks like I win again," I chide him. "You'll have to be faster next time."

He enters the corridor.

My mocking dies in my throat when I glimpse the hungry look

in his eyes. He strides forward, his soaking-wet shirt sticking to his chest. His every step carries him with urgency. With want.

He looks like he's spent a hundred years in the storm, and the first shelter he's found is me.

"Congratulations," he says. His voice is raw.

He continues forward. He's feet away from me now, and he doesn't stop.

25

I back up until my spine hits the column in the arched aperture. It's surprise, not displeasure, driving me—I'm unsure what Scott is doing, despite how his eyes burn with his intention. *Fighting or flirting? Rivalry or romance?*

His paces toward me pose another riddle. *Desire or diversion?* I no longer know where we stand with each other. Is this a game? A rebound? Is it . . . something more?

He walks all the way up to me, to where I'm flat against the unyielding stone. Water slick on his face, he reaches up and places his hand on the wall beside me. He presses forward.

I feel my breath halt in my throat.

Because Scott—*my* Scott, the man intertwined with my every ordinary workday, the regular life I use fantasy to escape from—has just done "the lean" *perfectly.*

Only the cold of my waterlogged clothing confirms I'm not literally dreaming right now. *You're stuck in a dream, Jennifer.* His words return to me. *Yes*, I could reply under the stone arch. *And right now you're the one holding me.*

I find myself looking up at him, my chest heaving. Exactly how "the lean" is designed. Scott dips his head, following the choreography like fantasy fulfillment is hidden instinct for him. His chin waits millimeters from my temple.

"You should never underestimate me, Jennifer," he whispers.

The rasp of his voice sends shivers racing over my skin. I don't know what he's referring to, honestly. The scavenger hunt. The lean. Or everything else. Fantasies I can't name.

I just know he's not wrong. Drops of water from the ends of his hair drip onto my collarbone—caresses, explosions, kisses.

"I'm going to kiss you now," he informs me.

I've read hundreds of words depicting characters in scenes just like this one. Yet I can find no words of my own. "Why?" I croak out. Honestly, Kethryn's eloquence in such moments is one virtue my queen possesses and I don't.

"Because I need to," he says.

The desperation in his eyes leaves no doubting his intention. It's written everywhere on his face, urging my pulse faster. I'm no longer shivering—with Scott over me, promising what he is, looking wrecked the way he does, heat rushes into me. The arch supporting me is welcome when the warmth weakening my limbs and dizzying my head has me ready to collapse into him.

I could unravel right here, I really could. *Here lies Jennifer. Her coworker flirted her to death.*

He lifts his other hand. He moves his fingers, exhilaratingly gentle. *His hand.* It's a thing of wondrous possibility. My out-of-control thoughts picture everywhere I'd like it. Of course, for the moment he only grazes my cheek with his fingertips.

I'm ridiculously attuned to his every movement. I'm watching the *Pride & Prejudice* hand flex over and over in real life in front of me. I could lavish whole Wintersian passages on every stretch and pause of his fingers.

Except, not right now I couldn't. Right now I remain without words.

His hand runs over the curves of my face, his fingers splaying against my neck, my jaw. Pinpricks of fire in every fingertip. Their caress props my chin up to his.

He looks into my eyes. I exhale, practically shuddering, staring into his.

"W–ell," I stammer, "let's see what you've got, then."

He doesn't waste a moment. No, he does—one moment, the perfect moment, the perfect prelude. His lips kick into a smile before they close over mine.

And under shelter from the rain, Scott Daniels does exactly what he promised. He kisses me. He kisses the fuck out of me. It's difficult to reconcile him with the man who ignores me in the office coffeemaker lounge, who reads itemized conference requirements and deadlines out of his notebook at meetings, in the *real world* hundreds of miles and endless infinities from here. Never, ever would I have imagined *this*. He isn't just kissing like he wants me. He's kissing like he wants to destroy me. He's kissing like he's wrestling with a dream so he can hold on to it forever.

Like *I'm* the dream, instead of stuck in one.

His body presses into mine, pinning me to the wall. I practically hear my heartbeat ricocheting on the stone. The archway holds me firmly in place. The clenching cold of Scott's wet clothing on my skin pairs with the heat of his mouth devouring mine.

I want to be devoured. I never want it to end.

I'm utterly lost in the feeling of him. The wanting in his lips, the way he's wrecking me right now, is limitless. For once, I dare to wonder whether he wasn't just performing, not just plying me with romance-hero rhetoric.

With pummeling clarity I recognize—like I never could, even when he's been feet away from me this week, because even feet away from me, he wasn't touching me like *this*—how much I want *him*. I want him like I never even knew to.

It's right out of a fantasy, possibly the greatest kiss ever to happen.

Except it's *real*, and it's happening with *Scott*.

He doesn't stop. While our mouths collide in frenzied passion, I'm unable to imagine him overwhelming me more. It's how *overwhelming* works. I can't get *over*-overwhelmed, right?

Wrong.

Scott's hand leaves my face. His grasp ventures down my damp neck, my wet collarbone. His fingers are magic, at once keeping me right where I am and flinging me into faraway realms. When he reaches my breasts, the gentle pressure has me arching forward to meet him. My unprepared knees nearly drop me to the flagstone. He uses the wall to his advantage, letting the rock hold me in place while he caresses me hard, opening up something dark and desirous in the depth of my stomach.

Ever demanding, he moves his hand lower. He finally has his fingers exactly where I want them—or, almost where. I damn the flimsy interception of my leggings. I *need* him, with a yearning, pounding pulse I can feel.

No longer satisfied with Scott writing my fantasy, in the penmanship of passion on my lips and chest, I lower my hands. I'm not just the reader of my own life. I don't have to pull the feelings off the page into my imagination, lavishing in invented lust. I'm living the fantasy. And I'm going to reach for what I want.

Clinging to his waistband, I pull him closer, which lets me feel the firmness in the front of his pants. Pushing hard, rubbing against me.

For the first instant since he dashed me into oblivion with his mouth, *he* falters. I feel his moan deep within his chest.

It's like finishing a chapter on a cliffhanger. I need more.

Writing in my own language of lust now, I slip my hand under his shirt. While I have cold fingers from the rainstorm, I doubt it's why he shivers when they meet the flat surface of his stomach. I leave my hand there—just over his belt—tempting and daring myself to reach down.

Urgent with frustrated desire, Scott moans into his kiss. He clenches firmer on me in retaliation, and I nearly gasp.

We push further. After he's dragged his lips to my neck and then returned to my mouth with new intensity, after his hands have roamed over my clothes everywhere he can given our state of dress, after I've panted into his neck while his leg parts mine, pressing into me—after I've swallowed his moan with my lips—only then do I decide it's not enough. In plain view in the graduate college archway, it could never be enough for what I need.

It's then that Scott withdraws. He looks smug, which, okay, he has every right to.

He raises his hand, in which he holds—the clue.

My clue. I reach on instinct for the pocket where I had hidden the scroll, finding it predictably empty.

"I told you. Never," he says, "underestimate me."

I'm half-outraged. Half, unfortunately, very turned on.

Scott looks all too aware of the effects of his ruse on me. He glances out of the archway. "Appears it stopped raining," he remarks, pocketing the scroll. "I didn't notice."

I say nothing, knowing my reply would come out gibberish if I attempted speech right now. He's right. Sun shines into our corridor instead of the pounding rain. *Of course* I hadn't noticed. Dragons could have flown down into the quad and I wouldn't have fucking noticed.

"Ready to return to campus?" Scott inquires. "Or would you like to try to steal this back?"

He slides the scroll into his front pocket, right near where I know he's still hard.

Part of me genuinely considers opening doors until we find an empty classroom. He would follow me in a heartbeat. Ruse or not, the desire I felt from him is impossible to fake.

I imagine ending this chapter of my fantasy the way it deserves. Shedding our wet clothes so I can take my revenge, and more.

He watches me, and I notice the same familiar cunning I've seen in his eyes whenever he contradicts me in a marketing meeting with some devastating detail, or his idea prevails over mine with our supervisor—the same Scott Daniels savvy, with new hidden stakes.

Which reminds me, merciless and swift, of why we can't do what I'm envisioning.

This isn't a fantasy. This is a guy I compete with every day at work. I don't even know what it is we'd be doing. Rebounding with each other? Redirecting the passion of our hatred into something new? I don't know which possibility worries me more.

I just know the choices have left me with none. I meet Scott's eyes coolly. "I'd say you earned this one," I reply.

While he smiles, disappointment flickers on his features, like I've managed to hand him a defeat hidden in victory. Saying nothing more, he walks past me out the entryway, commencing a walk to the Experience campus I anticipate we will make in silence.

I hunt in my heart for anger at his deception, or stress at how I've just made him only one clue from winning the Val prize.

Instead, with the clouds clearing over the storm-ravaged ground and the memory of Scott's hands on me—his mouth on mine—I feel only desire.

26

I forgot about the dance lessons.

When I arrive at the dining hall for dinner, I am already jumpy. Finding the tables moved to the sides of the room, providing the impromptu dance floor in the middle of the Great Hall, does not help my nerves.

I'm on high Scott alert. I can't help looking for him when I enter the grand room, where everyone else is adapting to the new seating arrangement with ease, carrying plates of the evening's delicious-smelling roast chicken. Well, *they* haven't just had a fantasy-making, heart-shaking hookup with their rival. Or, I assume they haven't.

I'm preoccupied enough that I mistake a blond man on Experience staff, carrying speakers, for Scott. I'm hopeless, looking for him everywhere. I spent the entire day daydreaming about him, honestly. Not the speakers guy—I spent the day daydreaming about *Scott.*

About the kiss.

I wasn't able to do anything else. Not even a forty-five-minute lukewarm shower—on the third floor, not our shared fifth-floor outpost, which is a freaking Scott Daniels flirting crime scene—cooled me off. The Experience's activities were wasted on me. I went to an Elytheum cooking class, hoping I could learn how to whip up a stew or night cakes for when I got home, and instead spent the hour scorching everything I attempted until I had to excuse myself on account of incompetence due to distraction.

The unfortunate episode left me wandering campus for the rest of the afternoon. The rain gave way to another gorgeous North Carolina day, perfect weather in which to get fussy about running into my work nemesis. When I happened to notice him leaving a lecture hall in front of me, I spun around and walked in the opposite direction.

I am fully aware I'm acting ridiculous. Not at all like a fierce, confident, sexy heroine. Instead I'm behaving like I did in middle school when I liked a boy and didn't know how to talk to him.

It's nonsensical. I *do* know how to talk to Scott! How could I not? I have spoken to this man, albeit often against my will, nearly every day for the past year of my professional existence.

And I do *not* have a crush on him. Only a fool would have a crush on the asshole she works with. It's unrealistic, and not in the flirting-with-a-fae-lord way.

And yet.

I'm heading for the servery, hoping dinner will fortify me against my volatile mood, when Scott walks into the dining hall, glancing around the room. *Is he looking for me?*

My stomach knots. *Oh no.* What if he's *not* looking for me? In moments like now, I do not appreciate my powerful, well-practiced fantasy reader's imagination. It's already providing devastating, dark-night-of-the-soul, all-is-lost plot points I would rather not live out. What if our kiss was just another of his schemes to outwit me? What's better than rejecting Jennifer once—the perfect culmination to a year of rivalry?

If it is . . . it's working. Which terrifies me. I'm here for the Elytheum Experience, not the Heartbreak Experience.

"You okay?"

I spin, finding Brit eyeing me inquisitively, which is understandable since I stopped short of the servery when I saw Scott. I'm presently standing motionless in the dining hall like a video-game NPC. She and Laurel are wearing long, flowing skirts. *Smart.* They'll learn how to dance in a dress. I'm in leggings and boots, having forgotten the evening's plans.

"Fine," I say with haste I know comes off weird. "I'm fine, yeah. Why? Did you hear something?" *Wow*, I am coming off jumpy. I could never be a courtly spy like Kethryn's ladies-in-waiting.

Brit peers at me. "What would we . . . hear?" she asks.

"Nothing!" I assure them. "Nothing. How was your day?"

Laurel looks like she hoped I'd ask. She leans in, quietly exuberant. "We found another clue, in the costume room!" she whispers.

Ordinarily, the news would stress me out. First Lord Scott the Deceptive, and now my friends—it seems like *everyone* has found their second clue except me. Now, however, I grasp on to the distraction from my own jumpiness and my not-crush. "That's amazing!" I cheer them. "Did you solve it?"

"Not yet. We . . . got distracted," Laurel replies.

I notice the shy restraint in her voice, halfway to embarrassment. Brit does, too. Shooting Laurel a quick glance, she explains. "Laurel's ex is getting married this week."

My eyebrows rise. Laurel fidgets with her sleeve. In just days I've come to understand she doesn't open up easily, and I count it an affirmation of friendship when she explains herself haltingly. "His name is Ryan. We dated for a year until he . . . cheated on me," she admits. "I wanted to hate him. I really did. I just couldn't. I was happy when we were dating. Really, really happy. I miss how he made me laugh, how he was always planning adventures and perfect nights and everything. I can't love him, and I can't stop," she croaks out. "Now he's . . . with her. Getting married."

"They posted from their venue today. Destination deal on Martha's Vineyard," Brit continues gently. "We . . . had a little spiral."

"I should've blocked him earlier," Laurel says morosely.

"I'm . . . I'm sorry, Laurel," I say earnestly. I remember her pointed commentary—*Revenge is makeover magic*. Maybe this week is a little bit of her own.

"It's fine. I'm fine," Laurel assures me. "What did you do today?"

"Nothing," I say.

The other women exchange a glance.

"Nothing?" Laurel repeats. "Are you feeling okay? I hope you're not sick."

"No, I'm not sick—" I start, then realize Laurel may have handed me an explanation preferable to reality. "I mean . . . yes, I think I might be. Sinuses. Or migraine. Probably from getting caught in the rain."

"Oh no," Brit says sympathetically. *Whew.* One point in the realistic-courtly-spy column for me. "Yeah, it really came down. You should get into bed after this."

"I agree."

Scott's voice startles me. I whirl, whacking my elbow into his chest.

"Ow," he says slowly.

"Scott," I greet him. He gazes down from where he's stopped, close to me. I wonder if he knows I recognize his simple black sweater from work. He probably *doesn't* know it's one of my favorites of his. "Um. Hello," I say. "Are you well?"

His eyes spark with amusement. "Exceedingly," he replies.

I wish I had something deft to reply. I would in other circumstances, circumstances in which I did not wish to end this conversation as soon as possible for fear of leaping at his kissable face or stomping on his foot for my stolen clue.

"Good. Good," I say instead. "Good to hear."

Brit narrows her eyes. "Um, is it? Isn't he the enemy?" she points out.

"What? Oh, right. No. Yes," I stammer. "That."

Everyone exchanges perplexed looks. Yes, if I were conducting espionage in Crimsonfell, they would certainly have flung me from the highest parapet by now. I push my nails into my palms, needing to get a grip on myself.

"You seem a little flustered," Scott remarks.

"No. Not at all," I protest.

He raises his eyebrow. Just the one.

Irritated, I decide I need to go on offense. "How was *your* day, Scott?" I ask.

Scott looks smug. I swear, I could chart his smugness like I chart social media hits on Parthenon's upcoming releases for work. His smug looks per day are up like five hundred percent in the past week. "My day was eventful," he replies.

"Memorable?" I press him.

"To some, perhaps."

I flush. "Not to you?" I glare, focusing on my annoyance with his evasion instead of the hurt of his insinuation.

He smirks. Then, though, the lofty playfulness of his voice softens. He nods at the open floor. "Want to dance?"

Promptly, I panic. I realize everyone is partnering up. I've gotten to dinner on the later side, without regard for the dance lessons—another unfortunate consequence of my distraction—and many people have finished the meal.

I cannot dance with Scott. What with the inevitable kissing and foot stomping. I look wildly elsewhere, around the room, not caring how paranoid I undoubtedly appear, and find—

Erik is walking past us.

I fling my arm out, grabbing him and dragging him over. "Sorry," I say hastily. "I already have a partner."

Erik blinks, understandably unprepared for my invocation. I give him a meaningful look, and like a skillful scene partner, he recovers. "Right. Yes," he agrees.

Scott shrugs like it's exactly what he expected me to do. I don't know if the flicker of disappointment in his gray eyes is real or wishful thinking. I've heard I have a problem with confusing those two.

"I didn't take you for a coward," he remarks.

Indignation flashes in me. "What could I possibly be afraid of?" I fire back.

"You tell me," Scott replies.

Now I'm pissed. I've finally run out of patience for whatever he's playing at. I'm not participating, even if it means no more kisses in the rain. Fine! Who needs those!

I pull Erik to the other end of the dining hall, where we watch the dancing instructors. I barely hear them over the blood roaring in my ears, and the pangs in my dinnerless stomach only make focusing harder. Erik, for once, says nothing, perhaps intuiting I'm not in the happiest of moods.

While the instructors demonstrate, I have the *here-goes-nothing* feeling I did in front of physics problems in high school. Fortunately, when the first practice dance starts, I find I can rely heavily on Erik, who appears to have had dancing training already. He leads us easily through the steps, his muscular frame directing me around the floor with poised confidence.

How often have I dreamed of jacked guys who looked exactly like him spinning me around a dance floor? I really, *really* wish I could enjoy the immersion instead of spending every minute hung up on a rainy kiss.

I do notice Erik's posture straighten even more perfectly whenever we pass in front of Heather Winters or Val—Fred, I should say, since it's who Erik is showing off for. Whatever. I'm lucky Erik unintentionally interceded in stuff with Scott. If he wants to use the opportunity to flaunt his Val vibes, everyone wins.

"Are you avoiding Scott because you kissed?" he asks.

The question comes out of nowhere, and I fumble in the midst of the dance, stepping squarely on Erik's toe. He winces but doesn't miss the step.

"How did—" I pause, realizing. "Of course he told you."

"We are in an alliance," Erik reminds me. "We share much with each other."

He's putting on the Elytheum heavy. I want to point out Heather isn't even in earshot.

I'm rolling my eyes when inspiration hits me. If Scott confides in Erik, for whatever reason . . .

"Did he . . . say anything about us?" I ask Erik. "Did the kiss mean anything to him?" I hardly dare share the possibility out loud, just like I've hardly dared entertain the idea itself. Hope is a page in an open book—fragile, and easy to rip out. "Or is it just part of his book boyfriend training, or whatever? Am I just practice? Just a data point for his journal?"

Erik pauses, considering, and my heart pounds. It's the feeling of figuring out my clues, except more intense—this question has eluded me, and the answer means everything.

Instead of responding, Erik spins me grandly away from him on the dance floor. When I return to his arms, he dips me with flourish. I hear *oohs* and *ahhs*. When I come up, I glimpse our spectators, and I realize—of course. Heather was watching.

"Did she see?" Erik asks eagerly.

It isn't just the head rush of the dance move sending a painful flush into my cheeks. Like cruel dance partners, frustration pairs with my embarrassment at how much the answer means to me. "Erik. I was talking to you," I say. "Can you focus on another person for two seconds?"

His eyes dart to me. I give him credit for the guilt in his glance. "Sorry. Right. I'm focused. You asked about Scott."

I nod eagerly.

"Oh, well, yeah, I can't tell you. You have to talk to him yourself. I will not forsake my alliance," Erik says.

Exasperated, I sigh. "Can we please stop pretending alliances are real? It's all just a game."

"If it's all a game," Erik replies, "then communicate with Scott for real. Or *maybe* you're avoiding it because you're afraid of being hurt."

He levels me a challenging look. I sag in his arms. "You're supposed to be too self-absorbed for that kind of insight," I say.

Erik laughs. "Don't worry," he says. "I'm still remarkably self-absorbed."

"I'll say."

The voice interrupting us is sharp like steel and smooth like silk. Val—no, Fred. He stands nearby, his presence halting me and Erik.

"May I cut in?" Val-Fred prompts Erik, nodding my way.

Erik doesn't respond, staring his brother down, probably weighing the pros and cons of making a scene in front of Heather versus letting his sibling in. "Am I stealing too much of the spotlight?" he asks Fred.

"Jennifer deserves to dance with *the one and only* Lord Valance," Fred replies.

Erik frowns. "For now," he mutters.

He walks off, and Val-Fred clasps my hand and leads me flaw-lessly into the steps.

"You didn't need to antagonize him," I say.

He stares at me, his expression unmoved. "His presence here is antagonistic," he replies. From his diction and his direct reply, I understand he's speaking like Val about the realities of Fred.

"I know," I reassure him. "Erik is in the wrong, too. You all need to work some stuff out."

Val-Fred's eyes narrow. "One could say the same of you and Lord Daniels," he observes.

My mouth drops open. It's not like *Fred* is in a whispery alliance with my enemy. "How did you . . . ?"

His gaze cuts past mine. He doesn't look curt, only serious. "While all of you are watching us, we are watching *you*," he says. "It is clear you care for each other, and yet you mask it in animosity. It is something I know much about."

His final words lift his lips in a wry, fond smile. While admit-tedly I appreciate his nod to Elytheum, his remark irks me. *Is* it clear we care for each other? It's not clear to me. I *wish* I had more clarity on whether I was just a pitiful pawn to the man with whom I just shared the hottest kiss of my life.

"Let me guess," I reply. "You think I should talk to him. It's what your brother just told me to do."

A little sadness stains Fred's smile. "Yes, well, I love my brother, and we're very similar. *Too* similar, perhaps."

I eye him, understanding. I hadn't considered it until now—how stressful Fred must find Erik's intrusion, amidst the pride Fred hoped to enjoy in his professional achievement. "Well, it's certainly worked in my favor," I say enthusiastically, hoping humor cheers him up. "A pair of brothers vying for my attention as part of their rivalry? I mean, who hasn't had that fantasy?"

It works. Val-Fred swallows his smile. I'm wondering if he remembers our chat about *The Vampire Diaries* over coffee, although of course he has to pretend he has no such memory. "Nevertheless," he says gently, "don't overlook what's right in front of you in favor of a fantasy, no matter how fun."

When he says it, I can't help my eyes straying to Scott. He's very earnestly practicing the dance steps, partnered with Amelia.

It's the real Scott, the one I met in that hallway a year ago. It's endearing to see him, the Scott who isn't Val-worn confidence and swagger. The Scott who's a little nerdy, who I once heard swapping favorite Excel shortcuts with our coworkers, who drinks mint tea out of a mug with *Star Trek* Captain Picard's "Make it so" quote on it during meetings. When this week is over, will I see him again? Or will he bring his book-boyfriend project back to the office?

I have to pull my eyes away. I face my dancing partner, only to find his gaze is also on Scott and Amelia. The expression of soft yearning on his face is all Fred.

"She's incredible, you know," I say gently.

"I know." His reply is immediate. Then he whips his head to me. "I mean, to whom do you refer?"

I smirk. "Nice recovery, *Fred*," I whisper. "Why don't you channel some of that Val swagger and ask her out?"

His gaze drifts to her side of the room again. "She'll say no. She doesn't see me beyond the character I play." He clears his throat, then speaks louder for the people nearby. "And I am sworn to my true love, my liege Queen Kethryn."

I laugh a little at his hasty cover-up, which prompts me to miss a step. Val steers me back on track unerringly.

"She sees you," I say quietly. "She just doesn't let herself get swept up very easily. Be brave, Lord Valance." I squeeze his hand, which I'm holding reassuringly.

He manages a halfway hopeful smile. "You are very inspiring. Queen Kethryn's court is fortunate to have you." Then, without Val's deep rumbling voice, he adds, "Thanks."

"It's easy to talk to you," I say to Val. "Like talking to an old friend."

Friend. The word echoes in my head.

Did I just friend-zone my one true book boyfriend?

I'm dancing in the arms of my favorite fantasy, and I . . . feel nothing. No infatuation. No giddiness. Instead, I feel like I've known Val for years. Which, in a way, I have, across five books and thousands of pages.

"With Scott . . ." I go on, slowly. "It's not easy."

Val watches me. His eyes still sparkle, but I find I'm not dazed. "No," he says. "It's not easy to face hurt. You can't be rejected by something that isn't real."

He spins me, and the world goes blurry for a dizzying moment before my vision can make sense of the dream around me once more. The moment it does, I know Val is right. None of the dance's continued steps are as complicated as the predicament I'm facing now.

I want to want Scott, and I'm afraid. Afraid he will hurt me if I reopen my heart, and not only because he rejected me once already. I'm afraid of how the *new* Scott, the one I've gotten to know this week, could dash the delicate new hopes I've started to have— not to mention how uncomfortable work would be if everything ends badly between us.

And then, deeper down, the darkest possibility. The antifantasy, the worst reality. What if the real reason I haven't had the relationships I wanted *isn't* because I don't try hard enough or communicate well, or because I push people away when they're not the fantasy?

What if the problem is me? What if *I'm* not good enough?

It makes punishing sense. Why would I have to hide here, ensconcing myself in fake fantasy, if I were the heroine I pretend to be? I'm not. I'm not a main character in the real world. I'm no one special. Why should I have an extraordinary love?

Val must notice. He slants his head to find my eyes while we glide around the dance floor. "Be brave, Lady Jennifer," he murmurs, echoing me.

Val-Fred is something more than smoldering, more than swaggering—he's sweet. Nevertheless, the nickname prods my sore spot. *Lady Jennifer.* Is she the character I deserve, or just the one I'm pretending I am?

I focus on the unambiguous part of what he's said. *Be brave.*

I force a smile, wanting to be.

27

Freed from my infatuation with Val, I decide to focus less on the scavenger hunt. I do still want to win, of course, only because it would be a fun part of the Experience. But I've decided I don't need to make it my preoccupation at the expense of everything else here. If I don't win, I'll survive. I hope whoever does—not Scott or Erik, please—has the perfect dinner date with our fae lord in residence.

For my part, I devote myself to enjoying the Experience's offerings. It's not hard, with the wonderful work Amelia and the other organizers have done. I stock up on Elytheum notebooks purchased in the craft store and fill my schedule with lectures, readings, and more, each held in gorgeous Gothic lecture halls.

Over the next morning's breakfast, everyone is eager for one event in particular. A women-owned sex toy maker has partnered with the Experience in a stroke—so to speak—of marketing genius and is offering a women's pleasure seminar. Of course, it's scheduled in the largest room on campus.

When I arrive, the lecture hall is *packed*. The only space I find is on the upper level, above the grand room. The hall must seat close to three hundred people, with blackboards running the length of one massive wall beneath high Gothic windows overlooking trees decked in green.

Everyone is noisily finding seats wherever they can. I suspect grad students have found out about this particular lecture and have snuck in. Good for them.

I wind up in the back, where the only open seats remain. On the worn wood of my chair, I find a small bag waiting for me. A quick glance around the room confirms there is one in every seat.

Inside, I find a vibrator. I pull the device out to examine it closer. It's what we're here for, right? No reason for shyness now.

"Interesting," I hear next to me.

None other than Scott stands beside the closest chair. Given the compactness of collegiate seating, the arrangement puts him inches from me—and my new vibrator, which, with heat flushing fast into my cheeks, I promptly fumble.

My party favor has almost fallen to the ground when Scott's arm shoots out. His precise grip stops it just short of hitting the lecture hall floor, near my ankles.

Scott does not waste the opportunity. Straightening slowly, he proffers me the pink vibrator like he's offering a Victorian lady her handkerchief.

"Thank you," I say, dying inside.

Holding my gaze, he grins. The mirth in his gray eyes crackles like lightning in storm clouds.

I clutch my vibrator awkwardly. "What are you doing here?" I ask, out of the vain hope he's gotten lost. Perhaps the neighboring lecture hall is screening *Star Trek* and he's in the wrong room. Perhaps I could *convince* the neighboring lecture hall to screen *Star Trek* in hopes of inducing him to—

"I'm here for the lecture on women's pleasure," he announces. "What about you?"

I feel my expression flatten. Scott notices my reaction.

"Oh, you think I don't need to attend? I know everything there is to know? You flatter me," he continues, raising his voice in comic self-aggrandizement.

Matters worsen when people around us chuckle. *Ladies of Ely-theum, I implore you*, I consider saying. *Instead of forsaking me like the Western Court forsook our queen, come to my aid. Encourage this man no further. He does not need it. I promise.*

If I'm honest with myself, part of the reason I don't is how charmed I am. Oh, I wish I wasn't. I don't want Scott to charm me. Not when I know his kisses conceal deception. Not when every reminder of his damningly charming qualities is a reminder of how he's only here to practice them to perfection.

Not when, I realize, he'll probably use whatever skills this class offers—maybe even the vibrator on his seat—on someone else.

My face falls. Scott notices. His humorous swagger disappears. The mirthful storms in his eyes part just like the clouds on the morning we kissed in the rain, leaving only the innocent day. He studies me sincerely.

"Can I sit here? If you'd prefer I go elsewhere, I will," he assures me. He's speaking in earnest now, without swagger or presumption. "I don't want to make you uncomfortable," he continues.

I look out over the filling lecture hall, feeling split down the middle. I want him to sit next to me. I want to sit next to him. It's impossible to ignore how the past days have made me feel. The Scott they've shown me is different in unimaginable ways from the man who once raised his hand on five separate occasions in one six-minute PowerPoint I was presenting, who rides elevators with me in complete silence when we have the misfortune of sharing one—who I could never, *ever* imagine kissing me like he did days ago. Increasingly, I find myself wanting to be near him always. Even now.

Which is why I'm afraid.

With Scott's eyes on me, I remember Val's words. *Be brave, Lady Jennifer.*

Resolute, I straighten up. If I'm not enough for Scott, it'll hurt, but I won't refuse to try. I won't be less than the best Lady Jennifer. "What would be uncomfortable about attending a sex lecture with your colleague who you made out with recently?" I reply, echoing Scott's own droll bravado.

When he grins, I add one more hope and fear to the list.

"My thoughts exactly," he says.

He sits next to me. Stowing his sex goody bag under his seat, he takes out his Moleskine. The Val notebook.

It makes perfect sense, and yet I have to ask. "You . . . plan on taking notes?"

"Diligently," he replies with a curve of his lips.

My stomach swoops, visions of tongues and fingers and rain crashing in my head. What else has he written about in there? Was the rain kiss in there somehow? *Wait for inclement weather to put the moves on the impressionable Jennifer?*

What other devious, delicious plans does Scott have? I covertly stretch my neck, trying to make out the small writing on the open page.

He's on to me immediately, damn him. He covers the page with his elbow.

"Snooping for clues? Nice try," he says.

Clues. Yes. I grasp onto the excuse. "You know, it's not too late. You could ditch Erik and join my alliance," I offer.

Amused, he spins his pen with his fingers. *His limber, deliberate fingers . . .* "I must decline," he replies. "There's no way I'm letting you go on a date with someone else, fictional or real, if I can help it. I must remain your adversary."

My stomach swoops again.

What does he even mean? Why keep me from dating anyone else, fantastical or nonfictional? Is this part of the Elytheum Experience—or the Scott Daniels Book Boyfriend Experience—or is it . . . real?

I have to ask him, I know I do. I just don't want to. It would interfere with whatever's going on here. I don't want to ruin this, don't want to open myself up to more hurt. Not when whatever we're doing is decidedly fun.

Like the rest of the week, it's an escape from reality.

I don't ask. I just enjoy myself. Is it following Val's words of wisdom? What's more courageous, venturing into disappointment or flirting with your rival? Who even knows.

"Are you jealous?" I pry, loading playful accusation into my voice.

The question doesn't put him on the defensive. He only gives me a long look—and then grins, pleased. Deliberately, he lifts his elbow from his notebook and flips a few pages, until he finds the one he wants. His pen moves to a line in the middle.

In one bold stroke, right in front of my eyes, he underlines what's written there.

Territorial jealousy.

I laugh. Out loud, in the lecture hall, where I'm relieved the lecture has not yet started. Scott's eyes crinkle with earnest joy, and I feel like making me laugh was *his* fantasy.

"What have you been up to today?" he asks me.

The question quietly startles me. No more fantasy flirting, no more goading insinuations. He closes his notebook in front of him, like he's found a pursuit preferable to imitating literature's finest master of swoon.

Just . . . him, and me.

"I went to some classes. Honestly, I'm afraid being here is inspiring me to go back to school," I admit. His gentle, unhurried curiosity encourages me to say more. "Maybe I want to get an MFA or something. I don't know."

"You should." Scott's reply is unhesitating. Not urgent, just . . . confident. In me, I realize. "I mean, if you've been enjoying this"—he gestures into the grand hall—"you absolutely should."

"Yeah?" I ask.

He nods like the equation I've laid out for him is rudimentary. "You love books. It makes sense you want to explore more sides of them," he explains. "Have you ever written before?"

Under other circumstances I would withdraw into shyness right about now. Scott's kindness is making me reckless with happiness. "Just terrible fan fiction that will never see the light of day," I share.

He leans in. "Any chance you saved any of it?"

"Not for you, Scott Daniels," I say, even though with the way the week has gone, he's no stranger to my fandom or my fantasies. It's only drawn us closer, somehow.

Grinning, he raises his hands in capitulation. "Fine, fine," he says.

"I still like my job, though. It's not like I want to give it up," I continue. "Maybe writing is just a dream I don't need."

The comment doesn't quite come out casual. I hear how deep the undercurrent of self-doubt runs in my voice.

Seriousness softens Scott's expression. "First, the Jennifer I know never gives up on her dreams," he says. *We're living in one for the week*, the knowing flicker in his eyes reminds me. "And second," he goes on, "it's not like you have to give up your job. You don't have to choose. Not right now anyway. If you want to go back to school, go back to school. Maybe it'll just be that—more education.

Education doesn't have to lead to anything more to be worthwhile. I mean, for a long time I thought I would get a PhD. I thought I would go to conferences and present papers in lecture halls like this one."

I glance over, not having expected the revelation. Scott's expression is deliberately unreadable, the gaze of someone who's practiced forgetting his own feelings on what he's saying.

He shrugs, as if comfortable in resignation. "Halfway through my PhD program, I realized how hard my dream was going to be. Impossible, even. I saw my cohort, the cohorts above me. Humanities academia was a miserable job market. My advisor sat me down and . . . said I would struggle to get the kind of job I wanted. I appreciated the honesty. The reality check," he explains, and I know he's in earnest. "So I changed course. I left with my Master's. I don't regret any of the time I put into it, even though it didn't lead me to my original goal."

Although I appreciate Scott's encouragement—honestly—I'm even more touched by the depth of what he's just shared. "I didn't know you wanted to be a professor," I say.

Scott looks down, like he's wrestling with a self-conscious shadow. I don't know who's winning.

"I don't dwell on rejection," he finally offers.

I study him. The explanation has me rewriting scenes in my head I only ever read one way, pieces I never understood of the dismissive, even cynical Scott I've known for the past year. Finding new meaning in comments he's made, observations and judgments. His comments on the riverbank—how I was cursed with idealism, damned to either cling to the wrong guy or push away the right one who wasn't my perfect fantasy.

I assumed they were just accusations. More easily flung criticism from my reliable rival.

Instead, I realize now that Scott is someone who's had reality shatter his dreams. His dismissiveness and cynicism hide a wary, wounded heart. Of course he would admonish me for pinning my future on fantastical hope, repeating the advice he received in the guise of grumpy criticism. Of course he *doesn't daydream*, the way he put it. Daydreams hurt, he knows.

I wish Scott still felt like he could find room in his heart for fantasies. I finally understand why he doesn't, though.

"Thanks," I say. "Really."

I don't only mean his kindness about my MFA idea. When Scott meets my gaze, I know he hears how much I mean it. I'm grateful for this conversation. For the gift of this piece of himself I never knew existed. It's what I asked for when we were horseback riding—the chance to talk to the *real* Scott. Not a performance.

"Of course," he says.

It makes me feel inexplicably excited. Like it's the start of something. While the final Experience attendees or venturesome graduate students fill the empty seats around us, I cross my arms playfully. "So," I say, "will you share your notes after class?"

His lips twist in a smirk. With one elbow on the closed leather cover of his Moleskine, he leans in once more. "In what medium, exactly?"

I reach out and shove his shoulder, rolling my eyes. It distracts neither of us from the heat pinking my cheeks. "So confident," I proclaim. "You know, I could give you constructive feedback on that kiss for your notebook. Since your project is all about self-improvement."

Perhaps I am cut out for my MFA. I am restarting my work in fiction right now. *Constructive feedback*. Ha.

Scott enjoys my foray into fabulism, although not the way I hoped. He tips his head back and guffaws.

"You do not have constructive feedback on that kiss," he declares.

I nod, absolutely bluffing. "I can think of a few things," I promise him.

He looks me right in the eyes. Half interrogation, half promise. Entirely Scott.

"There's nothing to improve. You would have nothing to write," he challenges me. "Unless you would like to write, *Perfect, no notes. I'll never stop thinking about this kiss*, in my notebook. Which . . ."

He slides his notebook out to the edge of his writing desk, closest to me.

"Be my guest," he invites me.

I return his smirk. Who says only handsome love-interest lords smirk and not heroines? "Only," I say nonchalantly, "in exchange for the clue."

Scott is unperturbed. "Nice try," he replies. "Anyway"—he retracts his notebook—"you've all but already confirmed your feelings on the kiss for me anyway."

One of the presenters has come onstage, holding—hey, a vibrator like mine. With her appearance, the lecture hall has started to hush.

The dutiful student in me wants to prepare for attentiveness. Unfortunately, Scott's comment won't let me. "Have I?" I ask, low and insistent. The effort makes my voice end up inviting and desirous. It's definitely due to scholastic politeness, of course. Only good manners.

Scott nods slowly, assured. "You're here. You're not hunting for clues," he explains simply. His sidelong gaze pins me in my chair. "I'm pretty sure you don't even *want* the date with Val anymore."

I swallow, his startlingly savvy deduction shattering my composure. At the front of the room, other women have taken the stage. The hush descends more fully over the lecture hall. "Oh look," I whisper, grasping onto the merciful diversion. "Class is starting. Hope you take copious notes," I add, unable to help myself.

Scott looks pleased. A little victorious, a little eager.

"For you, Jen," he says, "I will."

I face front, biting my lip to hide my smile.

28

"*You what?*"

I should have expected Amelia's reaction. I really should have. If I had, I would not have confessed to kissing Scott in the rain while Amelia was holding her fully globby paintbrush, causing her to fling magenta right onto my cheek with the violence of her exclamation.

Even Laurel and Brit's eyes widen. The four of us and, for some reason, Erik, are sitting splayed out across the grass in the quad nearest our dorm, painting masks for the masquerade. Or, Amelia, Erik, and I are painting. Laurel and Brit are stenciling and adding feathers and diamonds, far exceeding the rest of our artistic abilities.

"When did this happen?" Brit inquires. Her perfectly impartial interrogation reminds me she's a middle school teacher. I feel like I've just admitted to passing notes in Social Studies. I'm preparing to confirm my lapse in self-control when someone answers for me.

"Yesterday morning," Erik confirms. "In the rain. Do you think my mask could be blacker?"

While I eye him in irritation, he holds up his mask, which he has indeed painted entirely black.

"A full twenty-four hours ago?" Laurel presses me. Unlike her friend, she doesn't hide her delight at the detail. "Then didn't you go to the sex lecture together? And why does Erik know before us? No offense," she says to Erik.

He doesn't reply, obviously wanting to discuss his mask.

"It's black, Erik," Brit tells him. "It's impossible to make it more black. But if you add silver to the eyes, it'll pop more."

When the idea intimidates Erik, who inspects his mask like he's envisioning the unattainable silver eyes, Laurel sighs. "I'll do it for you," she offers, hand outstretched. Thrilled, Erik passes her his mask.

"Scott told him," I explain, wiping the paint from my face, confident I've left pink streaked on my cheek.

It's not like anyone will notice, what with how this conversation's embarrassment will change the color of my complexion. I don't know how to admit to my friends how much I wanted to kiss Scott outside the graduate college—how much I want to kiss him again—when I hardly dare admit it to myself.

"And we didn't attend the sex lecture *together*," I add. "We just wound up sitting together. It was . . ."

It was . . . a lot, I don't say. We might as well have attended together, from the way we spent the hour. Stolen looks. Heat pounding in me whenever I saw Scott jot something deliberate in his notebook in his quick, neat penmanship. Shared imaginings, I have to assume. Either we were preoccupied with the same fleeting figments of passion, or Scott was playing another game with me.

I didn't have a clue for him to swipe yesterday, however.

When the lecture finished, I had to rush from the room, overwhelmed. My second lukewarm shower in as many days awaited me. I headed straight to masks, hoping the artwork would distract me. Except when I found Amelia here, I realized I had to confess yesterday's kiss. If she found out later, or not from me, my conceal-ment would hurt her feelings.

"Awkward," Laurel finishes, with utterly off-the-mark sym-pathy.

I straighten, returning to myself. I can't quite force agreement with her, even when I desperately want to.

Amelia catches on. "Oh yes, sounds *very* awkward," she replies with gleeful sarcasm, prompting Laurel to look up from her work on Erik's mask.

She peers at me. "Do you have feelings for him?"

I know she doesn't mean easy-rebound feelings. Hearing the complicated combination of emotions in her voice, I recall our conversation earlier about her engaged ex. Laurel knows what I know—like hope, feelings are dangerous. They're just also impos-sible to fight sometimes.

Everyone has stopped what they're doing—except Erik, who eagerly watches Laurel's work on his paint job.

I look down at my own mask. It's blue and stormy. Like morn-ing rain. "I won't discuss this with spies present," I say, realizing Erik has provided me my perfect unexpected out.

He looks up, oblivious. "Me?"

"How do I know you're not here at Scott's request?" I press him, enjoying the opportunity to be interviewer and not interviewee.

"Dude." Erik looks skeptical of my skepticism, which, okay, he's right. I don't let on, staying stern in self-defense. "I'm just here to paint a sick mask," he declares.

The other women and I exchange looks. In fairness to Erik, his mask *is* obviously very important to him. His eyes have wandered again to the night-dark piece in Laurel's hands. Despite his avowal to his alliance, I doubt I can convincingly pin my secretiveness on him without my cohort jumping to conclusions.

I sigh. "Scott probably isn't even interested in more," I reply, evasively. "I mean, he as much as told me that the reason he rejected me once was because he thinks we're too different to even be friends. He could ask me out at any time, and—"

Right then, Scott enters the quad, striding with purpose right for us.

I fall silent.

Amelia follows my gaze. She smiles slowly, finding the man I'm watching approach us with absolutely no sign of slowing. None.

"You were saying?" she asks coyly, her enthusiasm apparent. Brit actually squeals.

Scott is fortunately out of earshot when she does. In seconds, however, he closes the distance. "Hello," he says when he reaches us.

I look up from pretending I was focused on my mask. "Hi," I reply. "Just passing through the quad?" I hear how overly cheerful and hurried my question comes out. Everyone else does as well. Laurel's lips squirm like she is fighting a smile. In no realm would anyone grant me the honorific of Jennifer the Chill.

"No," Scott says. "Erik texted me that you were here."

Of course. I round on the dastardly Erik, who has the grace to appear guilty.

"Okay, yes, I'm a spy," he admits. "I *am* really invested in this mask, though."

The glare I give him says *I'll deal with you later.* If I get a silver Sharpie and an opportune moment, he might just head down to the masquerade in a mask reading *Second Favorite Fae Lord.*

It's Scott I have to deal with now, however. "Is there . . . something you need?" I ask him, managing more casualness now.

"Very much," Scott says. "I was wondering if you would accompany me to the library tonight."

Everyone goes completely silent and still. Even Erik. I find myself *very* much hoping I got all the paint off my face.

Scott waits. I look up. His pleasant expression doesn't hide the urgency in his features. The gorgeous midday frames him in cerulean sky. It hurts my eyes to stare up. It hurts my heart to wonder if he's working some stratagem—or, possibly worse, only interested in forming an alliance or something completely impersonal.

From the intensity in his eyes and the morning we shared . . . I conclude he's not.

"Okay," I say.

"Excellent," Scott replies instantly. "I'll pick you up at eight?"

"Okay," I hear myself repeat.

His eyes lock with mine for a moment. I swear I see him stand a little straighter, like victory is coursing in his veins. *It's nothing*, I reassure myself, fighting down my own imagination. After a second, Scott looks to the rest of the group and nods in greeting. "Have a great rest of your afternoon," he says.

Then he's gone.

Amelia grins. Honestly, *grin* is an understatement. Not even my admiration of the Experience on the first night delighted her like my whatever-it-is with Scott just has. "Well, there you have it," she crows.

"It's not a date," I reply automatically.

Erik snorts.

"It's a date," he says.

My heart flips far too hopefully. I want to restrain my expectations instead of getting lost in the heavenly fog of a daydream. No, I *need* to. I need to be able to discern between fantasy and reality.

But it's becoming dangerously hard as the two merge in my mind.

"Oh, come on," Erik intones disappointedly, distracting me.

Shaken from my Scott thoughts, I follow Erik's eyeline out to the edge of the quad, where I immediately spot what he's reacting to. Val has started chopping wood—like literal segments of lumber with an axe—in view of the painting workshop and other spectators. He removes his filmy ebony shirt, for whatever reason. The gossamer garment's loose cut wasn't really impeding his freedom of movement.

Okay, never mind. Not for whatever reason. The moment Fred reveals his shirtless physique, I understand why. What was I saying about fantasy and reality?

Everyone stares. Including Erik. "Val doesn't even chop wood in the books," he complains.

"Who cares?" Amelia, Laurel, and Brit reply in unison.

It earns only discontented grumbling from Erik, who gently pulls his mask from Laurel's distracted hands and furiously starts applying more black paint.

I don't watch Val, although admittedly, no matter my feelings about Scott, the spectacle of Fred chopping wood is marvelous. No, I'm watching someone more interesting—Amelia. While she gawks like everyone else, I know she's seeing something different. Remembering something different. With every majestic swing of Val's axe, she's recalling Fred's enthusiasm about *The Vampire Diaries*, his hopeful flirtations with her, and probably a hundred other moments I didn't witness in the Experience's organization. The fan favorite infatuated with the fangirl. *Swoon.*

And she's not alone in her feelings. I'm the only one who knows who Val—or Fred—really has his eyes on with his little lumber-working display.

Sure enough, he sneaks a look over at *us*, not any other painting parties on the lawn, like he's making sure Amelia sees him.

I have to say something. "You're drooling," I inform my friend cheerfully.

Amelia snaps her mouth shut.

"Not more than anyone else," she replies, her dispassion not fooling me.

"Aaaand I'm done here," Erik announces grumpily. He stands, holding his precious mask. "Anyone know where I can get wood and/or an axe?"

"Yeah. Go share with your brother," I say.

He glares at me and walks off. I remind myself not to say anything at all about Scott in his presence, certain my comment will not earn me Erik's loyalty anytime in the near future. "Amelia, seriously," I entreat her gently, "go out with the guy. He's obsessed with you."

The same flat sheen I remember from the cafe falls over Amelia's face. It's honestly heartbreaking. "No he's not," she replies.

I inhale. I don't wish to repeat the results of our earlier discussion on the subject. And yet—never have I resented Amelia for *her* sometimes hardhanded advice about *my* life, even when it irritates me in the moment. I decide Kethryn and fantasy heroines aren't the only inspirations I can draw from when I need. "He is," I say firmly.

And what do you know—Amelia meets my eyes, half-conflicted.

"He's always watching you," Laurel adds. Even Brit, the non-lovelorn of the pair, nods in support.

I have a sudden, inexplicable pang of fondness, and sadness. When the week is over, we won't be able to hang out like this. In this place of fantasy, I've found very real friends. Who will return to jobs and cities in other parts of the country, or at least the coast. I'm certain we'll keep up over DMs, fan forums, and events . . . and I'll miss them nonetheless.

I wonder if it's something I might find if I returned to school.

In my undergrad years, I found friends eventually, but it wasn't easy or permanent. Many of my college friendships have faded now. I didn't know how to seek out friends who understood me, who loved what I loved.

Making friends the way I have here gives me hope. If I start again, maybe I won't just follow a new dream. Maybe I'll find what I've found in Elytheum—community.

Amelia fusses with her mask in her hands. "He did ask me to dinner, but I was too busy. It wasn't a date anyway," she admits.

Everyone groans now. Including me.

Is she kidding? The rest of us have spent the week scrounging around a college campus for clues—I fell in the fucking river for one—in hopes of winning a prize Amelia offhandedly scored with a few professional conversations and a coffee run . . . *and she declined?* My friend is officially ridiculous and must mend the error of her ways.

Yet her words ring in my head. *It wasn't a date anyway.*

I apply one final star to my mask and hold it up to admire it. Will I wear it for Scott to see? New fantasies fill my head, like the mask has summoned them with mysterious power. Decorated dance halls, gowns swirling like enchanted storm clouds. A man cut like no fae lord, yet made of magic entirely his own.

I'm scared of opening myself up to them. *And* I'm scared of closing myself off to them.

I know Scott had a point about not overlooking reality, but I don't want to shut down like Amelia, either, ignoring something incredible right in front of me.

It's a date.

Maybe it's just a silly fantasy, but maybe—just maybe—it'll be a dream come true.

29

I wait in the common room, ridiculously nervous.

Not helping matters, Erik is practicing his smolder in the mirror while the clock inches closer to eight, the dauntless minute hand carrying me ever closer to the not-date-okay-possibly-date. I attempted to read for distraction, and again, not even *The Exile Court* could call my mind from the uncertainties of Scott.

I realize I'm tapping my foot when Erik drops his Val demeanor and gives me a pained glance. "Please," he reprimands with artistic gravitas, "I need quiet to smolder."

Although I return his impatient, *you're-really-pushing-it* look, I still my foot. "A real Val can smolder under any circumstances," I inform him primly.

Erik is unamused by my critique. He lights the smoky-sweet leather-scented candle on the dresser, which he has commented on a couple occasions helps him capture his character's mindset. It is one of the parts of his process on which I have no complaints—I honestly love the scent.

"Since you're just sitting there nervously waiting for a date *at the library* with your coworker you *claim* to hate"—his judgment thicker than candle smoke—"can't you at least be my scene partner in the meantime?" he asks.

"No," I say.

"Come on," he pleas with the pouty persistence of a man not used to hearing *no*, which admittedly he probably rarely does. "We can do any scene you want. I saw you reading *Exile* earlier. We could do the one where the ladies-in-waiting catch Val asking Kethryn's cat whether he should ask her mistress to the masquerade."

"I will only perform the one where the Vengeant Men capture you on the journey into the Realms Past," I say.

Erik's brow furrows with recollection. "Val is unconscious for that scene!" he whines.

"Exactly."

He eyes me reproachfully. "I'm going to blast 'Cotton Eye Joe' while you and Scott are trying to get it on tonight."

I gasp. Not only at the horrible cruelty of his promise—also the, um, other insinuation. While I've maybe accepted this is a date, I've restrained myself from imagining what might happen *after* the library. I don't want to overdose on fantasy.

Just then, there's a knock on the door.

I look up. The clock reads eight p.m. exactly. It's very him. Assuming it *is* him.

When I open the door, I find Scott waiting. He's not in Elytheum costume. Instead he's dressed smartly, in a white knitted sweater and brown pants. While I very much enjoyed costume Scott, I'm definitely not mad about it.

"Hi," Scott says.

I love every word of Val's darkly delicious wordplay, every passion-aching pronouncement of his deeply felt declarations of love.

How is it, then, that *hi* is the most romantic word I've ever heard when spoken in the right voice, from the right mouth?

"Hi," I say.

Scott smiles. Not smirks, not exactly, although there's starlight in his eyes. Like he's promising something, and neither of us is sure what just yet. "You ready?" he asks.

"Scott, thoughts on 'Cotton Eye Joe'?" Erik interjects.

Scott frowns in understandable incomprehension. Eager to usher the moment forward, I step into the doorway with him.

"I'm ready," I say.

Scott's smile returns. "Good," he replies.

"*Good night*, Erik," I reply very pointedly over my shoulder.

I close the door, and we head into the hallway. Scott nods in the direction of my impudent roommate. "What was that about?"

"Nothing good," I assure him.

We continue into the stairwell. "How was the rest of your day?" Scott asks me with casual kindness, obviously unaware of what a coil of nerves he's wound me into.

"Laurel and I worked on our costumes for the masquerade. What about you?" I ask, avoiding confessing *and also I watched the clock for an hour waiting for you*.

"I had some work to catch up on," he says. "And otherwise, I was anticipating this."

I can't help the shy smile that springs to my face. I guess I could have admitted to anticipation of my own after all. "I hope it lives up," I say.

Swinging open the stairwell door for me, Scott grins. "I think that's my line."

I laugh. We walk down the stairs and into the warm evening, the campus lights golden in the darkness. The illuminated pathways feel like possibilities for the night—I don't know where they'll lead us. "And what exactly do you want to live up to?" I ask softly, playfully. "Would you care for a recap and evaluation at the end of the night?"

Scott smiles. "In a manner of speaking. Feedback comes in many forms," he replies.

His line is perfectly flirtatious, but still I don't know what this is to him. Another data point for the notebook? A fantasy he's conjuring for practice? Are we on our way to *experimental* nocturnal library perusing?

With effort, I push the doubts from my mind. *Enjoy this*, I remind myself. *Whatever it is.*

Scott guides us to the north end of the Hollisboro campus. Or, I think it's the north end. It feels northerly. Without my familiar landmarks, however, my sense of direction is once more failing me. Scott could be leading us to the parking lot, for all I know.

Until—there. The library.

It emerges past the archway we walk through. It's not the grandest building on campus, nor the largest or most decorated. Its Gothic tower doesn't reach higher than the surrounding rooftops. Nevertheless, there's . . . something hallowed here. Hushed invitation in the night air. The cicadas' hum is muffled, the murmur of traffic farther away.

Scott leads us up the front steps.

"Are we allowed in?" I ask, the logistic occurring to me for the first time. "Isn't it for students only?"

"One of the cool things about doing half of a PhD," Scott explains, "is having friends in academic places. I pulled a few strings to get us passes." When we reach the grand doors, he pauses to pull two name tags from his wallet. *Scott Daniels. Jennifer Worth.* He presents mine with chivalric flourish.

"Wow," I say, with playful overemphasis of my real admiration. "This is way better than impossible-to-get dinner reservations."

Scott smiles. "I know."

Quickly he clasps my hand in his, and I cover my reaction to the exhilarating sweetness of the contact. *Scott Daniels* is holding my hand like it's nothing. Experiment or not, it's . . . nice. My hand in his, we enter the library.

It's quiet, close to empty in the summer night. Lights illuminate the stone anteroom, stretching out shadows suitable for getting lost in. Similar to the quad outside, the silence is inviting. Welcoming. The only people here look to be a handful of grad students preparing for all-nighters. I even notice pillows propped up in the occasional carrel.

"What are we doing here?" I ask.

"We're on a date," Scott replies. "It may not be what you had in mind a year ago, but I think we can both agree we're not here to be friends."

Knowing his evasion is intentional, I roll my eyes even while my stomach flutters. While he's answered the question I've spent the afternoon fretting over, he hasn't answered the one I just actually asked. "Unusual date activity for me," I comment.

"Sort of the point," he returns. Dropping his coyness, he rubs my knuckle idly in our clasped hands. "I . . . want this to be the sort of thing you read about, Jen. Come on."

He draws us forward. I don't hesitate or ask more questions. Surprises have a sacredness when prepared with kindness, and I want Scott to unveil his in exactly the way he envisions.

Our footsteps sounding softly on the polished marble, Scott leads us into the stairwells descending into the stacks. I feel an irresistible giddy anticipation swell in me, and not just due to Scott's careful and mysterious efforts. I *love* university libraries. Their intricacy, their enormity, their unusual architecture accommodating generations of expansion and renovation. Labyrinths of learning sprawling out in every direction—including downward, where we continue, the flights of stairs offering glimpses of rows and rows of subterranean shelves.

We descend, and I have literally no expectation of where the library will lead us. Rare manuscripts confined in glass walls? Ooh, or a cozy reading room full of my favorite stories? We go minutes now without glimpsing another person. I hold Scott's hand, my curious heart picking up its pace.

Until we reach what is, without question, our destination.

The atrium reaches down into the ground, and up, with open balconies rising all the way to skylights in the ceiling. Scott has even set up small electric "candles" everywhere, surrounding us. In the low-lit space, they smatter the shelves like the starlit night has somehow spilled inside. It's stunning. It's magical.

I look to Scott, awed and wondering. Rationally, I know what's in front of me is his work. I just can't fully reconcile it with the guy who told me he didn't daydream. He certainly knows how to conjure them up.

Finally I find my voice. It's hushed, and not only because we're in a library. "This is . . . unreal."

Scott grins.

"Like I said," he replies, with soft charm, "sort of the point."

He releases my hand to reach into his pocket, from which he produces—the scroll, the clue I recognize from our memorable early-morning horse ride. When something playful enters his eyes, my stomach tightens in anticipation.

"The next clue," he explains, unrolling the parchment, "is a code. Here." He hands it to me and he continues. "I knew it was the library pretty easily. Took me a little longer to understand the mechanism. When I did . . ."

He shrugs shyly, as if to say, *Well, here we are.*

I read the clue in the false candlelight.

Where you find me, Lord Everbane, you find your reward,
in the place where all knowledge resides. In the volumes of
the start and end of our story, add each numbered page
where in darkness, light is found. Two numbers, one clue.

I understand Scott's library deduction. The clues have led us from *where knowledge continues*—the graduate college—to *the place where all knowledge resides,* the main college library.

And I recognize the words hiding in the description. *Where in darkness, light is found.* It's not a metaphor. "In darkness, light," is Val's friend Everbane's motto, uttered often to Val and Kethryn. Otherwise . . .

"*Add each numbered page.* Page numbers," I exhale, starting to understand. "Literal addition. You're supposed to take certain page numbers and add the numerals together."

"Page numbers," Scott repeats. "Like, say, the numbers of pages on which a certain character utters a certain memorable phrase."

"*Where you find me, Lord Everbane, you find your reward. Where in darkness, light is found,*" I recite. "We're looking for the numbers of the pages where that quote appears."

Scott leads me down the stairs to the ground floor of the atrium. We're near the general fiction shelves, hence the room's grandeur, I guess. On the table, surrounded by his electric candles, this man has assembled the library's Elytheum Courts copies.

Not the entire series. Scott has produced two copies—I'm pleased but not surprised to note the library has duplicates—of *The Shattered Court* and *The Risen Court,* the first and final volumes.

"*In the volumes of the start and end of our story,*" I repeat. "The first and last books of the series—that's where we're searching. And when we add up the page numbers where Lord Everbane's quote appears . . ."

Following my logic, Scott practically hums with anticipation. "We would end up with two numbers. One for *Shattered*, one for *Risen. Two numbers, one clue.* Here, *in the place where all knowledge resides.* And what"—he asks excitedly, and I have a glimpse of Professor Scott—"do you do with two numbers in a library?"

As he goes on, I understand the pieces he's putting into place.

"The Dewey decimal system," he explains, with the nerdy delight of someone who really did enjoy his years in academia. "A library is just a code with walls. Dewey uses one three-digit number, and then a decimal, and then another number. It's a scavenger hunt within a scavenger hunt," he summarizes proudly.

He moves to the table, where he unstacks the copies of *Shattered* and *Risen.*

"Using our knowledge of the series," he continues, "we have to find every page in each of these books where Everbane says 'In darkness, light.' Add up one set of page numbers for our first number, then the other for our second number, and we'll find a Dewey decimal number in this library," Scott concludes. "In these very stacks."

"Wait." Scott may have experience in academia, but Jennifer Worth, the former number-one patron of the YA section of the Southern Oaks Library in Oklahoma City, knows her own way around the Dewey decimal system. "A Dewey decimal number only gets you into the right section. How will we know what book we need?"

Scott nods like he anticipated the question. "I have a feeling we'll know, somehow. Remember the clue in the West College statue? Nothing about this scavenger hunt is random. Everything is planned. We'll know when we get there. And when we do . . ."

He pauses, and I realize it's as far as he's gotten—or let himself go.

"We'll find the final clue," he finishes with intrepid joy.

I feel it with him.

Until confusion cuts into the pounding of my heart when I realize what's just happened. Scott, who outran me on an obstacle course, who outwitted and outflirted me in the rain, has just explained how to solve his final clue. He's led me right to the solution.

I ask the obvious question. "You're telling me this *why?*"

Scott places one hand on the copies of *The Shattered Court*, steepling his fingers. He looks down, shyness stealing some of his enthusiasm, and underneath it, something else. His own cipher, written in sweetened ink.

"Because this game is only fun when I'm playing against you," he admits.

Quietly I wonder whether he's just confessed to something I never expected. I figured nothing except simple one-upmanship and a pattern of pettiness kept our rivalry continuing. Does Scott find the competitiveness, the drive to outdo each other . . . fun?

Do I?

Instead of asking him, I pick up one of the copies of *The Risen Court*. "You want to race," I clarify.

He raises an eyebrow—just one.

"What do you say?" he asks, quietly exhilarated, like he hears the pounding of hope himself. "Up for a challenge?"

I step closer to him.

He swallows.

Reaching up with my lips raised, I brush my mouth softly

against his. While his eyes flutter shut—while I kiss him—I gently pull the scroll from his hands.

His eyes open, and he doesn't reach for the clue I've claimed. His expression says he wishes I'd do it again and again.

"Game on, Daniels," I say.

30

"Excellent."

When Scott starts muttering to himself, I know how the night's going to go.

I'm reading *The Shattered Court*, wracking my memory for instances of Everbane's memorable motto. I have the heavy volume propped up on the copy of *The Risen Court* I'll get to once I've figured out the first component of the clue. Val's friend first enters the narrative after the coronation and before the other dignitaries come to court, I'm certain of it.

Which means I'm close. I flip past page 101, 102, my gaze racing over the paragraphs—

"Another," Scott says to himself. "Wonderful."

His enthusiasm distracts me. I can't help myself. I glance over, heart pounding with competitive frustration, and find him, sure enough, jotting something in his Moleskine with contented zeal—

Which is when I notice *him* look up at *me*.

Of course. He could be doodling in his notebook, for all I know. He's probably only making his victorious utterances to distract me!

And it's working, damnit. Sending him a glare, I receive only an absolutely devastating wink in return. I fume. Scott may have planned the literal perfect date, but if he wants competition, it's competition he'll get. Our previous clue-hunting duels were powered by no-holds-barred rivalry. No matter how he's made me swoon this evening, I've vowed to reengage my fighting spirit.

And when I notice his wink has stirred in me some rather noncompetitive feelings, I fume even harder. I'll fume all damn night if it means figuring out the Dewey decimal number faster.

He keeps up his efforts. I reread page 103 over again. Nothing. Nothing! I refuse the discouragement rattling the gates of my resolve—

"Fantastic. Right where I expected."

I do not give Scott the satisfaction of looking his way this time. So what if I have to read page 104 over again. He doesn't have to know. I continue in my labors, silently seething. *Finally*, I find an instance of "In darkness, light," uttered on page 112, and I flip forward, knowing Everbane has one ominous appearance among the final chapters.

When I'm hunched over the pages, getting lost in the exhilaration, suddenly he's hovering over me.

Not Everbane—Scott. Reading the very page I'm on.

Then he swiftly withdraws and jots something in his Moleskine, like he's found another quote. Only after a couple seconds of frantic hunting do I realize he didn't find anything on the page and was only messing with me.

It keeps happening. Wherever I am, he's there. Worse, his efforts start extending past direct subterfuge of my reading material.

Way past.

The *absentminded* mussing of his damnable hair while he reads. The confounded smirk he cuts me whenever he knows he's wrought my distraction. Every glance I spare his way, he's doing something I know is in his notes, strategically targeting weaknesses *I* handed over to him in the pages of my favorite books.

For no reason whatsoever, he carries his copy of *The Risen Court* over to one of the nearby tall shelves.

Where he *leans*, occupying as much space in my eyeline as he possibly can.

I struggle to stay focused on the climactic court assassination attempt, knowing Everbane is around here somewhere. Oh, I struggle hard. It's just—if a calendar were made of Attractive Men Reading Jennifer's Favorite Books, he would be, like, *January*. Or December. One of the real heavy-hitter months.

While I proceed to lose my place in the scene four times, lost in openly admiring him, Scott smirks. He makes victorious notations in his notebook.

No. No way.

I proposed a race. A game. What Scott's started is a *war*. And I won't let him win uncontested using his unfairly good hair and his leans. If Scott wants to play dirty, I'll play dirty with him.

On the flimsy pretense of needing to stretch my legs or inspire myself with a change of scenery, I carry my books in one hand over to the shelves. When I pass Scott, with my other hand I casually undo the top buttons of my dress. I walk into the stacks, putting a row of bookshelves between us.

I wait for him to peer through the shelves. Which, of course, he does.

Which, of course, I pretend not to notice.

Instead, while locating my next page number in *Shattered*, I sit on the floor. With my knees folded to my side, the hem of my dress rides up, exposing the skin of my upper leg. It's devious by design. I'm enjoying every minute.

Scott is as well. I watch his eyes catch on the exposed skin. I perceive the very moment he loses his place in whatever he's reading-slash-scavenger-hunting. *Shattered Court*? More like shattered concentration. I weigh sending him a wink, a Scott Daniels Special, and decide I'm not a sore winner.

Sure enough, Scott retreats into the stacks, giving each of us some space. It doesn't last long—in only moments, he returns, nonchalantly joining me in the stacks. He positions himself against the bookshelf across the aisle from me. Chess pieces staring each other down.

With enchanting coincidence, I find my final Everbane page in the first volume. I close the cover with a pleased flourish—immodest in more ways than one—ready to change over to *The Risen Court*, which I deposited on the floor when I carried it here with its counterpart.

Scott gazes on, charged with frustration and competition and maybe something else. Deprivation? It's convenient I've just spent the hour immersed in a Winters volume. I have every way of describing the ardent emotions waging war on his face ringing in my ears. Knowing he's eyeing me, I increase my siege. I get up onto my knees to reach for the book I've placed nearby, bending over for just a moment, knowing exactly how much of my skin I've flashed him.

Finally he speaks up.

"Jennifer, I'm finding it very difficult to concentrate right now, which I suspect you know," he says.

It's a victory like none found in the Dewey decimal system or the pages of my favorite prose. I glance at him over my shoulder, coy and content. "Feel like giving up?" I ask.

"Desperately," Scott replies.

Insinuation hides in his words. I won't let it make me flush—
not yet. "I hope you can last longer than that," I reply instead, managing to keep my voice ever casual. Flirting with Lord Valance
himself in the moonlit dining hall was the perfect practice, and
yet, I know it was nothing more.

Just practice for the real thing.

With my words, Scott's eyes *darken*. Somehow, he's managed to
do what every romance novel describes and I never knew how to
envision. I remind myself he's spent the week doing practicing of
his own. The intensity of his gaze has deepened, from sharp to
smoldering. Passionate to penetrating.

Then he removes his sweater, revealing an off-white button-
down. With his deft, deliberate hands, he proceeds to *roll the sleeves
up his forearms* right in front of me.

It's vulgar. Obscene. *Good god, we're in a library*, I want to
reprimand him, sternness hiding the heat pounding in every part
of me.

Except I don't want him to stop.

I understand, rationally, it's a completely ridiculous outfit to
wear in the middle of summer. Which means he's not wearing it
for comfort. No, he knows what it will do to me. What it *is* doing
to me. Never mind January or December. I could have a whole calendar of Scott in the academic allure he's putting on. He read every
one of his moves in the pages of a book, and he's weaponized them
beautifully.

"Is this interesting to you?" he asks, noticing my ogling.

I straighten. I don't need Kethryn right now—no, I'm pulling
from my favorite prim Victorian heroines. No hot thoughts for me,
no way. Just a Victorian lady with absolutely no knowledge of what
naked men look like! "Forearms?" I reply. "Please."

Please.

I hope it comes out as a scoff and not a whimper. Facing front, I'm ninety-nine percent certain I'm not drooling. However, one can never be too careful.

"Focus on your homework, then," Scott returns.

I scowl. *Focus on your homework* is a turn-on for me? Really, Jennifer? Sometimes I embarrass myself.

"I know what you're doing," I inform him, uttering my reply rigidly. If I let any emotion in, I'll let *every* emotion in.

"Winning?"

I shake my head. "You didn't just skim the books," I say. "Did you? Tell me what you thought of them. For real this time."

The library's silence surrounds us, and I remember we're the only people down here. The candlelit fiction section is hushed, waiting for Scott's reply, just like me.

The question is only half-strategic. Yes, I want to disrupt his practiced charisma with the reminder I know exactly where it comes from. Of course. Deeper down, I'm genuinely curious. He's not acting like the coworker who has insisted he doesn't understand the hype for my favorite series. No, he sounds like—

"I've read every page," Scott finally replies. "Multiple times."

In surprise, I close *The Risen Court.*

I watch Scott while he slides to the floor in front of his shelf.

We're facing each other now, seated, legs outstretched with feet nearly touching. I set down *Risen.* I say nothing, wanting him to know he's free to continue—and needs to, if he cares for me.

He sighs. "The first read, I was . . . intimidated," he explains. "Which made me dismissive. It was pathetic, really. My problem, not the series'. It wasn't until I read them again, recently, that I could . . ." He finds my eyes. "Appreciate them."

"*Intimidated?* By what? Because everyone calls Val their book boyfriend?" I frown. "You know that's just for fun."

Scott shakes his head. "It wasn't that. It was . . . the romance. The way Kethryn was captivated by Val. How he challenged her, how they helped each other grow. How every conversation they had was either deep or flirtatious. How they made love look."

Quietly, I accept his explanation. I've never understood the urge in commentary on art about or for women to compete with fictional characters—whether "over"-competent women or "unrealistically" noble, kind, or supportive men. I do understand what Scott's saying, which is different. How often have *I* wondered whether a love is waiting for me as grand as the one my favorite characters have found?

He goes on. "I . . . I didn't like how it made every relationship I'd ever had look. Like I'd only thought I knew what love was." He shrugs, hollow regret in his expression. "So I wrote it off. Convinced myself it was silly. Ridiculous. Fantastical."

And me with it, I nearly say. I remember Scott's first week, our first fight. Love of Elytheum is part of why Scott judged *me*, finding his overwrought coworker, Jennifer, frivolous in her romantic fantasies. It's not just that he thought we were too unlike each other to be friends. It's that he avoided anyone and anything that made his own feelings and relationships feel shallow.

He reconsidered Elytheum, though. His gaze found mine when he confessed he could appreciate the passion in my favorite pages.

Is he saying we're not too unlike each other now?

"I never understood it when people were hesitant or afraid to say *I love you*," he elaborates. "Or when they said they didn't know if they were in love. I couldn't fathom it. I thought . . . if you liked someone for long enough, of course you loved them. Didn't you? It was quantifiable. Measurable. Predictable, even. *One day of like* plus *one day of like* eventually equals love."

Quantifiable. Measurable. This is the Scott Daniels I know from work. *Something you could organize in a spreadsheet,* he's saying. *Or list in a notebook.*

He presses one fist gently to his knee, like he's fortifying himself to continue, despite the challenging conversation. "But it's different, isn't it?"

I nod.

The defeated confusion in his eyes inspires me to speak up. It *is* different, I want him to know. It's just not unreachable.

"I thought I could just make myself into this fantasy guy and then I'd have the kind of relationship I want. But . . . then you were here," he continues.

I smile, unable to resist the playful reprisal of our usual petty feuding. "And you realized, *Wait, I don't want to be the kind of guy* Jennifer Worth *is attracted to,*" I prompt him.

"Imagine my surprise," he returns, "when I realized quite the opposite."

My stomach flutters. The memory of our horseback ride, our kiss, sends my heart soaring for the night sky.

The courage of Scott's statement has quietly captivated me. The feelings you understand most innately in yourself are often the hardest ones to admit out loud. The fundamentality of them makes them fearsome. Yet here Scott is, confessing the fundamentals—he was wrong. He has feelings for me.

"At the risk of sounding vain, I don't think the problem was ever with who I was. The eyebrow stuff, the lean . . . they're fun, but they aren't a relationship," he continues. "The truth is, I called you overly romantic and optimistic because I don't have a lot of faith in relationships. I'm not close with my family. There's no reason for it, really, except feeling like my interests were uninteresting to them."

"I felt that way at school a lot," I reply. "Like the things I got obsessed with just weren't interesting to the people around me. It was . . . incredibly lonely. I'm sorry, Scott. I can't imagine how much worse it would be when it's your family." Sharing, I decide, follows its own lovely economics. The law of diminishing difficulty.

Scott meets my eyes. I have a hunch he's feeling the same. "When I saw your faith in love and relationships, deep down, I knew it wasn't just delusion. It was hope. And it . . ."

He presses his lips together. I hear the guilt and shame swallowing his words. What he's saying is hard for him.

"It made me angry," he admits. "Which made me judgmental, and pushy, and critical of what you loved to read. When someone has hope you wish you could feel, it makes you want to dismiss it. If I had been willing to talk about these things more, to be vulnerable in a way that is totally the opposite of dressing up and smirking," he continues with a graceful flash of humor, "I wouldn't have felt so embarrassed of it or lonely. I might've felt like it was . . . something that could bring me closer to someone, even."

I shift my leg so I can nudge his foot with mine. "We're close now," I remind him.

Scott smiles.

"We are," he says.

And I know, in the week of horseback riding and lawn wrestling, and obstacle courses and moonlit flirting and muddy showers, fighting and fandom—now is the moment I'll remember above all others. Him and me, sharing our real selves in hushed voices, far from clues and costumes and characters. What Scott's done to the library has made it enchanting. What he's said now has made it much, much more.

"I guess . . ." he goes on contemplatively, "I was sick of feeling rejected by the people and things I thought were supposed to be my whole life. I hoped that in love, I could have it all—someone to share a life with, yet who wouldn't have the power to hurt me if I didn't let them. All I had to do was not give them very much of myself, and then I wouldn't feel it when they rejected what little I'd given."

He hangs his head.

"So I played it safe in my relationships. I kept them insubstantial. Meaningless. I rejected people I was drawn to because that feeling scared me," he says.

I watch him closely. "People?" I repeat.

He understands my meaning. "One in particular," he admits. When he looks up, his gaze is penetrating, an utterly open book. "One I can never, ever quite manage to get out of my head," he says.

His confession explains every question and doubt I've had in our fraught year. Amid the candles, I'm not just surrounded by the starlight he's conjured. I'm full of it.

"In fairness to you," I say, "she really is prone to getting swept up in the idea of a romance instead of taking it day by day."

"Please consider how romantic it is that I'm not going to say anything about you admitting I'm right," Scott replies.

I roll my eyes. "I'm swooning so hard right now," I assure him—and the way he smiles when I say it really does have me swooning. "Okay," I say, "since I am prone to flights of fancy, let's get some things straight."

"Let's," Scott agrees. "Good to connect live. Tick through the points."

Hearing him reprise his emailisms, I fight laughter. We *are* in a library. "You said we're not here to become friends. What exactly are we here to become?" I ask pointedly, ushering the inquisition along.

"I like you, Jennifer. I do want to be your friend. But I also . . . want you," he replies, his gaze locked with mine.

His answer steals my breath, forcing my next question to come out hoarse. "When did you realize this?"

"I've always had eyes." With his words, he trails said eyes down my body.

Even if part of me wants to, I don't let his obviously perfect reply distract me. Practiced, perfected flirting is not the discussion I want to have right now. "Come on," I reply. "Please be serious. Don't just say what you think Val would say."

Scott exhales, looking like he needed the admonition. "Okay, fair. But that's not just a line. I guess . . ." he continues, "I consciously realized it when you came here. I had just watched you get dumped. I watched you carry a box of reminders of your failed relationship up to work," he marvels.

New heat lights in me now. Scott has managed to make my embarrassment feel like strength. Like courage. It's magic even I've never conjured. He's not exaggerating or overdoing his praise—and the measured honesty of it makes the sentiment mean more to me than poetry or prose.

"Then that same day you came here, not to wallow, but to experience something new. You had to have been hurting, but you didn't let it stop you. I thought you were really brave. And . . . well, I wished I had been that brave."

Brave. I want to hear him say it over and over.

Instead, I don't let myself indulge. *Not the point*, I remind myself. "But of course, you knew you never had a chance with me so you focused on making yourself into the perfect book boyfriend for someone else," I presume.

"Jennifer." The hint of a smile plays over Scott's lips. "I was pretty sure I had a chance with you."

Only with Kethryn's strength and the resolute temperament of the Northern Court's most devout Afterrealm guardians do I avoid the powerful pull of our old rivalry. It would be very easy to say *zero-point-zero-zero-zero-zero-one percent is a chance, yes* . . . "This is no time for cockiness, Daniels," I reply instead. "We're on to vulnerability now."

"Vulnerability means honesty," Scott argues. "And honestly it was obvious you were checking me out since I got here. Which is why"—he preempts me when I open my mouth to interrupt—"I was so annoyed when I heard you say you wouldn't even consider me for a rebound."

Even in the moment, I felt guilty for the way my overheard rejection would've hit. Now, though, new understanding settles over the memory.

"I don't think you want to be my rebound," I venture.

"I don't," Scott says.

The nighttime library is suddenly very quiet. Or, well, it *feels* quieter. Every shadow the shelves draw, every star summoned by the man sitting with me, seems to wait. I wait with them.

"You want vulnerability?" Scott murmurs. I nod. "When you beat me to that first clue, I realized I wasn't trying to become the book boyfriend for some future mystery girl. I was doing it for you. It was . . . all for you."

He won't meet my eyes. Hope is dangerous—the truth is, too.

"And then if it didn't work," he explains, "if you still didn't like me, then, well, it wasn't really *me* you were rejecting. It was a character. Something that only works on the page but not real life. I could write it off, the way I did whenever you shared your incandescent love for these stories."

I don't dare move, not wanting to disturb the pieces fitting into place. His notes, his winks, his Val-isms. His lean.

They were . . . for me.

It was all for you.

"And then . . ." He hesitates.

I remember him helping me—and Jelly Bean—in the rain. I remember us, filthy with mud, feuding in the forest, starting to understand each other. I remember him encouraging my newest dream, sharing what higher education meant to him, revealing parts of his own life I'd never known.

"Then you realized you could win me for real," I say, "by showing me *you*."

"Well, I do think the eyebrow thing helped, and I won't lie, I picked up some very nice kissing tips, but—"

I laugh, shoving his leg with mine. He grins—my favorite of his grins, knowing and wry and warm and very, very Scott.

"But yes," he says, "it wasn't about the book boyfriend. Or not in the way I expected. The more I tried to be him, the more I understood it. While the smirking and leaning and growling is very nice, it's not the whole fantasy, is it?" He picks up his copy of *The Shattered Court*, flipping pages with the reverent familiarity I've felt every time I open them. "He gets to know her. He listens. He shares. He loves her without holding himself back. The more I did those things, the more I felt something real between us. Something I desperately wanted."

He closes the volume.

"I never should've played it safe, Jennifer," he whispers.

When his eyes leap to mine, the darkness has parted in them. They're piercing. With love. With loss.

"I would risk everything for a chance with you," he says.

I feel emotion well up in my chest.

Everything he's saying is what I would want in a declaration of love written in a favorite author's hand, and it's happening to *me*. It's perfect. Impossibly perfect, so perfect it couldn't be real.

Except—what if it is? Hasn't this week taught me fantasy can be real?

I dare to welcome the deepest gift the Elytheum Experience has given me. Not the heart-pounding looks exchanged with the fae of my fantasies. Not the dance lessons, the delicacies, the details rendered in life from fandom-loved pages. Not the fun, not even the friends I've made on the lawns of the decorated college.

It's faith in fantasy. It's the courage to embrace dreams when they come to you in the guise of life.

Scott watches me with vulnerable hope. I move to my hands and knees, and with his eyes on me, I crawl across the aisle, closing the distance separating us, up his legs. I'm right in front of him now, my face only inches from his.

When he tilts his head back just slightly, inviting, I write the start of our first chapter in the soft kiss I press to his lips.

His hands find my waist, rising seemingly on their own, like he couldn't restrain them even if he intended. "Well," I murmur, sitting in his lap, facing him, "I seem unable to resist you, Scott Daniels," I inform him. Yes, it's fantasy. It's also the realest confession I've ever made.

His smile goes wonderfully wicked. The hot rush in me knows exactly what it's promising. He doesn't need to say it, and he doesn't.

"Why don't we finish this riddle," he offers, "and then we'll see about that?"

The riddle. Oh, the stakes have never felt higher. "You better solve it fast," I reply. "I don't intend to wait."

Scott fixes me with a devastating stare. He raises an eyebrow.

"In that case," he finally says, "I'll admit I solved it before you unbuttoned your top."

Affronted, I lean back. Honestly, his knowledge of the series continues to impress. Did he really know where every scene with Everbane's motto was? And will I never learn to assume Scott's hiding something in our scavenger-hunt showdowns? "Where was it?"

"Nearby," Scott confesses with no small amount of sly pleasure. "The organizers probably planned it that way. It was close to general fiction, where you'd find Elytheum, though a completely different section. Dewey number 822, 490. Few shelves down the aisle. 'English Drama'—plays from the 1600s and stuff."

He gestures in the direction I remember him retreating when I first turned up the heat on my own sabotage.

"I noticed the one right on the end of the shelf, by the playwright James Shirley. From 1653," he recounts. "It's called *The Court Secret.*"

Very clever, Amelia, I have to concede. Finding pages that would point to a section close to fiction, near Elytheum itself, and then in that section, finding something that would capture the notice of the intrepid fan. *The Court Secret.* You'd know it was what you were looking for if you were hunting our clue.

"Why didn't you say anything?" I ask.

"And miss out on what was going to happen after the top unbuttoning?" he returns.

I smirk. Fair enough, Lord Daniels. "I was going to let you win anyway," I inform him, settling onto his lap, enjoying the comfortable clasp of his hands on my hips.

Now his other eyebrow rises to accompany its counterpart. "Why's that?" he asks.

With the candlelit library surrounding us, with Scott speaking the plainspoken poetry I needed to hear, I don't know why I even need to answer. *Isn't it obvious?* I want to say.

"I'm pretty sure," I reply instead, "I just had my dream date."

I move close, heat humming in the library stacks. Scott's eyes devour me. And when I lean forward to kiss him, I don't stop.

31

Scott surges into the kiss, clinging to me while I straddle his lap. He moans into my mouth like he's dreamed of this moment for days.

Or longer, maybe. I feel his hunger, his release, in every explosion of his lips against mine now. With each rush of heat, he's rewriting everything I thought I knew about enemies becoming lovers. I know how the story works—every fight, every prickle of enmity, every disagreement alchemized into hot, ruthless foreplay.

This is . . . more. He's not just rewriting our enmity in the passages of passion he lays on my mouth. He's showing me the real him.

And it's more than any character or trope has ever made me feel. He's not my enemy, not my fae lord, not my book boyfriend. He's himself. Scott Daniels. He's giving me his entire self. Letting himself feel the hope of us fully.

From the way he kisses me, I know it's exhilarating.

It makes me want him more. Knowing I'm getting all of him, without reservation, without fear, I want everything.

I *need* everything. I need him.

I withdraw, my lips stinging pleasantly. Scott's eyes lock with mine from inches away. He knows what's on my mind. "Here?" I whisper.

"Anywhere you want," he replies without hesitation.

I know he's entirely serious. He's not holding anything back, even in his enchantingly indecent proposal. Glancing up and down the dark stacks, I feel a thrill shoot through me. Scott kisses my neck, waiting and urging in one press of lips. "It *would* fulfill a certain fantasy . . ." I admit.

Then my eyes catch on the cold stone floor, the staircases leading up to the main library . . . the long aisles of shelves where anyone could enter, innocently working on research projects. Noticing my hesitation, Scott smiles gently. He releases his grip on my waist, studying my fraught expression adoringly.

"Sometimes fantasies don't translate well in reality. Let's walk back," he suggests. "I have a luxurious twin bed waiting for us."

I laugh, more relieved than disappointed. When I've climbed to my feet, reluctantly leaving his lap, I reach down to help him up. He stands—close to me, a few inches taller, his ebullient hair mussed and yet perfect, and I'm having some serious *second* thoughts on the subject of location. I level him a look of coy challenge, knowing I need to distract myself. "Race you?" I say.

"If you thought I was motivated by the chance to have dinner with a guy with goat horns, you have no idea what I'm capable of now," he promises with urgency in every word.

In reply I lean closer, lifting my lips.

He's lowering his kiss to me when, right at the last second, I spin away.

"Oh, you'll pay for that," Scott vows despite the delight playing over his face while I reach down for my copies of *Shattered* and *Risen*.

"I hope so," I say.

We hurry to return our copies of the Elytheum volumes. Of

course, we're neck and neck replacing our copies in the fiction section. However, once we've returned our reading materials, Scott has to collect his plastic candles and put them in the bag I guess he left behind the shelves earlier, when he planned the loveliest date of my life.

In the meantime, I hit the stairs. I sprint up the flights and through the library, adrenaline and anticipation fueling me. When I reach the lobby, I don't stop as I draw curious looks from the students in their carrels. The way Scott and I have carried on recently, I'm pretty used to drawing the perplexed interest of graduate students.

I burst out the wide front doors into the deep blue night. It's no less dreamlike out here. Fireflies spark over the grass. The chill on my cheeks cools the heat of our makeout in the stacks.

I'd stop to immerse myself in the wonder of the scene if I were on an ordinary date.

I'm not, though. This date is real *and* extraordinary.

Breathless, I don't pause. I rush down the library steps, sprinting into the night. I don't know how much of a lead I have on Scott.

I run—only to see him emerge in the corner of my vision, leaving the library. He chases after me, looking like he's racing *for* me instead of racing against me, and my heart skips.

We dash across the grass, the joyous reprise of our chase for the first clue. I love the happy determination I glimpsed on Scott's face. Of course—once again—his runner's legs defeat my ordinary Jennifer legs. He reaches me quickly and pulls me in, catching me in a kiss.

It's heart pounding and spontaneous and unrestrained and everything. We part, chests heaving, and Scott looks right into my eyes—

"You're running the wrong way, baby," he says.

Releasing me, he starts off sprinting across the library lawn. In, unfortunately, the opposite direction.

I laugh, realizing my mistake. I still feel joyously dizzy from his first use of one little word. *Baby*. Giving chase, I notice his stamina flagging, or possibly excitement has me overcoming my own exertion, because I'm actually *gaining* on him. We fly over paved quad pathways and grass lawns under the impassive golden gaze of the campus lights. He maintains his lead as we reach our dorm.

On the second floor, I pass him. With footsteps pounding up the final flight of stairs, I reach our floor—where, victorious, I turn to wait for him in our hallway.

He joins me moments later. His whole face is glowing with joy despite his unlikely defeat. "I was going to let you win anyway," he repeats my own words.

"And why's that?" I reply in kind.

"Because I'll follow you anywhere," he says.

He walks closer. I wait for him, wanting him to reach me. He embraces me instantly, wrapping me in his arms, gentle and firm, loving and never letting go. With my elbows in front of me, forearms resting on his chest, I gaze into his slate-gray eyes.

"Anywhere?" I ask him.

I mean the word deep in my stomach, where desire pounds, and in my contented heart. I kiss Scott in the perfect stillness of our hallway, meanwhile sliding my hand into his front pocket.

I feel his smile against my lips, and then reluctantly he withdraws to speak. "If you're looking for the clue—" he starts.

He hushes when I pull out his room's key card.

Slowly, I reach past him to unlock his room.

Without a word and without hesitation, he follows me inside. He flips on the lights, and I spare a moment for my first look at his room. The quiet, inconspicuous place where the rival I know only from work returns to when we're not fighting or flirting. The Elytheum decorations look like my suite's—the candelabra, the accoutrements—although the art print is a different richly rendered landscape.

Otherwise, signs of Scott are sparse. His suitcase stands on the floor, against the wall. His laptop on his desk. I notice the sticker on his computer alongside the one for the New York Graduate Symposium for Lectures in the Literary Arts, the decal I clocked in departmental meetings immediately—I figured he attended. I never thought to ask whether he lectured or planned it or whatever else. They're details that aren't new to me, but I didn't know their significance before. Like understanding deeper meanings on a second read.

The feeling pulls my heart to him even more. I want to know everything about him. I want everything. I want him.

I sit down on the bed. It's difficult to keep still with the excitement humming in me. But like I'm opening the very first page of a story I know I'm going to love, there's pleasure in the expectation.

Scott closes his door deliberately, the lock clicking loud in the quiet room.

He approaches in fast, even strides. In one perfect, poised movement, he bends down to capture my face in his hands. I hardly even notice the moment he starts kissing me again—he just does, and I disappear into the rush of feeling, the perfect, intuitive continuation of the prologue of insinuated promises we made in the library.

He starts unbuttoning my dress, and I, on irresistible impulse, pull his shirt from his waistband and unbuckle his belt.

In synchrony, we stop. We stare at each other breathlessly for a moment.

And then it's like we can't turn the pages fast enough. We're flying, racing, pushing each other to make every fairy tale and fantasy real. Scott's hands find me, sliding up my thighs while I kick my shoes off. Then he's kicking off his, and he's half climbing onto the bed, one knee on the comforter, positioning himself over me. Closer, ever closer.

We kiss like we've spent the past year dreaming of this moment instead of feuding at every turn, parting only to remove more and more clothing. It's frantic, clumsy with desperate need—until nothing remains. Nothing but skin on skin.

Scott stands. He waits, next to the bed, *very* hard. Very, very ready for me.

I exhale, captivated. I reach for him, gripping him while he falls, in ecstasy and uncontrollable intention, onto one hand over me, caging me on the coverlet.

I could hold him here forever. The night has left the room pleasantly cool—not cold, only temperate enough for the air to remind me of my nakedness exposed to him. I could hold him, caressing him just like this, lost in the gentle rhythm I'm finding.

Scott has other plans. He pushes me lightly down until I'm lying flat, my legs still hanging off the bed. Then he sinks to his knees on the floor.

"Let me know how good the notes I took were," he says.

He doesn't hesitate. He puts his mouth on me, utterly in control of the heat ripping through my core. I gasp, and, oh, *fuck*, yes, I understand exactly how Scott got his Master's—with attention in lectures, followed by *very* diligent homework.

He recites his lessons on me with passion and precision, and I do nothing except let him drink me in while cascades of pleasure overwhelm me. When his fingers find me, gently thrusting with every intent stroke of his tongue, I go over the edge. Under the urging of Scott's mouth, the feeling lasts and lasts. Heat rushes over me in pummeling crests of light. My head feels full of the fireflies we saw dancing outside in the night.

The pounding ecstasy gives way to the softest pleasure weakening my limbs. Scott kisses his way up my stomach.

"Well?" he finally has the obliviousness to ask.

Well? Well, that orgasm changed my world forever? Well, how is it possible you've left me completely satisfied and completely insatiable at once?

I don't say those things.

"Pretty good for a guy without goat horns," I reply instead.

Scott laughs. His breath, hot on my ribs, is joyously spontaneous. It's so utterly *real*, in the midst of the impossibly dreamlike night. A laugh interrupting this fragile wonder. The kind of unexpected imperfections that make reality *more*. Like fights covered in mud while losing races, banter on horseback to distract from thunderstorms.

It pushes my desire ever further, my heart venturing into realms it didn't even know to explore until now. I remember every love scene I've ever read all at once, their pronouncements and poetics, metaphors and magic wrapping around one another in a chaos of feeling. I'm a girl made of spilled ink, a pure embodiment of the greatest passions I've ever read. It's not hyperbole—it's me. It's us.

Like he's similarly pulled, Scott climbs onto the bed while I slide up, my movement matching his on instinct, until my head is on the pillow. With his closeness, I'm immediately awash in the scent of him. Scott.

My Scott.

"Spread your legs for me," he says.

The command sends a throb of desire through me. Slowly, I do as he wants, unfurling myself, watching him watch me.

He stares, transfixed.

I'm impatient—needing him—and yet pinned in place, over-whelmed by the power of his hungry, adoring eyes. The power *I* have, to make him gaze at me, all of me, the way he is. "No need to spend all night looking," I finally say.

Scott looks slowly up, finding my face. His expression says he heard the sound of my breath struggling over my hurtling heart-beat, says he knows how difficult it was for me even to speak in such a situation.

I don't move. I keep my legs exactly where I have them.

"Jennifer, I thought you knew this better than anyone," he re-plies. His voice is gravel wrapped in silk. "When something is your favorite, you never get sick of it."

Heat floods my cheeks. It's one thing to study flirtation in the pages of a Moleskine notebook. It's another to have the creativity and confidence to spin material like this out of nothing. I can't help being impressed.

"You're far too smooth," I say.

He moves forward, fast and graceful, and positions himself over me. "You like it."

The wanting is unbearable now. I'm close to unraveling. "Since you're the expert on what I like," I say, "why don't you give it to me already?"

He does. Or rather, first, he grins. His face is close to mine, close enough to kiss. His hand glides down my body, pausing to linger *exactly* where I want.

He doesn't make me wait long. Quickly he reaches into his lug-gage, and in moments he's deftly unwrapped a condom and rolled it on. With the same hand, he guides himself into me. I go weak and ravenous at once, feeling him inside me, wanting ceaselessly while having everything I want.

How, I wonder, *is it possible*? How is it possible for a first time to feel so wonderfully familiar? How does every moment and movement, every paradox of passion, feel like recognizing what I never knew to imagine?

Magic, I suppose.

I cling to him, my legs rising to give him deeper access. He moves in me, finding our rhythm in desirous, purposeful strokes. I close my eyes, focusing myself entirely on the place where we meet. I want to miss none of this. I want the way Scott holds me—the way he rocks deep inside me, the kiss he presses to my neck while he does—inscribed on my heart in permanent ink.

It's a rebound and a fresh start in one. Desperate yet tender. An ending and a new beginning.

Of what, I don't yet know. It doesn't matter. I've never flipped to the ending pages of a book first, either. I don't need to know where something is going to enjoy it.

And *enjoy* is a woeful understatement. *Enjoy* is for four-star reads. Scott is on his way to shattering me with pleasure. Sweat slicks our bodies, our momentum mounting. I feel frissons of ecstasy shimmering in my hips, my legs, my stomach. I clasp Scott, wanting ever more.

When his breathing goes uneven, I lean up to whisper in his ear.

"Tell me your fantasy, Scott."

He stills, still sheathed inside me. His hand rises to sweep my hair from my face.

"You," he whispers. "Just you."

It undoes me completely. I kiss him, holding him close as he finds his release and the pure pleasure consumes me. There's nowhere I would rather be, nowhere. No magical world, no favorite pages.

Just here.

32

I wake up in Scott's arms, pressed close.

Yes, our position is partly due to the *luxurious* confines of the twin bed we enjoyed for the night. It's not the whole story, though. I have to think our proximity has more to do with the new closeness between us. Even if our sleeping situation were suitably sized, I'd want to sleep cozied up with him exactly like this.

I smile to myself. Scott has me romanticizing a mattress the size of a refrigerator. He really is magic.

I start to shuffle out surreptitiously from under the covers, wanting to run to my room to grab my toothbrush without waking him.

I fail. My gentle stirring rouses Scott. His hand, clumsy with sleep, finds my wrist, half caress and half constraint. "You're not slipping out on me, are you?" he asks. "I was hoping we could get breakfast together."

"*I* was hoping you could join me in the shower in twenty minutes," I reply.

He wakes up more fully very suddenly. "Yes, that's a better plan," he agrees.

I kiss him, lingering on his lips, damning my toothbrush for forcing me to leave his room. While he watches—I feel his gaze on me, content yet wanting—I pull on my dress. It's early. My phone clock corroborates the soft crispness of the daylight and the quiet in the hall. I slip out and tiptoe barefoot over to my suite. Once inside, I close the door quietly and head for my room—

"Now who's the traitor."

Erik's voice startles me. I whirl, having figured my roommate was sleeping. He sits up on the couch, where it looks like he spent the night. Waiting up for me?

Despite his words, he does not regard me with accusation. No, Erik looks . . . pleased. Even happy for me.

"I may have joined an enemy alliance," he pronounces, "but you *joined* with the enemy."

I frown, even though, honestly, it's kind of funny, and his delight in the pun only makes it more so. "Gross, Erik," I admonish him, not meaning it. Just the reminder of Scott, along with Erik's unexpected warmth, leave me incapable of holding my grimace for long. "But, yes, I . . . you're right. Obviously you're forgiven and we're all on the same side now."

Satisfied, Erik smiles. In the morning light, he stretches his arms over his head, showing off his ridiculous muscles. "Good. One big, happy alliance," he says.

"Right," I reply, smiling with him. I have to admit—I guess Erik is my friend, too.

"You can root for me in my duel against Fred," he goes on, his demeanor changing instantly, serious in strategy. "I know he'll have most of the guests on his side, so you and Scott need to cheer extra loud for me."

He stands up from the couch and promptly starts doing shoulder stretches in the middle of the common room, continuing on into pantomiming swings of a sword.

"Duel?" I ask, admittedly concerned despite my morning plans.

"Yes, I've challenged Lord Valance himself to a duel," Erik announces. "It's scheduled for tonight."

"Erik . . ." I say, shoulders slumping, not even sure where to begin.

"It's not a real duel," he assures me.

"I should hope not!"

"It'll be fun," Erik goes on, heedless of my horror. "I mean, it'll be very competitive with the highest stakes possible," he amends. "Brotherly bragging rights. *And* it'll be in front of Heather Winters herself. She looked intrigued when I challenged Val in front of her at campfire s'mores. I declared myself an enemy from the Lost Revenants, remember? From the visit Val makes into the Realms Past in *Ashen*? I knew she was impressed with my mastery of the lore."

"Oh, that is clever—" I begin, then stop myself. "I mean, that's not the point." Honestly, I really would love to buddy-read something with Erik. Maybe the next Winters release with him, Amelia, Brit, Laurel, and—

"The *point* is, we had a whole audience watching," Erik says. Stopping his imaginary sword fighting, he looks me right in the eye, imploring me to understand. "I know this is my chance. I'm not winning the scavenger hunt. And besides, a staged sword fight shows off my real skill set."

I let out my breath. I know he wants to impress Heather—I understand, I do. Nevertheless . . . "Is this really the best idea?" I ask. "Perhaps there's a lesson for you in what happened with me and Scott. That sometimes the person you think is your enemy"—I pause for effect—"is actually your greatest ally."

Erik makes a face.

"No. No way," he says. "That's boring."

Well, never mind my literary flourish.

"I mean, boring for me," Erik clarifies. "For you, it's lovely. We're all very happy you and Scott are together."

"Sure you are," I reply dryly even though Erik's loving sarcasm lights up familiar fireflies in me. *You and Scott are together.* "Of course we'll come support you, Erik," I say with a sigh, making sure he knows I still don't approve literally dueling his brother. "Not because we're in an alliance. Because we're friends."

Erik beams.

"But," I interject before he thanks me, "*because* we're friends, I'm going to insist you have a real conversation with Fred afterward."

Erik returns to the couch. He eyes me, petulant, while he considers.

"Maybe I prefer being just alliance members to friendship, then," he poses. The confrontation doesn't reach his expression. His grin gives him away.

I roll my eyes, fondly chastising. "You love us," I retort. Erik has no objection.

Leaving him in the common room, I head into my room to change into my robe and grab my shower stuff. As I reach for the hem of my dress, I hear the rustle of paper and feel something unexpected in my pocket. Reaching in, I pull out a folded piece of parchment, the kind all the clues are written on.

Scott, I realize, smiling. He stole a clue from my pocket once. It's a neat reversal he's done now.

Sure enough, I recognize his handwriting on the outside fold.

It's my hope to make all your fantasies come true. Even this one.

Swoon.

I feel my heart swell with joy, not to mention even more eagerness to get into that shower. I collect my towel and set the parchment down without opening it to read the clue inside. Riddles can wait—right now is for certainties.

33

Scott and I do not make it down in time for breakfast. Other pursuits occupy us for the rest of the morning. I really don't mind—I prefer what we spent the hours doing over any amount of puff pancakes.

Instead, we grab coffees and Danish from the student cafe and walk around the campus. It's surprisingly nice to experience the grandeur and greenery of Hollisboro this way, not as competitors prowling for clues. I stroll with Scott, hand in hand, sometimes speaking, sometimes not. *Hey, remember when you chased after me right there? Oh, yeah. Remember when we wrestled here in front of a group of students? Yeah, definitely.*

Eventually our morning walk carries us out to parts of campus our scavenger hunt didn't—the more modern parts, which Amelia and her cohort didn't want to use amid the Elytheum immersion.

We're passing the prismatic admissions center when Scott stops us.

"Wait here," he says urgently.

Without further explanation, he darts inside, leaving me perplexed on the steps out front. I do what he says, admiring the intense emerald lawn and the gentle, invigorating rustle of the leaves overhead. And in minutes, Scott returns.

He bounds down the steps to me, carrying a pamphlet in his hands. With flourish, he holds it out to me.

On the front are smiling students and Hollisboro's recognizable Gothic architecture. Over the familiar sights, however, is embossed the surprise.

Hollisboro Master of Fine Arts Program.

I look up, speechless. The gesture leaves me on the verge of quiet tears. Is there anything more meaningful, any greater gift, than someone daring to hope your hopes with you? It's magic of its own, making dreams, insubstantial like starlight, feel close enough to reach and firm enough to grasp.

"Just so you can see if it's something you want to pursue," he says.

"Thank you," I reply softly. How did the colleague who once called my season summary presentation reductive cover up the incredibly supportive and kind man before me?

My eyes fall back to the brochure in my hands. The dream expands, delicate like they get when they assume the weight of real possibility. I love this campus. I love the lecture halls, the dining halls, the dazzling green quads. I love the *feeling* of sitting in a classroom, ready to learn and explore my passions. I love walking the quaint streets surrounding campus. I could live here.

I have a life, though, I remind myself. I have a job, a good job. I have an apartment in New York. I have Scott.

Or—maybe I don't.

My heart drops, faster than a dragon plummeting from the clouds into combat. What if this is Scott's horribly gentle way of saying we have no real commitment between us?

What if I'm only getting caught up in my newest fantasy? Made not of queens or fae, but of unruly, powerful incantations like *long-term commitment* and *defining the relationship*? I fight their dangerous magic, remembering the facts. The facts are—we hooked up. It was wonderful, yes. And we haven't planned for anything more.

Scott, I realize, may have planned for *nothing* more. Reality reaches shrewd fingers into my happy fantasy, prodding, pulling off pieces. Replacing postgrad dreams with unforgiving probabilities. I picture myself sitting in a classroom fighting loneliness and loss. Strolling the streets of Hollisboro *without* Scott. Wondering, *What the hell did I do with my life?*

My mouth goes dry. Of course, he and I haven't had any conversations about what these past twenty-four hours have meant for us, logistically. We've made sweeping statements about wanting each other, but wanting and doing are very different. One is just a fantasy without the other.

What a reprise. Just hours ago I felt like the Experience had brought me to Scott. What if the story isn't over? What if it's only bringing me to heartbreak instead?

I need to be brave, I decide. I deserve to dream. Don't I?

"I was sort of thinking I would stay in New York, though," I say honestly, daring to envision how I could maybe have everything I want—or at least not lose it immediately.

Scott shrugs. "Sure, if that's what you want," he replies. "It helps to have the information either way, so you can compare. I've just noticed you admiring this campus."

"I have," I say.

I gaze out over the green. The day does my indecision no favors. The dappled campus spread out in front of us reminds me how I've fallen in love with this place. How I feel like I'm *home*, in ways having nothing to do with scented candles and fan art in my dorm or swords hanging in the dining hall.

"It's just so far from . . . everything," I venture.

"New York isn't going anywhere," Scott reassures me without hesitation. "And, you know, I wouldn't mind coming down here on long weekends. You're worth eight hours on the interstate." He winks. "Or we could find a place to meet in the middle. We could explore more of the Eastern Seaboard."

"Yeah?" I ask, feeling hope solidify around me.

Scott smiles like, *Wasn't it obvious?* "I wouldn't have handed you the brochure if I wouldn't. I'm not about to compete with an entire college campus for your affections."

I laugh. "I just wasn't sure if last night meant we were . . . you know," I say, "a one-time thing."

"It's already been a four-time thing."

I shove him despite the pleased heat stealing into my cheeks. *Yes, it has.* "It's just, you know, I have been told before I let my mind run away with me," I hesitantly explain. "I don't want to assume anything. I guess I'm . . ."

Nervousness finding me, I falter. *Doesn't every story have this part?* I remind myself. *Where the heroine needs to embrace adventure instead of resigning herself to disappointment or normalcy?* I wonder if it has a name in fancy literary circles like Scott's Master's program. Personally, I consider it the Fuck-It Moment.

Fuck it, I order myself.

"I guess I'm asking you to be my boyfriend," I say.

His eyes widen in shock for a moment. Then his expression turns serious. He takes my hand not holding the pamphlet in his, and there's quiet mirth under the open incredulity in his eyes. "Jennifer, did you miss the part where I beat you to this? I literally asked you out yesterday." Now he smiles, familiar and free. "Keep up, Worth."

I don't even rise to the challenge in his competitive goading. "Wait, so . . . you want to date?" I force myself to clarify. There will be no fragile fantasies, no dangerous magic of hope. Only the facts. "For real? I'm not imagining things here?"

"For real," Scott assures me. "I want to be with you, Jen. Here, when we go back home, if you go to grad school here or somewhere else. We can do long distance or . . . whatever. I just want to try. With you."

Now my heart soars for the sky.

For real.

I know what trying means for Scott Daniels. It's not just a word. I've watched him for the past year put everything into his work with precision and insight, determination and dedication. And he's *here*. Wrestling with romantic problems, he packed up his Elytheum costume and drove eight hours into the Northern Carolina woods to try to improve himself, equipped with tropes and a notebook.

Yes, I know what it means when Scott Daniels tries. It might be more magical even than hope.

I kiss him, knowing it's impossible to communicate the depth of my gratitude in one press of lips, and wanting to try anyway.

"Okay," I whisper when we part.

"Okay," Scott murmurs his refrain.

We continue walking the campus, eventually returning to our dorm and the Experience. Our fingers remain intertwined when we enter the dining hall for lunch. Of course, Laurel and Brit see us immediately. Erik is with them—winning adherents for his duel, no doubt—and when we near, the whole table applauds, drawing looks from the rest of the dining hall.

Scott bows with just a little fae-learned majesty. When he straightens, he gestures for me to do the same. Laughing, I shake my head.

"All credit is yours," I say honestly.

Scott smiles, accepting my judgment. He hugs me from behind and kisses me on the cheek. "You have *no idea* how long I've waited to hear you say those words," my former rival promises. "Sit," he says. "I'll get us lunch."

I do, knowing I'm glowing and all my friends can see it.

"I promise *no one* needs to say *I told you so*," I preempt them. "You were right and I freely admit it."

Brit preens. I remember she was one of the very earliest to encourage me to reevaluate Scott. She's earned it.

Laurel leans closer. "So . . ." she starts, "how was he?" The sparkle in her eyes makes it unambiguous what she's referring to.

I sit, knowing I'm not pulling off nonchalance. Or modesty. "You know chapter thirty-five in *Exile*?" I ask.

The girls nod eagerly.

"Better," I say. Eyes go wide at my pronouncement.

"I find that hard to believe."

The pompous judgment doesn't hide the amusement in the voice I hear over my shoulder. I look up, finding Val standing over me. His smirk holds genuine warmth, like the embers under a dead fire. I shrug, unembarrassed. One lesson I've learned from fandom is never to feel embarrassed when something makes you happy.

"I'm very pleased for you, Lady Jennifer," he says sincerely. I'm reminded of his character's deeper moments, when he isn't wry or flirtatious. When his conversations with his closest friends reveal his loyalty and kindness. "And for Lord Daniels."

I meet his ochre gaze.

"Thank you. For everything," I say with intimation, remembering a conversation during dancing—one that only somebody who really embodied Val's nobility would have had with his lovesick dance partner.

He nods in silent acknowledgment. Without saying more, he departs.

"Has anyone seen Amelia?" I ask. "I need to tell her, obviously."

"I think she's in her office. I saw her take her lunch back there," Brit says. She points in the direction of the hallway leading to the dorm's administration offices.

"I'll be right back," I promise everyone. I head past the bathrooms, deeper into the heart of the building.

When I find the door with Amelia's nameplate in the now-familiar Elytheum calligraphy, I knock. I wait until she calls me in.

I enter, and my enthusiasm dies on my lips.

I'm shocked to find the place is a complete mess. Amelia always had the most meticulously organized desk at Parthenon. Not just meticulously—*lovingly*, with colored Post-it notes galore, elegant journaling, and a full-desktop calendar. The office I've just entered looks like the Elytheum Royal Guard ransacked the place for evidence of espionage.

Amelia stands in the center of her court of chaos, glancing up briefly when I enter, dining hall coffee in one hand and the paper she's reading in the other.

"Whoa," I can't help saying, "what happened in here?"

Amelia waves the paper in a gesture of agitation. "Everything," she says. "I tried to stay on top of it at first, but it was impossible. Did you need something?"

"No," I reply, honestly worried what would happen if I said yes. "I just came to tell you Scott and I got together."

My friend looks up fully from her work now. "I'm so happy for you, Jen," she says earnestly. Her eyes have the fragile intensity of needing to push out a hundred other thoughts in order to focus on me. "Has he changed? Did he have a full Darcy transformation?" she asks.

"There have been Darcy-esque moments," I concede, "but really, over the past couple days we got to know each other in a deeper way than we ever had before." I close her door and come farther into the office. I have the feeling she needs to hear what I have to say. "And it's all because of this place. This incredible experience you put together. *Thank you.*"

Amelia's smile wobbles. "I'm so glad," she says, a little teary. "You give me hope. I want to hear everything when I'm—done here."

The impatience in her final words makes me pause, regarding the mess around us. "Are you okay?" I ask gently.

Her instant reply is pure Amelia. I recognize her caffeine-powered reflex for upbeat professionalism. "Oh yeah, I'm . . ."

She falters. The room falls silent. She lets the paper in her hand drop to her desk.

Her eyes shift from mine, and exhaustion extinguishes the optimism in them like a gust of wind over a candle. She looks . . . wrecked.

"No. Not really," she admits. "I think . . . No, I *know* I'm going to quit."

I startle. "*What?*"

"I've been thinking about it for a while, actually. I'm going to finish out the Experience, of course. But after that I'm giving my notice," she says.

I knew the Experience was demanding. I guess I figured it was the kind of intensity that Amelia lives for. "It was your dream job, though," I point out, not indignant, just confused.

Amelia sighs. "I don't know if those really exist. Once you start working, it's just another job. Even worse because the idealism fuels you until it runs out and the crash is . . . huge. I haven't been able to enjoy any of this, and I sort of just realized, why make myself miserable just because this is a job I wanted for years? It's not worth it," she goes on hollowly. "Next year I'll be able to attend as a fan, and it'll be better. I hope."

I open my mouth and close it, not knowing how to console her. *What would Amelia say?* I ask myself. *What would Scott?* "I'm sorry," I say. "I had no idea."

She smiles humorlessly. I recognize the feeling of having not let anyone know you were struggling, the doomed pride in getting away with your misery.

And I remember moments from the past week—when she said with hurried finality she was too busy to date, how she refused even to consider that Fred is interested in her, how she said she missed when Elytheum was her escape from everyday work.

"Although . . . I guess, looking back, I understand," I continue. Guilt cuts into me—the moments I remember now are ones I overlooked when they happened. I need her to know I'm not overlooking her now. "I'm sorry I wasn't here for you better."

"It's not your fault," she replies. "I didn't want to admit it. I mean, it's really fucking depressing, right? My dream job turned out to be a nightmare. I don't even know what I want to do now."

I hear fear filling up the vacancy in her voice. She stares out into the room, her gaze long.

Coming around to her side of the desk, I wrap her in a hug. "You don't have to figure it out right now," I reassure her.

She hugs me close. "Thank you," she says into my shoulder.

"Come find me when you need a break, okay?" I insist.

Amelia nods, and I leave. I feel guilty for abandoning her in her hectic office, although I know one often doesn't want company in the midst of overwork.

It's hard, honestly, seeing what she's going through and realizing I wasn't present for her until now. I'm glad she's choosing to do what's good for her. Giving up a disaster disguised as a dream.

I stop in the hallway, the uneasy feeling lingering with me. The MFA pamphlet in my pocket is suddenly impossible to ignore. I pull it out, my stomach twisting.

What if I end up like Amelia? Chasing some nonexistent ideal instead of just . . . living my life? I had misgivings earlier, including ones having nothing to do with Scott. Homesickness, uncertainty. What if Amelia ignored ominous omens of her own, or didn't recognize them? In our favorite stories, dark magic often hides the horrible debts it demands with the promises of pleasure and ambition.

What if I need to pull back on the fairy tale?

Being here is inspiring, but I need to remember my real life is valuable, too. Scott wasn't entirely wrong when he told me I live every day like it's a fantasy.

On my way into the dining hall, I toss the brochure into the trash.

34

"This is ridiculous."

I have no other word for what's unfolding in front of us. Erik faces Val, the men circling each other, wooden swords in hand. They watch each other with feigned fury, weighing their moves. Each is dressed in Elytheum garb, Val-Fred in one of his costumes and Erik having picked up black, muscle-emphasizing garments of his own from the student store.

"I think it's hot," Brit declares.

"Just because it's ridiculous doesn't mean it can't be hot," Laurel points out in agreement.

I shake my head in disapproval. The duel is held on the campus's soccer field, where there's plenty of room for Experience-goers to gather and cheer on their favorite fictional crush—Val, namely. The audience is heavily in his favor. When Erik darts forward, striking a tap of his sword on Val's shoulder, he raises his arms to the crowd, earning only gasps of worry for his opponent. Fred holds his shoulder, pretending the wound really hurt, and I notice Amelia biting her lip in worry.

Scott and I dutifully cheer for Erik, who drops his character's vengeful determination for only a moment to smile in our direction.

The pair continue their sparring. It's evident they've practiced stage fighting—each of them knows how to accentuate the moves and play up the emotion, enriching the choreography with natural drama. When Val evens the match, landing a strike on Erik, Erik exaggerates his recoil the way Fred had.

Even so, with the context I have on the duel, I know the pretend fighting draws on very nonfictional resentment. Real anger flashes in Erik's eyes—he's self-conscious, I know, of Fred showing him up in front of Heather.

Of course, Erik uses the feeling to fuel his performance. He flies toward his brother, who deftly dodges. They move fast, with impressive skill. "You stole what was mine!" Erik snarls. No one knows what the accusation means for his Elytheum character, but it doesn't matter. Everyone leans in.

"No, I did something much worse," Fred retorts, effortlessly continuing the half-invented scene. "I *won* it."

Erik roars and lunges forward, landing another hit. The audience cries out in dismay. Except Scott and me, of course.

"Then I," Erik vows dramatically, "shall win it back."

I can't help glancing at Heather Winters, who watches from the closest duel-side seat. The author looks quite amused, if impartial. She neither cheers nor gasps when Fred wheels his sword and sweeps a carefully controlled stroke close to Erik's chest.

As the fight continues, something starts to shift. The men's faces relax, their movements loosen. They almost look like they're . . . having fun, swinging and sizing each other up, planning each of their exciting maneuvers with more cooperation than competition.

Watching them, I find the duel ridiculous and hot—and kind of inspiring. Maybe they needed the guise of Elytheum to share their feelings out in the open, and now, freed in fantasy, they can enjoy each other's company and mutual joy in their craft. Or, possibly they just needed an outlet for their anger, which they've released in physical exertion. I wonder whether Erik, duel instigator, is a secret genius of sibling relationships.

Fred swipes at Erik, and Erik leaps back, a laugh escaping him for a moment. It makes Fred smile. Then they remember their audience and fix performed scowls on their faces. Or, they remember the audience until Fred's sword goes flying and he somersaults to retrieve it, earning an impressed whoop from his "opponent."

It's not only adorable. It's heartening. Their fantastical characters have somehow summoned their most real selves. The boys who probably work out and train together, who roughhoused as children.

Brothers whose dream can't divide them. Not really.

They rush together, swords crossed in front of their chests. In the midst of their wrestling to overpower each other, their lips move, inconspicuous words exchanged under the guise of combat. Although I can't hear what they're saying, I notice Erik nod and Fred smile.

Then they break apart, pushing each other away with duel-evocative intensity. Erik shouts out in anger, heightening the moment. They square off at opposite ends of the makeshift arena, eyeing each other like competing champions for a queen's hand or fierce enemies meeting on the field of war.

The whole audience hushes in rapt anticipation—I mean, honestly, I would watch an Elytheum show starring either one of them—until Erik charges, fiery conviction in his eyes.

Fred doesn't flinch. He waits, his stance ready. The perfect image of the fae warrior who stood down the darkest enemies of Elytheum.

When Erik rushes him, at the last possible moment, Fred swings his foot wide as if to sweep Erik's legs out from under him.

Although Fred makes no physical contact, the effect is marvelous. Erik manages to reverse his direction with what looks like incredible physical strength. Mastering his own momentum, he falls backward, pretending to impale himself on his own sword.

Fred—or rather, Val—picks up the moment's drama. Riven with sudden anguish, he rushes to his counterpart's side, where he drops to his knees. "Brother!" he cries out. "No!"

And Erik . . . Erik puts on a death fit for the screen.

In front of his rapt audience is not my enthusiastic, flirtatious, occasionally goofy roommate. Instead, it's the man who I know has devoted years of effort to his craft. He's Shakespearean. He's HBO-worthy.

"Forgive me," he exhales, imploring Fred. His eyelids flutter. He clutches Fred's hand with failing strength.

Even the audience, who had been rooting against him the whole time, has gone silent, immersed in his performance. I sneak a look and—yes, even Heather seems genuinely impressed. When Erik lets his head droop back, a hushed moment of reverence descends over the crowd.

Until Fred starts a slow clap. Immediately, Scott and I join in.

And when Erik opens his eyes, having given his "death" the proper finality, everyone is applauding him.

I recognize the look on Erik's face. Not just joy—it's more. It's the portrait of wanting to remember exactly this moment forever. The look of dreams coming to life. He regards his audience, grinning, a combination of humbled and exhilarated.

As I watch, his gaze *doesn't* find Heather. Instead, he looks up at Fred, who helps him to his feet.

"That was incredible," Fred exclaims. "The way you stopped

yourself while charging me? I know we worked on a variation of that, but to do it midair?" He shakes his head in earnest astonishment. "You've got to teach me that one."

Erik demurs, visibly delighted. "Well, you set me up perfectly. It wouldn't have worked with anyone else. And come on, I had to do *something* after you executed that somersault, man."

They clap each other on the shoulder, and in front of us, their enthusiastic crowd, they bow in unison. The duel concluded, everyone rises from the stands, dispersing into the daylight. I overhear the chatter of fans, and well, I expect a few scrolls with phone numbers addressed to my roommate will appear under our door in the coming day.

We don't depart with the rest of the crowd. Instead, we join our famous dueling friends. Erik and Fred have moved past recapping their fight to seeming to reenact their favorite moments in slow motion. When I near Fred while he's walking Erik through his somersault, I notice blood on the younger man's arm.

"Fred, you're injured!" I exclaim, nothing performed in my concern.

Neither the observation nor the reality appears to distress the brothers, oddly. Instead, they exchange a conspiring glance, one I don't have the chance to analyze when Amelia hears me from feet away and comes running over.

"Oh no," she gasps. She reaches unhesitatingly for Fred's arm, examining the long puncture intently.

"It's fine," Fred assures her. "It happened during the somersault. I hit a rock or something."

"You'll let our medic look at it, right?" Amelia presses. Her worry does not pass for professional diligence. I've never heard her this wound up, not over work deadlines or intimidating meetings. "I want to make sure you don't get an infection . . ." she frets.

"Of course," Fred replies readily. "Will you escort me there? I feel a little faint," he admits.

Having a way to help appears to fortify Amelia. With rather adorable resolve, she decisively pulls his massive arm around her slight shoulders.

"Lean on me," she says.

Fred does. As they walk away, he glances at Erik, who gives him a silent salute.

Scott puts it together. "Did you . . . plan that?" he asks my roommate with genuine curiosity.

"He gave me my moment in the spotlight," Erik says, "so I gave him what I knew he wanted." He nods after Amelia escorting Fred, who is playing up how valiantly he is withstanding the pain of his wound.

"It didn't happen in the somersault," I surmise.

Erik smiles. "The tips of these wooden swords are quite sharp," he observes.

I have to laugh. Even with their impressive performance, I wasn't giving them *enough* credit for their cooperation. "You two make a great team," I say honestly.

"We do, don't we?" Erik puffs up his chest. His gaze, ever eager, roams over the duel field as if he's remembering his past glory. He has every right. "We had the audience eating out of the palms of our hands," he says.

"You know who was included in that audience," Scott points out. Heather hasn't left—she's in conversation with a courageous fan who approached her after the duel. "Are you going to go talk to her? Now's your moment," Scott urges him. "Jennifer and I saw how impressed she was."

Erik looks at the author for a single moment of yearning. I know Erik has fantasies of his own flashing in his eyes—Hollywood meetings, red carpets, awards afterparties. His fantasies carried him here just like mine did.

Then his eyes refocus on us, returning him to reality.

"Fred is the better Val," he declares. "He's doing it all for the girl after all. What could be more in character than that? I cede to him," Erik concludes with courtly finality, fitting for the naming of the new Lord of Night.

I reach out impulsively and hug him. "I'm so proud of you," I say.

Erik looks pleased, if somewhat startled. When I release him, he sweeps his hair from his forehead self-consciously.

"Perhaps if I fall in love I can really challenge him for the role one day," he ventures, eyeing his former audience like his own queen or demoness could wait among them. "Alas, until then I will content myself with the many commercial gigs I am up for. I'm sure I can bring what I've learned from being Val to the deodorant ad I'm shooting next month."

He looks to us, inspired.

"Would you run lines with me, actually? It involves my working up a sweat walking dogs who can, of course, smell me," he explains seriously. "You would play the inner voices of the dogs."

I smile. Not only do I admire Erik's optimism, I have done plenty of acting over the past week. Acting like a lady of Elytheum, acting like I flirt with fae often. Acting fine with my rival showing up here unannounced. I can definitely handle the voice of a judgmental dog.

"Of course, Erik," I say. "We would love to."

35

I read with Scott in the candlelight, my head in his lap on the couch in my common room. We have my suite to ourselves while Erik has a reconciliatory dinner with Fred. It's quiet, the rustling of pages offering the only accompaniment to the dancing shadows the candles cast on the walls. Scott's scent surrounds me, and I feel his every gentle shift while the hours and the chapters pass.

It is incredibly romantic.

He's reading a book I recommended on my Kindle, which of course I packed with me—I would never find myself in an unfamiliar location without multiple means of escape into fiction. It's titled *Poisoned Legacy*, and it's romantasy, like Elytheum. It's an indie title he hasn't read, and I suspect he might enjoy it because it's set amid academia, featuring alchemists competing in their powerful studies.

I'm continuing my reread of *The Shattered Court*. Although, really, I'm focused on Scott. It's marvelous dating someone who loves reading the way I do. I can't wait for him to recommend his favorites to me, just like I can't wait to share with him more of mine. I continually steal glances at him, wanting to witness his every reaction while he reads. When he laughs, I look up with unrestrained eagerness, Kethryn and Val vanishing from my imagination. "What?" I ask him.

Scott smiles, amused, and clicks forward on the Kindle. "Are you going to ask me what I'm reacting to every time I make a sound or have a facial expression?" he asks with good humor while he continues reading.

I consider. "Possibly, yes. I like knowing what you find funny or surprising. In fact"—I sit up, ensuring he understands the importance of my edict—"when you get to chapter twelve you *have* to tell me. I want to watch you read."

He laughs. "You can't really just want to watch me read."

I lay my head back in his lap. "It might be better than reading myself," I say.

Scott sets the Kindle aside. When he leans down and presses the softest kiss to my lips, everything disappears. Elytheum and *Poisoned Legacy*, candlelight and the night outside and the couch under me. The whole world pauses.

"You're cute," Scott says.

"I like sharing things with you."

"I like it, too," he assures me, his sincerity unmistakable. "I'll let you know when I reach chapter twelve," he promises me.

"Good," I whisper. Happiness wells up inside me. Everything is perfect. Impossibly perfect. And I realize this night has surpassed even my wildest expectations for the week. I knew I wasn't driving down the interstate into the real enchanted land of Elytheum—I came here to experience something *like* a fantasy. Instead I found a fantasy itself, one I hadn't even known to imagine with the man next to me. I feel wonderfully, exhilaratingly content.

The very next moment, it scares me.

Impossibly perfect. What I'm feeling doesn't exist in the real world. Does it? It's ridiculous to hope everything will work out like this forever, my very own HEA. Hasn't everyone in my life reminded me it's unrealistic to expect fantasy from reality? Amelia? Jordan? My parents, who did not hide their dismay when I changed my major from Accounting to English? Even Scott himself?

Why would I ignore everyone—*everyone*—saying I need to remember life doesn't look like my daydreams? How delusional would it make me *not* to expect disappointment when reality resembles fantasy?

Something must be about to crack. My heart, surely.

I sit up, the notion making me dizzy, and reach for my laptop on the coffee table. I need something to ground me. Work. Bills. Anything. Feeling Scott's questioning eyes on me, I find the list of MFA programs I was looking into open on the screen.

They read like fantastical places now. *Hollisboro. Yale. UCLA. Elytheum. Nightfell. The Western Court.* No less out of reach. No less ridiculous. What's the difference? Who was I kidding?

I quickly close out of the page, feeling nauseated. I need an imperfection to hold on to, to press sharp points into my palm and remind me what's real. I need something disappointing enough to convince me the rest of my life won't fall apart.

"I don't think I'm going to go for an MFA after all," I declare, my voice coming out harried.

Scott glances up, startled. He doesn't respond right away, instead clearly considering the right response.

"Okay," he says calmly after a moment. "If that's what you want."

"I mean, I don't know what I want," I reply. Deciding against doing an MFA program is not helping, which scares me even more. Do I have a *fear* of fantasy now? Has it made my appetite for imperfection endless?

Scott puts down *Poisoned Legacy*. He gives me his full focus.

Focus I never saw in our fraught first year, not like he's determining my weaknesses and strategizing my professional demise—focus like I'm the greatest, most intricate love story he's ever known. It's perfect.

Dangerously perfect. Dangerously magical.

"What's going on, Jen?" he asks seriously.

I rub my forehead, spiraling. "I—I don't know," I manage. It's honest, if nothing else. "Maybe you were right when you said not everything is a fantasy. I have a good life. I don't need to risk it on some—dream, or whatever this is."

Scott studies me. When he reaches for my hand, I don't pull away, immediately greedy for his touch.

"This doesn't sound like you," he says. His voice is painfully kind. One more *perfection* for me to worry about. "You're the one who taught me to be unafraid of striving for everything," he reminds me.

"I know," I reply, my restless fingers fretting over his knuckles. "I guess I never expected I would really get it. And now, here you are and you're . . . just . . . perfect. Look at this moment!"

I fling my hand out in indication. Scott peers around the room, not understanding.

"It's perfect," I say miserably. "We're reading by candlelight. My head fits perfectly in your lap. Your hair is swooping in exactly the way I like. You're supportive and sexy and incredible and far *too* perfect."

Scott starts to smile. "I'm not sure my hair swoop is grounds for you to give up your dreams," he says delicately.

"No, it is!" I insist. "It's that good!"

"Thank you?"

"It's not a compliment! I wish it were less good!"

"Okay." Scott closes his other hand over mine, quieting my

fingers. "What is this? You're really not going to apply to MFA programs?"

Pulling my hand from his, I get up abruptly and pace the room. Indulging in Scott's measured compassion is like eating only puff pancakes for every meal. I know I would feel good in the moment—I just wouldn't like how I felt later.

I force myself to put my every fear into words. "What if I don't get in? Or what if I get in and I hate it?" I ask. The possibilities feel frighteningly immediate. Frighteningly real. "What if it pulls me away from you and from the life I already have?"

Scott watches me, his expression gentle. His calm is kind of comforting, and it's kind of maddening. If he's not as dizzyingly daunted as I am, he's obviously not understanding me. "You're scared," he summarizes. "That's okay."

"I don't want to be scared! I want to be Lady Jennifer!" I exclaim.

Scott cannot restrain his smile now, and while I know my fantastical invocation should embarrass me, it doesn't. Scott accepts me exactly as I am. Which just reinforces the problem. Why on earth—why in any realm, real or imaginary—would I jeopardize us for some flight of fancy I had in a lecture hall a few days ago?

"Who," Scott asks gently, "is Lady Jennifer?"

"She . . ." I struggle to put the inspiration I've found this week into words. "She's the heroine of her own life," I say. "The best, bravest version of me."

Scott understands. Of course he does. He nods in earnest.

"So be Lady Jennifer," he encourages me.

I fall silent. He makes it sound easy. Just like my favorite authors make fae feel like old friends, make dark curses feel like relatable problems, make fantastical realms feel like home—Scott makes it sound like I can just *find* the courage to chase the life I want.

I don't know if I can.

"What if some fantasies *can't* be real?" I venture, my voice fragile. "What if making them real only ruins them?" I go on. "And then you're left with nothing. Not even a dream."

It's why I'm here, in the end, isn't it? In this fake fantasy for the week. The sigils painted over my door hold no magical power. The scenery in the painting on my wall does not exist. I mean, it's not even a painting. It's Adobe Illustrator in a fancy frame.

The closest *I*, Jennifer Worth, can come to magic or daydreams is . . . imitation. Loving, but impermanent and fake.

In its own dark way, the Elytheum Experience is the perfect reminder that I live in the *real* world.

Watching me, Scott's expression shifts. Some quiet sadness invades his gaze. Unlike me, he does find his courage. I know he doesn't want to ask his next question. "This isn't just about the MFA," he guesses. "Is it?"

I skirt his eyes.

His question—this conundrum—is splitting me in half. I want to ignore these feelings raging inside me, but I know they won't go away. I push myself to follow Scott's own example. He was strong enough to ask the question. I can muster the strength to answer it. Just a little heroism. Just enough for now. "No," I say to the floor.

"It's okay," Scott says.

I look up, my heart clinging fervently onto his improbable reply. *It's okay? How the fuck is it okay, Scott?* Right now "okay" is the hardest fantasy to uphold.

Scott sees my lip wobble. Concern cuts deep down his expression. "Don't cry, baby," he hushes me.

I only cry harder. The words come easier now, at least, with the sobs. "This *can't* be real. It can't be something that lasts. Not because I don't want that—I desperately do. That's the problem. When I'm desperate for something, then I . . . want it too badly," I explain, needing him to understand how it's the happiest and hardest realization. "You know I do. You *told* me I do. I pretend the impossible is happening. I mean, a week ago, I really didn't like you. And now I'm falling for you? How is that possible?"

"I'm falling for you, too," Scott replies without hesitation.

I meet his eyes reluctantly. Hope? Or fact? He searches my face like he's looking for clues on what to say, on how to fight my fears with me.

"Just because you want something doesn't mean it's not real," he says gently. "This is real. Which is scary. It's terrifying having something so important to you. Something you care for deeply. I understand, believe me."

I know he does. I know he means how he kept his relationships insubstantial in hopes of avoiding the pain of rejection, how he knew the pain of dashed dreams and was determined to protect himself from losing more of them. And I remember what happened— he ended up hurt anyway.

"It was just easier when these feelings were only something I could read about," I say, the words choking my chest. "I could feel everything but at the end of the day, I could . . . close the book. And now . . ."

I look to the copy of *The Shattered Court* on the couch, then to Scott himself. His hair swoop. His inquisitive, kind eyes.

"Now you're—beyond anything I've read about, and if this ends badly, I can't just—close this book. I can't—I don't—"

He rushes up to me. He holds my face in his hands, urgent and desperate and loving. "No. No, you can't just close the book," he replies. "It'll hurt like hell if this falls apart. I know it will, Jen. I know."

He hugs me close.

"I know love is easier when it's a fantasy, but is it better? Or is it just safer?" he asks. When I say nothing, he continues. "You have to risk something to make it real."

I hold him, wrestling with myself. I know I've used fantasy as an escape, and the real world offers none of its forgiveness. It's devastating to imagine my dreams coming *true*, only to lose their luster when Scott and I fight, or I don't get into an MFA program, or long distance strains our relationship to breaking. It wouldn't just close the cover on us. It would rip pages out, whole chapters. The ending, even. Leaving me holding only the ruined remains of our once wonderful story.

What if I'm *not* brave? What if nothing goes the way I imagine, and my life ends up completely . . . ordinary? I would have nothing to write about. Scott wouldn't want me. Who would want Jennifer the Ordinary? I wouldn't be a heroine. I would be no one of note.

You have to risk something to make it real.

I want to say *You're right* or *I will* or *Okay.* Except those words would only come out disingenuous. Imaginary. Fake. No different from magic spells recited from the pages of my favorite stories of sorcery. The real world demands honesty. Not enchanting fictions about myself.

"I don't know how," I admit.

His hands lower to my waist, and he withdraws to look at me. He smiles sadly.

"Sometimes you have to fight for your fantasy. It's not an easy escape from reality. It's a dream you have to believe in even when it's hard. You taught me that," he says.

"Maybe I was wrong. I've been wrong so many times," I say weakly. "I've believed in a lie before."

Something crumbles in his eyes. "I'm not a lie, Jennifer. I'm real."

I pull out of his arms, knowing what I'm about to say will end this. And knowing I have to say it anyway. "You came here to become a character from a book."

Scott says nothing. It's horrible. He meets my gaze—like he's searching, scouring for clues in a scavenger hunt with no prize and no ending—and I hold his stare, my heart pounding painfully.

And then his expression closes up.

"You know deep down I've shown you the real me, Jennifer," he explains. His voice is unyielding, but not the dry dismissals of my rival. It's worse. "And yet you're pushing me away. Don't pretend you're doubting how real this is for me, how much I care about you. It's something else."

Panic shoots into me when he collects his phone and key card from the couch. "Where are you going?" I ask.

"If this was all just a flight of fancy for you—a fling with a guy who could halfway convince you that your fictional crush could be real—then I guess *I* was the romantic, swept up in a fairy-tale romance this time." His voice breaks. There's no fire of competition in his eyes, no anger, no friendship. Only disappointment. Heartbreak. "I should have known I never could have been what you really wanted. I'll leave you to enjoy the rest of the Experience without me," Scott says.

He walks to the doorway. I want to stop him. I want to erase these past minutes.

I feel new tears rolling down my face. "You *are* what I wanted," I say.

Scott shakes his head. "Not enough, though. I hope you win

that scavenger hunt," he says. "You deserve to experience what I can't give you." With one last look, he walks out and closes my door.

The quiet in my room, comfortable just minutes ago, is suddenly suffocating. The candlelight dances innocently on the walls. I sink onto the couch, staring at the door. I'm light-headed from how fast the night changed . . . and yet, I don't go after him. It's cleaner this way. On Monday we can go back to hating each other at work. It'll be like this week never happened.

The thought leaves me sobbing.

I hear his door open and close, and a few minutes later, open again. The sounds of his rolling suitcase follow his footsteps into the hallway. His door closes once more.

He's really leaving.

After his footsteps fade down the stairwell, I walk shakily into my bedroom. The night feels horribly like when I got here. I'm alone again. My heart hurts again.

It's frustrating to feel like the exact same girl who walked in here nearly a week ago, when everyone else has found what they needed. Scott embraced romanticism. Erik forgave his brother. Amelia has released something making her miserable.

And I'm just heartsick once more.

I look around the room, and the memorable details meet my gaze. The coverlet, the candelabra, the painting. The runes over the door.

It's the room of a main character, an occupant worthy of Elytheum. And if I sit in here and mope, I've failed in one of the main character's fundamental roles. I haven't changed. I need to grow. Val does. Kethryn does.

How can I have the Elytheum Experience without doing the same for myself?

In the midst of my determination, my eyes land on the folded clue on my desk. The one Scott found in the library and left in my pocket. I snatch it up, thumbing his handwriting on the outside. For the first time, I unfold the parchment to read the clue inside.

From the gates of the city, choose honor over power
Follow my journey and ring in the new day on the hour

The final clue.
I know the answer instantly.

36

I knock urgently on my friends' door, wired from too many Scott-related emotions to count, combined with my excitement for solving the final clue. I couldn't just sit in my room watching the clock, stuck in my head.

It's Brit who opens the door. "Hey?" she says, half questioning.

I find—for the first time—neither she nor Laurel decked out in Elytheum garb. They're in their PJs, getting ready for bed. Brit's T-shirt reads SYRACUSE UNIVERSITY in heavy lettering, and I make a mental note to ask her how she liked the campus and the city. Just in case.

Laurel looks up from her phone. "Hey, Jen. What's up?"

"Can we hang out? If you're going to bed, that's fine, I can go," I assure them, the words rushing from me. "It's just—Scott left, and I solved the final clue. I'm going to collect it at midnight."

Brit's eyebrows rise halfway up her forehead.

"Don't you dare leave after dropping that many bombshells! Get in here!" She ushers me in, and I step into their room, grateful. "Sit," Brit demands. "Spill."

I do. While the girls climb onto their beds, I sit in Laurel's desk chair, where I proceed to explain everything. Scott. My MFA and long-distance fears. I'm grateful for how sympathetically they listen. When I've finished the epic saga of my not-exactly-heroic journey, they comfort me. They tell me it'll be okay. They tell me broken hearts can always heal.

They have questions, however.

"Does . . . that mean you don't have a date to the ball?" Brit ventures.

I falter. With everything else going on, I'd honestly forgotten the upcoming masquerade. "I guess not," I say honestly.

Laurel smiles. "We'll all go together," she says. "It'll be fun."

It's not difficult to accept her reassurance. "Yeah. It will," I reply.

And I realize, I'm *not* in the same place I was when I arrived here. I have them, and Erik, and Amelia right nearby. Every story of heroism involves the enduring power of friendship, doesn't it? I guess I've done one part right.

"And if you've solved your final clue . . ." Laurel goes on indicatively, "you'll probably have a dance with Val anyway."

"I haven't solved it yet," I clarify. "I just know how to."

"Cryptic," Laurel replies playfully.

My instinct is to remain vague, hoarding my clues close like I've done for the entire scavenger hunt. We all have. But . . . why? I don't need to win a date with Val, or a dance. I've already won one prize—the friends in the room with me right now. And Val . . . Val isn't really the fantasy anymore, is he?

"How about," I say slowly, "instead of me telling you about the final clue . . . want to find it with me?"

I receive the response I expected. Brit jumps to her knees on her bed. "Obviously!"

"We just have to wait until midnight," I explain, flush with happiness. Erik's words of unexpected wisdom return to me. *One big, happy alliance*.

"Ooh, midnight," Brit echoes enthusiastically. "Vibes."

"What do you want to do until then?" Laurel asks.

I look around the room. My friends' masks are made, their dresses finished. There's no Experience programming. Just . . . us. Movies, gossip, trading music recommendations and favorite books. Just ordinary life.

No, ordinary *magic*.

I feel excitement rise in me.

"Anything," I say.

———

Erik texts me an hour later, having noticed my absence and Scott's unlocked door and empty room. I invite him to Brit and Laurel's, and he joins our hangout, visibly eager and flattered. I message Amelia as well and receive no response, which I figure means she's gone to sleep, probably needing an early morning tomorrow to set up for the masquerade.

With tomorrow being the last full day of the Experience, we empty out our mini fridges into one shared snack feast. I personally consider our collection of pretzels and peanut butter, yogurt and Oreos, tortilla chips and salsa no less fit for queens and heroes than night cakes, puff pancakes, or sweet-spiced stew.

We've just commenced dipping the Oreos into the peanut butter, like geniuses do, when Brit's phone rings. "You know what time it is," Brit says to Laurel.

While I watch, Brit picks up the phone. I don't need to hear the conversation to know what it's about. The crying piercing through the tinny speakers is clear enough. Brit puts the phone on speaker and a moment later she starts to sing softly into her phone, her voice traveling miles away to her daughter.

When she's completed four refrains, only silence greets us on the other end. Stephanie offers profuse whispered thanks, to which Brit urges her mom to get some sleep.

"Nice to get away for a week," I joke when she hangs up.

Brit's expression changes. In place of the larger-than-life, fearsomely passionate clue hunter and fae fashionista I've gotten to know, she looks introspective. Conflicted, even, but okay with it.

"Not really," she replies gently. "I miss her every day. I knew I would. It's not something I ever want to escape. But . . ." She presses one palm to her knee, thinking. "I want to be the best person *I* can be. I want to come home inspired, and patient, and joyful. Which sometimes means protecting my relationship with the things I love," she says. "I want my daughter to learn to do the same."

Laurel smiles softly. I remember my own rereads, realizing I understand exactly what she means. Fantasy is often equated with escapism, but *was* I escaping? Fleeing from my unsatisfying relationships into the comforting embrace of Elytheum's perfection?

Or was I seeking something else? Inspiration? Strength? Hope? Some of both, I think.

No further baby-related phone calls interrupt us, and the next hour passes quickly. We watch Erik's past commercials on YouTube while he mouths his lines from memory. We vow to start a virtual book club.

Finally, eleven thirty comes.

I announce it's time to head out for the clue. With my arm linked in Laurel's, I lead the group down the stairs and into the night. The warm summer wind fortifies us, not to mention the peanut butter and Oreos.

When the walkway leads us past the main hall, I notice lights on inside.

No, *one* light on. Amelia's office. I recognize my friend's silhouette pacing in front of her window.

"Wait here," I ask my fearless clue-hunting party.

While they do, I enter the hall. Minutes later, I emerge victorious, with a bleary-eyed but laughing Amelia. It only took one dramatic invocation of *Lady Amelia, the court—nay, the entire realm!—needs your courage and resourcefulness!* Obviously, it worked. The rest of the fellowship cheers when Amelia joins us, and we set off once more.

We pass the front gates of the College of Hollisboro—the gates I entered on my first night here, no idea what waited for me— where the grand wrought iron leads into the idyllic town. *From the gates of the city, choose honor over power . . .*

We don't go through them.

Instead, we continue on the campus path, heading deeper into the college, with just enough magic in the night to transform us from ordinary people into heroes on a quest. From fans brought together only days ago into friends.

37

"Are you sure?" Laurel asks.

I understand her hesitation. I really do. We stand at the base of the bell tower, which rises into the night sky.

High into the night sky.

"I don't want to climb ten flights of stairs for you to have gotten the clue wrong," Laurel explains.

I face my friends. Brit peers up the stone spire with uncertainty. Even Erik massages his duel-weary legs in what looks like reluctant preparation. Only Amelia reserves her practiced neutrality for our scavenger hunting efforts. My questing party needs inspiration. "You don't have faith in my Elytheum knowledge?" I return.

"I mean . . ." Laurel draws out the syllable. "After bedtime my faith in anyone's justifications for climbing a hundred steps diminishes greatly."

Brit looks to Amelia. "Can't you let us know if Jen is right?" she pleads.

"Absolutely not," Amelia says sweetly. Her unhelpfulness is impressive. Despite her disenchantment with organizing the Experience, she's devoted to ensuring we have an authentic scavenger hunt. Even if it means climbing a hundred wasted stairs.

"It's here," I say. I unroll the parchment, to at last reveal to them the final clue. I haven't yet explained my logic, and my questmates have gone on faith until now. "*From the gates of the city, choose honor over power. Follow my journey and ring in the new day on the hour,*" I recite. "It references Gatekeeper Gravesend. I know it does. Remember his chapter in *Risen*? In the start of the series, instead of having him executed for conspiracy, Kethryn has him stripped of his estate and assigned to guard the city gates. He goes from a lord to a foot soldier. A nobody. We don't hear about the guy for *five books*—until the forces of Darkness come to invade the city and offer him his old estate if he lets them in."

Amelia smiles softly. I remind myself it's probably just from the memory of one of our favorite parts of the series.

"He *refuses*," I continue. "They descend on him, and in the final moments of his life, Gravesend climbs the gate's bell tower," I cannot help emphasizing. "He rings the chimes, raising the city's defenses. Choosing honor over power. He dies unknown—having saved Kethryn and the court and everyone inside."

Everyone is solemn now.

"The '*gates of the city*' is meant to lead us to the wrong place," I insist. "Everyone is going to remember the Hollisboro gates we came through when we got here. Instead, we're supposed to follow the *story*. The character. *From the gates of the city . . . Follow my journey.*"

Honestly, I wouldn't have figured the clue out instantly without Scott's departure. In my room, I had character growth and change on my mind. While Gatekeeper Gowan Gravesend isn't exactly a fan favorite like Val, he represents one of the story's greatest messages. In an unexpected flourish, Winters devotes one single chapter of *The Risen Court* to Gravesend's perspective, where he makes his fatal, fateful decision. In his nine pages, he is the main character. Like anyone can be, the series implies, who experiences kindness and nobility and chooses to reflect it in themselves.

Amelia and the organizers wanted the final clue to resonate with Elytheum readers who understood one of the series' deeper messages. It's perfectly poetic. A reminder, in a week designed to make guests feel like intrepid court characters, that everyone has heroism in them.

Hence, the bell tower. *Ring in the new day on the hour.* Like Elytheum's unrecognized hero, we're meant to ring in midnight literally.

"I think she's right," Erik finally offers.

"Yes, I'm afraid so," Laurel joins in, her eyes traveling up the tower.

"You're welcome to stay behind," Brit replies. "*I* want to know what's up there."

Laurel looks indignant. "Hell no, I'm not staying behind."

Her pronouncement rallies the party. Everyone starts for the stairs—everyone, I notice, except Amelia. I pause behind the group. "You have to come," I implore her.

Amelia rubs her elbow. Yearning and restraint wrestle in her eyes as she stares up into the night. "I'm not sure I should," she replies.

"No," I insist firmly. I face her from the doorway to the stairwell. "You need to experience some of this for yourself. You've worked incredibly hard for everyone else," I insist. My friends, paused at the bottom of the steps, nod in agreement, all eyes on Amelia. "You deserve a moment off the clock," I say.

Amelia hesitates a second more.

With a smile spreading over her face, her gaze sparks. "Let's do it," she declares.

I grin. It's wonderful, witnessing the Amelia I know emerge

from her exhaustion. The Amelia who would urge me to stay up one more hour of a readathon, who would spend every lunch for weeks insisting I read whatever she was championing at Parthenon. Amelia isn't Amelia without fandom-level enthusiasm powering her.

We dash up the stairs. I have to admit, a week of hauling myself up four flights to my suite has prepared me for the challenge. Excitement does the rest.

I reach the top first, where I overlook the campus from the railing while the rest of the group follows. Everyone lines up with me, and we gaze out over the quiet world.

"I have . . . to say . . ." Amelia announces, catching her breath, "when I planned this . . . I did not anticipate . . . climbing those stairs . . . myself."

"It's worth it," Erik replies. His voice is hushed with uncharacteristic reverence, and I'm reminded he has his own compelling gravitas when he wants.

Amelia's gaze softens over the campus.

"Yeah," she says. "It is."

We stare out into the night. "It's magic," Brit says. "Look at the fireflies."

"Look at the stars," Laurel replies.

While we watch, lights dance on the inky expanse of empty lawns in front of us. Above the dark horizon, the stars shine in reply, midnight mirroring the sparkling earth.

I say nothing, emotion welling in my chest. It *is* magic. Magic lingers in inconspicuous places. It isn't unreachable. It's been here the whole time, merely waiting to be found. In a clear night, in a sky that has hung above the world unchanged for years. In middle school teachers, and commercial actors, and those who don't know what's next for them. In friendship and fandom, love and loyalty.

Magic and heroism exist in the ordinary as easily as the extraordinary. Something doesn't need to be untouchable or imaginary or even perfect to be a fantasy. It exists wherever you're willing to look for it.

"Well, Jennifer," Erik prompts me softly, "ring in the new day."

I smile, turning to the bell. With the world at my back—waiting for me, ready—I reach for the cord hanging on the post by the bell.

And with a hard pull, I send the bell ringing into the night, echoing the refrain of our victory.

While my friends cheer, my heart pounds steady and proud. I didn't need epic heroism to have this moment. I wasn't a demoness or a queen or fae. Just myself.

The greatest quests never end up where one expects. It's what makes them something more—it makes them stories.

Eventually, the night is still. Only us and the fireflies. Laurel stands next to me, and when I glance over, I notice she looks sad. "Hey," I say softly, murmuring too low for the group to hear. "You okay?"

I know I was right to ask when Laurel is quiet for a long pause. "I'm just not looking forward to going home," she finally admits.

She doesn't need to explain why. I know what going home really means. A broken heart and a return to reality. Brit was right, and fantasy doesn't have to be an escape, but sometimes escapes are what help us get through the darkest days.

"That's the magic of Elytheum, though. You can take it home with you," I reply. "It sounds to me like you might be due for a reread. I just started one myself. Maybe we can buddy read. I'll send you reactions at ungodly hours of the night with links to my favorite fics for expansions."

Laurel smiles. "Yeah? You're sure?"

"Are you kidding? There's nothing better than reliving my favorite moments and sharing them with someone new," I say sincerely.

"Good luck finding a fic I don't know about," she replies, her tone playful.

I smile, seeing the hope return to her eyes. "Oh you're so on. You know I love a challenge."

As the bell finally stops resounding in the night, Laurel turns to the group. Her voice stronger, she voices the obvious question. "Now what?"

I shrug. I don't have an answer. Which I'm okay with. Not having all the answers only means a story isn't finished yet.

The rest of my court, my questing party, is more curious. Everyone looks to Amelia, who rolls her eyes, feeling herself coerced into providing just one hint. "Nowhere to go but back down, right?" she offers.

I eye her, questioning. It's not what I expected. Did I get the riddle wrong? There's no way. *It's okay if I did*, I remind myself as I follow my friends down the steps. I had this moment, the perfect Elytheum Experience moment, with them, watching the night. Victory looks like sharing wonder with your companions. It looks like new friends and old. It looks like pride in yourself no matter what. Like continuing to find joy even when your heart is shattered.

The realization makes me gasp. *I'm okay.* I don't have to fear heartbreak. I can survive it, like I have this week.

This moment was exactly what it was meant to be, and it surpassed any prize. No scavenger hunt victory could match the experience of looking out over the glittering horizon, or the joy and adventure of finding each clue. No heartbreak could wreck sharing this with my friends.

Who, I notice, have gone quiet, congregated at the bottom of the stairs. I join them, following the group's gaze.

Heather Winters herself waits outside the archway.

The architect of Elytheum wears a smile and a shining crown. Otherwise—apart from her fans and the ceremony of the Experience, and outside the familiar confines of her author photo on dust jackets—I'm struck by how normal she looks. If I didn't know who she was, I would guess she was clue hunting just like me. I recognize her dress, one of the ones I almost picked out from the fan-made costume store on campus.

I'm reminded Heather Winters has woken up here for the week like the rest of us, and like the rest of us she'll return home, into a life full of her own ambitions and insecurities. Like heroes and heroines, I suppose storytellers can be anyone.

While the rest of the crew files out into the night, I notice Amelia waiting in the stairwell. She nods me forth, not following, clearly wanting me to win my prize.

When I join my group, we're all silent, I guess a little awestruck. No one speaks until Heather does. "Only someone who has followed three clues to their destinations knows the ending lies here—and now, at midnight," she explains. "Who among you claims the victory?"

Erik shoves me lightly forward.

Heather's smile falls on me. I say nothing. *Favorite author* puts my appraisal of Heather Winters lightly, and I've never had the courage to speak to her, even at the many release events I've attended.

I remind myself why I'm here. What I've done.

Heroine time.

"I do," I say.

Silently, Heather removes her crown. She hands the shimmering circlet to me.

While the group watches me, hushed, I stare at it in my hands.

It's lovely, full of Elytheum details. The emblems of every court are interwoven in the metal, reminding me of the first clue. Fogberry sprigs, courtly gates, and majestic horses. "Our very own Lord Valance would love to thank you personally for your valiant efforts over an intimate dinner before the ball," Heather invites me.

I return her smile. I remember how the Val dinner had me rapt on the first night. How desperate I was to heal wounds and fix problems with imagination.

I've realized I don't need a crown or a book boyfriend. I've always had everything in my regular, ordinary, extraordinary life. I look up from the crown. "Can I . . . give it to someone else?" I ask.

Heather's eyes widen for a heartbeat. "Of course," she replies evenly.

I look back into the stairwell, where Amelia peeks out.

I wave her forward. While Amelia reluctantly emerges, I face Heather. "We didn't cheat, I promise," I say, noting the author looks intrigued, not indignant. "It's just, Amelia deserves it more than anyone for everything she's done this week. And, uh . . ." I pause. When I started the sentence, I should probably have known how I was going to explain my friend's love life to our favorite author ever.

Heather smirks.

"And there's no one our Val would rather spend an evening with," she finishes for me. "That is"—she eyes Amelia now—"if she feels the same?"

Amelia startles. I do as well.

"How, um . . ." Amelia fidgets. Admittedly, I don't know what's worse, explaining your workplace crush to your favorite author or to your *employer*. "How did you . . . ?"

Winters's smugness could rival Val's himself. "Authors are masters of observation," she says loftily, her haughtiness not hiding her obvious delight for Amelia. "Where do you think we get our inspiration?"

I grin. Honestly, it's validating. I'm not the only one who knows Fred is perfect for Amelia. Only the greatest ship designer in literary history agrees with me!

When I hold the crown out for Amelia, cautious light enters my friend's expression. "Well?" I press her.

And like the first morning after the realm defeated the Darkness—*Risen*, chapter seventy-one—the light spreads. Amelia's expression dances with the inimitable promise of future joy. She clasps the crown decisively.

Erik whoops, which makes Heather laugh. Her cheeks red, Amelia perches the crown on her raven tresses. "You're sure it's okay?" she asks Heather.

"My dear," Heather assures her, "Elytheum is my creation. I have always made the rules."

Amelia's happiness makes my heart feel full. I look to Heather. "Thank you," I say spontaneously. It feels easy speaking with her now. Like Everbane has his motto, I now have mine. *In joy, courage.* "Thank you for everything," I go on. "Your books have gotten me through so much. Taught me so much."

Heather smiles. Although I have no doubt she receives the compliment often, her acknowledgment is not perfunctory. "I'm happy they were there for you," she replies. "I hope they have been mirrors, helping you to see the beauty, strength, and love already within yourself. I like to imagine my characters aren't merely creations of my own head, nor are they strangers to those who find them." She nods to me. "May you recognize your own bravery in Kethryn."

She looks to my gathered friends.

"Your friends' loyalty in her court," she says.

Her gaze returns to me with indicative sparkle.

"Your partner's love in Val," she finishes.

I say nothing. In her pronouncements, I realize I've found something unlikelier than magic, rarer than fae or dragons. If nothing else, I arrived here the ultimate fan, and yet, with Heather's words, I find I have more to learn about Elytheum. About reading. About fantasy.

My whole life, books were my refuge. I have cherished my favorite stories for their power to enchant and divert me, to carry me away from Oklahoma and New York, from loneliness and heartache, into the company of characters I considered friends and loved ones, and into places I viewed as wondrous escapes from my own world.

And I was . . . wrong. The purest gift of reading isn't finding escape. It's finding yourself.

"I have," I say with new honesty. "They've made me see that life is a fantasy we make real every day."

The author smiles. "Very well said," she remarks. "Are you a writer?"

I blush, which is a relief, because I kind of expected my favorite author complimenting my choice of words would make me explode into fireworks or fly one hundred feet into the air.

"I think so," I say.

"Well"—Heather looks pleased—"like I said, authors are observant. And I was told a very kind and handsome young man turned in his room key earlier this night to depart the Experience."

Panic grips me. What was I thinking? How could I push Scott away, let him think he's not enough? I feel like I'm in my own *Exile Court*, lost in the Realms Past. Which leaves me with only one option.

I have to return from exile.

And I'm ready. With my friends, this magical night, I've gathered the confidence to face down anything. If Scott and I don't work out, I'll be okay, because my life is rich in dreams of every kind. I have friends. I have professional passions. I have *myself*.

Heather intuits my resolve. Her smile grows.

"Don't worry," she reassures me. "As all storytellers know—there is *always* time for a grand gesture."

38

If Kethryn had only experienced the power of caramel cappuccinos, I feel confident she could have defeated the court's enemies in one book instead of five.

It is the conclusion I reach as a result of all the caffeine coursing through me, despite the five hours of sleep I'm running on. Although, admittedly, giddy excitement mixed with a dash of panicky fear and annoyance are probably also contributing to my wakefulness.

When we returned from the bell tower, Amelia lightly abused her Elytheum Experience power to let me know Scott had asked them for help making a hotel reservation for the night to prepare for his drive home in the morning. *He hadn't left*. When we completed the clue, he would have heard the chimes of our midnight victory.

It was going to be easy. Wonderfully easy. I would get some sleep—it was two in the morning when I left my friends to head to bed—and wake up at six, ensuring I could head him off the next day.

When I returned to my room, I found myself noticing the familiar details, remembering how when Scott left they embarrassed me with their falseness, their imitation of fantasy. The candle, the painting. The runes over the door. In the afterglow of the night, something made me see the fantastical flourishes anew.

Not imitation. *Aspiration*. The room, the actors, the Experience—even I myself when I arrived here—dared to imagine the impossible, the fantastical. In a way, I'm doing the same now, with stakes higher than I ever expected. I'm finding my fortitude. *Lady Fucking Jennifer*. Perhaps, I ventured to wonder, she and I are one and the same.

I decided I would find out in the morning. Determinedly, I set my iPhone alarm for six a.m. Nothing would keep me from Scott. Not self-doubt, not insecurity about the fragility of dreams. *Nothing*.

For the first morning of my life, I overslept.

When my alarm rang, I guess I shut it off without knowing what I was doing, half asleep. It wasn't until Erik shook me awake an hour later, about to start his morning mirror time, that I realized what had happened.

I rushed to the hotel, where of course they wouldn't let me know whether Scott had checked out or not. They called up to his room for me, but there was no answer. When I texted him, I received the notification that he had turned his phone on "Do Not Disturb While Driving."

Stupid, responsible man who just *had* to start driving at six a.m. sharp. He couldn't have, I don't know, spent a lazy morning in Hollisboro or enjoyed the hotel amenities for just a couple hours?

Returning to campus, I called Amelia and explained the plan starting to form in my head. It could come together, though timing would be tight.

Nevertheless, I had to try.

I scoured my email inbox until I located the exchange where Scott requested I drop off at his place the galleys he needed, which had been sent to me by mistake during the weeks when the office was closed for the holidays. Under his curt request, reflecting obvious reluctance to rely on or feel indebted to me, I found what I was looking for. *Scott's address.* There's something happily poetic in it—how our correspondence in mutual resentment was exactly what I needed to come home to him now.

I hit the road in my sister's Prius, the "Cherry Evening" air freshener mocking me like it had on my way to Hollisboro. The good fortune of leaving early in the morning is that traffic is light. Determined to only pause for one pee stop, a skill developed over Midwestern road trips in my youth, I make excellent time. The gas station has caramel coffee—my dark, delicious magic.

I'm in New York City by one thirty, which turns into two by the time I find parking outside Scott's place—parking in the city not being a skill I have developed at all.

Whatever. I did it.

I hurry into Scott's apartment building, heading straight for the stairs. I refuse to wait even one unnecessary minute for the elevator, and I hardly even feel myself flying up the flights anymore. Emotion urges on my heart rate relentlessly and I'm panting when I emerge into Scott's hallway.

His door. For whatever reason, his door is what makes my surroundings set in. I'm . . . here. Not in Elytheum, or what passed for fantasy this week. *I'm here.*

I rush to the door. I knock.

No one answers.

In the oblivious afternoon light from the hallway window, I knock again. Harder. *Wham wham wham.* What if he's—I don't know—listening to music while he's unpacking?

His door doesn't open.

The one next door does, however. "Hey, if you're looking for

Scott, he's out of town this week," Scott's neighbor informs me. "I've been getting his mail."

I plaster on my most pleasant smile. One I hope doesn't say *I just did something completely unreasonable and illogical in the name of love only for it to not work out, didn't I?*

Nothing like this ever happened to Kethryn or Val. This is a Just Jennifer problem. It's proof of just how close heroism is to ridiculousness.

"Oh. Uh," I start. She eyes me with the start of concern. "I think he should have gotten in today," I manage cheerfully.

His neighbor shrugs. "Not yet. I can mention you dropped by when I see him. What's your name?"

"Tell him Jennifer was looking for him," I say. "Thank you."

I retreat from the door, and she withdraws. Wondering what the hell I'm going to do, I absently pull out my phone and call Scott.

Surprisingly, the call *doesn't* go straight to voicemail. So he's off the road now, but he didn't come *here.* Where is he? Is he avoiding my calls? Is he too hurt, too pissed to give me a chance to apologize? I chew my nail in the hallway, giving myself over to the ridiculousness. This ridiculousness is the luck of a lifetime. A week ago, I honestly never expected I would get to share my greatest passions and my happiest self with Scott Daniels. A week ago, I was literally excited for nine days free of him.

Now . . .

He doesn't pick up, and when the voicemail beeps, I speak hurriedly and quietly, hoping Scott's neighbor isn't listening. "Hey. Hi. It's me again. So, funny story," I start. "I'm actually back in New York, but it doesn't look like you are? Or at least you're not at your apartment."

I swallow. No more playing it cool. I know what I want.

Everything.

"I have to admit I'm desperately curious where you went, but more than that, I just want to see you, so call me back, or I guess come home, because I'll be waiting in your hallway," I confess. "Which sounds creepy, but I promise it'll come off romantic if you—"

The elevator dings open.

Scott walks into the hallway, hauling his luggage.

His face. Weary from driving, with a little scruff from his early morning. *His clothes.* Dark gray shirt and jeans. Not Elytheum in the least. *His hair.* Swooped.

He stops hard in his entryway, shock stealing the color from his face.

I swallow. Talking to his voicemail is one thing. Finishing my declaration in person—well, it is demanding more courage than I expected.

I muster my reserves. "I'm sorry," I start. "For . . . everything. I . . ." Realizing I should have planned these words better on my drive, I falter.

Then I focus on Scott's eyes. Finding the man I know, waiting in his hallway. The eyes I've glared into in conference rooms, gazed lovingly into the past couple mornings. The real Scott, in front of me now.

It is everything I need to find my voice. "I was scared," I say, feeling the conviction in my words. "But I'm not now. Because being with you—believing in us—is a dream I'm ready to make real. I'm sorry I ever made you feel like you're not enough. *You* are who I want. Exactly the way you are."

The hallway is silent. I wait, counting my heartbeats.

"Maybe we're even now?" I offer, trying to smile. "You reject me once. I reject you once. The score is settled. Please . . ." I implore him, dropping my fragile humor. "Give me another chance."

Slowly, like hope is igniting within him, Scott's eyes—the eyes I know—light up. They snare the sunlight, dazzling in impossible happiness. His smile spreads like none I've ever seen on his face.

"I don't think the score can ever be settled between us, Jennifer," he says. "At least, I hope not."

Relief and joy crash into me. I hang up the phone and rush to his arms. He drops his suitcase, capturing me in his embrace and sweeping me into a kiss.

I press my lips to his—soft and then deep, gentle and then desperate with need and forever want—while familiar magic comes over us, erasing the entire world. Putting my newfound conviction into the kiss, I hope he feels exactly how magical I know we can be.

The way he kisses me back says he does. It says he's here, and he's ready to risk everything. It says he knew I would realize the truth. In his arms, I feel I've made the journey of a lifetime, into realms of magic and mystery, and have finally returned *home.*

His stare wanders past me when we finally part, and I see something register. "Hey," he says, "we had our first conversation in a hallway just like this."

Looking around, I realize he's right. Once more, I'm starting something unforgettable with Scott Daniels in a liminal space, the ultimate nowhere I'm hoping to make somewhere. *Our* somewhere.

He nods at our surroundings. "I know it's not as magical as the Night Grotto," he concedes, and I grin at the reference to the location where Val and Kethryn first meet, the hidden chamber where colorful auroras of dark magic pulse in the endless pit under the court.

"I don't know," I say. "It's pretty magical to me."

Scott smiles. He presses his forehead to mine, and I entwine my fingers with his.

"How did I beat you here?" I wonder aloud. I mean, there's magic, and then there's *magic*. I would not put my freeway driving in either category. "I went to your hotel and you had already left early in the morning."

He laughs, a little shyly. "I . . . um," he says. "I stopped at an indie bookstore on the way out. I was going to recommend it to you when you left. I just didn't know you'd already done so."

"Because you had your phone on 'Do Not Disturb.'"

"Because I am a very safe driver. I suppose that's not quite book boyfriend material," he concedes.

"Everything about you," I say, "is book boyfriend material."

His eyes gleam. He knows I mean every word, and I know he understands. The "book boyfriend" doesn't mean fiction or fantasy. It doesn't mean courts of hulking men, or glowers or glamours, wings or horns.

It only means kindness, loyalty, honesty, and loving hard enough to never let go.

"I'm ready for everything with you," I continue, devotion in every word. "For days that feel like fairy tales and for days that don't. Because together, we're more than a fantasy," I say. "We're a dream come true."

He squeezes my hand. When he says nothing, I know he's choked up.

"Scott Daniels," I joke lovingly, "you really are a romantic." I collect my hard-won resolve, and looking right into his gorgeous eyes, I ask the question I knew I needed to ask the moment Heather mentioned his departure. The reason I'm really here. "Will you go to the ball with me?"

Now Scott startles.

"The—the ball?" he repeats. "In Hollisboro?"

I nod firmly. "In *Elytheum*," I amend.

Scott smiles, still incredulous. "You . . . drove all the way here to ask me? You could have called and I would have set right back out on the road."

"I drove here," I explain, "to see you. I couldn't wait one more minute, not to mention eight hours. I know it's silly, going right back, and we might not even make it in time, but—"

He cuts me off with a kiss.

"It's not silly," he says finally, his voice hushed. "Yes. I'll go to the ball with you, Jennifer Worth. *Yes.* Even if it means eight more hours of driving. Even if we miss it. It'll be perfect, even if it's not."

No magic in this realm or any other could change how happy I feel.

"It already is," I say.

39

Even in traffic, love makes hours pass easily. Elytheum's most pow-erful sorcerers cannot hasten time the way laughing with Scott erases the minutes on the interstate. He drives, his hand on my leg, while the sun sets over the highway, the concrete painted in rosy light.

Night falls. We're probably going to miss the dance.

We drive on.

It is nearly eleven p.m. when we reach Hollisboro. The cute city is quiet, hushed in the illumination of the streetlights. We park outside the college itself, where the gates wait, unmoving and im-posing, in the darkness.

And, impossibly, lights are on in the dining hall. Music still floats out the doors into the night.

Scott meets my eyes. We exchange wordless smiles. *We made it.*

The realization sends us rushing. I run up to my room, where I pull my dress on hurriedly, not changing out of my sneakers under the shining fabric. Unable to find my masquerade mask im-mediately, I go without. In minutes I'm dashing back out into the hallway—half-fantasy, half-ordinary—and descending the stairwell.

In the downstairs entryway, I find Scott waiting for me.

He's not in full costume, either, having only grabbed his shirt before we left—a simple but elegant black collared one. He extends his hand, grinning with half of his mouth. Not exactly a smirk and not only a smile. *Lord Daniels of New York, High Master of Hallway Kisses.*

Just Scott. Man of my heart.

I wouldn't change a thing about him.

I put my hand in his, and we walk into the ball together.

It is magnificent, the hall remade in Elytheum finery. The room is packed—I underestimated the Elytheum crew's enthusiasm for dancing late into the night. The string quartet from the first night has returned, filling the air with romantic music. Underneath the dark vaulted ceiling, hundreds of candles light the room. I feel like we're walking into the midnight sky.

Everyone is here. When Erik, in his ebony mask, notices Scott and me reunited, he clasps us in one huge hug. We join him as he regales a crowd with his audition story. He's gotten better with every recitation. We continue on, finding Laurel and Brit—dressed and done up impeccably, with the finest masks in the room—near the fantasy cocktails.

Scott notices the nameplate under the light pink drinks with sprigs of rosemary. "Vesperynthe over rosewater," he remarks. His eyes light with recognition and shared joy. With what looks like fandom, I realize. "Just like what Val and Kethryn share when they're hosting the first Court Convergence," he reminds me.

Like I needed reminding. I only smile, feeling like I could combust from happiness—and, okay, pretty turned on by his love of my favorite books.

Speaking of fae lords, we find Amelia, who has donned the crown I gave her, on the dance floor in Val's arms. No—not Val.

Fred. I recognize the endless eagerness in his eyes. The man of a hundred fan fantasies, looking like he's living a fantasy himself.

I wave, and Amelia smiles warmly. When she puts her head on Fred's shoulder, I know I am not the only one having a perfect night. Dreams come in many forms, leading like paths into the sky, out to unknown horizons. While Amelia's "dream job" didn't work out like she'd expected, I'm inexpressibly glad she hasn't closed herself off to other dreams leading in new, wondrous directions.

"Well, Lady Jennifer," Scott murmurs like he's read my mind, "may I have this dance?"

I grin, although I have to say, the steps look like one of the harder ones we learned in class. "Do you know how?" I ask him.

"Oh, I know how," Lord Daniels assures me.

I'm laughing, putting my hand on his shoulder as he pulls us onto the dance floor. Scott may have more confidence than skill, I find as he leads us dauntlessly with the dulcet melody of the quartet.

It doesn't matter. His hand on the small of my back, his face inches from mine, the way the candlelight changes into golden streaks as we spin—I feel utterly swept away into a dream.

A dream of my own. One nobody is writing except me.

One I don't have to wake from, and one I won't reach the end of with the final words on a page. One that will stretch out forever, in pieces of wonder scattered in ordinary moments.

When we return home for real—from Elytheum, from this unforgettable week—we won't stop creating our fairy tale. It will be an enchantment woven in every kiss and every kindness, every hardship and every happiness.

And it won't be fantastical, but it *will* be magical.

Acknowledgments

In a way, every word of *Book Boyfriend* is one of thanks. This book is our recognition of the joy of reading, of immersing yourself in unforgettable stories and finding favorite characters your heart holds on to forever. It is our celebration of literary fandom and the comforting, enlightening, emboldening power of fiction. In this way, it is itself an acknowledgment of all those who make stories happen.

And in this regard, it is even more imperative we share our gratitude for everyone who made *this* story happen. Katie Shea Boutillier, our agent, none of our ideas would ever find their way onto the page without your enthusiasm, your insight, your constant care, and your vigorous championship. In particular, you have seen Jennifer and Scott through many versions of themselves over the past years, and we cannot thank you enough for the hope you have invested in every one. We look forward to many, many more stories with you.

Kristine Swartz, we are honored and deeply grateful to have worked with you on now *four* romances! With each one, we have felt incredibly fortunate to have your discerning judgment and sharp sensibility honing our efforts, and *Book Boyfriend* is no exception. Thank you for your patient and thoughtful guidance pushing Jennifer and Scott's story into its finest form and for challenging us not to write a second-chance romance!

Vi-An Nguyen, we cannot express how fortunate we feel to have your marvelous artistry once more inviting readers into this story. As ever, your cover captures all the charm and bookish delight we hope readers find with Jennifer and Scott. Thank you for continuing to grace our work with your dazzling design.

In Jennifer's favorite series, the Elytheum Courts are rich with lords and ladies, artisans and chefs, warriors and diplomats. *Book Boyfriend* could not have come into existence without the flourishing court at Berkley, which we're honored to call home. Thank you to the copy editor and proofreaders for the precise magic you've lent every page. To Kristin del Rosario, Christine Legon, Alaina Christensen, and Mary Baker, thank you for your care and coordination turning this story into a book with transformative power to rival the court's finest enchanters. Jessica Plummer and Hillary Tacuri, we're forever indebted for your inexhaustible work in reaching readers, and Kristen Cipolla and Tina Joell, endless thanks for your creativity and dedication in sharing this story. Working in publishing, Jennifer and Scott may not like each other, but we know they would love working with each of you.

Over the events of *Book Boyfriend*, Jennifer finds herself grateful not just for the "book boyfriends" she comes to cherish, fictional or otherwise, but for the friends she finds and depends on. We find ourselves lucky to feel the same way. Bridget Morrissey, Maura Milan, Gabrielle Gold, Gretchen Schreiber, Rebekah Faubion, Derek Milman, Brian Murray Williams, Farrah Penn, Carlyn Greenwald, Alicia Thompson, Emma Alban, Kalie Holford, Sophie Sullivan, Kate Golden, thank you for enriching our lives with love and inspiration. To the incredible authors who have lent kind words to this book, you know how deeply meaningful your generosity is. Jodi Picoult, your epic talent is rivaled only by your surpassing kindness, and we are fortunate to call you a friend.

Finally, thank you to our family, without whom none of this would be possible.

EMILY WIBBERLEY

Book Boyfriend

AUSTIN SIEGEMUND-BROKA

READERS GUIDE

Discussion Questions

1. Who's your book boyfriend? What fictional character would you love to meet in real life?

2. Jennifer struggles to decide whether hope and idealism help or harm her. What's the difference between chasing your dreams and having unrealistic expectations?

3. Is it possible to invest too much time and emotion in fiction, at the expense of one's "real" life?

4. How does reading fantasy help us relate to or process daily life?

5. Jennifer finds herself living the college life for the first time during the Elytheum Experience, and contemplating pursuing additional higher education. Would you ever want to go to or go back to college?

6. Jennifer and Amelia each put their heart into their job. What are the upsides and downsides to making your passion your job?

7. If you went to an immersive experience or into the world of a book, what genre would you want to live in?

8. Jennifer makes new friends at the Elytheum Experience over their shared love of their favorite series. Do you find it important to have common interests with friends, or do other things bring you together?

9. Where do you find magic in everyday life?

Keep reading for a preview of

Emily Wibberley and Austin Siegemund-Broka's

THE BREAKUP TOUR

Prologue

RILEY

There's nothing like the sound of heartbreak.

I lower my lips from the microphone, exhaustion deep in my chest, head humming with restless melody. I've immersed myself for weeks in the hardest memories of my life, the deepest hurt, searching them for inspiration. It's where I'll find what I need, I know it is. I just need to keep listening.

I'm frustrated, honestly. When I've spent fifteen hours in the studio, I expect to have polished whatever I'm working on to perfection.

Instead, nothing is working. The chorus is cheaply grand, synthetically sorrowful. The verses have no culmination, no urgency. The instrumentals have come out well enough—it's my singing I can't get right. I sound like I'm performing, not like I'm *myself*. It's left me here, rerecording vocals. The more I wrestle with the song, the further I get from the music in my heart, refrains insisting I let them free.

I wish I could. It physically pains me how much I wish I could.

This song was supposed to be my masterpiece. It needs to be my masterpiece. It deserves to be my masterpiece.

He deserves to be my masterpiece.

Sighing in exasperation, I roll my shoulders under the shining studio lights. In the expansive soundproofed space, it's easy to forget it's one in the morning. Nothing changes in the windowless, sterile room of microphones and minimal furniture. Usually I welcome the emptiness, the lack of distraction, the freedom to pursue whatever musical inspiration I'm hearing.

In this moment, however, it just reminds me of the progress I'm *not* making on the song I can't finish.

Part of me wants to resign for the night. I'm half-desperate to surrender to the impersonal comfort of my suite, my home for the past few months. The Victory Hotel off San Vincente near Sunset, one of Los Angeles's highest-powered entertainment industry neighborhoods, has hosted me in discretion while I procrastinated on house-hunting, instead hurling myself headlong into my music.

I couldn't help it. After my divorce, what else could I do?

The end of my marriage was a summons. I knew I could write us unforgettably. The whole perfect, painful ruin. Everything I hoped with him, everything I imagined. I chased the promise of the *song of us* until finally, "One Minute" was finished.

Moving out of our house, packing my possessions into suitcases, I listened to the demo on repeat. Over and over, the reminder of the music I found in the hurt kept me from sobbing. My ex wasn't home—he let me relocate in peace, one of his few recent kindnesses. I packed rhythmically until, in one unassuming moment, it happened.

Inspiration.

I was proud of how I'd rendered our whole relationship in one song. It gave me the idea for my entire next album. I pitched my label the premise, which they loved. I started writing, and once I started, I couldn't stop. It consumed me. Writing shifted into recording, and many days I did some of each.

I've practically lived here in Stereosonic's huge recording studio, spending wild hours of productivity playing and polishing, often sleeping on the couch. When I'm chasing inspiration, sacking out on the cushions is just easier. Honestly, I'm probably the Victory Hotel's favorite guest.

The songs emerged, each memorializing a relationship. I worked and worked until they were exactly the way I wanted. The process was like no inspiration I've ever experienced. I could hear *everything* I wanted. I worked relentlessly until I executed them flawlessly. Eleven of them.

Everything was magic. *The sound of heartbreak*. It was going startlingly well.

Until now.

At first, I didn't even know whether I wanted to write the song I'm struggling with. Our relationship was long ago, in the privacy of the past. It holds no public recognizability, unlike my infamous flings and marriage. It's not even a footnote in the many, *many* stories of the musicians and movie stars I've loved and lost.

Yet I decided I had to include him, for one undeniable reason.

I know, quite simply, I loved him most. I heard every harmony. I could feel the wonder of every coming reprise. I was unforgettably in love with him.

The song I wrote for him has eluded me for days. Once I finish the recording, the album is done. In the weeks since I wrote the lyrics, I've recorded plenty of passes—none of them satisfying. Whenever I fell short, I would procrastinate, redirecting my efforts to one of the album's other songs.

Now I'm out of unfinished songs.

Fuck, I feel wrecked. My voice is sore. My back hurts from the stool where I've sat for hours in front of the studio microphone.

The Victory is nine minutes from here on the empty streets of midnight in West Hollywood. I imagine the cool comfort of the marble floor under my feet, the windows' gauzy curtains letting the light of the low skyline into the room, contouring the furnishings in gentle gray-white. The pillowed comforter of my California king, solitude I reassure myself is independence.

Instead, I wander over to the studio couch. I won't permit myself the comforts of "home," I decide. Not when I've failed so profoundly. Spending the night in the studio is my reminder to myself of the work yet undone.

In the dark of my mind, a dangerous possibility lurks. *What if I only have eleven songs of heartbreak in me?* This song is desperately important to me. What if importance isn't enough? What if I've exhausted myself in months of divorce and relentless heartsick songwriting?

It's unimaginably depressing. I force the idea away.

However, I do need sleep. What I'm feeling now is no way to record. I'm miserable. Defeated, frustrated, hopeless. I feel like—

I sit up straight.

What if it's the perfect way to record?

With every urge in me demanding I rest, I return instead to the microphone. My heart is racing. This album is about the deepest hurts of my life, the struggles. The wounds of love. It's dedicated to devotion and defeat.

It's supposed to sound this way, I realize. *It's supposed to hurt.*

I start the recording, having put in enough hours here recently to know how everything works without the help of my engineer or producer, who have gone home, given the hour. The piano fills my ears.

When the verse comes, I sing. I sing like it's the last chance I'll give myself. I sing like I'm giving up. I sing like I'm saying goodbye.

I put everything into the music like I know my everything isn't enough. Like I know I can't be what the song needs.

It hurts. It hurts so much.

With the emotion I'm devoting to every note, it never fails to surprise me how fast three verses, three choruses, and one bridge pass. The music ends, and the rest is silence. Withdrawing from the microphone, I wipe my eyes with shaking hands. I didn't even know I was crying. Of course I was, I guess.

In the hushed studio, I hesitate. I'm out of inspiration, out of fight, out of everything except one fragile hope. I don't know how I'll cope if this song breaks my heart like the man who inspired it.

I play the recording. The song I've worked on for days, weeks, months fills the room. I listen closely.

It's . . . perfect. Fucking perfect.

It was worth it, I remind myself while I walk with heavy steps over to the couch, knowing I'll nod off in the Uber if I head for the hotel. The pain I gave it was worth everything I'm certain this song will give me.

The recording feels . . . life-changing. Undeniable. It feels like my hit. It sounds like my legacy.

It was worth it, I repeat to myself, my only lullaby in this windowless room. *You made it worth it.*

Four
Months
Later

MAX

I remember exactly what song was playing when I started my car on the night I got my heart broken.

I cranked the key in the ignition. The radio came on—Joni Mitchell's "The Same Situation" filled the interior of the used Camry I'd gotten for two thousand dollars when I graduated from high school. Feeling foolish, pretending I was fine, I let the song play, even while I knew it would entwine itself with the day's sad memories. I drove home on Los Angeles's silent freeways, recognizing in the pit of my stomach how Joni's voice would haunt me from then on.

Which is why a decade later I find myself hovering my finger over my laptop's space bar, unable to press play.

Open on Spotify is Riley Wynn's new album, framed on my screen in the small office I share with my sister in Harcourt Homes, the senior assisted-living facility I run with her help. It's just me in here right now, waiting for myself, ignoring the spreadsheets printed out on my desk. January is the coldest the San

Fernando Valley gets. The California chill surrounds me, invading my fingertips, expectant, urging. *Listen, Max. Just listen.*

I know what will happen when I start the first song. *If* I start the first song. The voice of the country's new favorite pop prophetess will steal into my soul the way only she can.

I should listen, I know I should. Hit play. Let Riley's music—her magic—ensnare me. Especially "Until You," the undisputed song of the year. I've had to work to escape hearing it because it hides around every corner in the labyrinth of the same songs every radio station plays.

I haven't entirely succeeded, instead hearing snatches in the supermarket or when I'm changing stations. Then there are the billboards, Riley looming over my commute on Sunset. She stands in the wedding dress she's wearing on the album cover, looking caught off guard while fire licks the edges of her veil. The *Rolling Stone* email with her featured interview hit my inbox a week ago.

Yet, I've resisted Riley's new music until today, when I suddenly knew I could hold out no longer—gravity was pulling me. Of what heavenly body, I don't know. Stars have gravity, but so do black holes. Like one inside the other, Riley's eyes stare out from my laptop screen.

My hesitation is sort of pathetic, I know. In fairness, however, not many people in the world face the question I do when it comes to Riley Wynn's new album.

How do you listen to *The Breakup Record* when one of the songs is about you?

Maybe we should form a support group—me and the eleven other people Riley's immortalized on her chart-smashing second LP. It's the gripping, genius conceit of her new collection of songs—each one centers on a romantic split of Riley's life.

Which means our nine months together in college are presumably included in the company of Hollywood-headline relationships, of short-lived flings, of her notorious divorce. Nine months when I dated the woman who would become one of the most famous musicians in the world. Nine months in which I felt like I'd found the chorus to my verse in Riley Wynn—whose lips made me ignite, whose smile looked like stage lights, whose laughter played secret chords on my heartstrings.

There's a chance I'm not included, some hopeful part of me whispers. What if our relationship didn't register enough to make the cut?

On second thought, that might be worse.

Riley is known for her breakup songs. Renowned or infamous, depending on the source of the judgment. On her first album and EPs—when she was popular, just not yet the most loved figure in the contemporary music industry—the songs of heartbreak were the hits.

It was easy to understand why. When I listened to them once or twice, out of nostalgia or masochistic indulgence or some combination, Riley's preoccupation with the pain or pleasure of romantic endings was evident in the power of her voice, the sharpness of her structures, and the keenness of her lyrics.

Her reputation was made. "The Breakup Queen," the music press calls her.

The Breakup Record is her meta-manifestation of her own reputation, self-commentary and self-realization in one. It's ingeniously Riley, making masterpieces out of misadventures, conferring ironic honor on romantic failures memorable enough to spawn songs. While I'm pretty much the opposite of fame-hungry, even I would prefer Riley Wynn's songwriting scalpel over the ignominy of being the forgotten ex.

I know there's only one way to find out whether she wrote us into song. It's just—how do I prepare myself for what feels like walking into the fire on the album's cover?

Melodies hold memories. Like nothing else on earth, they recall feelings, places, moments—the needle dropping into the groove of the soul's record player. I remember what song was playing when I had my first kiss, what I put on while having dinner alone the night I moved into my first apartment, what was on the radio while my father stiffly said I would need to run Harcourt Homes if I wanted it to stay open, because my parents could no longer manage the property.

Whenever I listen to them, I'm there.

The same will happen here. When I play whatever Riley's written for us, I'll find myself reliving a part of my life I'm not sure I'm over, even ten years later.

"Did you listen yet?"

The sound of Jess's voice has me snapping my laptop shut. Instantly, my furtiveness embarrasses me. It's not like I was watching porn or something.

Sure enough, my sister smiles. She's opened the door just a little to poke her head into the office. The loose curls of her chestnut hair hang past her collarbone. The sparkle in her green eyes says she knows exactly what hell I'm presently in. We're obviously siblings, matched in every significant physical characteristic—the perfect pair for, say, the "About Us" page on retirement home websites.

"I've heard it," I say neutrally.

"Liar," Jess replies. She slouches in mock desperation. "Come *on.* I need you to listen and tell me which one is about you."

"You don't know if any of them are about me." Hearing my own lack of conviction, I wince.

Jess rolls her eyes. "Um, you and Riley were obsessed with each

other. I'm one gazillion percent certain there's a song about you."
She shrugs, pretending she's indulging in casual speculation,
which I know she is not. "My guess is 'Until You,'" she says.

I frown. Surely Jess is messing with me now. I probably have *a*
song—not *the* song. The lead single. No fucking way. I'm surely
relegated to the second-to-last track or something. The filler. The
one that barely made it onto the album.

"I'm sure 'Until You' is about that guy," I say.

Jess looks incredulous. "Her ex-husband, Wesley Jameson? He's
an Emmy-nominated actor, collective crush of the internet. He's
not '*that guy*,'" my sister informs me witheringly.

"Whatever. Him," I say, feeling my face heat. I definitely know
exactly who Riley's ex-husband is. I don't know why I insinuated
otherwise. "The song is about him. Isn't that what everyone is saying?"

It's not like I seek out gossip headlines. When it comes to Riley,
however, they're hard to miss. Riley has shot to the kind of star-
dom that makes speculation about her love life a national pastime.
Everyone online is saying the biggest hit on the album is about
Wesley, Riley's husband of three months.

Had it surprised me when Riley married one of prime time's
hottest stars? No, absolutely not. Riley is . . . everything. She's gorgeous, smart, quick-witted, uncompromising. She'd want someone who could complement her. Who could keep pace with her
own relentless incandescence.

Jameson made sense. He's machine-pressed handsome, with
sharp, planar features, his eyes squinted ruggedly in every one of
his numerous photoshoots. Like Jess remarked, he's undeniably
internet-crushable, with his wavy dark hair, his sinister somberness. He's captivating on-screen, launching himself from a conflicted criminal on HBO to the leading man of fans' fantasies.

His relationship with Riley captured the public's obsession instantly. Photos of them close, of him whispering in her ear, found their way online from one charity event or magazine party or other. They weren't world news, not yet. Riley wasn't famous like she is now. In fact, *he* was the famous one then. Rumors followed his potent combination of popular and prestige, of roles in consideration, of other women.

The photos of them together were what caught fans' imaginations—the dazzle of Riley's delight, the glint in Jameson's eye. The dark prince who snared the sharp-tongued starlet. Each garnered more and more retweets and comments until Riley Wynn and Wesley Jameson were iconic "main characters" on the public stage.

Two months later, they were married. Three months later, they were divorced.

It was the perfect reflection of the differences in the lives we'd led. Obviously I wasn't just home on the couch swiping through photos of Riley with Wesley Jameson—I've had relationships of my own, some of them serious.

They're passages of memory unnerving in their finitude, disappearing from my life so completely it's hard to remember how much of it they once occupied. Kendra, who had her MFA in design and worked on the new progressive mayor's campaign, and loved herbal tea and her sister. Elizabeth, one of our residents' granddaughters, who worked in employment law, never liked Los Angeles, and dreamed of living in France.

In the year I spent with each woman, I meant it when I said I loved her. It just . . . never worked out. It wasn't right.

Or, *I* wasn't right. I can claim fault for the end of each relationship. The same thing happened—when the idea of moving in arose, I withdrew. Not immediately, yet unmistakably. Dinners got quieter. Futures faded into uncertainty. I could feel something missing, or I convinced myself I could. Either way, it scared me, and I ran.

In the meantime, I've enjoyed myself well enough with the one-night stands the right combination of tousled hair and glasses will earn.

Jess is watching me with skeptical wonderment. "You really haven't listened to it, have you?" she asks.

I stand, knowing it's confirmation enough. "I'm late," I say instead, struggling to keep annoyance out of my voice. The problem with working with your family is that you can't hide from them, even when you want to. "I'm due in the dining room." I pass Jess in the doorway, hoping she'll let the subject drop.

Of course, she doesn't.

"One of those songs *is* about you, Max," she says.

I don't reply, heading into the hallway on the second floor. My sister's inquisitiveness is expected, honestly. Everyone who knows me personally—which, okay, isn't very many people outside of Harcourt Homes, where the residents don't exactly listen to the SiriusXM hits station—has asked me eagerly which song is about me.

I've found refuge in saying I don't know. I don't *want* to know. Ten years isn't enough time to get over Riley Wynn. Maybe twenty years will be. What is it Springsteen sings? *In twenty years, I'm sure it'll just seem funny.*

I head down the wide staircase into the lobby, ignoring patches of peeling paint near the carpet curling up from the floor. Details our residents don't notice, or I hope they don't. They stand out sneeringly to me, though. Guilty indications of places where I couldn't keep up with the demands of the property.

Once our parents' business, now our own, Harcourt Homes is the legacy I carry proudly despite its heavy weight. In the Valley's flatlands, only minutes outside of, yet unmistakable for, Los Angeles, we keep residents' lives from changing. It's the point of what we do, conserving health, comfort, consistency. It's the business of waiting, of holding on.

Holding on despite what I found in the spreadsheets on my desk, the monthly financials I've printed out, no different from last month's.

I've pored over them, searching for costs to cut or secret efficiencies to exploit, struggling to do right by this place. There's nothing—except for the outright cruelty of raising prices on our residents, which we would never do. Planning for retirement is nearly impossible. When someone doesn't correctly calculate how many years they need to save for, we work out new rates with their family based on what they can pay. Unfortunately, it's left Harcourt Homes on the edge of bankruptcy.

I wanted to help. It's why I changed my major from music to business. I even *did* help, for the first few years, keeping the home running. Only when I faced the ongoing downward spiral did I realize I couldn't find the fixes we needed, which left me in this precarious position, learning habits for cost-cutting wherever I could.

I know the *real* conversation is coming. The one where we face the music, so to speak. Where I gather everyone and admit Harcourt Homes cannot continue. I just can't dwell on it right now.

Not with the piano waiting for me.

In minutes, I'll play for everyone, our residents and their families. I don't want my stress over the home's finances to bleed into my performance this evening, but of course it would if I let the harsh realities preoccupy me. Everything I feel finds its way into my music.

Music is the life in the lungs of Harcourt Homes, the sustaining spark in these walls. Whether it's old standards I let echo from the record player into the halls, or me playing for residents during dinner, music helps us forget life's peeling paint. Since high school, I've hardly ever missed my Sunday piano revue.

The dining room is full of familiar faces when I enter off the main hallway. The four octogenarians who always wear Navy hats occupy one corner. Keri eats with Grant, the pair having become inseparable since they realized their names combined into one old Hollywood star. Imelda regales her indulgent daughter with resident gossip—of which, make no mistake, there is plenty. I cross the room, nodding to the residents.

When I sit down at the ancient upright piano, I feel like I'm home.

"*Finally*, Maxwell."

I smile, hardly surprised. The voice is Linda's. Of course, my favorite Harcourt Homes resident is seated right next to the piano.

"My potatoes are already cold," she remarks, playful petulance in her eyes.

"I'm sorry," I say earnestly. "How about Sinatra to make up for it?"

Linda smiles magnanimously, satisfied, and I start playing.

The home's upright is the piano I learned to play on. It's *not* the nicest piano I've ever played, not by far, but it's my favorite. The rich sound, the worn feel of the keys—it's perfect. Part of the reason I never went on to pursue music despite initially majoring in piano performance is this wonderful instrument's unwieldy logistics. I can't just pack the piano up and haul it to gigs with me.

I place my fingers on the keys, feeling the warmth of their welcome. This piano is part of me. When my foot finds the pedal, I feel like I'm stretching my hamstrings to sprint. When I inch forward on the bench, it's like inhaling deeply.

I play, and it's like coming to life.

The song spills from me, rolling like the wind over the hills of Mulholland Drive ten minutes from here. "Come Fly with Me" is one of the residents' favorites, ebulliently quick on the keys and sprightly syncopated. It plays like its title, the rush of landing gear lifting off the runway.

Half the dining room hushes to listen. The other half continues conversing. I don't mind. Music doesn't have to demand everyone's attention. It's there for those who need it. Not every song preaches from the pulpit—some hold your hand from the passenger seat.

I run down my repertoire of the residents' favorites, from Sinatra to Elvis, Bobby Darin to Etta James. When I play, I forget the minutes drifting past on weightless currents of melody. I'm perfectly content. Everything else vanishes—the financial pressures of Harcourt Homes, the idea of returning to my empty apartment, the pattern of watching my friends from music school either make it or give up their dreams for steady jobs and families they find equally fulfilling.

I forget about the hit song I've possibly inspired. I forget *The Breakup Record.* I forget—

Well, no. I never quite forget Riley.

Dessert signals the end of my dinner revue. While staff serve key lime pie, my father's recipe—one of the ways in which my parents' presence lingers here, despite them having retired to Palm Springs—I finish my final song and stand, bowing my head to scattered applause. Not every table is occupied, I note with discomfort clenching in my chest, reminding me we're not at full capacity. I can't move in anyone new, though, not without the money for more staff.

It's remarkable how quickly stress wraps me again in its clenching wires. How quickly the respite of music's exhilarating ease has disappeared into the past. Looking out over the residents enjoying meals in this home, the idea of everyone we might fail is overwhelming.

"Encore!"

The single word rings out over the applause. The voice is young, female, and flickering with confident humor.

Saying it distracts me is the understatement of the century. It stops my heart.

Glancing into the back corner, I blink, certain I'm hallucinating. The figment of my overwrought imagination, the result of the billboards I saw on my drive in this morning. Of staring at the album art on Spotify.

Of remembering the sound of her small intake of breath before she would strum the first chord of her songs in college.

The figure seated inconspicuously near the entrance to the kitchen is miragelike. I feel my heart pick up its pace, emotions I can't name crescendoing into one forbidden harmony.

While her hair is dyed sun-spun gold, her roots remain dark. She's dressed in jet-black jeans, with the black fabric of the top she's tucked in clinging to her frame, covering her chest and carelessly and recklessly revealing the skin of her sides. No bra. She never wore one when I knew her. If she turned to the left, I could see the first word of the line of poetry tattooed under her breast. It's Mary Oliver, her favorite.

Who ever made music of a mild day?

She's heart-stoppingly gorgeous and looking right at me. With her head slanted coyly to the side, her smile says she knows she's walked out of my daydreams.

In honesty, *daydream* isn't half description enough for her sense-warping effect on me. She's a symphony when you're expecting a solo. She's heartbreak. She's my first favorite song.

In the corner of the room, Riley Wynn raises her hand *hello*.

The Roughest Draft

*Sometimes the best love stories start
with The Roughest Draft . . .*

Three years ago, Katrina Freeling and Nathan Van Huysen
were the brightest literary stars on the horizon, their co-written
book topping bestseller lists. But on the heels of their greatest
success, they ended their partnership on bad terms. They
haven't spoken since, and never planned to – except they
have one final book due on contract.

Forced to reunite, they hole up in a tiny Florida town,
trying to finish a new manuscript quickly and painlessly.
Working through the reasons they've hated each other
for the past three years isn't easy, especially not while
writing a romantic novel.

While passion and prose push them closer together in
the Florida heat, Katrina and Nathan will learn that
relationships, like writing, sometimes take a few
rough drafts before they get it right . . .

Do I Know You?

After five years of marriage, they're about to have their first date . . .

Eliza and Graham's marriage is quietly failing. With their five-year anniversary approaching, neither of them is thrilled about the week-long getaway they've been gifted. The luxury retreat prides itself on being a destination for those in love and those looking to find it – so for Eliza and Graham, it's the last place they want to be.

But when a well-meaning guest mistakes Eliza and Graham for two single people and introduces them at the hotel bar, they don't correct him. Suddenly, they're pretending to be perfect strangers, and it's unexpectedly fun. Eliza and Graham find themselves flirting like it's their first date.

Everyone at the retreat can see the electric chemistry between Eliza and Graham's alter egos. But as their game continues, they realize this performance could be the very thing that saves their marriage . . .

MIKE YOON PHOTO

Emily Wibberley and **Austin Siegemund-Broka** met and fell in love in high school. Austin went on to graduate from Harvard, while Emily graduated from Princeton. Together, they are the authors of several novels about romance for teens and adults. Now married, they live in Los Angeles, California, where they continue to take daily inspiration from their own love story.

VISIT EMILY AND AUSTIN ONLINE

EmilyandAustinWrite.com